**Read what reviewers are saying about**

# DINAH MCCALL

# DINAH MCCALL

# MIMOSA GROVE

**MIRA®**

ISBN 0-7783-2029-4

MIMOSA GROVE

Copyright © 2004 by Sharon Sala.

All rights reserved. Except for use in any review, the reproduction or utilization of this work in whole or in part in any form by any electronic, mechanical or other means, now known or hereafter invented, including xerography, photocopying and recording, or in any information storage or retrieval system, is forbidden without the written permission of the publisher, MIRA Books, 225 Duncan Mill Road, Don Mills, Ontario, Canada M3B 3K9.

All characters in this book have no existence outside the imagination of the author and have no relation whatsoever to anyone bearing the same name or names. They are not even distantly inspired by any individual known or unknown to the author, and all incidents are pure invention.

MIRA and the Star Colophon are trademarks used under license and registered in Australia, New Zealand, Philippines, United States Patent and Trademark Office and in other countries.

Visit us at www.mirabooks.com

Printed in U.S.A.

This story is about faith, for it is only in faith that you can believe in something you cannot see. And it is about love, for in love, and only love, will you ever know the joy of selflessness. And it is about family, for without them you know nothing about being accepted just as you are. And it is about eternity, for without it, yesterday is forgotten, today is taken for granted and tomorrow never comes.

Learn to love who you are, accept what you cannot change and trust in truths you cannot see.

I dedicate this book to all God's children.

# 1

Laurel Scanlon was in love. Had been for more than four months now. It was what got her through the days and filled her lonely nights. Knowing the tenderness of his touch, the patience and passion of his lovemaking, and the fulfillment of dying bit by bit each night in his arms as he took her to a climax that left her breathless and often trembling, was more than she'd ever hoped to have in her life.

And tonight was no exception.

After another mindless and seemingly endless night of playing hostess for her father, federal prosecutor Robert Scanlon, it had been all Laurel could do to get undressed before crawling into bed.

She wanted her lover with a need that made her shiver. Longed for the mindless, weightless feeling of coming apart beneath him. Yet even in the deepest part of her soul, she was sorry for the fact that she saw him only in her dreams.

But how could she regret someone who, nightly, was breathing life into her heart and reminding her why she'd been born a woman? She needed him as much as she needed oxygen to survive, craving the freedom of his touch, getting lost in his kisses and ultimately experiencing the mind-numbing shock of sexual release. No one knew he existed, and she would not admit, even to herself, that he was not real. Tonight was no exception.

It was with eagerness that she crawled into bed, rolled over on her side and wearily closed her eyes, waiting for consciousness to subside—waiting for him.

And as she waited, her subconscious slipped into that state between cognizance and sleep, bringing back to her the joke of her existence, wondering why she'd been born different from other women and always the butt of jokes—tolerated only because of her father's status in the upper echelons of Washington politics.

She rolled onto her other side and plumped the pillow beneath her head, trying to block out the pain, but it was with her as surely as the blood that flowed through her veins.

People smiled to her face, but she knew they talked when her back was turned. She knew what the people in the elite circle of her father's life thought about her. They said she was unbalanced. Some even called her crazy. The kinder ones thought she was just given to high flights of fanciful imagination, but nearly all of them figured she would end up in an expensive but distant institution, just as her mother, Phoebe, had done before she had taken her own life.

No one gave credence to the provenance of Laurel's family, or to the legend that the oldest daughter in every family directly related to Chantelle LeDeux, who had disappeared from her family plantation in Louisiana in 1814, had the gift of "sight."

Laurel's so-called gift had been an embarrassment to her father since the day she learned to talk. It had ostracized her during her school years and made her something of a cult oddity in college. Her reputation became the source of amusement at parties, as her so-called friends urged her to "see" into their future. But the day she "saw" one commit a crime before it happened was the day her popularity came to an end.

Trying to hide her disability, as soon as she graduated college, she got a job at a local newspaper, but that, too, soon ended, along with her three-month engagement to the editor's oldest son. Her second engagement to a stockbroker occurred two years later and lasted until he began urging her to give him tips on the market.

For Laurel, it was the last straw. Having to face the fact that he'd believed in her only enough to further his own goals had soured her on ever supposing she would find someone who could ignore the gossip and love her for who she was. Now, at twenty-eight and sick of the vicious cycle that had become her life, she was ready for a change.

Unknown to her father, she was planning to leave D.C. But until she could decide what she wanted to do and where she wanted to go, having an affair with a man who existed only in her mind seemed like a damned good idea. For now, sleep had become her escape.

And so she waited with expectation, praying for sleep to come. She took slow, deep breaths to clear her thoughts from the meaningless chitchat she'd endured throughout dinner, exhaled softly. Moments later, she was asleep.

And, just as she'd hoped, he came to her. In her

dream…in her head…in her heart—slipping into her thoughts without warning. One moment she was alone and dreamless, and the next thing she knew, his hands were on her body, caressing her shape. Then his mouth touched her skin, leaving a thin, wet trail on her breast as he traced its shape with the tip of his tongue.

Laurel moaned and then sighed as she unconsciously rolled over onto her back and parted her legs. She felt his hand sliding across the flat of her belly, pausing just long enough above the juncture of her thighs to make her moan with longing.

She wanted more.

She wanted him.

She wanted it now.

As if he'd sensed her thoughts, he moved from beside her to on top of her. She thought he whispered something shameless as he slid between her legs, but she couldn't quite hear the words. For a heart-stopping moment, he held himself poised above her; then she wrapped her legs around his waist and pulled him in, arching uncontrollably toward the hard, pulsing length of him as he began to rock her world.

Moonlight filtered through the pale blue sheers of the second-story bedroom, bathing the room in an eerie light, but Laurel didn't know and wouldn't have cared. She felt nothing but the impact of their bodies in the ebb and flow of making love.

Her climax came without warning and in the form of a belly-deep moan, shattering Laurel's dream, leaving her awake and shaking and trying to reconcile the loneliness of her existence with the intimacy of where she'd just been.

With a stifled sob, she thrust her fingers through

her hair, swept the dark red curls away from her face and then rolled out of bed. She stumbled as she got up, then staggered to the bathroom, hoping to salvage her sanity with the shock of a cold shower.

*Same time: Bayou Jean, Louisiana*

Justin Bouvier woke with a gasp, then sat straight up, searching the shadows in his room for a glimpse of the woman who'd been in his bed. When he realized that, once again, it was nothing but the same dream he'd been having for months, he rubbed the heels of his hands against his eyes and cursed. How was this happening? It had seemed so real. He inhaled sharply, then frowned, imagining he could still smell the scent of her in the room.

With a muffled groan, he got out of bed and strode to the bathroom, flipping on lights as he went. Within seconds he was in the shower and standing beneath the stinging jets of cold water, and yet no matter how long he stood, the feel of her was still on his skin.

Half an hour later, Justin was still up, trying to come to terms with the fact that he was having a love affair with a phantom. Not even the sturdy walls and cool, bare floors of the home that had been in his family for three generations were enough to ease his frustration tonight. Finally he took a cold can of beer from his refrigerator and walked out onto the back porch.

The Louisiana night was still, the air warm and sluggish. Beyond the perimeter of his house, the racket of tree frogs and crickets almost masked the less-prevalent sound of a nearby bull gator's boom. This was his world—the world in which he'd been raised. But not even the bayou and all it concealed was as frightening to him as the last four months of sleep had been. He was no high school boy having wet dreams about sex. Whatever was happening was locked into his soul. He didn't know why, or if it would ever happen again, but he knew, as well as he knew his own name, that if she existed, he had to find her.

And so he stood, staring off into the darkness as a fresh layer of sweat beaded on his skin, reminding him of the heat they had generated while making love. Finally, he laid the cold can of beer against the back of his neck.

"God give me strength," he said softly, then popped the top on the beer. Lifting it to his lips, he tilted his head and drank until it was gone.

Robert Scanlon was just finishing his breakfast when Laurel entered the dining room. He frowned as he watched her walk straight to the sideboard and pour herself a cup of coffee.

"You overslept," Robert said. "Are you ill?"

Laurel took her coffee and moved toward the table. "No. I'm fine."

There was no other answer she could give him. He already thought she was crazy. Telling him she was losing sleep over a love affair with some phantom from her dreams would send him over the edge.

"It's almost nine," he said, persisting in pointing out the fact that she was late coming down to breakfast.

Laurel lifted her cup, looking at her father over the rim as she blew across the hot surface, then took her first sip. She knew it infuriated him that she had yet to give him a satisfying answer, and while it was somewhat childish, she savored the small rebellion. After a second sip, she set her coffee cup down and smiled at the woman who was coming into the room.

"Good morning, Miss Laurel. What would you like for breakfast?"

"Good morning, Estelle. Please tell Cook I'm only having coffee this morning."

Her father's frown deepened as the housekeeper left.

"You should eat something, Laurel. It's not healthy to—"

"Father, for heaven's sake. I'm twenty-eight, not eight. I know whether I'm hungry or not. Besides, I'm having lunch with Mr. Coleman at one o'clock."

Her delayed arrival at breakfast and the fact that she wasn't eating properly were forgotten as he absorbed the fact that she was having lunch with their family lawyer and he hadn't known about it.

"Coleman? Why? And why didn't he let me know?"

"Really, Father, it's not like I'm doing anything illicit. He called. I agreed to lunch. I supposed it might have something to do with Mother's trust fund, which is my business, not yours."

"Still," Robert muttered, "one would have thought he'd contact me, not you."

"Why?" she challenged.

"Well, because…"

"I'm not my mother," Laurel snapped, her voice rising with each word she spoke. "I'm not disturbed. I'm not unbalanced. I'm not crazy." Then she shoved her chair back from the table and stood abruptly. "Have a nice day at the office, Father. I have some letters to write…and some spirits to channel,'' she added, knowing the last shot would infuriate him even more than he already was.

She walked out with her head held high, refusing to let him know how badly she hurt.

''Damn him,'' she muttered as she took the stairs back up to her bedroom. ''Damn all men to hell and back.''

But the moment she said it, she thought of the man from her dreams and knew that unless she found him in someone real, she was the one who would be forever damned.

Albert Coleman was, for all intents and purposes and except for the Scanlon family, retired. He would have given them up, too, had it not been for Phoebe's daughter. If he abandoned Laurel the way Phoebe had, then she would be standing alone against the world, because her father certainly wasn't taking her side. More than once, Albert had been a witness to Robert's coldhearted treatment of Laurel. In a way, he understood a bit of why Robert was so stringent. He'd been helpless to stop his wife's self-destruction, and it was fear that drove him to ride Laurel so hard. But Albert knew something about Laurel that Robert didn't seem to get. Laurel wasn't Phoebe. She was strong, self-assured, and more her father's daughter than either one of them realized.

He fiddled with his napkin as he waited for her to arrive, while wondering what his latest bit of news was going to do to the very fragile balance of her world.

Then he looked up, saw the tall, beautiful redhead walking his way with her father's attitude and

Phoebe's smile, and felt his heart skip a beat. He laid down his napkin as he stood to greet her.

"Laurel, darling, it's been too long," he said, then kissed her cheek and seated her at their table.

Laurel smiled at her old friend and, not for the first time, realized that the older he got, the more he resembled Abraham Lincoln, sans beard.

"It has been a while, hasn't it?" She reached out and patted his hand as he sat down beside her. "We must remember to do this more often."

Albert signaled their waiter that they were ready to order. As soon as the waiter was gone, Laurel put her elbows on the table and leaned toward him in a confidential manner.

"So, what's up, doc?" she asked, expecting to see a smile break across the somberness of Albert's face. Instead, he frowned.

"Albert?"

He cupped her hand, then patted the side of her face.

"I have some sad news for you, dear. Your grandmother, Marcella, has passed away."

Laurel's smile faded. She had only vague memories of her maternal grandmother, but what she remembered was all good. Going to Louisiana—to Mimosa Grove, the family estate where her mother had been born and raised—had been like going to Disneyland, only without all the rides.

The country had been hot and green and wet, and, to her, somewhat like a jungle. And it was the first time she'd ever felt completely accepted. No one minded that she "saw" things others didn't, and no one chided her for her flights of fancy. It had been one of the most memorable times of her life.

But after Phoebe's disintegration, Laurel had never seen her grandmother again. To her shame, she realized that she'd never considered going back on her own after she'd become an adult.

"When's the service?" Laurel asked.

Albert shook his head. "Again, I'm sorry, but it's over. Marcella Campion was buried in the family plot at Bayou Jean over two weeks ago."

Regret hit hard, followed by shame.

"Oh, no," Laurel muttered.

"That's not all," Albert said.

Laurel waited for the other shoe to drop.

"She left everything to you."

Laurel was still wrestling with indecision when Robert came home from work that same evening. And she could tell by the look on his face that he was geared to continue the argument they'd started that morning.

"Good evening, Dad. Would you like a glass of wine before dinner?"

Instead of an answer, he hit her with the same question he'd asked earlier.

"What did Albert want?"

"To tell me that Grandmother Campion had died."

The smile on Robert's face shocked her.

"Dad! Really!"

He shrugged. "What? You'd rather I be hypocritical? We didn't like each other. There's no need pretending at this late date. Besides, her demise puts an end to the ridiculous notion that crazy family continued to champion."

If he'd slapped Laurel in the face, she couldn't have felt any more betrayed.

"Crazy family? You married one of them. If you believe that so wholeheartedly, then what does that say about your judgment?"

"That I was blinded by your mother's beauty," he snapped, then strode angrily toward the wet bar and poured himself the drink she'd offered moments earlier.

"I see," Laurel said. "Well, that explains my existence, but it doesn't solve all of your dissatisfaction."

Robert spun abruptly, his eyes narrowing angrily as he snapped, "What do you mean?"

"Marcella's death does not change me. Chantelle LeDeux's blood still runs in my veins, too."

Robert's face turned a dull, angry red.

"Shut up!" he said, and then pointed his finger at her as if she was a recalcitrant child. "I'm sick and tired of hearing about visions and spirits and 'seeing' things that aren't there. There's no such thing as being psychic."

Then he flung his drink into the empty fireplace, shattering the glass and splattering the wine into a thousand directions.

"Why?" he shouted. "Why do you keep harping on that goddamned claim as some kind of gift? It ruined your mother. It ruined our marriage, and it's going to make you crazy, just like it did her."

In that moment, both Robert and Laurel would have been startled to realize how alike they really were.

"I'm not crazy, and I'm not my mother!" she shouted back. "But since we're harping on the same old subject again, then let me tell you something right now. You aren't going to get the chance to put me away like you did Mother. I'm leaving in the morning, and I'm not coming back, which should make you exceedingly happy. You will no longer be embarrassed by having to explain to your colleagues that your daughter is a half bubble off plumb.''

Robert didn't know whether to argue or be glad that the break had finally been made.

''Fine. A trip to Europe will probably do you some good.''

''Oh, yes,'' Laurel said. ''I forgot to mention the other part of Albert's news. I'm not going to Europe. I'm going to Louisiana. I'm going home. Grandmother Campion left everything to me, including Mimosa Grove.''

Robert felt as if someone had just yanked the ground out from under him.

''What the hell are you saying?''

''I'm moving. Tomorrow. To the family estate in Bayou Jean, Louisiana, that's what I'm saying. Maybe my absence will give your life some peace. God only knows what it will do to mine, but anything will be better than this.''

Having flung down her personal gauntlet, Laurel strode out of the room.

For once in his life, Robert Scanlon was speechless.

Laurel exited the New Orleans airport terminal with the keys to her rental car clutched in one hand and dragging her piggybacked suitcases with the other. The heat and humidity of Louisiana sucked the air from her lungs and stuck her clothes to her body as she struggled to pull the luggage up over a curb.

''Help you, missy?''

Startled by the unexpected voice, Laurel jumped as

a young black man came out from behind a concrete pillar and pointed at her bags. His features contorted in a constant shift of jerking muscles as he waited for her to answer. Instinctively, her fingers curled around the suitcase handle and she took a nervous step back.

"No. No. I'm fine, thank you," she said quickly.

Instead of leaving her alone, the young man moved closer. Now she could see his bloodshot eyes and the droplet of spittle at the corner of his mouth. When he pointed at her bags, she could see the muscles in his forearm twitching, too. What in God's name was wrong with him? Did he mean her harm?

Suddenly he grabbed her by the wrist, and before she could scream, the air shifted. The man's face began to dissolve before her eyes, and the flesh on his hand melted away, leaving what appeared to be a skeletal hand with fleshless fingers wrapped around her wrist.

Laurel gasped, then yanked out of his grasp. Immediately, the vision disappeared.

"Don't touch me!" she cried, her voice trembling from shock. "I don't want you to touch me!"

His expression crumpled as he started to cry.

"Sorry, lady. Didn't mean to scare you. Just tryin' to help. Mama says to help people in need."

Almost immediately, Laurel felt sick. This young man couldn't be more than twenty-two, maybe twenty-three years old, and now that she could see him clearer, she could tell he was simple. And she knew one other thing about him, too. He was going to die. She didn't know how, and she didn't know when, but it was going to happen as surely as she knew her own name. Once she would have tried to tell him what she'd seen in hopes that she could stop the inevitability of fate. But she'd learned the hard way that fate could not be changed and people did not welcome such news.

So instead of spilling her guts, she took a deep breath and made herself smile.

"It's okay. Please don't cry. You just startled me."

He jammed his hands in his pockets as he ducked his head, then looked up at her from beneath his dark, shaggy brows.

"You not mad at me, lady?"

Laurel sighed. "No, I'm not mad at you."

"Okay, then," he said, and walked away.

Laurel gave him one last glance and then started on into the parking garage. A few feet away, she felt the urge to turn. As she did, she saw the strange young man walking toward the terminal in a slow, shuffling motion. His head was down, his shoulders hunched around his neck, as if bracing himself for a deadly blow. Laurel quickly turned away, willing herself not to think of what she'd just "seen" and wondering if there was anybody in his life who would grieve for him when he was gone.

A few minutes later she found her rental car and wearily stuffed the suitcases in the trunk. With a map of Louisiana unfolded on the seat beside her, she settled a pair of sunglasses on her nose, turned the air conditioner up to high and drove out of airport parking.

It was just after eleven in the morning as she hit the highway and headed south toward the little town of Bayou Jean, which, according to the map, was located somewhere between Houma and the Atchafalaya Bay on the coast. If nothing happened, she would reach Mimosa Grove by late evening.

* * *

Robert Scanlon parked his BMW in the garage, pressed the button on his automatic garage door opener and waited for the door to slide shut before he got out. As a federal prosecutor, being careful about everything was part of the job. Once he was satisfied that he was alone inside his own garage, he grabbed his briefcase and got out.

He entered the house through the utility rooms, at once smelling the inviting scent of beef Stroganoff that Cook was waiting to serve. He started to call up for Laurel to come down, then remembered that she was no longer here. Regret was not a familiar emotion for Robert, but his shoulders slumped as he realized that, unless he was entertaining, he would now be eating all his meals alone.

"Mr. Scanlon?"

He looked up. Estelle was standing in the doorway.

"Yes?"

"Will you be wanting dinner soon?"

"Whenever Cook is ready, let me know."

"Is thirty minutes all right?"

"Perfect," Robert said. "It will give me enough time to enjoy a glass of wine beforehand."

Estelle eyed him curiously, then hurried away to deliver the message, once again leaving Robert to himself.

He tossed his briefcase on the sofa, took off his suit coat and draped it on the back of a chair, reminding himself that this was all for the best. He and Laurel had been spoiling for this break for years, and while it would be damned inconvenient to be without a hostess the next time he entertained, he felt a separation would be in their best interests.

Still, the wine he poured seemed flat despite the

fine vintage, and when he sat down to dinner, the beef
Stroganoff was not as satisfying as he'd expected. All
in all, Laurel's absence had left a bigger hole in his
world than he would ever have believed.

When Cook served dessert, he waved it away, took
his coffee to the office and opened his briefcase. Earlier this week, a woman had come to the federal prosecutor's office with allegations that had blown their
minds.

The woman's name was Cherrie Peloquin, and she
was claiming that her boss, Peter McNamara, was involved in illegal activities. Robert had been in on the
initial meeting and had been the first to suggest that
she should have taken her suspicions to the D.C. police and not the federal prosecutor's office. At that
point, she'd dropped the rest of her bomb when she'd
fixed her gaze on Robert.

"Mr. Scanlon, isn't it?"

Robert nodded.

"I know you're telling me I've come to the wrong
place, and if I have, I apologize. But I was under the
impression that anything that had to do with the
United States military would come under the auspices
of the federal government. Was I wrong?"

Robert frowned. "No, Miss Peloquin, you were
not. But please explain yourself."

Her hand was shaking as she tucked a wayward
lock of hair behind her ear. He could see she was
wavering between continuing the conversation and
getting up and leaving before anything else was said.
At that point, something told him that she was on the
up-and-up.

"It's all right," he said, softening his voice just
enough to give her the courage to continue.

"You don't understand," she whispered. "I really like Peter. I kept trying to tell myself I had to be wrong about him, but I'm not, and I know it."

"Please continue," Robert said.

She took a slow breath, as if bolstering her courage with the momentary delay; then it all spilled out.

"I work for Peter McNamara—"

"Of McNamara Galleries?" Robert asked.

She nodded.

"Sorry, please continue," Robert said, hoping that he'd masked his surprise, but everyone who was anyone in D.C. knew of Peter McNamara, and to think he was about to be implicated in any way in something illegal was shocking, even to him.

"About two months ago, I was getting ready to go out of town for the weekend when I realized that I'd left my plane ticket at the office. I tried to call Peter, hoping he was still at the gallery, and that he could get the ticket and drop it by my apartment, but there was no answer. My flight was very early the next morning, so I felt I had no option but to go back that night or take the chance of missing my plane. I let myself into the gallery and started up the stairs to the offices. I was hurrying, not thinking about anything but what I still had to do when I got back home, when I realized I was hearing Peter's voice. At first it surprised me, because I'd called and he hadn't answered, remember?"

Robert nodded.

"Anyway, I stopped." She flushed as she looked away. "I'm not in the habit of eavesdropping, but I didn't want to walk in on Peter and one of his women friends, you know?"

"Were there lots of different women?" Robert asked.

She shrugged. "I guess, but he wasn't married, and to my knowledge, neither were the women he dated."

"So you waited," Robert echoed, urging her to resume the story.

"Yes, but I soon realized he was alone…and talking on the phone." Tears pooled, but she pinched the bridge of her nose to keep from crying as she continued. "He was speaking Russian…. I knew because I'd had a friend in college who was from Odessa. I didn't understand all the words, but I knew enough to know something was wrong, you know?"

"Yes," Robert said. "Continue."

"He was angry. And there was a tone in his voice that I'd never heard. He sounded cold, almost frightening. I didn't know what to do, but I knew I didn't want to be found outside his door."

Robert frowned. "You had to hear more than some Russian words to make you suspect something was going on. Am I right?"

Tears rolled from her eyes and down her cheeks.

"I recognized enough of what he was saying to know it wasn't good."

"You might have misunderstood. Remember, you said you don't speak the language."

"No, but I understand enough to get by."

"So what did you hear?"

"I heard him telling someone that the money had to be wired to the account before they got the goods."

"Look, Miss Peloquin…he sells art objects. This in itself could be completely innocent."

"I know. I'm not a fool," Cherrie said, swiping

angrily at the tears on her cheeks. "But how innocent is it to say that what he had to sell would change the art of war?"

Robert's heart skipped a beat. "Okay, I'm listening," he said.

Cherrie sighed. "Then he said something to the effect that it was easy to steal from fools. That was when I took off my shoes and ran back down the stairs to make a reappearance, one that Peter would hear. I opened the door again, letting it slam as I came in, and started singing 'Do You Know the Way to San Jose,' because that's where I was going.

"He heard me coming up the stairs and came out of his office. His phone was still in his hand, but he was smiling.

"I should have gotten an Oscar for my performance. He told me my serenade was darling but unnecessary. I laughed and told him I'd forgotten my ticket, sailed past him as if I didn't have a care in the world, retrieved it from my desk, waved it in his face on my way out the door and cried all the way home."

Robert nodded. "I'll need to make some calls, see if anyone in the military is aware of any wrongdoing. Would you be willing to testify if it becomes necessary?"

She hesitated.

"We can make sure you're kept safe."

"But can you do it forever?"

Robert wanted to assure her this was so, but he couldn't, and she knew he couldn't.

"Look, Miss Peloquin, for now, let's play this by ear. We'll stay in touch. If we can corroborate your accusations, we'll go from there."

"Can you keep my name out of this?"

"Right up until the moment you testify," Robert said.

"Then that will have to do," she said.

Moments later, she was gone, leaving Robert and his staff with what amounted to a smoldering bomb.

A year ago, Peter McNamara had been named one of Washington, D.C.'s, most eligible bachelors, and four days ago he'd made the headlines again by being arrested for selling government secrets. Once his name and face had gone international, it hadn't taken long for the new Russian regime to start denying any knowledge of his crimes.

The Russian ambassador had been caught between a rock and the proverbial hard place. Older than McNamara by ten years, he was well versed in the games his country had once played with the most powerful government on earth. But that had been then and this was now, and the Cold War was supposedly over. The Berlin Wall was long gone, and a half-assed order of democracy was trying to take root in what was left of the USSR. But having the truth of McNamara's background emerge would destroy the ambassador's tenuous credibility.

Bit by painful bit, that truth finally came out. McNamara wasn't really Peter's name. He was actually Dimitri Chorkin, and as a young man, he'd been planted in the U.S. by the old Russian KGB. It was still up in the air as to whether or not he'd been spying for his government all these years, but the accusations were strong enough for an indictment. Added to that, he had been making big bucks for the past eleven or so years by selling military secrets to enemies of the United States, which really put the ambassador on edge. He'd had two meetings with the President and was scheduled for a quick flight home to Moscow tomorrow to update his superiors there. He didn't have any kind of news they were going to like and daily wished Chorkin to hell on a fast-burning boat.

During this time, Robert Scanlon had been officially named lead prosecutor, becoming part of the process that would bring an end to Peter's charade. But by refusing to admit he was regretting his daughter's absence, Robert was stuck with nothing but work to keep him occupied. Having gotten himself in this situation with his temper, he now decided to get a head start on things by reviewing the files on the impending case. There was no need worrying about a daughter who didn't wish to comply with society's standards.

Despite his public persona, Peter McNamara had always been something of an enigma. He owned a popular, upscale art gallery, which put him high on the party-circuit guest list. He enjoyed the popularity as well as the notoriety that went with being in the public eye. With district attorneys, senators, even foreign ambassadors, as friends and clients, McNamara had lived secure in the knowledge that his circle of friends represented the crème de la crème of Washington, D.C. But the truth of his existence wasn't that simple. He was a rich, single, remarkably handsome and fit fifty-four-year-old heterosexual male who was living a lie.

Dimitri Chorkin was born in a small village outside of Minsk in the old Soviet Republic of Russia, and it had soon become evident to those around him that his intelligence was far beyond that of his humble parents'. At that point he'd been removed from his home by government officials and taken into a state-run institution for education. By the time he was eleven, he'd acquired the equivalent of two Ph.D.s, one in mathematics, the other in the sciences. At that point, another branch of the government had taken over his education, and by the age of eighteen, he knew everything there was to know about subversive activities. With forged papers and a new identity, he appeared on the campus of Harvard University in the fall of 1968 as a freshman named Peter McNamara and began to assimilate himself into American society, fully expecting to be called upon at any time to do what he'd been trained to do.

But the years passed without further communication from the government that had created him. During that time, the lines between reality and fiction began to blur. Dimitri liked the freedom of the United States as well as the opportunities. By the time he was thirty, he rarely thought of Dimitri Chorkin, and when he did, it was only in the past tense.

He lived as others around him lived, making friends, celebrating holidays and Christmases with his woman of the moment, but never letting anyone see past the obvious. Then he moved to Washington, D.C., opened an art gallery with money he'd made on a dot-com company before it went bust, and after getting drunk at a party with a general's son and some hooker he'd been trying to impress, he became what he'd been trained to be.

Selling military secrets had been an easy and productive addition to his financial portfolio, and it had lasted eleven good years. When they'd arrested him, he'd been stunned. Even after he'd hired a lawyer and been told there was the possibility of a witness in the offing, as well as a traceable connection to the military, he'd scoffed. He was too brilliant to make mistakes like that and felt confident that there was nothing solid linking him to anything illegal, only the revelation of his true identity.

Except, of course, that general's son.

# 2

It was nearing seven in the evening when Laurel drove into Bayou Jean. The heat waves coming up from the concrete hung like a curtain of steam between her car and the town's only stoplight as she waited for it to turn green. An old hound lay immobile on the street corner, immune to everything, including the flies buzzing around his ears. A small child on the opposite corner of the street was so curious about Laurel's presence that what was left of the Popsicle she'd been licking melted and ran between her fingers as she stared.

The light turned green. Laurel grinned and wiggled her fingers at the little girl. Startled, the child ducked her head and turned to run back into the nearby grocery store. As she did, she caught the toe of her sandal on a crack in the sidewalk and fell face first onto the concrete.

Laurel gasped, then winced as she witnessed the impact. She could see blood spurting from the child's lower lip, and without hesitation, wheeled toward the curb and parked. By the time she got out, the little girl was bloody and screaming with pain. Laurel reached her just as the mother emerged from the store.

"Melanie! Melanie! What happened?" the mother cried.

"She tripped and fell," Laurel said. "I saw it from the street."

By now, several other people had come out of nearby stores to see what all the fuss was about. When the little girl, who Laurel now knew as Melanie, realized she was bleeding, she began to cry even louder.

"I've got some medicated wipes," Laurel said, and ran back to the car. She dug through her purse for a small pack of aloe-vera-coated wipes, then hurried back to the little girl, who was now sitting in her mother's lap.

"Easy now, darling," Laurel said softly. "These will make it feel all better, okay?"

She pulled two separate wipes from the packet, unfolded them and laid them gently on the little girl's knees, then handed the rest of the packet to the mother so that she could clean the child's elbow and mouth.

"Thank you so much," the woman said, then pressed a nervous kiss against her daughter's cheek before easing the damp tissue against the child's rapidly swelling bottom lip.

"Oww, Mommy. It hurts," Melanie cried, then hid her face against her mother's breasts.

Laurel delicately fingered a flyaway curl at the side of the little girl's cheek, then asked, "Melanie? Your name is Melanie?"

The little girl nodded without looking up.

"So, how about a new Popsicle?" Laurel asked. "I'll bet your lip would feel a whole lot better with something cold and sweet against it."

There was a moment of silence, and then the little girl nodded.

"Cherry?" Laurel asked.

She nodded again.

"Be right back," Laurel said, and hurried into the small grocery store. "Where is the frozen-food section?"

A curious clerk pointed toward the south wall.

Laurel found the small freezer section, picked up a box of Popsicles and headed toward the checkout counter. She tossed a five dollar bill toward the cashier and hurried toward the door.

"Hey, lady, your change!" the clerk shouted.

"Keep it," Laurel said as she ran out the door.

When she got back to the curb where the mother and child were sitting, she eased down beside them and quickly opened up the box.

"Look, honey! Want to pick out one for Mommy, too?"

The little girl nodded as Laurel handed her a new icy treat. She took one long lick on the cherry-red ice, then took a fresh one out of the box and gave it to her mother.

"Mmm, green," her mother said. "My favorite."

"You, too," Melanie said, and handed one to Laurel.

"Why, thank you," Laurel said. "It's orange...and that's *my* favorite."

She pulled the paper from the frozen treat and then wrapped it around the stick to catch the drips as she began to lick.

Laurel handed the box around to the remaining bystanders.

"Help yourselves before they melt."

A couple of the older women shook their heads and smiled before walking away, but a teenage boy and his girlfriend, as well as a woman with two kids in tow, accepted the offer.

"This is good," Laurel told Melanie as she tried to keep up with the quickly melting Popsicle. "Thank you."

Melanie ducked her head but continued to lick, looking at Laurel only when she thought Laurel was not looking back.

Now that the small drama was over, the young mother also took time to assess the stranger who'd involved herself in her daughter's plight. The Cajun accent was thick in her voice as she glanced up at Laurel and spoke.

"My name is Yvette Charbonneau. This is my baby girl, Melanie."

Laurel smiled. "Nice to meet you, Yvette…and you, too, Melanie. I'm Laurel Scanlon."

Melanie giggled once, then slurped noisily to catch a big drip before it fell on her T-shirt.

"You just passin' through?" Yvette asked, then took a big bite of the green Popsicle, letting it melt on her tongue.

Laurel hesitated, took a bite of her own Popsicle, then did something she'd been taught not to do and talked with her mouth full.

"No. My grandmother lived just south of here. She died recently and left her property to me. I was on my way there when I saw your little girl trip and fall."

Yvette's expression fell. "Oh…I didn't mean to pry. I'm sorry for your loss."

"That's all right," Laurel said, and then finished off the last of her Popsicle before standing. "I'd better be going. I want to get to Mimosa Grove before dark.''

The shock on Yvette Charbonneau's face was obvious. She stood abruptly, clutching her little girl against her breast.

''You goin' to Mimosa Grove?''

Laurel nodded.

''Miz Marcella was your grandmama?''

Suddenly Laurel realized that the friendliness she had seen on the people's faces was gone. She took a step back, bracing herself for judgment.

''Yes.''

An old woman who'd been standing nearby suddenly moved out of the shade toward the curb.

''You be Phoebe's girl?''

Laurel nodded, and wondered if she was going to have to defend the honor of her family name down here, as well.

''Praise be,'' the old woman said, and then made the sign of the cross.

The others who'd been staring at Laurel began to smile, echoing similar murmurs of encouragement and welcome as Laurel stared at them in disbelief.

''Miz Marcella was a good woman,'' the old woman added. ''We gonna miss her, yeah.'' Then she eyed Laurel up and down, hesitating only briefly before asking. ''You got the sight…like Miz Marcella?''

Between the shock of their obvious welcome and the thickness of the old woman's Cajun accent, Laurel wasn't certain what she was hearing. But if she wasn't mistaken, not only had these people acknowledged Marcella's psychic abilities but had revered her for them.

"Uh…um, I…"

The old woman saw the fear on Laurel's face and suddenly understood.

"It be a great thing…dat gift of sight," she said softly. "Miz Marcella and me…we friends, yeah, from way back. Been missin' her somethin' fierce. But you here now…so a piece of her still wit' us after all." Then her expression shifted to one of concern as she added, "You gonna stay, yeah?"

The muscles in Laurel's throat tightened as she nodded.

The old woman smiled. "Ain't no seer, me…but I heal some. If you get da malaise, you come see old Tula. I fix you up good, yeah?"

Laurel took a deep breath. "Yes. I'll remember that."

Then she glanced nervously around at the others who were still present. No one seemed wary or offended. She gave them a tentative smile, which they quickly returned.

Then Tula spoke again. "Marie LeFleur…she know you comin'?"

Laurel frowned. The name was vaguely familiar, but she couldn't remember why.

"Who's Marie LeFleur?"

The old woman smiled. "You find out when you get to Mimosa Grove. When you see her, you tell her, Tula, she say hello."

"Yes, all right," Laurel said, and with a quick wave toward Melanie and Yvette Charbonneau, started to leave. But before she could get off the curb, a police car pulled up beside her car and parked. When a stocky, middle-aged man got out with a glare on his face, she stifled a groan.

"Somebody got trouble?" he asked, eyeing Laurel warily before looking at the others gathered on the sidewalk. Then he saw the little girl's injuries and frowned. "What happened here?"

Melanie pointed at Laurel. "She gave me a new icy," she said.

"Well, that's right nice of her," he said, then eyed the blood all over her clothes, as well as the cuts and scrapes. "How come you bleedin' there, darlin'? You didn't run into the street, now, did you?"

Laurel felt an angry flush spreading across her cheeks as she glared at the officer.

"I did not hit that child with my car and then try to buy her off with a Popsicle, if that's what you're trying to imply," she snapped. "The child fell. I saw it happen and stopped to help. Now, if you all will excuse me, I want to reach Mimosa Grove before dark."

The policeman's expression shifted instantly. Before he could ask, Laurel stomped toward her car and got inside.

Frowning, Yvette gathered her child up in her arms. "Now, Harper, you know what you just went and done? You insulted Miz Marcella's granddaughter, that's what."

She shook her head at him in disgust, then hurried back inside the grocery, anxious to finish her shopping and get her little girl home so she could better tend to her injuries.

Harper Fonteneau paled, then shoved his hat to the back of his head, watching with unconcealed dismay as Laurel drove away.

"Now, why didn't somebody introduce me before I shot off my mouth?"

"Ain't nobody able to tink dat fast," old Tula countered, muttering to herself as she shuffled away.

By the time she passed the city-limits sign, Laurel's good mood had returned. She wasn't certain what awaited her at Mimosa Grove, but it was obvious that the people of Bayou Jean were not of a mind to run her out of town on a rail. Just the thought of being accepted for who she was made Laurel smile, and she was still smiling as she glanced down at the map on the seat beside her. According to the lawyer's directions, she should be close to her destination.

A short distance down the road, she saw a rural mailbox mounted on a rusting scroll of decorative wrought iron. She slowed down, then tapped the brakes, giving herself time to read the faded name on the side of the box.

Campion.

Her heart skipped a beat. This must be it! According to the lawyer's letter, this marked the front boundary to Mimosa Grove. She turned the steering wheel sharply to the right, then accelerated slowly, maneuvering the car through a narrow drive bordered on both sides with overgrown bushes. Within seconds, she emerged onto the grounds with a slightly obstructed view of a massive, three-story structure.

Once it must have been majestic in its elegance, but no longer. Everywhere she looked, there were large, spreading mimosa trees in full bloom, as well as a solid wall of them surrounding the grounds on three sides. As she drove closer, she could see that the roof of the old mansion was in obvious need of repair, as were the railings on the second-story veranda. Four massive Corinthian pillars marked the

length of the front of the house, standing three stories
tall and doing what they could to hold up the slightly
sagging roof. Paint peeled and flaked without preju-
dice, giving the entire house the appearance of having
some horrible, scaly disease. Overgrown landscaping
that should have framed the old house's appearance
only added to its encroaching demise.

Laurel sighed. It wasn't what she'd expected, and
it certainly wasn't how she remembered it, but it
didn't change the fact that it was hers. As she drove
farther, she noticed a pair of peacocks near a large,
scum-covered pool of green water. She had a vague
memory of standing near the edge and tossing bread-
crumbs to a pair of oversize goldfish. Obviously the
fish were no more, because that murky water couldn't
possibly sustain life other than bacteria and mosquitoes.

As she drove past, the peacocks squawked their
disapproval, then fanned their tails before strutting toward the shade of a huge mimosa. A faint breeze
shifted the fragile, spiky blooms on some trees near
the road, causing a few of them to come loose and
shower down on her car, while others were caught on
the air and sailed past. Another memory surfaced, of
standing beneath such trees while loose blossoms
drifted down upon her face and hearing her mother
tell her the blooms weren't really flowers, but pink-
and-white fairies. She knew if she closed her eyes,
she would be able to hear the laughter that had come
afterward.

Quick tears blurred her vision when she realized
how long it had been since she'd thought of her
mother in a positive vein. If only Phoebe hadn't died.
If only she hadn't let her father control her life after-

ward, she might have known Marcella Campion as more than just a name.

"Oh, Grandmother, forgive me. I should have come back."

Seconds later, a large parrot flew across her line of vision in a blurred swath of red, green and yellow, followed by a smaller blue one. Looking closer, she realized there were dozens of parrots, some perched in nearby trees, others flying from tree to tree in a colorful game of aerial hopscotch.

Moments later she pulled to a stop only feet from the steps leading up to the veranda. She killed the engine and got out, anxious to see if the interior of the house looked as abandoned as the exterior. She circled the car and had started up the steps when suddenly a large peacock appeared on the porch above her. Its tail fanned to full display as it let out a piercing and territorial shriek.

Laurel paused nervously, uncertain whether to broach the peacock's territory or wait until it moved away. Before she had time to decide, the front door was flung open, and a tiny, cocoa-skinned woman of indeterminate age, wearing a red-and-white muumuu, her hair wound up in a bun and yellow flip-flops on her feet, came out on the run.

"Shoo! Shoo!" she cried, waving her arms over her head. "Get on with you!"

Like the bird, Laurel took a nervous step back, not quite sure if the warning was meant for her or the peacock. Moments later, the peacock gave one last shriek, which set the hair on the backs of Laurel's arms on end, then moved away in slow, elegant steps, its long, multicolored tail now dragging behind in grand, sweeping motions.

Now that the bird was gone, Laurel found herself motionless beneath the woman's dark, piercing stare.

"Hello. I'm Laurel Scanlon. Marcella's lawyer sent me a letter about—"

"You didn't look much like Phoebe when you was little. You still don't. Look more like Chantelle herself, I think."

Laurel's mouth dropped open. She knew, because she felt air moving between her teeth, but for the life of her, she couldn't find the will to close it. Mesmerized by the intensity of the little woman's dark stare, she stood, waiting for whatever came next.

"Yeah, like Chantelle," the old woman muttered, then reached forward, first touching the dark copper strands of Laurel's hair, then running the back of her forefinger down the side of Laurel's cheek.

"So," the old woman said. "You came." Then she nodded approvingly. "Marcella said you would. I should have known better than to doubt her words. Come. Come. You must be exhausted."

All the breath went out of Laurel in one instant. Until the old woman had mentioned it, she hadn't realized how tired she really was. Still, she needed clarification of a few simple facts.

"Are you Marie?"

A wide smile shifted the wrinkles on her face.

"You remember me?"

Laurel was embarrassed. "No, I'm sorry to say I do not. But I met a woman named Tula back in Bayou Jean who mentioned your name."

Marie nodded. "Ah, yes…Tula. She and Miz Marcella grew up together. Friends from way back, you know."

Laurel nodded. "I gathered as much." She hesitated, then had to ask. "Marie…the people here—"

"What about them?" Marie asked.

Laurel wasn't sure how to approach the subject.

"Speak up, girl," Marie said. "You never learn answers if you don't ask questions."

"When the people I saw in Bayou Jean learned I was Marcella's granddaughter, they seemed pleased."

"But of course," Marie said. "What else would they be?"

"But they had to know she was…that she could—"

"You mean, did they know she had the sight? But of course! Over the years, many came for help. She turned no one away."

Laurel shook her head in disbelief. "Somebody pinch me or I'm going to think I've just died and gone to heaven."

Marie frowned. "This is not so where you come from?"

"Hardly," Laurel said.

Marie shrugged and then tugged gently at Laurel's wrist.

"So it is good you are here, yes? Now come. You must be tired. Your room is ready, and when you have rested, we will have supper."

"Wait," Laurel said. "I need to get my bags."

"No…no, this I will do for you."

"But, I—"

"It is my job. It is my honor," Marie said. "Now, no more arguments."

Laurel could tell it would not be wise to mention that she was far more capable of carrying luggage than a woman of Marie's age, so she did as she was told and followed her inside.

The moment Laurel stepped into the foyer and saw the grand staircase curving upward to the second-, then the third-floor landings, she had a feeling of déjà vu. She looked down at the pink-marble flooring and then up at the flocked but fading designs on the wine-colored wallpaper and could remember playing jacks in a corner of the foyer and hearing her mother's laughter nearby. From where she was standing, she could see into two different rooms, and both appeared to have been furnished with pieces straight out of a museum. Moments later, the door swung shut behind her. The thud echoed within the three-story foyer like a shot. Even though she knew it had been nothing but a draft that made the door swing shut, she had to shake off the feeling of having been entombed.

"Welcome to Mimosa Grove," Marie said, then added, "Welcome home. You come this way to your rooms."

Laurel felt a ridiculous urge to cry. If only this place would be the home she'd never had. Then she realized Marie was already halfway up the staircase and hurried to follow.

Almost immediately, she was struck by a faint feeling of despair. The farther up she went, the stronger the emotion became. A few steps shy of the first landing, she was forced to stop. She grabbed onto the stair rail and closed her eyes, physically unable to move any farther.

The house was silent, only the sound of her own breathing could be heard, and yet the sobs of a woman were vivid in her ears. At that point she was wondering if she'd made a mistake in coming and toyed with the thought of returning shamefaced to her father. Within seconds of the thought the crying stopped, and she felt as if she was being urgently begged to stay.

Suddenly Marie was at her side, her bony fingers curling around Laurel's wrist.

"Tell her who you are and then say a prayer for her," she said swiftly. "Say it now."

Laurel's legs went weak. "Say a prayer?"

Marie nodded briefly. "*Oui*, quickly now," she urged.

"For whom?" Laurel asked.

"For the lost soul," Marie said.

Ignoring the ridiculousness of the order and accepting that she was out of her element in this strange but wonderful place, Laurel did as she'd been told.

"I'm Laurel, Marcella's granddaughter," she whispered, and heard the fear in her own voice. Then she began to murmur, asking God for forgiveness and blessings for any and all who lingered here, beseeching those who were lost to go toward the light.

Almost immediately, the heaviness that had weighed on her heart was gone. She opened her eyes and then started to shake. Marie was still standing at her side, still clutching her wrist.

"My God!" Laurel asked. "What just happened?"

Marie shrugged. "I am sorry. I should have told you sooner. It won't happen again, now that the house knows who you are."

The skin on the back of Laurel's neck began to crawl, as if plagued by a thousand tiny ants.

"What do you mean, now that the house knows?"

Again Marie shrugged. "Forgive me…that was a poor choice of words. But Mimosa Grove is old, and with age come eccentricities. She has seen much happiness…and much sadness in her time. Even though physical bodies of previous residents no longer exist, the echoes of their laughter and grief are still here for those who are sensitive enough to feel. I should have thought to warn you.'' Then she smiled, and the action shifted a thousand wrinkles on her face into new positions. ''Like Mimosa Grove, I, too, suffer a lapse now and then.''

Laurel tried to smile back, but she was too shocked to speak.

''You come now,'' Marie urged. ''Lie down for just a bit. I'll call you when it's time for the evening meal.''

Laurel let herself be led up the stairs, then down the hall, as if she were a child. It wasn't until Marie pushed a door open and stepped aside that Laurel found her voice again.

''These will be your rooms,'' Marie said. ''Your grandmother enjoyed them. It is good that they will be occupied again.''

Too startled to hide her dismay, Laurel took a small step back.

''These were my grandmother's rooms?''

Marie nodded.

Laurel shivered. She could hear the panic in her voice but couldn't stop herself from asking, ''Please, I'd rather stay somewhere else.''

Marie frowned and then shook her head.

''But no, my dear. Marcella would be so pleased that you are here. Besides, the other rooms are not fit for habitation.''

Then she shrugged, as if to say the discussion was

over, put her hand in the middle of Laurel's back and gently pushed her forward.

Laurel shivered as she entered the rooms, eyeing the dark burgundy upholstery fabric and the even darker mahogany paneling on the walls. The sagging drapes at the windows had been hanging so long that the colors of the paisley print had long since been bleached by the sun. And yet, as depressing as the rooms should have been, almost immediately upon entering, the anxious emotions Laurel had been experiencing disappeared.

"In here is the bedroom, *ma petite,* and the bath just beyond. Mimosa Grove is ancient, but her accommodations are not. Miz Marcella had the plumbing redone a few years ago, and all is as it should be. You will be much at home here, as she was, yes?"

Laurel nodded, then turned to Marie with a smile. "Yes, this is wonderful."

Marie's smile widened. "I knew it would be so." Then she gestured toward the bed in the adjoining room. "For now, you rest. I will call you for the evening meal."

The bed looked soft and inviting, and the linens carried the scents of both wisteria and fresh air. With the exhaustion of travel and the unexpected connections she'd experienced from unsettled spirits, there was nothing left in Laurel with which to argue.

She nodded once, then stepped out of her shoes and crawled onto the bed. By the time Marie returned with the bags and a bouquet of fresh flowers for the writing table in the sitting room, Laurel was fast asleep.

# 3

Justin Bouvier logged off the computer in his office, then leaned back in his chair and combed his fingers through his hair. If he'd still been in New York, he would have gone for a massage at the gym before going home to dinner. But the only people giving massages in Bayou Jean were the Gatlin girls, and their idea of a massage could get him arrested.

He got up from his chair and walked out of the office, ignoring the active screens of the other two computers. The stock market was closed, so it was time to relax. If he'd wanted to live his life making money twenty-four hours a day, he would have stayed in New York.

He took a cold bottle of lager from the fridge, popped the cap and took the first drink. The chill of the amber liquid and the tang of hops on his tongue hit the spot. He ambled into the living room, flopped down in his father's favorite recliner and then slung his right leg over the arm as he turned on the TV. Almost immediately and out of habit, he shifted his sitting position to a more proper one and, not for the first time, wished his parents were still alive to tell him to sit up straight and quit slouching.

His sigh was more regret rather than weariness as

he flipped the channels, intent on catching the national news. It had been four years since he'd walked out on Wall Street to come home and care for his ailing parents. They'd died within months of each other, leaving him free to return to that high-paying, high-powered job. But for reasons he had yet to identify, he hadn't gone back. Now, three and a half years later, he was still here. The fact that there were enough residents in Bayou Jean who were interested in mutual funds and stock market investments still surprised him, but he'd come to believe that nothing happened by accident.

About a month after he'd buried his last parent, the president of the local bank had passed away. Less than a week later, Marcella Campion had approached him and asked if he was interested in taking over her portfolio. He'd done it as a favor to his mother's old friend, then, before the year was out, he had acquired ten other clients. Between the money he made from them and the income derived from his own investments, he was sitting pretty without the hassle of a big city. The only thing lacking in his life was purpose. Living his life in the pursuit of fortune seemed a bit empty without a woman to share it with. God knows his life was lonely. And while he could have settled for any one of a number of single young locals, he wanted the life his parents had enjoyed. He wanted a wife for life, not just a partner in bed, and he had yet to fall in love. Then he thought about the woman he'd been dreaming of and frowned. If only she were real, he would be a happy man. As he sat there, it dawned on him that she'd been absent from his dreams for the past two nights. His pulse rocked slightly, then stuttered back into a normal rhythm. What if she was gone? What if she never came back?

Sighing in disgust at his flights of fancy, he took another drink and decided he was losing his mind. Weary of his own company all the way to his soul, he upped the volume on the television just in time to hear an update on the growing scandal coming out of Washington, D.C.

He shook his head, listening in disbelief as the news anchor began repeating what they'd learned about a well-to-do D.C. local who'd been arrested for selling military secrets to numerous enemies of the United States. But that wasn't the biggest hook to the story. Discovering that the local, Peter McNamara, was really a man named Dimitri Chorkin, a Soviet spy who'd been planted in the United States years ago, had caused a horrible backlash between the American and Russian governments. Despite the Russian president's reassurance that Chorkin was a man whose existence had been overlooked and forgotten by the old hard-liners and unknown to the new democratic presence in their nation's capital, the implications of his existence were causing enough repercussions to resurrect the Cold War.

Justin stared at the man's picture on the screen. He looked so ordinary—so like someone who might live next door. He thought of how much he'd adored his parents and wondered how someone could give up homeland, family and friends to live a lie in a country that was not one's own, never mind the added danger of being a spy.

Then a series of rapid knocks sounded at his door, and the national news and Dimitri Chorkin were forgotten as he hurried to answer.

*   *   *

It had been less than forty-eight hours since Laurel's arrival at Mimosa Grove, but she felt like she'd lived there forever. She'd returned the rental car and was having Marcella's Chrysler detailed and inspected by a local who'd given her a cold bottle of Coke and a ride home, then gladly offered to bring it out to her when he was done.

The friendliness was so heartwarming and so unexpected that she was doing something she'd never done before—letting down her guard.

The memories of the falsely cordial lifestyle she'd lived in Washington, D.C., were fading by the hour. The longer she was here, the more familiar her surroundings became. What had appeared strange and foreboding upon arrival now welcomed her—except, of course, Elvis the peacock, so named for his flashy garb and macho attitude. Despite all Laurel's good intentions and offers of special treats, the young peacock would have none of her and continued to challenge her at every turn. Marie laughed aloud each time Laurel exited the house, watching with unfeigned delight as the young woman tried to make peace with the big bird.

With a small bag of sunflower seeds in her hand and determination in every step, Laurel sneaked out the back of the mansion, intent on taking a walk. But to do that, she had to get past Elvis without losing face again. It didn't strike her as the least bit odd that while she took spirits and visions as a matter of course, she was in danger of losing her cool with what amounted to a turkey in drag.

Marie LeFleur was right behind her, eyeing the tall, leggy redhead who was Marcella's granddaughter and shaking her head in disapproval at the bright blue spandex bike shorts and red sports bra she was wearing. Mimosa Grove had never seen anything like Laurel Scanlon. Then she smiled to herself. Maybe that was what the old place needed. New blood. She would love to be able to live long enough to know joy and laughter in this place again before she died.

"It gonna rain before dark," Marie warned as Laurel stepped off the back porch, then stopped to retie the laces of one of her tennis shoes.

"I'm not going far," Laurel said. "I just want a little fresh air. I'm used to a daily workout at the gym, and while it's nice to be a little bit lazy, I don't want to get too out of shape."

Marie frowned. "Your shape just fine like it is," she said, eyeing Laurel's lush curves. "You built like your mama, who got her height from Etienne."

Laurel stopped and turned. "Etienne?"

Marie clucked her tongue in disapproval. "Girl, you don't know nothin', do you? Your papa should be ashamed of hisself for keepin' you away from your family. Etienne was your grandpapa."

"Mother never once mentioned him," Laurel said. "Why is that?"

Marie crossed herself, then shrugged. "You were little when she started getting sick. Besides that, he died a month before she was born. She never knew him, so I guess talkin' about him to her baby girl didn't seem important."

"How sad," Laurel murmured. "What happened to him?"

"He died during World War II on a beach in a place they called Normandy. Miz Marcella knew the moment he died. Swore she felt his spirit pass through her body on his way to heaven. Everyone thought she was just nervous about her man being gone when she gave birth to their first child, but they kept their opinions to themselves after she got that telegram. By the time the army shipped his body home, your mama had been born. We interred his body and had Phoebe's christening service at the same time.'' She frowned, remembering the sadness accompanying the memory. ''Your grandmama…she wasn't one for waste. The parish priest had come all this way to bury Etienne, she thought he might as well christen their baby while he was at it.''

''She was tough, wasn't she?'' Laurel said.

Marie laughed aloud. ''Lord, yes.''

Laurel sighed. ''It's unfortunate I didn't inherit some of her guts. I might have fared better in D.C. if I hadn't been so worried about what everyone was thinking of me.''

''No matter,'' Marie said. ''You here now. Everything gonna be all right.''

Laurel eyed the overgrown shrubbery she was going to have to pass to get to the mimosa grove and frowned.

''Not unless I make peace with Elvis,'' she muttered, then looked back at Marie. ''How come I'm the only person he doesn't like?''

''Who knows what's on that bird's mind?'' Marie muttered. ''Remember, honey. It may have feathers, but it's still a male, and I ain't seen one yet worth his salt who could walk and chew gum at the same time.''

Laurel laughed aloud.

''What would my grandmother have done…about the bird, I mean?''

Marie's laughter echoed as she slapped her leg.

"Probably figured out a way to make peacock pie."

Laurel grinned. "Well, he looks too tough to eat, so I guess I'll just practice my sprints and hope for the best."

Marie was still chuckling as she went back inside, leaving Laurel to deal with the problem alone.

Laurel glanced into the thickets, making a mental note to hire someone to help restore the landscaping, and started off on her walk. Before she'd gone fifty feet, Elvis glided down on outspread wings from a nearby tree. He landed between her and the mimosa grove, fanned his tail, then began to strut back and forth, blocking Laurel's path with an intimidating series of shrieks.

"Elvis, darling," Laurel cooed. "Look what I have for you."

She dug into the small bag and pulled out some sunflower seeds, then tossed them on the ground between them.

Elvis might as well have been blind for all the attention he paid to Laurel's seedy bribe.

"Fine, then," she said, and started walking again, telling herself that it would be all right, that this RuPaul of the bird world was nothing but a bunch of noise and feathers, and that there was nothing to be afraid of.

But the moment she moved, the bird gave chase. In a panic, she threw the sunflower seeds toward him, sack and all, and began to run. She didn't look back, but she thought she could hear Marie's laughter as she sprinted into the trees.

Entering the grove was like entering another world. The humidity in the air seemed thicker. Moisture gathered on the leaves, only to drip on Laurel's head and shoulders as she passed beneath the trees. The ground was littered with the fallen pink-and-white blooms, carpeting the floor of the grove in an exotic pseudo-Persian pattern.

Every now and then a parrot would swoop across her line of vision in a startling flight of color and sound on its way to somewhere else. The rackety sound of cicadas blended with the intermittent croaks of tiny tree frogs, reminding her of Marie's warning that it was going to rain.

Intent on getting a little exercise before being shut in for the night with the storm, she took a moment to orient herself within the massive span of trees, then started to jog.

Within minutes, both her hair and clothing were wet, as much from the humidity as from exertion. But it felt good to be working up a good sweat, so she pushed on through the grove, following a faint but distinct path without knowing where it led.

She didn't know how long she'd been running when she heard the first roll of distant thunder. She paused, her heart pounding, her muscles at the point of burning from the run as she bent over and grabbed her knees, bracing herself as she struggled to catch her breath. There was a slight stitch in her side, and she was mentally chastising herself for not bringing some water, when the thunder rumbled again, only closer. She straightened, swiping away straggling bits of hair that had escaped from her ponytail and now clung to her face, and began to retrace what she thought was the way back to the old mansion.

She hadn't gone more than a few feet when she looked down.

"Oh, no," she mumbled, realizing the path on which she was walking was untouched.

She stopped, then turned around to retrace her steps, but she could no longer see the path. The wind was rising, causing blooms and the fernlike leaves alike to fall from the trees in wild abandon. The faster they fell, the more densely the old path was covered.

Her heart skipped a beat.

The storm was almost upon her, and she didn't have the faintest idea which way to go. The wind was whipping through the trees now, and although the heavy canopy above her head might normally have formed a shelter, she could already feel the first drops of rain upon her face. It wasn't as if she minded getting wet, but the gathering clouds had sucked up all the light. Between one moment and the next, night had come.

Before she could focus, a bolt of lightning slammed to the ground, shattering the trunk of a tree less than fifty feet behind her. She screamed, then raced forward just as the rain began to fall in earnest.

*Not that way.*

Immediately, Laurel stopped, her heart hammering against her rib cage, her legs trembling with fear as she made a three-hundred-and-sixty-degree turn. No one was there, yet she'd heard the words as clearly as if the speaker had been standing right behind her.

"Where, then?" she yelled. "Tell me which way to go."

*With the wind at your back.*

She spun abruptly and began to run, taking care to keep the force of the storm at her back, letting the wind push her when her legs were too tired to move.

Several minutes passed, and still she could see

nothing but rain and the dark, verdant thrashing of storm-tossed limbs. Then, just as suddenly as she had entered the grove, she was out, running across the grounds toward the blessed safety of the old house.

Marie was standing at the back with the door open, waving for her to hurry as Laurel bolted up the steps and all but fell into the kitchen. Her eyes were huge, her heart hammering so hard she could barely hear Marie scolding her for being gone too long. She looked down at the puddle she was making on the old linoleum flooring and started to shake.

"I'm sorry," she mumbled. "I'm getting everything wet."

Marie made a clucking sound with her tongue as she began tugging and pulling at Laurel's clothes.

"Take these off right here, baby girl."

When Laurel hesitated, Marie scolded her again.

"There ain't nothin' under those clothes I never saw before, and you gonna catch your death if you don't get yourself dry. Lord, Lord, honey, you worried me right out of my mind. I was afraid you'd gone and gotten yourself lost in there."

Laurel began pulling at the sopping spandex, which was all but glued to her skin.

"I did get lost," she said, shivering as her teeth began to chatter.

Marie kept shaking her head as she helped Laurel peel off the wet clothes and shoes.

"It's good you find your way out," she said. "It's 'bout dark as night out there now, and it ain't even seven o'clock."

"But I didn't," Laurel whispered.

Marie pulled an afghan from the arms of an ancient rocking chair and threw it around Laurel's shoulders, wrapping and patting until it had covered Laurel's nudity all the way to the tops of her knees.

"There now," Marie muttered, then realized what Laurel had just said and looked up with a frown. "What you mean…you didn't? You standin' here big as day, ain't you?"

"I was lost. When it started to rain, I began to run. Then she told me I was going the wrong way."

Marie frowned. "She who? Ain't supposed to be anyone else in the grove."

"I didn't see anyone else. I just heard her voice…in my head. She told me to put the wind at my back, so I did. That's how I got out. That's how I found my way home."

Marie's expression blanked. She took a deep breath, then stared at Laurel before she began to nod.

"What?" Laurel asked.

"She likes you."

Laurel pulled the soft, well-washed blue afghan tighter around her shoulders.

"What are you talking about?"

"Remember the day you arrived? Remember the feelin' you had on the stairs?"

The skin on the back of Laurel's neck began to crawl. It was all she could do to answer.

"Yes."

"That was her. She don't welcome just everybody into this house." Then she patted Laurel's back and then took her by the hand. "Come with me, baby girl. We gonna get you all warm and dry, and then we'll have us some supper. Yep. You're gonna be all right now. Don't ever have to worry 'bout anything again. She likes you. She'll take good care of you."

Laurel paused. "For Pete's sake, Marie. Quit talking in riddles. Who likes me? Who's going to take care of me? Are you trying to tell me that my grandmother's spirit is still in this house?''

"Lord no, honey," Marie said. "Your grandmama was ready to go. She met her Maker with a clear conscience and His name on her lips. She's with her Etienne again and got no need to stay in this place."

"Then what are you trying to tell me?"

Marie looked at Laurel in disbelief. "Why, honey, I thought you knew. It's Chantelle LeDeux."

Laurel stared at Marie as if she'd just lost her mind.

"But didn't she run away from here almost two hundred years ago?"

Marie shrugged. "That's what they say."

Laurel frowned. "Then why would her spirit stay in a place where she hadn't wanted to be?"

Marie shrugged again. "Maybe because she all guilty for running away and leavin' her husband and her babies. Maybe she's doomed to spend eternity here at Mimosa Grove because she didn't stay and care for it in life. Who knows? I'm just the housekeeper round here. You're the one who's supposed to know all that kind of stuff. Come on with you, now. You need to get you a bath before the power goes out."

Laurel followed the old woman upstairs, letting her fuss and scold, because she knew it was her way of showing that she cared. Later, after they'd shared bowls of soup and cold sandwiches by candlelight while the storm still raged beyond the walls, Laurel gave up trying to read and went to bed, hoping that power and rationality would both return with daylight and the passing of the storm. And hoping that somehow she would reconnect with her dream lover, who'd been noticeably absent since her arrival in Louisiana.

Parish police chief Harper Fonteneau and his men had been searching for the little girl for hours, but with no luck. When it started to rain, their hopes dropped. Whatever clues might have led them to four-year-old Rachelle Moutan's location were being washed into the river that connected with the Atchafalaya Bay. Tommy and Cheryl Ann Moutan were pale and quiet as the dead, which bothered Harper even more than if they'd been screaming and cursing his name. But losing a child in the bayou country was dangerous in broad daylight. It was now almost midnight, it had been raining for hours, and he was at the point of praying they'd at least find her body before the gators did.

While little Rachelle's parents clung to each other in desperate silence, her uncle, Justin Bouvier, had been manic—almost driven to find her himself. Upon his arrival three hours earlier, he'd taken to the bayous in a shallow boat with an outboard motor for power. And with a two-way radio for communication, he'd covered a large portion of the waterways on his own, leaving the others to search higher ground, where they believed the little girl to be.

It wasn't until a few minutes ago that one of his deputies had bemoaned the fact that Marcella Campion had passed. If she'd still been alive, they were certain she could have given them a direction in which to search, if not an exact location. It was then that Harper had remembered the woman he'd accidentally insulted in Bayou Jean.

"Holy Mother of God," he muttered. "I forgot she was here."

"Who you talkin' about, Harper?" one of the deputies asked.

"The granddaughter! Miz Marcella's granddaughter is at Mimosa Grove."

"She got the sight like her grandmama?"

"I don't know, but I'm damn sure gonna find out," Harper said, and ran toward the lost child's parents. "You got anything here that belongs to Rachelle?"

Tommy only shook his head and started to cry, but Cheryl Ann had a different answer.

"Her jacket," she said, and ran toward their car. "I brought it in case the mosquitoes got too bad before we got home from the picnic." Moments later she thrust it into Harper's hands. "Are you gonna use the dogs? Maybe it's not too wet for them to track her, right, Harper?"

"No, darlin'," Harper said. "Not the dogs. They couldn't get a scent in this rain. I'm takin' this jacket to Mimosa Grove."

"That won't do any good. Miz Marcella is dead…like my baby." At that, she started to wail.

"Her granddaughter is at Mimosa Grove. I don't know if she's got the sight, but I'm gonna find out."

# 4

Laurel was dreaming about Christmas and a flashing string of lights that kept falling off the Christmas tree when she realized that the flashing lights were really outside and not just in her dreams. She rolled out of bed and stumbled to the window just as the doors of a police car opened and two shadowy figures dashed through the rain toward the house. Without giving herself time to think of why they might be there, she grabbed her robe from the back of a chair and put it on as she ran.

She could hear them pounding on the door before she reached the top of the stairs. As she started down, Marie appeared out of nowhere carrying a flashlight and a baseball bat.

"Marie! What's going on?" Laurel cried.

"Don't know, but I'm gonna find out," Marie said. "Be careful comin' down the stairs. The power is out." Then she yelled through the door, "Who is it? Who's knockin' on the door?"

"It's me. Harper Fonteneau!" the police chief shouted back. "Let me in, Marie. It's an emergency."

Marie set the bat aside and then opened the door, shining her flashlight right in his eyes.

"What wrong with you, Harper? Don't you know it's the middle of the night?"

Harper flinched as the lights blinded him, then pushed his way past Marie and into the foyer. From the corner of his eye, he saw movement on the stairwell and turned to look. It was the woman from town, standing midway up the stairs.

"Ma'am," Harper said, "I need to talk to you."

"You wait a minute!" Marie yelled, and grabbed Harper by the arm as he started up the stairs.

Harper pulled a small pink jacket from inside his coat.

"You see this? It belongs to Tommy and Cheryl Ann Moutan's little girl, Rachelle. She's been missing more than six hours in this storm. We need help, Marie." He waved the jacket toward Laurel. "Can she do it? Is she like Marcella?"

"What's wrong?" Laurel asked.

Harper ran up the stairs as Laurel was coming down. Impulsively, he thrust the jacket in her hands.

"Please…please, lady. Can you see her? Can you tell us where she is?"

All she saw was a tiny pink jacket with the name Barbie embroidered on the front and then the room went dark. She fell backward onto the stairs with the jacket still clutched in her hands. She didn't see Marie rush toward her or feel the police chief's hands as he caught her just before her head hit the stair rail.

"Mommy…I want my mommy."

The small, high-pitched voice that came out of Laurel's mouth raised goose bumps on Harper Fonteneau's arms.

"Holy Mother of God," he said softly, and made the sign of the cross as he stared down at the woman on the stairs.

"Where are you?" he asked. "Where are you, Rachelle?"

"I'm afraid," Laurel cried in that same little sing-song voice. "The gators are gonna eat me up."

Then she started to weep. At that point, Harper began to shake. He didn't want to go tell Tommy and Cheryl Ann Moutan that their baby girl was dead. He didn't want to have to recover her in bits and pieces floating in the bayous.

"Sweet Jesus...no," he muttered, and stifled the urge to throw up.

Laurel flinched, then threw her arms above her head as if covering her face.

"Daddy...Daddy...the water is comin' over the stump."

Harper gasped. Wherever the child was, she was in danger of drowning, which had to mean she was somewhere in the bayous. This wasn't good, because most of the search had been conducted on dry land. He frowned, trying to remember which searchers had been assigned to the waterways, then remembered that Rachelle's own uncle, Justin Bouvier, had gone there on his own. He turned to the deputy who'd accompanied him into the house.

"Give me your radio," he said, pointing to the handheld two-way the deputy had on his belt. As soon as he had it, he keyed it up. "Justin...this is Chief Fonteneau. Do you read me? Over."

There was a crackle of static; then a faint voice broke the silence there on the stairs.

"I read you, Harper. Any news? Over."

"I'm at the Grove," he said. "I need you to listen and listen close."

Justin swiped at the rain beating down on his face.

As he did, a large chunk of a rotting tree came sweeping through the arm of the bayou in which he'd been searching. It hit his fishing boat, causing it to lurch suddenly to the left. His heart skipped a beat as he tightened his hold on the steering arm of the outboard motor, then let the accelerator idle down as he pressed the radio tight against his ear, straining to hear above the storm.

Harper held the radio close to Laurel's mouth and began to feed her questions.

"Rachelle…can you hear me?"

"Yes."

Harper shuddered. It was too damned eerie hearing that voice come out of this woman's mouth.

But Justin didn't have the privilege of knowing where the voice came from. All he knew was that it sounded like his niece's voice.

"Rachelle! Rachelle! Are you there?"

When there was no answer, it dawned on him that Harper had not released the key on the radio, which meant no one could hear him talking. Panicked, he grabbed a piece of canvas from the bottom of the boat and then ducked under it, using it as a buffer between him and the rain. Even though the rain was still pelting down, thanks to the heavy canvas, the exterior sounds had been muted. He could hear Harper's voice and what sounded like Rachelle's. And yet, it wasn't Rachelle. If Marcella Campion was still living, he would have known what was happening. But he'd been to her funeral. He'd watched them carry her casket into the family crypt. So who was at Mimosa Grove? Desperate for answers and willing to try anything, he focused on the faint voices coming to him through the storm. He heard Harper's voice, asking another question.

"Rachelle...can you tell me where you are?"

Laurel shuddered, then wrapped her arms around herself, as if she was freezing.

"In the rain. I'm in the rain."

"What do you see? Can you tell me what you see?"

"It's dark. I can't see nothin' but the dark."

"Is there still lightning?" Harper asked.

"Yes. I'm scared. It's too bright. It hurts my eyes."

Harper looked down. The woman held Rachelle's jacket in a wad beneath her chin, as if trying to absorb it.

"Yes, I know it's bright...and it's scary...but the next time lightning comes, I need you to keep your eyes open. I need you to look around and tell me what you see."

Seconds later, Laurel screamed, but she didn't hide her face. Harper watched her eyes widen and would have sworn that he was looking into the eyes of a frightened child and not the woman lying prostrate on the stairs before him.

"Tell me, Rachelle...tell me what you see."

"A big cypress tree that's broke in half, but still growing and...and...there's a little house on long wooden legs. It looks broken, like the tree."

Justin's heart stuttered to a stop and then jump-started itself as his pulse leaped. That sounded like Marcus Sweeny's old fishing shack, and it wasn't far away. He threw the canvas off his shoulders, checked his compass to make certain he was going in the right direction, readjusted the big searchlight mounted on the bow of his boat, then accelerated carefully.

The wind was at his back now as he moved cautiously through the inky darkness. The rain continued to fall, adding to the misery and difficulties he was facing, but he kept thinking of Rachelle out alone in the storm and knew he would do anything to get her back. He kept the radio close to his ear, listening for more clues as he drew closer to the location of the fishing shack.

Harper's hands were shaking as Marie slipped past him, only to take a seat on the stairs so she could cradle Laurel's head in her lap.

''She wearin' out,'' Marie warned as she eyed the pallor of Laurel's skin and the frantic tic at the corner of her right eye. Even though she understood what was happening and had assisted her old mistress, Marcella, in the same manner over the years, she was still superstitious enough to be made uneasy by the supernatural.

Harper nodded, then lifted the radio. ''Justin…it's Harper. Where are you? Over.''

Justin waited for a shaft of lightning to illuminate more than the small tunnel of light that the searchlight emitted. When it came, he could tell he was about a quarter of a mile from his destination.

''About ten minutes from the location,'' he said. ''Over.''

''Stay tuned. I'm going to question her more. Over.''

Justin had to ask. ''Who? Who are you talking to?''

''Marcella's granddaughter. Over.''

The skin crawled on the back of Justin's neck. Like everyone else in Bayou Jean, he'd known Marcella's daughter, Phoebe. What he hadn't known was that she'd had a daughter, or that she was now at Mimosa

Grove. Even though he'd grown up knowing that the women of Mimosa Grove had gifts beyond the norm, it was unbelievable to think that she was able to tap in on a lost child miles away from where she was.

"Come on, lady," Justin whispered, as he took a chance and accelerated through the night. "Guide me to our little angel before she actually becomes one."

Harper put the radio back to Laurel's mouth.

"Help is coming," Harper said. "Your uncle Justin is coming to find you. Tell me if you see a light."

Laurel lay without moving, but it was her silence that brought their fear to a frantic peak. If she wasn't answering, did that mean they were going to be too late?

"Rachelle...tell me! Tell me what you see."

A soft, almost nonexistent moan slipped from between Laurel's lips, and then she gasped.

"The water...it's over the stump. My shoes are wet. Mommy gonna be mad at me."

Harper swallowed around the knot in his throat. God help them all. The water was rising. He spoke quickly into the radio, knowing his panic was evident from the tremor in his voice.

"Justin! You've got to hurry. I think she's standing on a stump or a bunch of logs...she says the water is over her feet."

The moment Justin heard this, he gunned the engine, despite knowing full well the dangers of running blind in the dark. But if he was too late to save Rachelle, it would be far easier to die than to go back and face his sister without her baby girl.

And while he was racing through the bayou, Laurel suddenly jerked, then sat straight up. She was staring past Harper's shoulder so intently that he turned to look, half expecting to see a ghost of some kind awaiting him at the foot of the stairs. But when she stood abruptly and started waving her hands, Harper knew their prayers had been answered.

"I see the light! I see the light!" Laurel cried.

"Where is it?" Harper asked.

"There," Laurel said, pointing over Harper's right shoulder toward the front door of Mimosa Grove.

"You're on her right, Justin! She sees you! She sees you!"

Justin swerved immediately, just missing a large growth of cypress knees jutting up from the bayou.

"God help me," he whispered as he peered through the intense downpour, seeing nothing silhouetted in the light but swamp and rain.

"Help me...help me!" Laurel cried, and started waving and jumping up and down.

Within seconds, the spotlight on the bow of Justin's fishing boat swept past her, but he'd seen the motion. He corrected his direction, and then he saw her—looking even tinier in the dark, but alive and moving just the same.

"I see her! I see her!" Justin yelled, then stuffed the radio into a waterproof bag in the floor of the boat and gunned the motor.

As he drew closer, it appeared as if Rachelle was standing on water. The image made him think of the story in the Bible where Jesus had walked on water; then he remembered hearing her say that she was standing on a stump.

He idled the boat as close to the little girl as he could get, but each time he tried to reach for her, the rapid flow of the water would pull his boat away. If she'd been a little older, or if he had not been alone, retrieving her from the submerged stump would have been easier. Each time he came toward her, she was too blinded by the searchlight to see what he was trying to do.

Then, after several futile tries, he realized she was trying to walk to him. If she stepped off that stump and into the swiftly moving flood waters, she would be gone and there would be nothing he could do to save her.

"Hang on, *bébé*. Stay there! Don't move!" he yelled. "Uncle Justin will come to you."

All the time that Laurel had been clutching the jacket, she'd been so locked into Rachelle Moutan's fear that she'd been unable to voice her own thoughts. And even though she'd been aware of the other voice on Harper Fonteneau's radio, she'd been unable to connect to him in any way.

Through Rachelle's eyes, she'd seen the first glimmer of the searchlight as the boat had come through the storm. She'd felt the acceleration of the little girl's heartbeat. The sound of her sobs had torn through Laurel's heart as surely as if they'd been her own. Then she'd heard the man shouting, telling the little girl to stay there. She'd felt the child's urge to move, and she'd added her own silent plea to make her stay still.

The light on the boat was in her eyes now. She could hear the sound of the engine blending with the wind and the rain. The smell of gasoline scorched the insides of her nostrils as the man turned the boat sideways, trying to get close enough to snatch the child from the stump.

She felt Rachelle's hesitation again, and again she

silently told her to wait for help to come to her. Once she felt the child touching her own face, as if in disbelief that she was hearing voices from within, but Laurel couldn't lessen her connection to the child for fear she would come to harm. So she waited, watching through Rachelle's eyes as the light centered on the stump, watching as a shadowy figure suddenly went over the side of the boat and started swimming through the swiftly moving waters toward her.

He was close now. She could hear the sound of his labored breathing as he fought the current to get to her. Suddenly he loomed, a large and imposing silhouette, separated from the storm by the searchlight at his back. Laurel watched him reach for the child, heard him shouting—pleading with Rachelle to jump.

"Come to me, *bébé*. Jump to Uncle Justin. You can do it."

The sound of his voice sent a shiver of recognition sliding through Laurel's consciousness, nearly shattering her concentration. But she made herself focus on the child. She felt her fear, sensed her hesitation, then urged her forward.

*You can do it, Rachelle. Jump, as if you were playing in your own backyard and it was your own little wading pool. He will catch you, and then you can go home to your mommy and daddy.*

Rachelle heard her uncle's voice, but it was the voice in her head that gave her the courage she needed. Without further hesitation, she jumped off the stump, falling directly into Justin Bouvier's outstretched arms.

At the moment of impact, Justin wrapped his arms around her and struggled with the urge to weep. They'd been looking for her for so long, and he'd been so afraid that the end to this day would be one of tragedy. Instead, their precious little girl was alive and well.

"That's my good girl," Justin said softly, clutching her close against his chest as he headed back toward the anchored boat.

And as he turned, the searchlight momentarily wiped the shadows from his face. In that moment, Laurel saw him through Rachelle's eyes and heard herself moan in disbelief.

The chin was just the least little bit square. The nose was strong, and once upon a time, might have been broken, because there was a tiny bump just below the bridge. His hair was seal black and slicked down upon his head from the rain, and she knew, although she could not see, that his eyes were as black as the night. Through Rachelle's tiny hands, she could feel the muscles in his back as they stretched and flexed while getting her safely to the boat.

But she'd seen him before and knew well the power in his body as he'd thrust repeatedly into the valley between her legs. She knew the cut of his cheek, the taste of his lips, the softness of his breath as his mouth moved upon her skin. And she knew the gut-wrenching sound of his groan when he came.

It seemed impossible, but it was the man from her dreams.

Unaware of the drama being played out back at Mimosa Grove, Justin lifted Rachelle into the boat and then climbed in with her.

At the same moment, Laurel Scanlon dropped to the stairs in a faint. That scared Harper in a way nothing else could have done. Unaware of the rescue Laurel had witnessed, he read the unconsciousness as death.

"Justin! Justin! This is Harper! Can you hear me? What's happening? Over."

There were a few moments of silence; then he heard a brief bout of static as Justin keyed his own radio.

"This is Justin. I found her. She's alive. You find Cheryl Ann and tell her that I'm bringing her baby home. Over and out."

Harper leaned back against the stairwell, then dropped his head.

"Praise God," he said softly, then reached down and lifted the little pink jacket from Laurel's clenched fist.

He looked down at Marie, then at the woman she was cradling.

"Is she all right?"

Marie nodded. "She will be."

Harper stared for a moment, then lifted his hat and combed a hand through his hair.

"I don't know how she does it, and I wouldn't admit to many that I'd ever seen it happen, you understand. But tonight I thank God for the blood that runs in this woman's veins."

"Yes," Marie said. "I will tell her so. Later."

Harper hesitated, then pointed down at Laurel.

"Want me to help you get her up to her bed or something?"

Marie sighed. "It would be better for her if you would. I am no longer as strong as I once was."

Harper pointed at Marie's flashlight.

"With the power still out, I'm gonna need some light to negotiate these steps."

Marie aimed the flashlight as he lifted Laurel out of her arms. Together, they started up the stairs. A few moments later he laid Laurel in her bed, gave her shoulder a brief pat. Slightly embarrassed by the tender gesture, he faked a cough, then readjusted his rain-soaked hat into a different position before looking away.

"You gonna be all right here?" he asked.

Marie glanced toward the bed, then sighed, unaware that her shoulders slumped wearily with the sound.

"Yes. We will be fine."

Suddenly anxious to leave this place where magic happened, Harper nodded.

"I'll let myself out and lock the door as I go. No need you goin' back down those dark stairs just to see me out."

Marie nodded her thanks. She could hear Harper's receding footsteps as she pulled a rocking chair up beside Laurel's bed, then sat herself down. She heard the police car start up, then heard it drive away, and still she sat, rocking slowly as she kept watch.

It was nearing dawn by the time Justin pulled up in front of his home and got out. The storm had finally passed, leaving the air with a fresh, rain-washed scent and the ground soft beneath his feet. The aftermath of the search was finally starting to sink in as he started toward the house, his feet dragging with every step.

He kept picturing the joy on his little sister's face and his brother-in-law's tear-filled eyes, both of them too moved to speak as they tore Rachelle from his arms, then held her close in a desperate embrace.

They'd tried to thank him, but he hadn't been able to listen. Not now, not when all their emotions were too raw. He wanted to fall on his knees and thank God for the woman at Mimosa Grove, but he knew that if he went down, he would be too weak to get up. And there was the fact that he didn't even know her name. So he'd gotten back in his truck and taken himself home with the promise that before the sun went down on this day, he would know the name and the face of the woman who'd saved his family from tragedy.

Back in D.C. that same night, Peter McNamara was going through his own brand of drama—one just as deadly, but one he was determined to survive. Even though he'd grown accustomed to the luxuries afforded U.S. citizens, he wasn't a fool. He'd forgotten none of his Spartan upbringing, or what he'd been trained to do under the old Soviet regime. Despite the government's outrage toward him, which was being displayed through the media, he knew there was no paper trail linking him to dirty money. Everything had been done through telephone instructions, then later through the Internet, and bounced off so many other stations that it was impossible to tell where it had originated or ended. The monies were always paid directly to a numbered Swiss bank account. No one he'd done business with had ever seen him, so there were no witnesses to testify against him—except Trigger, the general's son. Trigger didn't know it, but even though Peter had believed himself untouchable, he'd still left a back door through which to exit, while implicating Trigger as the man to arrest—and the only man who'd betrayed his country.

Unless the prosecution knew something he didn't

or Trigger had panicked and talked, most of their case was being based on the fact that the military had discovered their files had been hacked into, and somehow they'd learned he was a Russian spy who'd been living under an alias in the United States of America. He figured they'd put two and two together and were trying to make it add up to five to fit the scenario.

He figured his best bet was to persuade his lawyer to set up a meeting with the federal prosecutor. He didn't have a genius IQ for nothing. He figured he could explain and negotiate, and make a far better case for himself than anyone he could hire.

After a phone call to his lawyer, he went to bed with an easier spirit. Tomorrow he would talk to the prosecution and be out of prison in time for dinner.

It said something for Peter's state of mind that he believed his situation could be solved so easily.

And so he slept without dreaming, certain that his plan would not fail, while Justin Bouvier sat on his front porch, waiting for daylight to meet the woman who'd saved his niece.

# 5

Laurel woke up the next morning feeling restless. She'd dreamed of the rescue over and over in the night—seeing the face of Rachelle's rescuer had been startling, then confusing. It was most certainly the man from her dreams, and she'd seen him through the little girl's eyes, so she hadn't been imagining him there. The police chief had called him Justin. Now she had a name to go with the face. But she didn't know what to do next. Should she force the issue and go in search of him, or wait and let the fates that had brought them together in sleep finish the job in their own time? When nothing brilliant occurred to her that would make sense of the latest chaos in her life, she dragged herself out of bed and headed for the bathroom.

After showering and getting dressed, she did something very out of character. When she went downstairs, instead of going to breakfast, she went to the library to call her father.

Robert Scanlon had overslept. It was so unlike him that even as he was finishing his first cup of coffee, he was still rattled by the fact.

Estelle was bringing a plate of toasted English muffins and a small crystal dish filled with strawberry preserves into the breakfast room as he was getting up from the table.

He glanced at the short, stocky woman without really noticing she'd recently colored her salt-and-pepper hair a light brown, applied both mascara and lipstick, and was wearing nice shoes with short, but sensible heels instead of her normal flat-soled Hush Puppies.

Robert eyed the pools of melting butter on the toasted muffin halves and manfully ignored the pangs of hunger.

"Estelle, I don't have time for that," he said, and began stuffing the files he'd been reading back into his briefcase.

Estelle took a freshly ironed napkin from a sideboard and laid it beside his plate.

"Now, Mr. Robert, you know you won't take care of yourself at work. You eat something or it will be dinnertime before you stop long enough to eat again."

Before Robert could argue, the phone rang. Estelle jumped, then bolted toward the phone. Robert Scanlon had no idea that she had a new admirer, nor was she going to tell him. She'd worked for him for more than fifteen years, and not once had he inquired as to her personal life or health.

"You're probably right about eating," he said, then waved her away from the phone. "And I'll get that. It's bound to be someone from the office wondering where I'm at."

Disappointed, Estelle left the room, praying it wasn't her friend, Charlie. She didn't want to have to explain to her boss about the personal calls she got when none of the family was at home.

Luckily for Estelle, it wasn't Charlie. As for Robert, he'd guessed wrong about the caller, too. It wasn't his secretary. It was Laurel.

"Good morning, Dad. I called your office, but they said you weren't there yet. Are you ill?"

Robert was surprisingly touched by her concern. He didn't know it, but his voice softened as he answered.

"No, dear, I'm fine. I just overslept."

Laurel frowned. "Are you sure? You never oversleep."

Still off kilter from her call, he popped off before he thought and unintentionally resurrected their antipathy.

"Yes, Laurel, I'm sure," he said. "How is Mimosa Grove? As dilapidated as ever, I assume."

Laurel resisted the urge to snap back. Just once, she wished he could be positive about something.

"It's very beautiful down here, Dad, although we had quite an event during the storm last night. A little girl was lost, but the searchers finally found her."

"That's good," Robert said. "I'm sure her parents are very grateful."

Laurel thought about telling him her part in the recovery, then changed her mind. There was no reason to assume he'd changed his opinion of having a daughter with psychic abilities.

"Yes, I'm sure they are," she said. "Is everything okay there? I miss seeing Estelle's monthly make-overs."

"What makeovers?"

Laurel laughed. "Her hair? Her makeup? Dad...for such a brilliant lawyer, you are horribly unobservant.

Estelle is a fervent *Oprah* watcher. She saw a program six months ago that was about getting out of a life rut and trying new things.''

Robert grunted. He didn't like to be accused of missing the point on anything.

''I'm sure I would have noticed if anything was that out of the ordinary,'' he muttered.

Laurel laughed. ''So what color is her hair this week? Is she wearing makeup?''

Robert frowned. ''I'm sure I don't know. I'm not in the habit of staring at the help.''

Laurel sighed. ''She's not help. She's Estelle.'' She didn't bother to add that, until Marie, Estelle was the only mother figure Laurel had grown up with.

Uncomfortable with the personal turn the conversation had taken, Robert glanced at his watch.

''Laurel, it was good to talk to you, but I'm late for work. I've got a big case coming up. You probably heard about it on television.''

''No. I haven't been watching any television since I've been here,'' Laurel said. ''What's up?''

''Remember Peter McNamara of McNamara Galleries?''

''Yes, of course.'' Then she gasped. ''Are you saying he's involved in the case you'll be trying?''

''No. I'm saying, he *is* the case.''

''Oh, my…whatever is he supposed to have done?''

''He was arrested for selling military secrets, but that's not the kicker. And this is a fact that's already made the news, so I'm not divulging any confidential info. He's not really Peter McNamara. His real name is Dimitri Chorkin. He's a Soviet plant, left over from the Cold War.''

Laurel was hearing his voice, but she'd lost the train of thought to a growing unease. The more he talked, the more convinced she became that her father was in some sort of peril.

"Dad."

He kept talking, talking, talking.

"Dad."

"...so they've confiscated everything in the downtown gallery and..."

*"Daddy!"*

Robert flinched. "What?"

Her heart was pounding, and she felt sick to her stomach.

"Do you have to take that case?"

He frowned. "Of course I do. An assignment is an assignment, and you know that. It's my job."

She didn't know what form it might take, but she knew something bad was going to happen if he persisted.

"But couldn't you pass on it if you wanted to?"

His frown deepened—his dissatisfaction transferring itself to his voice.

"But I don't want to."

Laurel felt the same way she'd felt the day her mother had died, but she didn't know why.

"Dad, I think something bad is going to happen."

"Oh, for Christ's sake, Laurel. Don't you ever stop?"

His anger was expected, but it was the derisive tone in his voice that hurt most of all.

"I'm sorry I bothered you," she said softly. "Have a nice day." Then she quietly laid the phone back in the cradle and convinced herself she'd been imagining things. Her hands were shaking, her eyes burning with unshed tears. "Well, that was a mistake."

Marie walked into the old library just as Laurel was hanging up the phone.

"You talkin' to me, sweet child?"

Laurel turned around, then stood for a moment, looking at the love and approval on the old woman's face. Calling her father might have been a mistake, but coming here was not.

She smiled through tears. "No, ma'am, but I should have been. It would have made the morning much better."

"You come with me. I'll take that frown off your face for sure," Marie said. "I got your breakfast all ready. Mamárie will make you better and that's a fact."

"Mamárie?"

Marie looked slightly embarrassed, but she still reached up to caress the side of Laurel's face.

"I never had me a daughter like Marcella did, but when she was little, your mama, Phoebe, used to call me Mamárie. You know, Mama Marie, only she said it short, like babies often do. I sure miss Miz Marcella...and her little Phoebe, too. It's gonna be real nice having you here. Almost like old times."

Laurel's eyes filled with tears as she gave Marie a quick hug.

"I haven't had anyone to call Mama since I was twelve."

Marie could tell that something had disturbed Laurel's morning, but she was determined she would be the one to put it right.

"Now you do. Come to the kitchen with me. My grits is gettin' cold."

"I like your grits," Laurel said as she gave the old woman a last fierce hug.

"'Course you do," Marie said as she hugged her back. "You might have been raised up north, but your soul is southern, just like your people. Stands to reason your tummy would be, too."

Laurel laughed.

By the time they sat down to eat, the bad feelings she'd had from her conversation with her father had disappeared. They shared the meal and the table, talking about everything and nothing, and once they'd done the dishes and cleaned up the kitchen, the morning was half gone. Marie took off her apron, changed her shoes and began fussing with her hair.

"Yesterday Tula sent word by her nephew that she'd be comin' here this mornin'. We need groceries, so I'm gonna ride into Bayou Jean with her. Anything you want me to pick up for you?" Marie asked.

"No, but wait a minute and I'll get you some money."

Marie waved her away. "Shoot, honey, you don't have to do that. I always get what we need. The store sends the bill to the bank. They pay the bills for Mimosa Grove, and that's the way it works."

Laurel shook her head, realizing that she had a lot to learn about how things were set up around here. Then she remembered there was something she'd been meaning to discuss with Marie.

"I've been wanting to see about getting someone to come out and redo the landscaping. It's a bit overgrown. What do you think?"

Marie nodded. "Yes, Miz Marcella fussed some about it during her last years but didn't have the heart to tackle it."

"So do you think we could get some help?"

"Oh, sure," Marie said. "I'll ask Tula. She always know who needs a little extra money round here." Then she glanced at the clock and added, "I won't be long. When I get back, I'll fix us a late lunch."

Laurel frowned. "Absolutely not. You have fun with your friend. Eat lunch in town if you want. I'll find something to snack on, then help you fix supper tonight."

Marie frowned. "You not supposed to wait on me."

Laurel ignored Marie's nervous look. "Maybe I want to," she said, then saw an old blue sedan coming toward the house. "Looks like your ride is here. Go have fun. I'll be here when you get back."

Within minutes, Marie was gone, and for the first time, Laurel was alone at Mimosa Grove. She'd seen a good deal of the grounds outside, but had yet to explore all of the mansion itself. She'd been through the entire downstairs, and her favorite room was the library. It was a dark-paneled room with floor-to-ceiling shelves crammed top to bottom with books that would take a lifetime to read.

But she had vague memories of the top floor of the home, as well as a half dozen secluded cubbyholes that had once been full of dusty trunks and boxes she had wanted to explore, only her mother wouldn't let her. She wondered if it was all still there, then knew there was only one way to find out.

She started up the stairs, and although she'd been here almost four days now, this was the first time she'd ventured up past the second floor. As she climbed, she couldn't help but notice the dust on the carpet runners and the occasional spiderweb between the spindles on the stair rail, and she made a mental note to get some day help for Marie, even if it was only a couple of times a week. Laurel didn't want to give Marie the impression that she thought she was too old to do her job, because she'd already seen how important the place was to her, but if she was going to live here, the spiders were going to have to go.

The rain from last night's storm was already mixing with the heat of the day, making the air feel like the inside of a sauna, so the higher Laurel climbed, the hotter it became. She was almost at the top of the stairs when she realized she was starting to get cold. Instinctively, she stopped, acknowledging the presence she sensed.

"I'm just looking," she said softly.

The air moved against Laurel's cheek, as if someone near her had sighed. The air shifted again, and between one breath and the next, heat slammed against Laurel's face like a slap. Whatever entity had been on the stairs had bowed to the inevitable and moved on. Still, she waited, trying to absorb the difference in this feeling from what she'd felt out in the grove. It took her a few moments to realize the energy she'd felt just now had seemed male. Confrontational. Like the man of the house. She frowned. From what she knew, the women in this family had been the powerful ones. Then she shrugged off the thought and told herself that if she wasn't careful, she would turn out just as her father constantly predicted. She had no intention of morphing into some old maid psychic who had a dozen cats, or, in this case, a peacock with attitude.

Shaking off the feeling of unease, she reached the third-floor landing and found herself staring down a long, narrow hallway. She frowned. This wasn't what she remembered. Where was the big room with all the trunks and boxes? But there was an interesting aspect of the floor that she didn't remember. There were a good dozen portraits of women hanging along the east wall. Laurel moved toward them and soon realized that she was seeing the progression of her ancestors, from her grandmother, Marcella, whose portrait was at the head of the line, all the way down the hall to the last, which in reality had been the first.

The name engraved on the small copper plate on the frame was Chantelle LeDeux. Laurel stepped back, squinting slightly in the dimmer light for her first glimpse of the infamous woman.

She was more than slightly surprised by what she saw. Unlike Laurel, who was taller than average, the woman appeared small, almost tiny. Her hands lay folded in her lap and appeared hardly larger than a child's. Her dress was ornate and low cut, revealing small, rounded breasts, and her beaded slippers, barely visible from beneath the hem of her gown, looked like a child's shoes.

But it was her face and the color of her hair that were startling to Laurel. Like Laurel's, her hair was a dark, fiery red, and they shared large, expressive blue eyes and wide mouths. Chantelle's nose was slightly smaller than Laurel's, but it still had the same shape—slim and straight, without a hint of foolish tilt.

Laurel took a slow breath and started to trace the shape of the name with the tips of her fingers when she heard the sound of a car engine pulling up at the front of the house. She hurried toward a window to look out, but it was so dirty and the view so blurred that all she could see was the shadowy figure of a man getting out of a truck.

"Rats," she muttered, then gave the portraits a last, lingering look and hurried back down the stairs.

The knocking was constant and measured. "I'm coming, I'm coming!" Laurel cried as she started down the last flight.

Seconds later, she was at the door.

The distinct crack of a gunshot brought Justin upright in his bed. He hit the floor running, pulling on his jeans as he went. As he ran, the loud thump of his heartbeat against his eardrums irritated the dull ache at the back of his neck, and he was vaguely aware of a pain in his knee, compliments of his search for Rachelle. He yanked the front door open and ran out onto the porch, only to find his neighbor, Claude Shiffler, with a dead snake dangling over the barrel of a shotgun.

"What in—"

Claude grinned as he raised the gun barrel.

"Big sucker, ain't he, Justin?"

Justin shoved a shaky hand through his hair as he groaned with relief.

"Damn it, Claude. Next time, try knocking. It would be a hell of a lot easier on my heart."

Claude's grin widened. "Didn't mean to startle you none. But this big cottonmouth was between me and the house, and I didn't figure the fine state of Louisiana was going to mind the existence of one less snake."

Justin eyed the large water moccasin, or at least what was left of it, then sighed. From the angle of the sun in the sky, it must be close to noon.

"Looks like you nailed him right in the head...and parts south."

Claude tossed the snake into the back of his pickup truck, then stowed his shotgun behind the seat.

"I'll toss him out down the road," he said, and started toward the porch. It wasn't until he was coming up the steps that he realized Justin had been asleep. "Dang it, Justin. I forgot you might still be in bed after last night's search and all. Real sorry I woke you."

Justin shrugged. "No matter, Claude. Come on in. I'll make us some coffee."

"No need," Claude said as he took a long envelope out of his back pocket, then handed it to Justin. "I was just stoppin' by to drop this off."

"What is it?" Justin asked as he took the envelope.

"Two thousand dollars. Wanted you to invest it for me."

Justin frowned. He knew Claude's situation. Two thousand dollars to the Shiffler family was a whole lot of money.

"Now, Claude, you understand that it might take a while for any investment to pay off."

Claude nodded. "Don't matter. My twins are only five. I just want to be able to give them a good education when they're ready to go to college. Don't want them havin' to live like me, trying to raise a family on a roofer's pay."

"I understand. Do you have any particular stocks in mind?"

Claude grinned. "Hell no. I don't know nothin' about that stuff. Your judgment will be good enough for me."

"Thanks," Justin said, and shook Claude's hand.

"I'll try to take good care of you. When I get your portfolio set up, I'll send you the information."

"Whatever," Claude said. "Once again, I'm real sorry about waking you up, but it's sure good to know your sister's baby is safe. I heard you was the one who found her. Is that so?"

Goose bumps broke out on Justin's skin as he relived last night's terror.

"Yes, I did."

"Man, you sure were lucky," Claude said.

"It wasn't luck. It was divine providence, my friend. Did you know Miz Marcella's granddaughter is living at Mimosa Grove?"

Claude's eyes rounded with surprise.

"For sure?"

Justin nodded.

"Does she have the sight?"

"If it hadn't been for her, we would have lost Rachelle for certain. Which reminds me…it's a good thing you came by, because I intend to go thank her in person."

Claude nodded. "Isn't that somethin'? Reckon she's Phoebe's girl, right?"

"Yes."

"Reckon she'll stay?" Claude asked.

"If we're lucky," Justin added.

"Well, I'll be seein' you," Claude said, and headed back to his truck as Justin retreated into the house.

He put the envelope with Claude's money in the desk drawer of his office, then started toward the kitchen. The coffee would be brewed and ready to drink by the time he got out of the shower. After that, it was off to Mimosa Grove.

Thirty minutes later, he had showered and shaved,

downed two cups of coffee and pocketed Claude's money to be deposited in the bank in Bayou Jean.

He drove out of the drive, heading down the road that led to the blacktop that would take him to Mimosa Grove, but his thoughts were as scattered as his neighbor's guinea hens that were pecking in the road. He honked as he slowed down, giving them time to get out of his way without thought for why the Gunthers let them roam. Out here, people and animals pretty much did as they pleased.

As he moved past the hens, his thoughts returned to last night and the rescue—and the disjointed sound of a voice coming to him from miles away, guiding him to his niece just in the nick of time. He thought of Marcella and tried to picture what her granddaughter might be like, then thrust the thought away and concentrated on his driving. His body still ached from the rigors of last night's search, and his mind continued to wander. He was well aware that he could have spent the day sleeping, and when he took a curve too fast and came close to running off into the ditch, he wondered if he should have stayed in bed.

Finally he neared his destination. When he came to the Mimosa Grove mailbox, he tapped the brakes and took the turn off the highway. Even though he'd driven this way many times before, as soon as he drove onto the grounds of the old estate, he always felt as if he'd taken a step back in time.

Justin pulled up in front of the old three-story mansion and killed the engine. Rarely did any sounds of civilization ever reach this far back off the road. As the silence and the heat of the day quickly seeped into his consciousness, he knew that unless he moved, and moved quickly, he was likely to fall asleep where he sat. With a weary sigh, he opened the door and got out.

His steps were measured as he walked up the steps of Mimosa Grove and then under the shade of the veranda. Even as he was walking toward the door, it seemed impossible to believe that Marcella would not be here. He'd been at her funeral, but this was the first time he'd come to her home since she'd passed. The woman had been larger than life. Thinking of this place without her seemed strange.

A large peacock hovered at the end of the porch, as if trying to decide whether to attack or retreat. Not sure of the bird's attitude, he began knocking on the door, hoping to be inside before the peacock made up its mind. When it started toward him, he knocked a little harder and tried a friendly hello, hoping the familiarity of his voice would deter what was coming.

"Hey, Elvis. How you doin', big boy?" Justin murmured.

He winced as the bird fanned its tail, then uttered an ear-piercing shriek. At the same moment, the door swung inward. He was still smiling when he turned with Marie's name on his lips.

But it wasn't Marie who met him at the door.

He stared at the woman in the doorway, then wiped a hand across his face, certain that when he looked again, she would be gone. But she was still there, and he would have sworn he heard her breathing.

"Sweet Mother of God," he whispered, convinced he was losing his mind.

It was then the thought hit him that he might never have left home, or that he hadn't talked to Claude, or seen a dead snake. He hadn't showered and shaved, or driven the fifteen miles between his place and this one. He was still in his bed, sleeping. He knew, because this was the woman from his dreams.

Accepting the explanation, he moved forward.

"I've been missing you," he said softly, and took her in his arms.

Laurel's shock at seeing this man on her doorstep quickly turned into acceptance, then joy. The fates had been kind to her after all. But before she could speak, he took her in his arms and then kicked the door shut behind him. She heard him sigh, then felt the warmth of his breath against her neck. It was straight out of her dreams. But was she dreaming? Hadn't she been upstairs only moments before? Surely she hadn't imagined the chill, or felt the temporary disapproval of the specter on the staircase?

Then Justin's mouth centered on her lips, and questions disappeared. All she could remember was how he made her come apart in his arms, how lonely she'd been without him. Whether he was real or not, she didn't want this to end. She slid her arms around his neck and gave him back kiss for lonely kiss.

All the aches and pains, all the weariness that had been dogging Justin's footsteps that morning, were gone in a heartbeat.

"Ah, *chère*...where have you been? I've missed you."

The softly whispered words sent chills down Laurel's spine. He'd missed her? But how? He'd been in her dream, not she in his.

Then he put his hands on her breasts, cupping the fullness as if measuring them for fit. At that point she sighed, giving herself up to the inevitable as an intense longing surged through her. She wanted this—

even needed it. He'd become an addiction she didn't want to kick. If this was a dream, she didn't want to wake up.

"I've missed you, too," she said softly, then kissed him again.

Justin lifted his head long enough to look around. "Are you alone?"

She put a hand to his cheek. He felt the warmth of her skin against his face.

"Not anymore," she said, and took him by the hand.

They went up the stairs hand in hand, as if they'd done it a hundred times before—looking into each other's eyes, recognizing the need, remembering the power of their lovemaking.

Justin couldn't take his gaze from her face. Never had the dream been so lifelike—so intense. He had not remembered how soft her skin was to the touch, or how her eyes crinkled at the corners when she smiled. But he knew what it felt like to come inside her, and he wanted that bad—and he wanted it now.

Laurel led him to her room, and the moment the door closed behind them, they began taking off their clothes. The bedclothes were still in a tangle from last night's troubled sleep. Justin swept them aside, tossing them to the foot of the bed as he pushed her backward onto the sheet.

She wrapped her arms around his neck and pulled him down with her as she fell. When the weight of his body pressed her deeply into the softness of the mattress, she moaned, wanting him inside her just as deep.

"Hurry," she whispered.

A muscle jerked at the corner of Justin's mouth.

He was rock hard and hurting and knew just how she felt. Without foreplay, without so much as a kiss, he parted her legs with his knee and slid inside. She was hot and wet, and he was in danger of losing control. She moaned once—a low, guttural sound that raised the hair on the back of his neck. He was inside her—hard, pulsing, but motionless.

"Look at me."

It took everything she had to focus on his demand, but she did it and lost herself in the black depths of his gaze. Only then did he begin to move, rocking against the cradle of her pelvis in hard, hungry strokes, with each thrust shoving her farther toward the headboard until she was pinned. Laurel reached above her head, her fingers curling around the spindles as she held on, while riding the intensity of their lovemaking. The heat between them was rising just as she'd known it would, churning and curling into a tight, hungry knot in the pit of her stomach. Then, suddenly, it began to crash.

"Oh...oh..."

She didn't see his jaw clench as he struggled to maintain his control. At that moment, there was nothing that mattered except the rhythm of their bodies and the shattering climax that came upon her.

She screamed.

The sound tore through Justin's head like a bullet, scattering his concentration. He shuddered, then groaned, his body arching as he came. Wave after wave of unbearable ecstasy rolled through him, leaving him weak and shaking. Without waiting for it to ebb, he took her in his arms and rode the climax all the way down.

They both lay without moving, unable to think past

the need to draw another breath. And even as the lust was passing, Justin was already aware that this joining was different. He kept waiting for the dream to move forward—for the moment when he would wake with a start, then sit up in bed. Slowly, he raised himself up on both elbows, easing the weight of his body from her, and as he did, he felt the heat of her breath against his face. At that moment a bead of sweat rolled out of his hairline and into his eyes. The saltiness of the moisture immediately burned his eyes, and as it did, he flinched.

"What the hell?"

Laurel's smile turned to a frown.

"What's wrong?" she asked.

Justin didn't answer. In fact, he couldn't answer. Instead, he rolled off her, then to a sitting position at the side of the bed.

"Justin?"

His heart skipped a beat. How did she know his name? In fact, why was he even hearing her voice? The dream had never been like this before. Gently, he lifted a damp curl from her forehead, and as he did, he felt the silkiness of the dark, fiery strand against his finger. He knew he was staring, but he couldn't stop. He reached toward her, running the back of a finger down the side of her face.

"Am I still dreaming?" he asked.

Laurel's heart dropped.

"Have I been in your dreams?" she asked.

He nodded.

She sighed. "I suppose that's fair, since you've also been in mine."

He frowned. "What the hell are you saying?"

"You come to me in my sleep." Laurel's face

flushed with embarrassment. "And then we make love. I feel you inside me, but I never hear you speak."

Justin started to shake. "This...what we just did...we're still dreaming...right?"

"I don't think so."

He touched her face, then her hair, then her face again, running the ball of his thumb down her cheek, then across her lips.

"You're real? This is real?"

Laurel nodded.

Justin grabbed his clothes and started putting them on. The need to put something more than distance between them was suddenly uppermost. When he picked up his shirt, he paused, then turned around, staring as if he'd seen a ghost.

"You came to me," he said. "You walked into my bedroom every night..."

Laurel picked up where he left off. "...just after I went to sleep. One moment I'd be alone in my bed, and the next thing I knew, I'd feel you pulling back the covers, then..."

Justin dropped his shirt onto the bed. "...I'd take you in my arms and..."

Laurel finished the story. "...make love to me."

He grabbed his shirt and quickly pulled it over his head.

"I don't know what to think. This is crazy."

Laurel wouldn't let herself think about how deeply the ugliness of that last word cut.

"I felt the same way last night when I saw you rescue your niece."

He blanched. "You what?"

Laurel shrugged, then looked away, unwilling to see the disbelief on his face.

"I saw you through Rachelle's eyes."

"You...ah, God...so that's how you..."

There was a long pause, but he didn't curse, he didn't laugh. In fact, if she hadn't known better, she would have sworn he'd just accepted her answer as gospel.

"So this isn't a dream?"

"No."

"And we've been making love to...no, dreaming of making love to each other for months?"

Laurel hesitated, then nodded.

"Jesus," he whispered softly, then took her in his arms.

His breath was warm against her face, his grip firm yet gentle. But it was the urgency in his voice that pulled at Laurel's conscience. What had happened between them was startling, but not out of the realm of her beliefs. It was Justin who looked as if he'd just been broadsided.

"You don't think it's...that I'm crazy?"

Justin didn't realize until she spoke that he'd been holding his breath. He exhaled slowly, then cupped the side of her face.

"If it had not been for you, my sister's little girl would have died last night. You saved her life."

Laurel shuddered as he traced the curve of her lower lip with his thumb. She couldn't quit staring. She was tall, a little above five feet, eight inches, but she had to look up to meet his gaze. His hair was the color of a raven's wings and just brushed the collar of his shirt. His eyes were so dark she couldn't tell if they were brown or black, and his lips were wide and full. His jaw was strong. His chin had something of a stubborn curve, and now she knew the sound of his voice as he came inside her.

"I quit dreaming of you after I left D.C.," she said, then added, "I missed you."

Justin's heartbeat stuttered as his mind went blank. Without asking, he knew she was referring to the fact that they'd been absent from each other's dreams for several nights now. His ache was sudden and fierce, and while he was not a man who took foolish chances, he could no more have lied to her than he could have quit breathing.

"I missed you, too," he said.

Laurel sighed. His voice rumbled roughly against her cheek. She knew he was rattled, but she had to give him credit for standing his ground.

"I know we've just met," Laurel said.

Justin smiled. "*Chère,* what just happened between us wasn't a meeting, it was, at the least, a revelation."

Laurel blushed.

Justin laid his cheek against the crown of her head.

"I came to say thank you to the woman who saved Rachelle's life. I didn't know she would be the same woman who's been haunting my nights."

Laurel didn't know if the haunting was good or bad.

"As you have mine," she reminded him.

He put a finger beneath her chin and tipped her head back until they were looking eye to eye.

"How did this happen?"

"I don't know."

"If I was superstitious…"

Laurel flinched. "Are you?"

He smiled, then shook his head.

"No."

"So?"

He brushed his mouth across the surface of her lips, then broke away with a soft groan.

"So…hello, Laurel Scanlon. It's very nice to meet you."

Laurel smiled.

"It's very nice to meet you, too."

"Oh. Before I forget the real reason I came… Besides thanking you for leading me to Rachelle, my sister and her husband are having a big party Saturday night. It's sort of a thank you to all the people who helped search. I've been given strict orders to tell you that you are invited. In fact…you're to be the guest of honor. Please say you'll come."

Laurel was floored and made no move to hide it.

"Are you serious?"

He frowned. "Yes. Why wouldn't we be?"

"Where I came from, what I can do is not looked upon with favor."

His Cajun accent thickened with emotion.

"Then, *chère,* I'm sorry to say you have lived among fools. Down here, we honor those touched by God."

*Touched by God?* It was all Laurel could do not to weep for joy.

"You tell your family that I would be honored to meet them and to come to their party."

"If you would allow me, I will be your escort."

"And you don't think it strange that today was our first meeting, Saturday will be our first date, and we've been making love for months?"

He grinned. "*Chère,* not only is it strange, it's a

downright miracle. But, then, who am I to question such a heavenly gift?''

It was then that Laurel began to believe her life was truly taking a turn for the better.

# 6

Justin was gone by the time Marie came back from Bayou Jean. His appearance and their subsequent lovemaking had so rattled Laurel that she had abandoned her curiosity about the third floor of the mansion for a cooler day and changed the sheets on her bed instead. As she gathered up the discarded sheets to take downstairs to the laundry room, she got a whiff of Justin's cologne. Without thinking, she buried her face in the bundle and inhaled slowly, savoring the memories and the scent of the man who'd made them with her. What had happened between them was extraordinary, even in Laurel's life. She had no explanation for their connection, but she was guessing that since he lived near the estate she'd just inherited, it all had something to do with proximity—and, of course, fate. And while she wasn't about to question the gift of such a man in her life, she had no intention of letting anyone else know. Thus the need for clean sheets.

After she'd put the bedclothes in the wash, she'd wandered through the downstairs, sifting through the books in the library. As she poked about, it occurred to her that there were probably books on the top shelves of the floor-to-ceiling library that hadn't been looked at in years. She thought about exploring them and began testing the built-in ladder that ran the length of the shelves, making sure that the rungs were secure. Satisfied that they would hold her weight, she climbed partway up, then changed her mind when a spider ran out from behind a bookend, leaving minute tracks in the thick film of dust covering everything on the upper shelves.

"Eeew," she muttered, grimacing as the oversize eight-legged critter disappeared between two books. "This place is going to get a thorough cleaning. And whether Marie likes it or not, we're going to need some help."

Having decided that exploration would have to wait for another day, she decided to take herself outside. Elvis was perched on the corner of the roof over the veranda. When he saw her coming, he let out an ear-splitting shriek of disapproval, which sent Laurel over the edge. When she saw him flying down from the roof, she decided she'd had enough of him, too. After dealing with Elvis, she found a pair of clippers and a hoe in a shed out back and was hard at work, putting a new look to the overgrown shrubs around the front of the house, when Tula and Marie returned.

Marie's shock at seeing Laurel in such sweaty disarray quickly turned to shame. It was her fault that the place had gone to seed, but for the past few months, it had been all she could do to get through a day taking care of Marcella's needs. Seeing to the grooming of Mimosa Grove had been so far down on her list of things to do that she'd never gotten to it. To see Laurel doing what she should have done herself reduced her to tears.

She got out of Tula's old truck before the engine

had stopped running, waving her arms as she hurried toward the house.

"No, no, baby girl…you got no need to go and do all that. I went and found us some help just like you wanted. Tula got a grandson needin' work. He'll be here tomorrow to start cleanin' up this place."

Laurel smiled as she tossed a handful of clippings into the refuse pile and then wiped her forearm across the sweat on her forehead.

"That's good, Mamárie, but I like doing this." She spied a small green inchworm on the front of her shirt and flipped it off. "Except maybe for worms. I have, however, been having such a good time that I think I might have missed my calling."

Marie looked properly horrified, while, on the other hand, Tùla was grinning. It wasn't every day that someone got the best of Marie LeFleur.

Suddenly it dawned on Marie that there was something missing in the front yard.

"Where's Elvis?"

"In his pen," Laurel said.

"How did you make that happen?"

Laurel's chin jutted mutinously. "I put the fear of God into him—and a broom against the backside of his ass."

Marie looked startled, then smiled while Tula laughed aloud.

Laurel laid her gloves on the porch steps and then went to the truck to help carry in the groceries.

Again Marie seemed bothered, and when Laurel turned around with a sack in each arm, she couldn't hide her dismay.

"You're the mistress of Mimosa Grove. What will people think of you actin' like this?"

What she didn't say was "What would they think of me?" She didn't want to be viewed as incompetent or unable to work. The fear of being turned out in favor of someone younger had been uppermost in her mind ever since Marcella's death. And even though she and Laurel had hit it off, she didn't want to be thought of as too old to do what needed to be done. Mimosa Grove was as much a part of her life as it had been Marcella's. It wasn't just a place where she worked, it was her home. The fear of having to finish out the end of her days elsewhere was horrifying.

Laurel laughed at Marie's indignant expression.

"Oh…Mamárie, you're asking the wrong person if you think I care what other people think. Now, get yourself in out of this heat. You can put up the groceries while I carry them in, how's that?" She pointed at Tula, who was still sitting behind the steering wheel. "And you…Ms. Tula…you get yourself inside with Mamárie. I made some lemonade. You two go in and cool yourselves off. I'm right behind you."

Tula slapped her leg and then rolled out from behind the wheel. She'd planned on being home in time to watch an *Oprah* rerun, but she wouldn't have missed this for the world.

"Don't mind if I do," she said.

Her gait was slow but steady as she made her way up the steps.

"Come on, Marie. Looks like we finally got ourselves a proper mistress for Mimosa Grove. She knows her own mind like I do mine, and I'm thinkin' I might like some of that lemonade."

Marie frowned, but secretly she was proud. Tula was right about Laurel knowing her own mind. And it had been a long time since there had been anyone at Mimosa Grove who cared about anything but the past. It would be good not to have to carry the entire burden of this place alone. Still, she didn't want Laurel to think she could be manipulated easily.

"I'll just be carryin' in this little sack as I go," Marie said, then snatched up a sack before walking past Laurel and Tula, and into the house.

"After you," Laurel said.

Tula paused, giving Laurel a long, studied look.

Laurel felt off center, not knowing what the old woman was really thinking.

"So?" she asked.

Tula's eyes squinted until they all but disappeared beneath the caterpillar fuzz that passed for her eyebrows.

"So...I think you gonna do. You gonna do just fine," she said.

Laurel felt an inordinate amount of pleasure from the old woman's simple praise.

"Thank you," she said, then impulsively handed the two sacks she was carrying to Tula. "If you don't mind, would you take these the rest of the way to the kitchen while I go back for the others?"

"I be proud to help out," Tula said.

Laurel hurried back outside, anxious to get the groceries out of the heat. A few minutes later, they were in the kitchen, emptying the last sack, dividing the purchases between those that went into the pantry and the ones that needed refrigeration.

"Here, Mamárie, this is the last of the cold stuff," Laurel said as she handed a gallon of milk to Marie.

Marie scooted a jug of orange juice to the side and set the milk onto the shelf beside it.

"Now, then," Marie said. "Where's my lemonade?"

"Coming up," Laurel said as she opened a package of Oreo cookies and put some on a plate. "Who wants cookies, too?"

"I don't mind if I do," Tula said.

"Help yourself," Laurel said, then began to pour the lemonade.

Marie frowned as Laurel puttered around the kitchen.

"It don't seem right...you waitin' on me like this," Marie muttered.

"I do it because I want to."

Marie's lips pursed, but there was a smile in her eyes as she reached out and patted the back of Laurel's hand.

"Then I thank you," she said gently.

Tula handed Marie a cookie.

"Here, woman, put your teeth around this."

"I might be wantin' more than one," Marie said.

Tula scooted the plate of cookies toward her old friend.

"Then help yourself."

Laurel felt a sense of loss as she watched the two old friends squabbling back and forth. She sat down with her lemonade, then leaned forward, satisfied to be nothing more than an observer to their friendship.

It was Tula who first noticed Laurel's wistful look.

"What you thinkin' about, girl?"

"About how lucky you are to have each other as friends."

Tula winked at Marie, then laughed.

"Shoot, honey. We aren't friends. We don't even like each other."

Marie cackled. "That's right. We don't."

Taken aback, Laurel didn't know what to say. Then she caught the look that passed between them and knew they'd been teasing.

"You're putting me on, aren't you?" she asked.

They nodded in unison; then Marie put her hand on Laurel's arm.

"Honey...the first thing to learn about havin' a friend is knowin' when to laugh."

Then Tula added, "And knowin' they're there when you need a good cry."

"I've never had a friend like that," Laurel said.

Tula took a cookie from the package and handed it to Laurel.

"Here's the way I see it. Marie, here, is gettin' old."

"So are you," Marie muttered.

"True enough," Tula answered. "Anyway...as I was sayin'...it seems to me that we're in dire need of another friend to take Marcella's place. One of these days, one of us is gonna pass just like she did, and if we don't have a backup, we're gonna be all alone."

Laurel nodded, because right then, speaking aloud would have been impossible without crying.

Marie winked at Tula, then picked up where she'd left off.

"It's a serious thing...bein' a friend," she said. "You have to love without judgment, and you don't offer an opinion unless it's asked for. But you do have to be there whenever the need arises. Think you can handle that?"

Laurel took a deep breath, then nodded.

"Then that's that," Tula said, and lifted her glass of lemonade. "Friends forever."

The glasses of lemonade were lifted off the table, clinked gently one to the other, then the women holding them drank to the foundation of the bond that had just been laid.

Laurel thought of Justin, of what had passed between them and what had yet to occur. Back in D.C., she'd had no one, yet her world had been continuously expanding since she'd set foot in Bayou Jean. She looked at their faces, open and waiting. She'd shared laughter and food. Was it possible that having friends could be this simple?

"Now that you're my friends, I have something to tell you."

The two old women leaned forward, subconsciously drawing closer.

"I'm going to a party Saturday night with Justin Bouvier. You need to tell me what to wear."

"Party? Justin Bouvier? When did all this happen?"

Marie shot three questions at her before Laurel could answer one.

"When he came over to thank me for my help last night, he said his sister's family is having a big party Saturday night to thank everyone who helped with the search."

The frown on Marie's face lifted somewhat, but Laurel could still hear her mumbling beneath her voice about social etiquette and doing things right. Before Laurel could justify herself, someone started knocking on the front door.

More than ready to reestablish her position as the woman in charge, Marie jumped up from her seat.

"I'll be gettin' that," she said, and strode out of the room.

Laurel smiled as she watched her go. If the simple statement about attending a party got her on edge, she could only imagine what she would think if she knew what had gone on upstairs. And that thought reminded her that she had yet to put the sheets in the dryer.

"Tula, I need to put a load of clothes in the dryer. Help yourself to some more lemonade. I'll be right back."

"Take you time, *bébé*," Tula said, and palmed another cookie.

A few moments later, Laurel was setting the timer when she heard Marie calling her name.

"Just a minute," she said. "I'm in the laundry room."

She punched the start button on the dryer and then headed back into the kitchen. As she started down the hall, she could tell that whoever had been at the door was now in the kitchen.

"What's—"

It was as far as she got before she lost her train of thought. All six feet plus of the man she'd just been naked with was standing beside Marie, but looking at Laurel as if he might eat her alive. Laurel was caught off guard by his reappearance. The look on his face wasn't helping. His gaze was fixed, his posture stiff. She couldn't imagine what had brought him back.

"Justin! It's nice to see you again, but I didn't expect another visit so soon. Did you forget something?"

He took a deep breath and then reached for her.

"After I left here, I drove into Bayou Jean, deposited some money in the bank, bought groceries and then started home. The closer I got, the more confused I became. The road still made that S curve just outside of town. Mose Reynolds' vegetable stand was still in the same place. I waved at him just like I do every time I pass by. The sun was beaming on the hood of my truck just enough that when I headed west, it ricocheted into my eyes…and I began to doubt what I was seeing…and what I'd seen.''

When his hand brushed the side of her face, Laurel froze. She was afraid to look at Marie or Tula. Then he spoke, and she found she could not look away.

"I had to know," he said softly.

"Know what?" she asked.

"If you were still here…if you were still real."

Laurel smiled. "So is the consensus in?"

Justin leaned forward, kissing the smile she was still wearing and satisfying himself that he hadn't lost his mind after all.

Marie's shocked hiss complemented Tula's throaty chuckle. Laurel was too stunned to react one way or the other.

Suddenly remembering they were not alone, Justin reluctantly let her go.

"Six o'clock Saturday?"

She nodded, then remembered what she'd been about to ask Marie and Tula and asked him instead.

"What should I wear?"

A slow smile spread across his face, and she knew he was remembering her wearing nothing at all.

"Anything casual and comfortable," he said. "They'll cook outdoors…eat outdoors…dance outdoors. Whatever's going on will be under Louisiana stars.''

"Okay, and thank your sister again for the invitation. I'm looking forward to meeting some of my neighbors.''

Marie snorted none too lightly.

''You know you and Tula are invited, too,'' Justin said. ''It's a celebration for the life of Rachelle.''

Marie's lips pursed, but she didn't voice her disapproval of the fact that they'd kissed.

''Thank your sister for me, but my dancing years are far behind me. I'll be in bed long before the dancing starts.''

''I might come with my nephew, Jean,'' Tula said.

''Then we'll see you there,'' Justin said. He looked back at Laurel, as if reassuring himself one last time that he had not imagined the previous events of the day.

''I'm here,'' Laurel said, then added, ''And I'm not going anywhere.''

He shook his head, as if still unable to believe what had happened.

''Okay then,'' he said softly. ''See you Saturday?''

''I'm looking forward to it,'' Laurel said.

''I'll let myself out,'' he told Marie, and left before she could grill him with her own set of questions.

The moment the front door closed, Marie turned.

''Girl...what on earth was that about?''

Laurel lifted her chin, hoping she wasn't going to insult Marie, but well aware there was no way she could explain.

''Mamárie, I know our relationship is new, and I'm already loving you dearly, but there's something we need to get clear. I am not a girl, I am a woman. And since I believe it's rude to kiss and tell, you're going to have to trust me on this.''

Marie's eyes widened; then she started to grin.

"Well now," she said. "If I didn't know better, I'd be thinkin' that Miz Marcella was back in this house."

"Then you're not mad at me?" Laurel asked.

"Nope," Marie said, then pointed at Tula. "And I know you're keepin' this to yourself, too, aren't you, old friend?"

Tula acted as if she'd just been insulted.

"Since when have I betrayed a confidence and told something you didn't want told?"

"You told my daddy I went to New Orleans with Oliver Stanley."

Tula rolled her eyes. "Lord have mercy, old woman. That was more than fifty years ago. And it was a good thing I told, or your daddy wouldn't have known where to look to bring you back."

Marie sniffed. "Did it ever occur to you that I didn't want to be brought back?"

Tula laughed. "Lots of times, but that don't change the fact that I was right in tellin'." Then she turned to Laurel. "That Oliver Stanley was a good-lookin' man for sure, but good looks don't mean a thing. They sent him to Angola for killin' a man, and if he hasn't already passed, he's still there."

Laurel stifled a grin. "We've all had our weak moments, haven't we, Mamárie?"

"It took longer than a few moments. That Oliver had more goin' for him than good looks," Marie said, and then laughed aloud when Laurel's mouth dropped.

Laurel could only imagine the stunts these two old friends had lived through in their lives and decided it was time to change the subject.

"Tula, I'm looking forward to your grandson coming to help clean up the grounds and wonder if you know of two or three more people who'd be interested in doing some work inside? It would involve climbing on ladders, cleaning and polishing woodwork, and the like.'' She heard some muttering and hissing behind her and added quickly, before Marie ignited, ''Mamárie would be in charge of everything, of course. There's a lot of cleaning to do, but I can't have my best girl climbing on ladders and getting dust in her hair.''

The hissing turned into a sort of clucking sound. Laurel didn't dare look for fear she would laugh.

''I'm sure we can come up with some help,'' Tula said. ''Lots of people loved Miz Marcella. They'd be happy to help you clean up a little.''

''It will be more than a little,'' Laurel said. ''But if they work out, there might be a permanent position for one or two of them. Ultimately, it will be Mamárie's decision. If they don't respect her authority, then they just won't work out.''

All was silent behind her now. Laurel figured it was the perfect time to ask.

''Mamárie, is that all right with you?''

''I could use some help. But I won't stand for any foolin' around.''

Laurel nodded seriously. ''That's what I figured. You tell Tula what you need, and she'll have a better idea of who to ask. Now, if you two don't mind, I'm going to take a shower and wash off the evidence of my gardening.''

''I'm making blackened catfish for supper to-night,'' Marie said.

''Sounds good,'' Laurel said. ''I'll help you later.''

Marie started to argue, but she was coming to realize that none of this had anything to do with getting too old. Instead, it was Laurel who had the need—a need to belong.

"That would be good. And you can tell me about growin' up in Washington, D.C., while we're workin'."

While Laurel was finding her balance in her new home, her father was struggling with her absence. To compensate, he'd thrown himself into his latest case. He had investigators digging through every piece of evidence that he'd been presented with, making sure that there would be no surprises come the day of the trial.

He'd interviewed Cherrie Peloquin, McNamara's secretary, and knew that the defense could poke enough holes in her testimony to render it useless. Any number of interpretations could be attributed to what she'd heard McNamara say. But the facts could not be misinterpreted. McNamara was an alias for Dimitri Chorkin. He had been planted in the U.S. years ago as a Russian spy. The military had finally admitted that certain top-secret files had been tampered with, and there was information recovered from a computer confiscated from McNamara's home that could be interpreted as evidence that he'd been in contact with enemies of the U.S. through e-mail. Separately, none of the facts were hard-core proof that Chorkin was anything but a fake. It wasn't against the law to live under an assumed name, and they couldn't prove that Chorkin had ever done anything illegal in the U.S. under his real name. But add it all together and the feds believed they had a fairly solid case.

But Robert wasn't satisfied with "fairly." He wanted a lock.

However, no one was more surprised than Robert when he got a call from Carter Murphy, McNamara's lawyer. McNamara wanted to talk to the prosecuting attorney, and not even Murphy knew why. Robert agreed to the meeting, but with reservations.

Carter Murphy was a small man in appearance, but he had the IQ of a genius, which was fortunate, because it was going to take a genius to keep Peter McNamara from a life sentence in a federal prison. Part of his problem was McNamara himself. McNamara, or Chorkin, whatever he called himself, was of the opinion that he could finagle his way out of this "situation," as he called it, by giving up some players who were in a much bigger league than himself. But Carter knew something about the federal prosecutor that McNamara didn't. Robert Scanlon didn't bargain and he didn't make deals—not with men who sold out their country. Of course, technically speaking, McNamara hadn't sold out his country, because he wasn't a United States citizen. But under the circumstances, Carter seriously doubted Scanlon would see it that way.

He glanced at his watch, then up at the door of the visiting room, and wished to hell everyone who was supposed to be here would show up. He didn't like prisons. Then he leaned forward, resting his elbows on the conference table, and reminded himself that being a lawyer had been his idea. He could have gone into the mortuary business with his father and saved himself the hassle of dealing with the living.

While he was feeling sorry for himself, the door

opened. Robert Scanlon came in, nodded courteously to Carter Murphy, and then took a seat on the opposite side of the table.

"Mr. Murphy, it's been a while," Scanlon said.

Carter nodded. "The Tyler case, right?"

Robert Scanlon grinned. "Yes, I believe it was at that."

Carter resisted the urge to tell Scanlon to wipe that damned grin off his face, but it would have been childish, considering that he'd been the attorney for the defense that had taken the loss. Marshall Levon Tyler, convicted of ten serial killings, was sitting on death row, awaiting his termination, thanks to the relentless prosecutor.

Robert glanced at his watch, then back at Murphy. "What's this all about, anyway?"

Murphy frowned. "I'm as much in the dark about this as you are. I advised him against this, but Mc-Namara has a mind of his own."

"I don't make deals," Robert warned.

Murphy shrugged. "I have none to pitch. However, I cannot speak for my client."

Before anything else could be said, the door opened. McNamara entered in handcuffs and leg irons, and accompanied by two armed guards. The odd thing was, despite the chains and prison garb, McNamara still managed to look somewhat stylish.

"Mr. Scanlon, isn't it?" McNamara asked as he seated himself in the only empty chair.

"Mr. Chorkin, I'm going to ask you to be brief. My time is valuable."

Peter grinned. By calling him Chorkin, the prosecutor was taunting him with the reminder that he was not an American citizen.

"Of course it's valuable," he said. "As is what I have to tell you. I want to make a deal."

Robert stood abruptly, glaring at both Murphy and his client.

"I told you, I do not make deals."

Peter was leaning back in his chair. His head was tilted to one side, and there was a big smile on his face.

"But you will this time," he said.

Robert's heart skipped a beat. There was something about McNamara's grin that made his stomach knot. Still, he maintained his stance. He glanced at Murphy.

"I'll see you in court," he said, and started toward the door.

"Confiscate my property...have me deported... drop the charges of treason, because we both know that your evidence is circumstantial at best."

Robert stared at the man in disbelief, then glared at Murphy.

"This is ridiculous. You should have more control over your client than to waste my time like this."

Without another look at McNamara, Robert started toward the door again.

"Wait! Hear me out!" McNamara said, jumping to his feet.

Carter grabbed Peter by the arm. "Sit down, and for God's sake, why don't you stop while you're ahead?"

McNamara stared at Carter and then sneered.

"Small man...small mind...why did I ever think you'd be of any use to me?" He looked up. Robert Scanlon was standing at the door. "The U.S. suffered some major setbacks during the war with Iraq that didn't play very well in the media."

"What are you talking about?" Robert asked.

Peter sat back down, his hands resting in his lap as he spoke.

"I'm talking about the deaths of U.S. soldiers under friendly fire."

Robert frowned. "It's war. It happens, but you have no right to talk about anything that has to do with our military. You betrayed them. You betrayed us all."

Peter shrugged. "Still, it's very bad press to shoot one's own men, which is why the FFR is so valuable, and why it would be in your best interests to have it back."

Robert stifled a groan. Have it back? That meant it was gone, and he didn't even know what it was. As much as he hated to admit his ignorance, he had to ask.

"What the hell is the FFR?"

"Call your friends in the Pentagon and ask them," Peter said.

Robert started to tell him to go to hell, but the smirk on the man's face made him nervous. Instead of leaving, caution won out. He pointed at Carter.

"I'm going to make a call. Don't either one of you leave."

Peter leaned back in his chair.

"Where on earth would I go?" he asked.

Again that self-serving, satisfied smile on McNamara's face was too easy. Robert wanted out.

"Guard! Guard!"

The prison guard opened the door.

"My cell phone was confiscated when I came in. I need to make a call."

The guard pointed him toward a pay phone, then buzzed him out of the containment center.

Robert punched in the numbers, cursing beneath his breath when he hit a wrong button and had to start over. There was nothing in his notes about anything called FFR. He had no idea what McNamara was talking about and hated looking less than prepared, but instinct told him this could be serious.

"Department of Defense. How may I direct your call?"

"This is Robert Scanlon. I need to talk to Secretary Fredrich."

"I'm sorry, but Mr. Fredrich is in a meeting and—"

"I'm the prosecutor for the McNamara case. It is vital that I talk to Mr. Fredrich now. It's an emergency."

"Just a moment, Mr. Scanlon. I'll see if I can reach him."

Robert leaned against the wall as he waited, absently noting a camera high up in the far corner of the hall. Robert began to relax, reminding himself that he was the one in charge. McNamara was just desperate, posturing and threatening without a snowball's chance of making any of it work for him. He wasn't going free. Not if Robert had anything to do with it.

"Sherman Fredrich here."

Robert flinched, then straightened, as if they were face-to-face, instead of speaking on a phone.

"Mr. Secretary, this is Robert Scanlon. I'm lead prosecutor on the McNamara case."

"Yes, how can I help you, Mr. Scanlon?"

"What is an FFR?"

The silence that came afterward was just as telling as the smirk on McNamara's face had been.

"Secretary Fredrich?"

The friendly tone in Fredrich's voice was gone.

"I need to know where you heard that term and who said it."

*Crap.* "I'm in a meeting with McNamara and his counsel. He's trying to bargain with me to make a deal, and is using the FFR as a reason for me to consider his requests."

Robert thought he heard the man curse but wasn't sure. However, from the reaction he'd gotten, it was possible that McNamara might have them by the short hairs after all. If this was true, the case could get tricky.

"So is this something we need to check out?" he asked.

"Yes."

The abruptness of Fredrich's response was disheartening.

"When can you let me know if this…FFR has been tampered with?" Robert asked.

"Give me a phone number."

Robert repeated the number on the pay phone.

"Wait there," Fredrich said.

Obviously the dial tone in his ear was all the goodbye he was going to get from the secretary of defense. He hung up the receiver, then glanced at his watch. It was ten minutes after two in the afternoon. He had promised to attend a dinner party that evening but was wondering if he was going to have to send last-minute regrets. Down the hall, he saw the door to the containment room open. Carter Murphy stepped out into the hall and glanced his way.

"What's going on?" he asked.

Robert waved him back into the room.

Carter frowned but retreated. He was the counsel for the defense, for God's sake, and didn't have a clue as to what was going on.

Seven minutes later, the pay phone rang. Robert picked it up on the first ring.

"This is Scanlon."

"Fredrich here. We have a problem."

"What the hell do you mean?" Robert asked.

"We have reason to believe that McNamara has the FFR."

Robert sighed. "Okay. My first question is…what the hell is an FFR?"

Fredrich hesitated. Few outside of the department even knew it existed, but considering the high profile of this trial, it stood to reason that the world would soon know. It was only fair that the prosecutor had a head start.

"One of the biggest tragedies of any war is killing our own under friendly fire. It happened far too often during our last conflict in Iraq, when we were after Hussein."

"True. It seemed to me that each time it happened, the media was all over it, looking for a way to make the accident seem sinister…which made it even more of a tragedy than it already was. As if someone on our side did it on purpose."

"Exactly," Fredrich said. "Which led to something so simple it's a puzzle why we didn't think of it sooner."

"The FFR?"

"Yes. Friendly Fire Radar. Only it's not exactly radar. To put it simply, something similar to a computer chip becomes part of every existing missile, as well as those that have yet to be built. It will recognize an answering signal that will be installed in every United States military vehicle, from jeeps to tanks. Basically, it initiates a self-destruct sequence before contact. Anything that moves on the ground will be safe from whatever comes from the sky...if it's one of ours. In other words, we will no longer be killing our own.''

''And you know for sure that McNamara has this?''

''Someone does. The fact that he even knows of its existence tells me we're in trouble.''

''Goddamn it,'' Robert said. ''Don't you keep that stuff locked up?''

Fredrich snorted lightly. ''You have no idea.''

''And yet he still got to it, which backs up the intel we have on him. Some child prodigy that the old U.S.S.R. got hold of and turned into a stone-cold spy. Ironically, we think they forgot about him, so, left to his own defenses, he used every skill they taught him and went into business for himself.''

''We need to know where the schematics are and who else knows about it.''

Robert tensed. ''I don't make deals.''

''You will this time.''

''Goddamn it!'' Robert roared. ''Do you know what kind of a message this sends to our enemies? Besides, once this becomes public knowledge, the FFR won't be a secret anymore.''

''Then make it go away.... Make McNamara or Chorkin or whatever the hell his name is go away. Give him back to Russia. Let them deal with him.

They're pretty embarrassed about the whole thing as it is.''

"That's what he wants!" Robert yelled. "You're playing right into his hands. Have you wondered what other secrets he's sold? Or how many people have died as a result? Let me bury the son of a bitch. I'll put him so deep into the federal prison system that he'll never see daylight again.''

"Do what I told you to do," Fredrich said.

"Go to hell," Robert said, and slammed the phone onto the hook.

Then he stood there, shocked by what he'd just done. He'd spent his whole life playing by the rules, ashamed of his wife's bizarre behavior, ignoring his daughter to the point of alienation, and now he'd defied the system.

He stared back down the hallway, trying to picture himself groveling to that son of a bitch and his lawyer. He couldn't see it happening. Not in this lifetime.

And the sooner he dealt with the bastard, the better off they would all be.

# 7

Robert's hands were curled into fists as he strode back into the prison conference room. Carter Murphy looked up, then flinched as Scanlon pointed his finger in McNamara's face, his voice rising in anger as he spoke.

"I will not make a deal with you. Not now. Not ever. It is my opinion that whatever you stole has already been compromised. Whether we get it back or not does not change the fact that its existence is no longer a secret. Therefore you have nothing with which to bargain."

"I don't believe you!" McNamara shouted, and started to get up when Carter Murphy shoved his client back into his chair.

"Sit down, damn it, and for once do as you're told."

"He's lying!" McNamara shouted. "I know what I have. He's got to be lying."

The flush on Robert's face gave him away.

"See?" McNamara said.

Even Carter was surprised that Scanlon would do something this rash.

"Are you?" Murphy asked.

Robert's fury was evident. "I told you before. I don't make deals."

McNamara raised his fists, the handcuffs rattling as he pointed in Robert's face.

"You will deal with me, or I'll make you sorry."

Robert stiffened. "Don't you think you're already in enough trouble without threatening a federal prosecutor?" Without another word, he left the room.

Carter Murphy threw up his hands and grabbed his briefcase.

"This meeting is over." Then he glared at his client, angry with himself and with McNamara that he'd let him get by with this. "This was a mistake from start to finish. You are not in charge of your case, I am, and I advise you not to say anything more."

"Then you're fired!" McNamara shouted.

"Thank you," Carter said, and followed Robert out of the room. "Scanlon! Wait!"

Robert paused.

"There's no use arguing with me," he said. "I'm not changing my stand on this."

"McNamara fired me," Carter said. "Just wanted you to know."

Robert smiled grimly. "When the attorney general finds out what I've done, I'll probably be fired, too."

Carter's eyebrows rose. "They told you to deal, didn't they?"

Robert hesitated, then nodded. "Yes."

Carter grinned. "I'll say this for you. You've got balls. As for our Monty Hall/*Let's Make a Deal* reject in there, I'm leaving before he changes his mind."

Robert was mildly amused at Murphy's reference.

"I can tell you for certain, there is no Door Number

Three. The attorney general will have something to say about this case, but it won't come through me."

"Or me," Carter said. "Never been so happy to be fired in my whole life."

"Wish I could say the same," Robert muttered. "It will probably be the end of my career."

"Worse things could happen," Murphy said.

They shook hands and then went their separate ways, but what Carter Murphy said stuck with Robert. Worse things *could* happen. It set him to wondering what would happen if he left the prosecutor's office. It hurt him to admit that the world would go on. In fact, he wondered if there was anyone in this whole city who would miss him, then set the thought aside. Time enough to feel sorry for himself later. For now, he was going to remove himself from the case before they had a chance to fire him.

Trigger DeLane had known ever since the day of McNamara's arrest that this call would come, yet when he heard Peter's voice on the other end of the line, his stomach knotted. If only he could take back the last four years and start over, he would never have gotten mixed up with this bastard, no matter what the reward.

"Trigger, it's me."

"You shouldn't be calling me," Trigger said.

Peter sneered. "Why? Afraid Daddy's little boy might be implicated?"

Trigger cursed softly but stood his ground. "That isn't possible."

"Well…actually, yes, it is," Peter drawled. "I

mean, after all, a man has a right to cover his back when necessary, don't you agree?''

The taste in Trigger's mouth was suddenly bitter. He felt like he needed to pee.

"What the fuck are you talking about?"

"Oh…how do you Americans say it? Oh, yes…that's for me to know and you to find out.''

"You're bluffing."

"Try me."

Trigger shuddered, thinking of his father's face should he learn of his involvement, and knew he was lost.

"What do you want?" he mumbled.

"That's better," Peter said. "Now, here's what I want you to do. Robert Scanlon is the lawyer for the prosecution in my case and he's balking at making a deal. I want you to find out what he treasures most, then use it against him until he agrees to my demands.''

"That's probably his daughter," Trigger said. "She's a looker, and single, too."

"Really? Then that's perfect. Get her. Don't hurt her…but don't let her get away. We're going to need her to convince her father to my way of thinking."

"Damn it! I'm not going to get myself involved in kidnapping."

"Why? You're already involved in treason. What's a little kidnapping compared to that?"

"For starters, the death penalty."

"You're already facing the death penalty if they catch you, so just be sure you don't get caught," Peter snapped. "Do you still have the same cell phone number?"

"Yes."

"Then get her and put her somewhere for safe-keeping. I'll call you in a couple of days to let you know what to do next."

Saturday dawned hot and still. The air was muggy, seemingly too thick to breathe. The air-conditioning in the old house was spotty at best, and today was no exception. Laurel woke slowly, coming to her senses before opening her eyes. Her grandmother's bed cradled her comfortably as the weak flow of breeze from the air-conditioning vent blew down on her back. She knew it was late, but her sleep last night had been restless. All night she'd dreamed that someone was standing beside her bed and watching her sleep. Even when she'd gotten up in the night to go to the bathroom, she'd remembered the feeling and given the room a quick search, although no one was there. It had taken her a long while to relax enough to get back to sleep. Now she was awake, but reluctant to move.

It would be easy just to turn over and go back to sleep. The notion was on her mind when suddenly she realized it was Saturday. Her body quickened. Tonight was the night of the celebration party for the safe return of Justin's niece. He was coming to get her around five. The thought of spending the evening in his company made her shiver with longing. It was crazy to feel this connected to a man she'd just met, but it had happened just the same.

Without giving herself time to change her mind, she threw back the bedclothes and sat up on the side of the mattress. As she did, her gaze automatically went toward the windows opposite her bed. She glanced out, wincing at the already white-hot, cloudless sky, and headed for the shower, stripping out of her gown as she went. Later, as she was dressing, she heard the sound of a small engine running and hurried to the window. A tall, lanky man wearing a pair of faded blue overalls and a baseball cap was pushing a lawnmower about the backyard. A long brown ponytail was hanging out from beneath the back of his cap, and when he turned the corner of the yard and started back toward the house, she could see bare skin burned teak-brown by the sun.

It appeared that Tula's grandson, the one who was going to clean up the grounds, had arrived and was off to a good start. Clippings flew out from beneath the mower as he pushed it through the tall, uneven grass. Off to the west, she could see Elvis's tail feathers hanging down from the lower limb of one of the mimosa trees in the back yard. She grinned. It appeared that Elvis had taken refuge from the mower. For all she cared, the darned bird could spend the day up there.

She gave herself a quick glance in the mirror, eyeing the pale yellow T-shirt and black shorts as proper attire for the weather, poked an unruly strand of her copper-colored hair back behind her ear and started to step into a pair of backless sandals when she happened to glance back up at the mirror. A reflection of something behind her caught her eye. She turned, curious as to what she'd seen, but when she looked, there was nothing there. Still curious, she looked back in the mirror, and as she did, her heartbeat stuttered, then started to race. Whatever it was, was still there, and as she watched, what appeared to be a face began to appear in the air above her left shoulder. Suddenly the notion that her sleep had not been as solitary as she'd believed seemed more likely.

As she stared, more and more of the specter took shape, composing its form from the dust motes and sunbeams hanging in midair. Every instinct Laurel had made her want to run, but she felt rooted to the spot. She took a deep, shaky breath and then slowly turned again. This time the image remained. She could see what appeared to be the upper two-thirds of a female, and while the details were vague, Laurel felt as if the hairstyle and clothing were from a time long gone. Transfixed by the sight, she just stared, and as she did, she was struck by an overwhelming burden of sadness. Tears sprang to her eyes, and without thinking, she clutched her hands to her chest, as if to alleviate the pain within.

Slowly the shape of the spirit before her began to shift, and the longer she stared, the more convinced Laurel became that it was beckoning to her to follow.

"You want me to follow you?"

Almost immediately, the evanescent shape before her began to move, dissipating in substance as Laurel headed for the door.

The moment she opened the door, something passed beside her, then moved out into the hall. Although the spirit was no longer visible, she felt led by an unseen source.

As she started down the stairs, she heard pans banging in the kitchen and knew Marie was fixing their breakfast, but the moment she reached the first floor, the need to turn right toward the old library down the hall became clear. Hurrying now to keep up with the thought, she was running by the time she entered the room. She knew immediately that she was alone.

Groaning with frustration, she had to accept that either she'd taken a wrong turn and lost where she was supposed to have gone, or she was here without knowing why. Her shoulders slumped as she stared about the room. Nothing was any different from what she'd seen before. The lower shelves were full to overflowing, while the upper shelves nearest the ceiling were less so, as if all the previous residents of Mimosa Grove had forsaken the climb it took on the ladder to make use of that space and opted for what was within reach from the floor instead.

"I'm sorry," Laurel whispered. "I don't understand."

Nothing sounded. Nothing appeared.

Disappointed, she moved about the room for a few moments but felt no urge to go to a particular place. Giving up the chase as a lost cause, she left the library without looking back, and followed the scent of frying bacon and fresh coffee permeating the air.

"Something smells wonderful," she said as she entered the kitchen.

Marie glanced up, then smiled. "Good morning, sunshine. You hungry for one egg or two?"

"I'll have one, please. I'm saving my appetite for the party tonight."

Marie turned, her eyes alight with curiosity. "Oh, yeah...tonight is the fete for little Rachelle, *oui?*"

"Yes. Justin is coming to pick me up around five. What would you suggest I wear?"

"Somethin' like what you have on...only less."

Laurel looked down at her long bare legs and almost bare feet, and felt herself starting to blush.

"You're joking. Tell me you're joking," she muttered.

"I'm jokin'," Marie said, then turned around and calmly cracked two eggs into the skillet.

It took Laurel a moment to realize she'd been had; then she started to grin.

"You really had me going there for a minute," she said.

Marie chuckled. "Scared you some, did I, girl?"

"Yes, ma'am, that you did."

"Just wear something comfortable that's not too fussy, 'cause most people round here don't have a lot of money, and you don't want to shame them by dressin' up."

Laurel nodded, then glanced out the window as Tula's grandson passed by, still pushing the mower.

"I see Tula's grandson has arrived."

"That's Claude. He'll do whatever you want."

"I'll talk to him after breakfast," Laurel said, then took her elbows off the table as Marie carried their breakfast to the table. "That looks good."

"And I 'spect it tastes good, too," Marie said.

Laurel laughed as she dug into her food. "Am I forgiven for hiring help?"

Marie pretended to frown. "I'll let you know."

Laurel was still smiling as she took her first bite.

"Mmmm, it's marvelous," she said. "Especially these biscuits."

Marie's frown completely disappeared. At that point, Laurel knew she was back on solid ground. She listened as Marie began to count off the tasks she had scheduled for the day, including the fact that two women from Tula's family would be there later to begin cleaning.

"I'm going to start them in the library," Marie said. "It's probably the biggest job. All those books...they just settin' there gatherin' dust."

The mention of the library made Laurel shiver. She wondered what Marie would say if she told her what she was seeing and feeling in this old house. More than that, she wondered if her grandmother had experienced the same thing. But to know, she would have to ask.

"Want another biscuit, darlin'?" Marie asked, then proceeded to take a biscuit and put it on Laurel's plate before she could answer. "Here...try some of my orange marmalade. Your grandmama loved my marmalade."

Laurel considered it an answer from above that her grandmother was mentioned. It gave her the perfect opening to bring up the subject of ghosts.

"Mamárie...can I ask you something?"

"Sure you can, baby girl...ask away."

"Remember the day I arrived...and the ghost that met me on the stairs?"

Marie laid down her fork, the smile gone from her face.

"I remember."

"Did my grandmother see things like that?"

Marie's eyes widened. "See? You mean, did she see apparitions?"

"I guess...yes...did she actually 'see' ghosts, or did she just feel them?"

Marie grabbed Laurel's hand.

"What's been goin' on with you here? Are you tellin' me that you seein' things?"

From the look in Marie LeFleur's eyes, Laurel had a feeling she should have kept the news to herself. Still, it was too late to take back the words, and she'd been taught that the truth would set her free.

"Yes."

Marie quickly crossed herself as she stared at Laurel in disbelief.

"Then you got some real mojo, baby girl. To my knowledge, your grandmama never saw spirits...only things that had happened, or were going to happen." Then something else occurred to her. "Are they talkin' to you, too?"

Laurel shrugged. "I don't hear actual words, but I get what feels like emotions. Like she's wanting me to find something, but I can't understand what."

"She? She? You seein' Chantelle, the first mistress of Mimosa Grove?"

"I don't know who she is," Laurel said.

"It's her.... I know it's her! Lord have mercy," Marie said, then winked. "Your grandmama would be jealous. Proud, but jealous."

"Really?"

"Yes, really. Now eat that biscuit before it gets cold. Just 'cause you seein' spirits and all, don't mean you can waste my food."

"Yes, ma'am," Laurel said, putting the subject of ghosts on the back burner. She toasted Marie with the biscuit, then took a big bite.

Marie was drinking the last of her coffee when someone began knocking at the door. She frowned at Laurel, then pointed her finger at her.

''That should be Tula's nieces. I'm tellin' you now, if they don't do right, I'll be sendin' them home.''

Laurel held up her hands. ''Don't yell at me. You're in charge, and you know it. I'll just be outside talking to Claude. Call if you need me.''

''Humph.''

Marie's grunt was just shy of a snort. Laurel carried their dishes to the sink, rinsed them, then loaded them in the dishwasher before going out the back door. Despite all her fussing, Laurel knew Marie was secretly glad to have the help. Within a short time, she and Claude had made friends, as well as plans as to what to clean up first. But when she started wielding an oversize trimming saw toward some low-hanging branches, he balked.

''Miss Laurel, you need to go on back in the house now and let me do what you're paying me to do.''

''Absolutely not,'' Laurel said. ''I'm perfectly capable of doing—''

''Yes, ma'am, I'm sure you are. But I'm a proud man, and you wouldn't want to put me to shame by showing me up, now, would you?''

Laurel sighed. She hated to admit it, but she was already exhausted. Plus there was the party tonight. And Justin. Marie thought it was something that she was seeing ghosts. She could only imagine what the old woman would think if she knew what had been happening between them. She eyed the determined jut to Claude's jaw and knew the gentle smile on his face was just for show.

''All right,'' she said. ''If you have questions, just let me know.''

"I'll be fine," he said. "You go take yourself a rest. Can't be dancing all night if you're too tired."

"How did you know I'm going to a party?" she asked.

Claude smiled. "Shoot, Miss Laurel, everyone knows everyone's business here in Bayou Jean."

She grinned. "Well, I hope not *all* of it."

"Enough to cause trouble," he said, then wandered off toward the toolshed to get a wheelbarrow. Laurel gave up and went back into the house.

The scent of lemon oil mingled with that of dust as she crossed the hall to the library.

"I've been fired," she announced as she walked into the room.

"Don't come in here," Marie said, waving a feather duster in Laurel's face. "Go boss someone else around and leave the business end of this to us."

"Claude ran me off of the landscape clean-up, and you won't let me in the library. I think the term 'boss' is highly overstated around here. We both know who the boss is, and she's a whole lot shorter than me."

The two women standing on ladders chuckled.

Marie frowned as she pointed. "The funny one with dirt on her nose is Wanda Jo. The scrawny one is her sister, Frances."

"Thank you so much for coming to help out," Laurel said.

"Yes, ma'am," they echoed.

"Not ma'am...Laurel, please."

The one named Frances immediately picked up on the offer.

"Laurel...can we ask you something?"

"Sure," Laurel said.

"Are you like Miz Marcella? Do you have the sight?"

Laurel hesitated, then answered. "Yes."

"You gonna stay here at Mimosa Grove?" Wanda Jo asked.

"Yes."

"Good."

Again Laurel was overwhelmed by the instant acceptance, when it had been just the opposite where she'd grown up.

Marie nodded approvingly, then waved Laurel out of the room.

"Take a rest...read a book...write some letters. Or better yet, make yourself pretty for that Justin Bouvier. You never know what will come of new friendships."

Even though Laurel wanted to say more, she held her tongue. This was going to be their first date, but she and Justin had definitely moved beyond the boundaries of friendship.

"Okay for now, but call me if you need me."

"Oh! Well, my goodness!" Frances suddenly cried. "What's this, I wonder?"

Laurel turned quickly, curious as to what the other woman had found.

"What is it?" she asked as the skinny little woman quickly climbed down the ladder. As soon as both feet were on the floor, she ran to Laurel.

"Look at this. It looks real old. It was on that top shelf behind a stack of books."

"What you got there?" Marie asked, and took the small package away from Frances. She frowned as she turned it over in her hands. "Some kind of book, I think...wrapped in a piece of old leather." She handed it to Laurel.

The moment Laurel touched it, she knew what it was, and who it had belonged to.

"It's Chantelle LeDeux's diary," she said.

Both Frances and Wanda Jo turned pale.

"How you know something like that without looking?" Wanda Jo asked.

"You getting goofy in your old age?" Marie asked. "She done told you she's got the sight like Miz Marcella, and touchin' stuff is how she 'sees.'"

Wanda Jo looked decidedly uncomfortable. Apparently it was one thing to know someone was psychic, but it was another to witness it firsthand.

Laurel laid the pack carefully on the desk, then unwrapped the leather from around a small book. When she opened it, a small picture fell out. Upon closer examination, she realized it was a painting, rather than a photo, then remembered that when this woman lived, photography had yet to be invented.

She stared at the small oval face framed with dark hair pulled severely away from her features. Her neck and shoulders were bare, with only a hint of lace and some kind of dark scarf at her bosom. There was a very distinctive cameo hanging from a bit of ribbon around her neck and nestling securely in the valley between her breasts. She was an attractive woman, but her expression seemed sad. Then it dawned on Laurel that this was the first ancestor to whom the psychic abilities of the family could be traced.

"Let me see," Marie begged, and when Laurel

handed her the painting, she cradled it in the palms of her hands, as if afraid she would damage it. "Oh, my...would you look at that." Then she eyed the small book from which it had come. "What you reckon she got to say in there?"

Laurel already knew that, whatever it was, it was sad. She'd felt that from the beginning. As she picked up the diary, she realized that this might be what her ghost had been trying to show her.

"Okay...okay," she said softly. "Let's see what you've been trying to say."

Marie frowned. "You talkin' to me?"

"No," Laurel said, then took the picture from Marie, wrapped the book back in the leather and left the room.

Wanda Jo and Frances looked at each other, then rolled their eyes.

"I saw that," Marie said. "Ain't nothin' happened here except you found an old book, understand?"

"Yes, ma'am," they echoed.

"So get back to work. I want to be done in here by the end of the day."

"Yes, ma'am," they said again, and climbed back up their ladders with clean dust rags in their hands as Laurel climbed the stairs to her room.

She closed the door behind her as she entered the room, kicked off her shoes and crawled up in the middle of the bed with the packet. It was only a bit after nine o'clock. She had plenty of time to read before she needed to begin getting ready for the party. Again she unwrapped the diary, then set the picture of Chantelle aside and opened the book to the first page.

February 10, 1814
I am a married woman. For the rest of my life I am to sleep with, and give birth to the children of, Jean Charles LeDeux. The rest of my life is forever. I pray I will learn to love him.

February 25, 1814
I don't know how I feel. Part of me is proud to be a married woman. Jean Charles is a good man. Mimosa Grove is beautiful, like God's Eden. The house is quite grand and stands three stories tall, with four magnificent pillars along the front. The house servants have been with his family for years. Old Mary seems as if she's waiting for me to fail. Joshua is kind, but he will not look directly at me. I don't know if that's because they're taught to do that, or if they are afraid to meet my gaze. At first they were courteous, but now they are afraid of me. I feared this would happen, but I could not stay silent about what I had seen. If I had, the child would have died.

Laurel's arms went limp, letting the diary rest between her legs as she sprawled on her bed. Even though the writing was old, Chantelle's spirit was so strong on the pages that she could see what had happened as clearly as if it was on film.

*February, 1814*

It was nearing sundown and people were beginning to arrive for the party. Jean Charles LeDeux had invited all the surrounding plantation owners and their wives to his home to meet his new French bride. Her beauty was the talk of Bayou Jean, and the wealth of her dowry had gone a long way toward helping fill the lean coffers of his bank accounts. Although this year's crop looked good, the last two years' cotton harvests had been poor. After losing four of his best field hands during the past eleven months—three to malaria, one to a snake bite—he considered his marriage a fresh beginning to Mimosa Grove. The fact that he was eighteen years older than she was hardly mattered. Her youth was a plus, assuring him a wife with plenty of childbearing years ahead of her.

The party was in full swing, and Jean Charles was gloating over his friends' envious glances at Chantelle. Even the married men were charmed by her beauty and innocence. Then he noticed her standing by the doorway, and it occurred to him that she'd been there for some time. He nodded cordially to the woman at his elbow and excused himself before making his way toward his wife. It was obvious she needed a gentle reminder that since she was the hostess, she must mingle with her guests.

He cupped her elbow.

"Chantelle…"

She moaned. Almost immediately, he feared she'd taken ill. He turned her toward him, then laid the back of his hand against her cheek. Despite the warmth of the room, her skin was cold and clammy. She was looking at him, but he could have sworn she could not see. Her gaze was empty, but somehow frantic. He could see her eyes moving from side to side, as if she was watching players on a stage.

"Chantelle…talk to me."

She took a deep breath, then wailed. The sound that came up from her throat and out of her mouth was like the wind blowing through a partially opened window—like a high-pitched moan.

Suddenly everyone in the room became silent as all eyes turned to Jean Charles's new bride.

Joshua, one of the house servants, quickly moved toward the master, sensing a need for assistance.

"Massuh?"

Jean Charles wondered if he looked as panicked as he felt. This couldn't be happening to him. Surely to God his child bride had not already succumbed to this damnable country with its agues and fevers.

"Get Mary," he said shortly.

The large black man set the tray he was carrying on a table and bolted out of the room, heading for the kitchens.

Jean Charles put his hand beneath Chantelle's elbow, intent on leading her toward a chair, when she pulled away from his grasp and pointed toward the window.

"The child...the child...somebody save the child."

Jean Charles ran to the window, thinking that she'd seen something horrific that they'd ignored, but there was nothing in sight but fireflies and the hanging lanterns that Joshua had hung on the veranda. He turned back to Chantelle and, in his panic, shook her harshly.

"*Mon Dieu... Chère,* talk to me...talk to me. What's wrong with you? There's no child."

"In the quarters...she's in the quarters. The second cabin on the left. Snake in her bed. Hurry, before it's too late."

Then she dropped to the floor, unconscious.

Jean Charles hardly knew what to think as he picked his bride up from the floor and carried her to a chaise near the fireplace. At the same time, he realized that both Mary and Joshua were standing in the doorway. The look of horror on the old woman's face was nothing to the terror on Joshua's. It was then that he realized that the cabin Chantelle had spoken of was where Joshua's family lived.

"Massuh...please."

Jean Charles realized Joshua was asking permission to go to the quarters.

He hesitated, wondering how it would appear to his guests if he gave in to a Nigra's request, then stifled the thought. This was his home. He was master here. He could do and say what he chose.

"I'm sure all is well, but you may go. However, I expect you back here in five minutes.... Hear?"

"Yes, Massuh, thank you, Massuh," Joshua said, and bolted out of the room, while Old Mary put her apron over her face and refused to look at Chantelle.

Jean Charles cursed beneath his breath.

"Mary...attend to your mistress this moment, do you hear me?"

"Massuh...no, please don't make me."

"What's wrong with you?" he snapped. "Don't think I won't have you whipped just because you're old. Tend to your mistress."

Old Mary fell to her knees and pulled her apron over her head.

"I can't, Massuh, I can't. She's got the voodoo sight. Don't let her witch me."

Jean Charles heard the soft gasp of his guests as

they stared in disbelief. In the midst of his embarrassment, he felt as if he'd been slapped. He leaned over the old woman and grabbed her by the arm.

"What on earth are you saying?"

Old Mary looked up, her eyes brimming with tears, then pointed at Chantelle.

"She a witch, Massuh. She a witch woman."

He was on the verge of slapping the woman for her insolence, but a sound from outside the house stopped him. Loud shouts and cries of dismay echoed from the slave quarters. Always fearful of an uprising, the women cried aloud while clinging to their husbands, certain they were about to be murdered where they stood.

Within seconds, Joshua came running back into the room. He, too, was crying, but tears of joy. His arrival was much less startling than that which he was carrying. A huge, steel-gray snake of great circumference and length was dangling from his fist. Even from this distance, the people recognized the snake as a cottonmouth—a water moccasin whose deadly venom often claimed the lives of those who lived in the bayous.

"Massuh...Massuh...she was right! It was in my baby's bed. Praise God, Massuh, she saved her life."

Old Mary wailed even louder, then scrambled to her feet and dashed from the room.

All Jean Charles could think was that this had to be a nightmare from which he would soon wake. This couldn't be happening. Not in his house. Not on his estate. But Joshua was still there, holding the dead snake. His guests were aghast, staring from the snake to Chantelle and back again. And Chantelle...she was still there on the chaise, looking for all the world as if she'd just fallen asleep.

"Goddamn it!" Jean Charles suddenly shouted. "Joshua! Get that thing out of here at once." Then he turned to his guests. "My friends...I know you will understand when I ask you to excuse me. I must attend to my wife's health. She has simply fainted from the stress of planning our fete. However, I am sure all will be well in the morning. Please enjoy yourselves. I will have more champagne sent up from the cellar."

Without looking at their faces, he scooped Chantelle from the chaise and carried her up the stairs, shouting for Mary to follow as he went.

Laurel shuddered, then came to with a gasp. With tears in her eyes, she picked up the diary, laid it back in its leather wrapping and put it on the table near her bed.

"Poor Chantelle," she said softly. "Poor, poor Chantelle. Mimosa Grove was not your Eden after all."

# 8

Justin had been working on the computer most of the morning, catching up on e-mail as well as posting some new info to his client lists. Normally he could go through such a task in only a couple of hours, but this morning he'd been unable to concentrate, and he knew why.

His thoughts were on Laurel.

It was unbelievable to think of how well he knew her passion but not her tastes. He didn't know if she liked mustard or mayonnaise, but he knew the sound of her sigh as he moved inside her body. He wanted to know her favorite color, her favorite food, what made her laugh, what made her sad. And most of all, he missed sleeping with her, yet they'd never actually shared a night together. From what he could tell, their nighttime connection had been broken about the time she'd arrived in Bayou Jean, which didn't make sense. They were geographically closer now than they'd been before, but she no longer came to him in his sleep. Even though they had truly made love only once, and in the bright light of day with no one but the ghosts of Mimosa Grove as their witnesses, it wasn't enough.

He groaned, then shut off the computer and walked out of his office. No need trying to work anymore.

Not when a tall, leggy redhead was so deep in his head that he couldn't think.

As he walked down the hall, his grandmother's old clock began chiming the hour. Surprised that it was already two o'clock and he had yet to eat lunch, he dug through the refrigerator without success, then opted for an apple and some iced tea, saving his appetite for the party that night.

The apple was sweet and crisp as he took the first bite. A tiny droplet of juice escaped from the corner of his mouth and slipped down his chin. He caught it with the back of his hand and then took another bite. The sweetness reminded him of Laurel's kisses.

Lord. Three more hours before he would see her.

He finished his apple as he walked through his home, struck by the solitude and silence of his existence in a way he'd never been before. As he did, he caught a glimpse of himself in the hall mirror. He looked the same. But he wasn't. Laurel had changed him in ways he could only feel. He tossed the apple core outside, grinning to himself when his old hound jumped on it as if it was a big juicy bone.

"Come on, Big Red...leave it for the chickens."

But the old dog had gulped it down too fast to taste it. Justin was laughing as he went back inside. His hand was on the doorknob when Laurel's face popped into his mind. He didn't know how he knew it, but he was certain that something had happened that had made her sad. Without thinking, he reached for the phone, dialing the number to Mimosa Grove from memory.

It rang once, twice, then Marie answered on the third ring.

"Marie, it's me, Justin. May I speak to Laurel?"

"You better not be callin' to break your date with my baby," Marie said.

Justin laughed. "You know better than that."

"Well...okay then. Hang on a minute. I think she's still upstairs."

"Marie! Wait! Don't walk all that way upstairs just to tell her about the call. It wasn't anything important...just tell her I called."

"If you want to talk to my girl, then it's important," Marie said. "You just wait."

He heard her lay down the phone, then heard her footsteps as she left the room. Still regretting his impulse, he could do nothing but wait. Then he heard Marie shout Laurel's name and knew that she must be standing at the foot of the stairs. A few seconds later, he heard someone pick up on an extension.

"Hello?"

"Laurel...it's me, Justin."

"Justin? Is something wrong?"

"You tell me," he said softly as he heard Marie hang up downstairs.

Laurel's breath caught; then she sighed. The lingering sadness of reading Chantelle's diary was still with her.

"I was doing some reading."

"Have you been crying?"

Goose bumps broke out on Laurel's skin.

"I'm the one who's supposed to be psychic. How did you know that?"

"Don't ask me. I was minding my own business, eating an apple and having a glass of iced tea, when your face popped into my mind. Then I felt sad...really sad. Only it wasn't my emotions, it was yours."

"Weird," Laurel said.

He laughed softly. "Coming from you, that's priceless." Then he added, "I've been missing you."

Laurel smiled to herself. "I've been missing you, too."

"Do you still dream about me?"

"No...do you dream about me?"

"No."

"Why is that?" he asked.

"I don't know."

"I want that back," he said.

Laurel's throat tightened. "So do I."

"Laurel..."

"What?"

"I want so much from you, maybe too much."

"I know," Laurel said. "A love affair in my sleep is one thing. Making love to a stranger is another."

"Please...don't call me that."

"Call you what?"

"A stranger. Too much has passed between us for that."

"I didn't mean—"

Justin sighed. "Never mind. I shouldn't have said anything. You're right. We don't know each other, at least not well enough. But tonight can be a new beginning for us. I want that. I want that very much."

His voice was in her head; his promises were stealing her composure. If not for Marie and the workers downstairs, she would be begging him to come over now. Remembering the tenderness of his lovemaking made her weak with longing.

"I want it, too...that, and more."

Justin closed his eyes, remembering the softness of

her breasts pressing against his chest as he slid deep inside her.

"Have mercy, *chère,* you're making me crazy."

"Then I guess we're even, because according to most, I'm already there."

He groaned beneath his breath. "Are you sure you're okay? I could come over earlier. We could take the long way to my sister's house. Maybe you'd feel better."

His offer was unexpected and so sweet.

"I'd love to spend more time with you, but it's not necessary to come earlier just for me. Thanks to you, I feel better already."

"You sure?"

"Yes."

"Okay…but tonight…"

"Yes?"

"I'm not making any promises about keeping my hands to myself."

"Good," Laurel said. "I'd hate to be responsible for broken promises."

His laughter was soft against her ear as he disconnected. Laurel hung up the phone, then pulled her knees up beneath her chin and hugged herself. It was obvious that whatever was going on with her and Justin was out of her control. She didn't know what had connected them, but she didn't want it to stop. For the first time in her life, she was beginning to believe she'd found a place in which she belonged—and maybe a man to belong to. It was more than she'd hoped for when she'd left D.C.

Once she thought of D.C., she thought of her father. After he'd mentioned the high-profile case he was working on, she'd taken to watching the national

news broadcasts, as well as *CNN Headline News.*
Only now and then was mention made of McNamara's arrest, and when it was, it seemed that the
focus was on his past in Russia—of his genius intellect and of being planted in the U.S. for espionage
rather than the charges for which he'd been arrested.
The only specifics mentioned were for selling "military secrets," which could mean anything.

Again the notion came to her that her father was
going to be in danger, but she couldn't tell how. All
she knew was that she got a sick feeling in the pit of
her stomach when she heard McNamara's name.

Trigger DeLane cut a line of cocaine on the marble
surface of the bathroom vanity and sucked it up his
nose. The hit was immediate and strong, and the feeling of euphoria eased the anxiety he'd been living
with since McNamara's arrest. He knew the addiction
he'd been hiding for almost fifteen years was completely responsible for the mess he found himself in
now, but he lacked the intestinal fortitude to kick it.

As the oldest child and only son of four-star general
John Franklin DeLane, it had become apparent at an
early age that Trigger was expected to follow his father's path into military service. The pressure had
been too much and the desire to do so completely
absent. Instead of standing up to his father and announcing his intent to become a chef, he'd lied to
everyone, including himself, quit high school at the
age of sixteen and reluctantly attained a GED at
twenty-four, thereby bypassing college altogether and
eliminating himself from the possibility of ever attending West Point. The fact that his father considered
him a failure in every way was almost a relief. At

least now nothing was expected of him. But it was what he'd expected of himself that was eating him alive. He'd never planned to be a traitor to his country. He'd never meant to sell himself out. But he'd done it because it was easier than standing up to the man who was his father.

He glanced down at the other line of coke still on the counter, bent over and inhaled, running the line up his nose with a straw just as he'd done with the first.

"Whoa, mama!" he yelled, then laughed out loud when the drug hit his brain. This was what he'd needed. Now he was untouchable. McNamara wanted Robert Scanlon rendered useless as surely as if he'd been castrated, and Trigger DeLane was the man to do it.

Robert Scanlon handed a stack of folders to his secretary and then shut his briefcase. His confrontation with the attorney general was over. The fact that he still had a job was nothing short of a miracle, but his refusal to make a deal with McNamara had been looked upon as mutiny. Had he been a military man, he would be facing a court martial. As it was, he'd been given specific orders to make himself scarce, with an unpaid leave of absence. He considered it a bargain. He headed for the parking garage, intent on stopping by the travel agent before going home to pack. He hadn't taken a vacation in years, and considering the atmosphere under which he was leaving, it was high time he did.

A short while later, he had tickets to Belize in his pocket, with a short side trip to Louisiana. Despite the fact that he could not condone Laurel's lifestyle, she was his only child, and he was uncomfortable with the circumstances under which they'd parted. The least he could do was go to Mimosa Grove and make peace with her before leaving the country.

Satisfied with his decisions, he started toward home, wondering what Cook was making for dinner and hoping that Estelle had remembered to have the cleaners deliver his laundry. There were a couple of items that he wanted to take with him.

Trigger DeLane pulled up in front of the Scanlon residence and parked on the wide, tree-lined street, taking advantage of the large swatch of shade that the giant oaks in front of the Scanlon home were providing. He glanced at his wristwatch, then at his reflection in the rearview mirror. It was twenty minutes after two in the afternoon. The perfect time to pay a call on Miss Laurel Scanlon. They'd met each other briefly at a New Year's Eve party at his father's house over two years ago. He didn't know if she would remember him, but all he had to do was throw his father's name into the conversation and he would be in the door.

He'd come to talk a woman into taking a ride with him. The fact that she would not be coming home from that ride was moot. Thanks to his predilection for "blow" and McNamara's fuck-up, he was being forced to kidnap a woman with whom he'd shared nothing but a brief New Year's Eve kiss on the cheek.

He smoothed his hair with both hands, then slipped on a pair of sunglasses. He was reaching for the car keys when he caught a glimpse of a car coming slowly down the street. Deciding it might be prudent to wait until it passed, he sat, watching the car. To his dismay, the car did not pass but instead turned into the Scanlon driveway and then drove around behind the house toward the garage.

Trigger had seen just enough of the driver's face to recognize Robert Scanlon. Cursing his luck and the fact that McNamara had ever been born, he decided to wait. It was too early for Scanlon to be home from work, which meant there was the possibility he would be leaving as abruptly as he'd arrived. As he sat, he decided to give Laurel a call. That would make his mission even easier. It never even occurred to him that she might not be interested in going out with him. All the unmarried women wanted a piece of John Franklin DeLane's son.

Satisfied that he'd solved his immediate problem, he picked up his cell phone and dialed information. A couple of minutes later, the phone in the Scanlon residence began to ring.

Estelle was near the phone and answered on the second ring, fluffing her new hairdo and admiring her blond highlights in the gleaming tabletop as she answered the call.

"Scanlon residence."

"Laurel Scanlon, please. Trigger DeLane calling."

"I'm sorry, Mr. DeLane, but Miss Scanlon is no longer at this residence."

Stunned by the news, he sat up with a jerk, almost dropping the phone in the process. The blow he'd snorted was losing its buzz, and the news he'd just received didn't help his disposition.

"Uh...is she on vacation? Where did she go? It's imperative that I talk to her."

"No, sir, she moved. Would you care to speak to her father?"

"No, that won't be necessary," he said quickly, and disconnected.

"Who was that?" Robert asked as Estelle was hanging up the receiver.

"A gentleman for Miss Laurel."

"Really?" Robert muttered. To his knowledge, men did not call the house to speak to his daughter. Her reputation had preceded her, scaring off any would-be suitors. "Who was it?"

"I think he said his name was Trigger DeLane. It's an odd name, but I'm pretty certain that's what he said."

Robert frowned. Everyone in the city knew Franklin DeLane's son was a loser. Definitely not the kind of man he would want his daughter seeing. Then he sighed. What he wanted for Laurel was moot. She'd removed herself from his influence.

"Mr. Scanlon, are you ill? Is there something I can get for you?" Estelle asked.

Robert grinned wryly. "No. I'm not ill. I'm officially on a leave of absence. In fact, I'm going to Belize in a couple of days."

"Oh, my!" Estelle gasped, wondering what would happen to her. With Laurel gone and Robert Scanlon leaving the country, she hoped her job was not in danger.

"I hope you'll be comfortable staying on, even though you'll be on your own. As long as the house is maintained, you can feel free to keep your own hours. I don't like the idea of leaving the place empty."

Estelle breathed a sigh of relief. "Oh, yes, sir…certainly. How long do you plan to be gone?"

He frowned. "About a month. You'll have my cell

phone number, and I'll call to check in on you from time to time. Certainly to let you know when I'm due home."

"Yes, sir. What about Laurel? Is she going with you?"

"No. She has her own life right now, although I *am* going to drive down to Bayou Jean and see her before I leave."

"Please give her my best," Estelle said. "I miss her."

Robert sighed. "Yes. I miss her, too," and as he said it, he realized he really meant it. "I'm going upstairs to pack. I'll be leaving first thing tomorrow morning."

Laurel was shaking, partly from nerves, partly from excitement, as she fixed her hair at the mirror. Tonight she would be with Justin, in the midst of his family, facing people who knew she was different. Justin had not seemed to care, but her experience had proved that he was the minority. She wanted to make a good impression on him and his sister, not freak them all out, but she never knew what was going to happen or what she might "see." Being in the midst of so many strangers could set off all kinds of bells and whistles, and the last thing she wanted was to embarrass herself or Justin.

"Honey girl…you gonna brush that hair right off your head if you don't stop."

Laurel looked up. Marie was standing in the doorway to her bedroom with an armful of clean towels. Even though it was close to sundown, her pink cotton dress was still as clean and fresh as when she'd put it on this morning. Her only concession to the end of the day was that she was now wearing house slippers rather than her usual yellow flip-flops.

Laurel sighed, then laid the hairbrush down on her dresser.

"I'm sort of nervous about tonight," she said.

Marie carried the towels into the bathroom and put them in the linen closet, then stood back with her hands on her hips and gave Laurel a once-over.

"Well, you look fine to me. You wearin' those jeans just fine, and that pink T-shirt looks real nice on you, too. Justin gonna have a time keepin' his hands to hisself."

Laurel blushed. She didn't want him to keep his hands to himself, but she could hardly tell that to Marie.

"Mamárie...I didn't think to ask, but are parties like this potluck? Should I be bringing something?"

"No. You the guest of honor, remember?"

"How can I forget?" Laurel muttered, and flopped down on the side of the bed.

Marie moved in front of Laurel, then tilted Laurel's chin.

"Look at me, baby."

"I'm looking."

Marie grinned. "You're gonna be fine. People down here loved your grandmama. They gonna love you, too."

Laurel looked long and hard into the old woman's face, past the years and the wrinkles, into dark eyes rich with wisdom. Finally she leaned forward and wrapped her arms around Marie's waist.

Marie pulled Laurel's head onto her breast, then rocked her gently against her where she stood.

"You just trust Mamárie.... I'll take care of you, just like I took care of my Marcella."

Laurel was so moved she wanted to cry.

"Why, Mamárie?"

"Why what, honey girl?"

"Why do you stay here at Mimosa Grove? You could go anywhere, do anything, and yet you've all but buried yourself in this place."

An expression crossed Marie's face that Laurel didn't see. By the time she looked up, Marie had regained her composure.

"For as long as there's been a Mimosa Grove, there's been a member of my family here, as well. It's hard to explain, but our lives are intertwined with Chantelle LeDeux's descendants as surely as if we shared the same blood."

"I suppose I should stop second-guessing my good fortune," Laurel said. "You've made me feel welcome...even loved. I'm very glad that you're here."

"No happier than I am to have you," Marie said, then gave her a quick kiss on the forehead. "Now quit worrying about things that have yet to happen. Just have a good time and don't let that good-lookin' Cajun talk you into anything you don't want to do."

Laurel hugged Marie tight, but before Marie could say anything further, they both heard a car driving up.

"Someone's coming," Marie said. "Probably Justin. Go powder your nose and wash those tears out of your eyes. I'll tell him you're on the way down."

"Yes, ma'am," Laurel said, then sat there on the side of the bed, listening to Marie's footsteps as they moved along the hallway, then down the stairs.

She was still sitting on the side of the bed when she heard the rumble of Justin's voice in the vestibule. She stood; then, drawn like a magnet to his presence, she hurried down the stairs.

# 9

Justin was teasing Marie about not bringing Laurel home before sunrise when he heard her coming down the stairs. The smile was still on his face as he turned around. As he did, the setting sun was reflected in a mirror opposite where he was standing and momentarily blinded him. He shifted one step to the left and then froze. For a fraction of a second, he would have sworn it wasn't Laurel who was coming down the stairs but a small, slender woman with thick red hair piled high upon her head. She wasn't wearing the blue jeans and T-shirt that Laurel had on. Instead, it appeared she had on an off-the-shoulder, floor-length white ball gown with what looked like a gardenia behind her right ear.

Breath caught in the back of his throat. He blinked, and as quickly as the vision had appeared, it was gone.

"Uh...I—"

Laurel's smile faltered. "What's wrong?" she asked, then pulled nervously at the hem of her T-shirt. "Am I not dressed right?"

Marie winked, then blew Laurel a kiss before she left, as Justin went up the stairs to meet her.

"No. No. You're perfect," he said softly, then took her hands and turned them palms up, kissing one, then the other. "Forgive me. For a moment there, the sun was in my eyes. I thought I saw…uh—"

"What?" Laurel asked. "What did you see?"

"Nothing," Justin said quickly.

Too quickly for Laurel's satisfaction.

"Justin?"

He shrugged, then grinned wryly, expecting her to laugh when he admitted what he'd seen.

"For a moment there, I thought I saw a small, red-haired woman in a white ball gown coming down the stairs. But like I said, the sun was—"

Laurel glanced around the foyer almost wistfully, wishing she was the one who'd seen her.

"I guess it was Chantelle," she said softly. "I've been reading about her. I think it's stirred up her ghost."

Justin's eyes widened, but he managed to refrain from looking over his shoulder. "Really?"

"Yes, the house cleaners found her diary in the library earlier today."

Justin kept feeling as if someone was standing behind them, watching them talk. Unwilling to admit his fears to Laurel, he tugged at her hands instead.

"We'd better go," he said. "Since you're the guest of honor, we don't want to be late."

"If you're sure I'm dressed all right, then I'm ready."

Justin eyed the curve of her hips, then the thrust of her breasts against the T-shirt, and whistled softly beneath his breath.

"You're not just all right, honey. You're fantastic."

The wanting in his voice made her shiver.

"You don't look so bad yourself," she said. "Besides, I'm starving."

"Then we're going to the right place," Justin said, and led her outside.

They were starting down the steps when Elvis sailed off the veranda roof and landed between them and Justin's truck. Before either of them could react, the bird started to shriek.

"Oh, good grief," Laurel said.

Justin started to grin as the peacock fanned his tail and began to strut back and forth.

"You know what I think? I think Elvis has a crush on you."

"You can't be serious," Laurel muttered.

"Well, let's say I recognize the behavior. It's similar to the way I behaved around the age of ten. I had a great big crush on Yvonne Martin, and to show my love, I pestered her constantly on the playground. Wouldn't leave her alone. Couldn't stand it if she wasn't looking at me in some way. Of course, it never occurred to me that chucking handfuls of gravel at her hair wasn't going to endear me to her."

Laurel laughed. "You didn't."

Justin grinned. "Yeah, I did. And that's what that stupid bird is doing. He's always in your face, isn't he?"

"Well, yes, but—"

"Does he always fan his tail like that?"

Laurel stared at the big bird, absently admiring the magnificent colors as she thought back to her arrival.

"You know, I think he does."

Justin laughed. "Just what I thought. Male peacocks show off their 'stuff,' so to speak, when flirting with a possible mate. So how do you feel about feathers?''

"Oh, my lord," Laurel said.

"Don't worry," Justin said. "All he needs to know is that you're already taken."

"That's silly," Laurel muttered. "How on earth can—"

"Like this," Justin said, and took Laurel in his arms.

Before she could think, he was kissing her.

At first he was gentle, laughing beneath his breath at the absurdity of staking his claim before a bird. But the softness of her lips and the slight moan he heard when he put his arms around her waist dragged him further under than he'd intended to go. They forgot about the peacock. They forgot about the party. And they almost forgot about where they were. It wasn't until Justin started to pull her T-shirt over her head and lay her down beneath a sheltering mimosa that they came to their senses.

"Have mercy," Justin said, turned loose of her body, then took a single step back.

Laurel was flushed and shaking, bereft by the distance between them after being anchored to the man and his need.

He ran a hand through his hair, then looked at her in disbelief.

"I'm sorry. I didn't mean to…oh, hell. Truth is, you drive me crazy," he said softly, then added, "But in a really good way."

Laurel swallowed past the knot in her throat, then straightened her clothing.

"I know the feeling," she said, then combed shaky

hands through her hair. "Besides, I think Elvis got the message."

Justin looked. The peacock was gone.

"Come on, honey," Justin said. "Let's party."

There were cars lining both sides of the dirt road in front of Tommy and Cheryl Ann Mouton's home, leaving just enough space for a car to pass through. Hundreds of tiny white Christmas-style lights had been strung about the yard and beneath the porch, illuminating the area and adding to the festivities already in progress when Justin pulled up and parked.

Laurel took one look at the yard full of people and tensed. She'd served as her father's hostess for many years, knowing—and eventually not caring—what they thought of her. But tonight was different. She wanted to be accepted by these people so badly she could taste it. The hunger to belong was making her sick. Without thinking, she reached for Justin's hand.

"I didn't know there would be this many people."

He lifted her hand to his lips and kissed her fingers before leaning over and kissing her lips.

She sighed, then melted when he gently bit her lower lip before turning her loose.

Laurel touched her lower lip with her fingertip, then shivered.

"Since we've been intimate sexually, we were going to turn it around and take our relationship slow."

"Bad decision," Justin whispered, then tucked a dark red curl behind her ear and winked.

Laurel sighed. "I'm nervous."

Justin frowned. "Of me?"

"No, silly. Of them."

She pointed toward the crowd. He grinned. "Don't be. They're just like me."

Laurel eyed the crowd. "Oh, Lord."

He laughed out loud. "Not in that way. But they're harmless, just the same."

"You're not," Laurel argued.

Justin's grin widened. "*Chère,* where you're concerned, I am helpless to resist you."

"Helpless and harmless are two different things," Laurel muttered. "So take me to the party before I back out of this deal."

He gave her hand a last comforting squeeze and then helped her out of the truck.

"Hey, ya'll!" Justin called. "Did you save us some crawfish?"

A small, dark-haired woman and a tall, sandy-haired man quickly separated themselves from the crowd and came to meet them. Almost immediately, Laurel was engulfed within the man's big arms, then lifted off her feet.

"Hey, Tommy, put her down, she's mine," Justin growled.

Tommy Mouton put her down but did not immediately turn her loose. His eyes welled quickly with tears, which ran unashamedly down his face.

"You saved my baby," he said, his voice gruff with emotion. "Know that I am forever in your debt. If you are ever in need, all you have to do is call."

Justin slid an arm across his brother-in-law's back, then looked at Laurel.

"Honey, this is my sister, Cheryl Ann, and her husband, Tommy."

"It's a pleasure to meet you," Laurel said.

Cheryl Ann Mouton clasped Laurel's hands.

"No, dear lady, the pleasure is all ours, and Tommy is right. 'Thank you' is a pitiful pair of words compared to what you have given back to us. Rachelle is our everything." Then she started to cry. "I don't know how...there aren't words to—"

"Enough," Laurel said. "It was Justin who found her."

"But only because you showed me where to look," Justin said softly. "It's true. Rachelle is the jewel of our small family. The loss of her life would have been devastating to us all. I add my thanks again for what you did."

Laurel started to look away, then lifted her chin and faced them instead. It was time she started acknowledging the truth.

"It is my gift."

"Then we will praise God for your blessing," Tommy said. "So come, come. Everyone is anxious to meet you."

Justin tugged at her hand, urging her to follow Tommy and Cheryl Ann as they waved to silence the band. The music stopped. When it did, everyone turned to see why. When they saw Justin with the stranger, the murmur of happy voices and laughter stopped as quickly as the music.

Once more Laurel felt herself on display, but it didn't last long. Tommy's voice rose into the air.

"Everyone, this is Miz Marcella's granddaughter, Laurel. If not for her, our baby, Rachelle, would have drowned."

There was a huge round of clapping and cheers. More than one person stepped forward to pat Laurel on the back. A woman handed her a can of cold pop, while another remarked on her resemblance to her grandmother, Marcella. In the middle of all that, Tommy beckoned to Justin. "Go rescue your lady before she decides to abandon you."

Laurel turned and smiled at Tommy.

"That's not likely," she said.

"Come with me," Justin said, and slid an arm around Laurel's waist as they followed his sister through the crowd. Laurel ducked to miss a low-hanging string of lights, and when she looked up, realized they had stopped.

"What's going on?" she asked.

Justin pointed at his sister, who was bending down to pick up a little girl. "Sis said Rachelle has something she wants to say to you."

Laurel saw a dark-haired, wide-eyed child looking at her from over her mother's shoulder, and stilled. Then she took a deep breath and smiled. She remembered the little girl all too well, only the last time she'd seen her, she'd been scared out of her mind and on the verge of drowning.

"Hello," Laurel said softly. "It's very nice to meet you."

The little girl ducked her head; then Cheryl Ann whispered something in her ear. Finally the child raised her head and looked at Laurel.

"Thank you for helping Uncle Justin find me when I was lost."

There was a stray curl near Rachelle Mouton's right eye. Without thinking, Laurel reached out and tucked it behind the child's ear.

"You're welcome," she said softly, then added, "You were very brave, you know. You did everything your uncle told you to do."

Rachelle's lips pursed as she studied Laurel's eyes.

"At first I was scared," she admitted. "Then I heard you in my head and I wasn't scared anymore."

Breath caught in the back of Laurel's throat. She tried to speak, but all she could manage was a smile.

"Praise God," Cheryl Ann whispered, and stared at Laurel as if she were a ghost.

Laurel's heart sank when she realized what had been said. Now they knew that she'd been inside the child's head, urging her to wait for her uncle instead of jumping into the water. They were bound to think she knew what everyone was thinking, which was far from the truth. She sighed. It had started off so well. She should have known it wasn't going to last.

"It's not what you think," Laurel muttered. "I didn't really...I mean, she was going to walk off that stump and I just..."

Tommy shuddered, then stared at their child anew.

"We didn't know," he said, and then started to cry. "Dear God, she didn't tell us that. If she hadn't listened to you, Justin would not have been able to save her."

Justin slipped an arm around Laurel's waist, then impulsively turned her in his arms and kissed her soundly.

"Way to go, Justin!" somebody yelled.

"Hey there, pretty lady...if you don't like that crazy Cajun, I'm available!" someone else shouted.

It was exactly what had been needed to ease the tension of the moment. But Laurel knew how moved Justin had been by what had happened when he finally pulled back. He was grinning, but his eyes were filled with tears.

"I don't know why I've been so blessed to have you in my life, but I'm not stupid enough to mess this up. Whatever you want…whatever you need… just say the word and it's yours.''

Laurel put her hand on Justin's chest, letting the steady rhythm of his heartbeat settle the thunder of her own.

"I already have it," she said.

"It? Exactly what is *it* that you have, sweet lady?"

"Something I've been looking for all my life. Acceptance."

"Who stopped the music?" Tommy yelled.

"You did," Cheryl Ann said, and then laughed.

"So…start it again!" Tommy yelled. "Hey, Clyde…make that fiddle sing."

Almost instantly, fiddle music filled the air, along with the carnival sounds of a concertina, and the gaiety returned. Justin swept Laurel into his arms, then lifted her up onto a makeshift dance floor that had been set up in the yard.

Laurel looked nervously at the rollicking dancers and then at Justin.

"I don't know how to dance like this," she said.

"There are no rules for this," Justin said. "Just listen to the music and follow my lead."

And they danced.

After that, the night became a series of moments caught in Laurel's mind as surely as if they'd been snapped by a camera.

A tiny bead of sweat glittering on Justin's upper lip as he swung her around in his arms.

The feel of his cotton shirt against the palms of her hands as he waltzed her off the dance floor and away from the crowd.

The urgency of his mouth against her throat.

The flash of hunger in his eyes.

The shouts of laughter and thanksgiving as four-year-old Rachelle Mouton fell asleep in her daddy's arms.

The taste of boiled crawfish and buttered corn on the cob.

The shy yet welcoming smiles from people whose names she had yet to learn.

The dappled patterns of moonlight coming through the trees and shining down on the long row of cars.

The crowded dance floor, and the mingling scents of heat and women's perfume.

Blood running down a pretty woman's face and into her open, sightless eyes.

Laurel gasped, then moaned and covered her face.

Justin grabbed her before she fell. Believing that she had been overcome by the heat and the excitement, he quickly carried her off the dance floor, then set her down in a nearby chair beneath the stars.

Cheryl Ann had seen the incident and was there almost immediately with a cold drink and a damp cloth for Laurel's face. Anxiously, she handed the cloth to Justin as he knelt at Laurel's feet.

"Did she get too hot?" she asked.

"I don't know…maybe," Justin said as he wiped the damp cloth across Laurel's brow, then took the cold drink from her sister's hand. "Here, honey, drink this."

Laurel heard him, but she couldn't pull back from where she'd gone.

"Hitting her. He's still hitting her," she mumbled. "Tell him to stop. She's already dead."

Justin rocked back on his heels as if he'd been slapped.

"Jesus," he whispered prayerfully, then looked at his sister for direction.

"Get her in the house," Cheryl Ann said. "I'll get Tommy."

"Don't make a scene," he said. "If anybody asks, just tell them she's taking a rest."

Cheryl Ann nodded and ran off in search of her husband, as Justin picked Laurel up. She leaned against him as if she were drunk, although he knew for a fact that she'd had none of the whiskey or beer that had been floating around.

"Too much party?" someone asked.

"Poor baby," another said, and patted Laurel's head as Justin carried her through the crowd to the house.

Justin kept grinning and nodding, only breathing a sigh of relief after they were inside and the door had closed behind them.

The muted sounds of the party could still be heard, but it was the steady ticking of a clock on the fireplace mantel that steadied Justin's nerves. He laid Laurel down on the couch, then hurried into the kitchen to redampen the cloth for her face. When he came back, she was sitting up and staring at the corner of the room, but he could tell by the dazed look in her eyes that while she was physically there in the room with him, her mind was somewhere else.

Moments later, Cheryl Ann rushed in with Tommy behind her.

"What happened?" Tommy asked, and started toward her. Then Justin grabbed his arm.

"Wait," he urged, then sat down on the couch beside her and took her by the hand. "Laurel…tell me what you see."

Tears welled, then spilled from her eyes and down her cheeks. Her shoulders slumped dejectedly.

"She's dead."

"Who? Who's dead?" he asked.

She shook her head. When Justin laid his hand against her cheek, she flinched as if he'd hit her. Slowly she began to rouse. He could tell she was coming back to herself. And while it had been nerve-racking to witness this part of her, he wouldn't let himself think about what it might mean to their lives. Not now. Not until they'd dealt with what she'd just seen.

Laurel felt a bit sick to her stomach and reached for the damp cloth in Justin's hands, then laid it against the heat of her face.

"What happened?" she asked. "How did I get in here?"

"I carried you," Justin said.

Laurel's eyes widened; then her cheeks flushed with embarrassment as she looked up.

"I'm so sorry," she said. "I can't imagine what you must have thought about me. I don't know—"

"Laurel...honey...that doesn't matter," Justin said. "Tell me what you saw."

Her face crumpled as she struggled not to cry.

"He kept hitting her and hitting her, even though she was already dead."

Tommy Mouton took a startled step backward, then muttered a quick prayer beneath his breath as he pulled his wife to his side.

"Who?" Justin asked. "Who is dead?"

Laurel frowned, trying to remember if she had known the woman's name, but nothing came.

"I don't know. One minute we were dancing and

laughing, and then someone jostled us. Remember? You steadied me in your arms as I fell against your chest?''

Justin nodded.

Suddenly Laurel understood. She stood abruptly.

"Take me back out there," she said. "If I see the woman from my vision, then that means what I saw is in her future. But if the woman isn't here…then the person who bumped against me is the killer."

Cheryl Ann groaned, then clasped her hands against her stomach.

"I can't believe that anyone we know could be a murderer. You have to be wrong."

Justin stood, then put his arms around Laurel's shoulders.

"She wasn't wrong about Rachelle," he said shortly. "Come with me. I'll take you back out. Don't say anything. I'll do all the talking. You just look."

Laurel nodded, then turned to Cheryl Ann.

"I wish I was wrong. It's times like this when I wish what my father thinks about me was true."

"And what does he think about you?" Cheryl Ann asked.

"That I'm crazy," Laurel said, then followed Justin out the door.

# 10

Justin helped Laurel out of the house, then into a chair on the porch. Night air shifted lazily, enough to lift the ends of her hair away from her face.

"You all right, darlin'?" an old woman asked.

Laurel nodded and smiled. "Yes, thank you. Just got a bit too hot."

The old woman smiled, revealing a three-tooth gap as she nodded with understanding.

"Dis old bayou country, she take some gettin' used to, yeah. You drink sometin' cold. Feel much better soon."

She handed Laurel a glass of something wet and cold, then winked as she walked away.

Justin bent down and whispered near her ear, "Do you see the woman from your vision anywhere here?"

Laurel glanced up and around, her gaze searching the constantly moving crowd. Then her shoulders slumped.

"No."

"It's all right," Justin said. "Just keep watching. She's got to be here."

Laurel grabbed Justin's wrist. "Not if I connected with the killer instead."

The smile in Justin's eyes went flat. "Yeah…right. Let me know if you recognize her, though."

Laurel nodded.

"Cheryl Ann is bringing out dessert. How about I go and get us some?"

"Yes, all right," Laurel said, although food was the last thing on her mind. She could still see the wide, shell-shocked look in the dead woman's eyes and the way the blood turned her fair hair a dark, coppery red.

She watched Justin walking away, absently admiring the way the fabric of his jeans cupped his backside and remembering all too well what lay beneath. But now wasn't the time to remember how Justin Bouvier made love. This was about saving a woman's life. She took a drink from her glass and once again began searching the faces of the women circling the dance floor with their partners.

Mattie Lewis loved to dance more than anything, and yet she'd married a man who did not dance. She sighed as she watched the couples dipping and swaying around the dance floor, laughing with them, clapping to the music while keeping time to the tunes with the toe of her shoe, even lifting her voice to sing along. But she didn't dance. Not even when old schoolmates offered. Not even when her brother started to take her hand. Martin wouldn't like it. And even though they were still in the honeymoon stage of their marriage, she'd already learned not to make Martin mad.

In fact, she wouldn't even have come to the party, but her brother, Aaron, had insisted. Mattie had been instrumental in furnishing hot coffee and food for the

searchers during the time that Rachelle Mouton had
been missing, and she'd been specifically named as
one of the special guests. But with Martin gone to
New Orleans, there was no way she would have gone,
until Aaron offered to escort her. She kept telling herself that it would be okay. Martin approved of her
brother. Aaron approved of Martin. Everyone was
happy about the arrangement—except, of course,
Mattie. But she'd made her bed by marrying Martin
Lewis after knowing him only six months, and as her
mother had often said, now she would have to lie in
it.

The music stopped, and as it did, Mattie saw her
friend, Lorraine, trying to get her new baby to sleep
while her older child begged to be held.

"Here, Lorraine, let me," she offered, and held out
her hands for the baby.

Lorraine Girraude smiled a weary thank-you and
gladly handed over her six-month-old daughter, along
with a bottle of milk, then picked up her three-year-
old son.

"Come here, little man. Let Mama rock you to
sleep."

"Wanna go home," the little boy whined.

Lorraine looked up at Mattie and winked, then nodded toward her husband, who was playing fiddle in
the band.

"Daddy's not ready to go home yet," Lorraine
said.

Mattie moved away from the crowded dance floor,
crooning softly to the baby as she headed for a seat
on the porch. The baby's weight against her breasts
made her ache for a child of her own. Maybe she
would have twins. She and Aaron were twins. He had

twin daughters. Maybe she would have twin sons. Boys would make Martin happy, although Mattie really didn't mind what she had, as long as they were healthy.

The baby squirmed in her arms as the last of the milk disappeared. Mattie shifted the baby from her breasts to her shoulder, intent on burping her, when she felt a hand on her arm. She turned, a smile on her face, and realized that it was the woman who'd come with Justin Bouvier.

"The baby…she is darling, isn't she?"

"Your name…what's your name?" Laurel asked.

Mattie frowned. "Mattie. I'm Mattie. You're Miz Marcella's granddaughter, Laurel, aren't you?"

Laurel nodded.

Mattie eyed the pretty woman's wide eyes and red hair, and wondered what it was like to be psychic. Curiosity won out as Mattie shifted the baby to her other shoulder.

"Can I ask you something?" she asked.

Laurel shuddered. She'd never had a conversation like this before. She knew she was standing beside this woman. And she was hearing the lilt of laughter in her voice, but she was seeing her as she would be in the future—lying still, bloody and dead. She needed to tell her, but she knew from experience that the news would not be well received.

Justin kept one eye on Laurel as he moved through the crowd, looking into women's smiling faces and wondering which one of them would be dead before morning. The knowledge that Laurel always saw the truth made him anxious. He'd grown up with some of these people, while the elders had watched him grow up. They were friends and family, even neighbors. He couldn't imagine a one of them capable of murder or becoming the victim of such a horrible crime. But if he accepted Laurel's abilities, of which he had no doubt, then time was of the essence. They needed to find the woman Laurel had seen before it was too late.

Someone laughed out loud behind him; then a woman squealed. He turned abruptly, then laughed along with everyone else at the couple in the middle of the dance floor. Jack Cowan and Bettina Townsend had been dancing; Justin had seen them only moments before. But now Jack had swung Bettina off her feet and was swinging her around as if she weighed nothing at all. Justin laughed along with the others as Bettina kept begging, between giggles, to be put down.

Out of habit, his gaze slid again to Laurel, only she wasn't where he'd left her. He took a couple of steps to the left for a better view of the house; then his heart skipped a beat. She'd gotten up from her chair and was staring blindly at the fair-haired woman beside her. Justin couldn't tell who it was, but he began to move, hurrying through the crowd without drawing undue attention to himself or to her.

Laurel was swaying on her feet when she felt a hand on her shoulder. Without looking, she knew it was Justin. She reached behind her and grabbed hold of his hand, frantically squeezing his fingers.

Justin felt her panic and knew his guess had been right. This must be the woman she'd seen in her vision.

"Laurel?"

She knew why the question was in his voice. She nodded.

Justin felt sick to his stomach. He'd grown up with Mattie and Aaron Clement. The fact that they'd been twins had made them something special to their classmates. Justin had even had a crush on Mattie when he was about twelve, though it had lasted only until his parents had bought him a new pup. After that, the small, brown-eyed puppy had captured his newfound devotion.

Mattie smiled at Justin.

"Hey, friend. Long time, no see," she teased.

He cupped the back of the baby's head she was holding and winked at her.

"Hello, Mrs. Lewis. Whatcha got here? Practicing for the real thing?"

Mattie smiled. It was still something of an oddity to realize that she was a married woman with a new name other than the one under which she'd been born.

"Sort of," she said. "Lorraine had her hands full trying to put both her babies to sleep. I offered to help." Then she gently rubbed her cheek against the baby's soft skin. "It wasn't much of a sacrifice. This little doll is too sweet for words."

Laurel stifled a moan, but Justin heard her. He could tell by the blank look in her eyes that she was seeing something they could not.

He cupped Laurel by the elbow, then put a hand on the back of Mattie's waist.

"Mattie, why don't you come inside with Laurel and me? It will be quieter there, and easier to get the baby to sleep."

"Yes, good idea," Mattie said, then glanced around, searching the crowd for sight of her brother, but didn't see him. "Oh, well, Aaron can come find me when he's ready to go."

The absence of noise and the cooler air made a welcome change from the revelry of the party outside. Mattie scooted a rocker away from the direct flow of air from the window-unit air conditioner and then sat.

Justin guided Laurel back to the couch, then sat down beside her.

Laurel shuddered. Leaning forward, she put her elbows on her knees and covered her face with her hands.

Justin wasn't sure what to do, but something had to be said. "Honey...are you feeling any better?"

She looked up, her eyes swimming in tears.

"No."

His heart dropped.

"Are you sure?" he asked softly.

She didn't have to look at Mattie again to know.

"Yes."

Mattie frowned. "I'm sorry. I didn't know she was ill. I can go back outside and—"

"No," Justin said. "It's not that, honey. She's not sick." Then he stared at Mattie, helpless to find the words to explain the horror of what Laurel had seen.

Laurel swayed where she sat, but she lifted her head and looked straight into Mattie's face.

"Out there...on the dance floor...I bumped into you."

Mattie smiled. "You must have me mixed up with someone else. I wasn't dancing."

"No...I don't mean like that," Laurel said. "I bumped into you. I think Justin almost stepped on your feet, didn't he?"

Mattie's smile widened as she cuddled the baby against her neck, patting its little back as she rocked.

"Yes, but it was okay. He always did have two left feet. I just pushed him back in the right direction."

"I felt your hand on my arm," Laurel said.

A slight frown creased Mattie's forehead as she continued to rock.

"I'm sorry. I'm not understanding what—"

"Touch is how I 'see' what I see," Laurel said.

Suddenly the rocker stopped. The smile on Mattie's face slid sideways, then disappeared. She looked at Justin for support but saw only pity—and something else, something frightening, in his gaze.

"Justin…you two are scaring me," she said.

"You're in danger," Laurel said. "Someone is going to kill you tonight."

The other woman moaned and would have dropped the baby had Justin not grabbed her out of Mattie's arms.

"What are you saying?" Mattie whispered. "Why would you tell me something this awful?"

"Because it's true," Laurel said. She took a slow breath, trying to still the pain, but it wouldn't stop. Tears that had been welling in her eyes began to spill down her face. "Whatever you were going to do tonight, don't do it."

"I'm only going home," Mattie said. "I came here with my brother, and he's taking me home afterward. And there's no one at home who would hurt me."

The moment she said it, she knew that was a lie. Only, Martin wasn't home—wouldn't be home until sometime late the next night, so she couldn't mean him.

Justin laid the baby on the love seat next to the

fireplace, then covered her with a blanket before turning back to Mattie.

"Couldn't you and your husband just spend the night with Aaron?" he asked.

"Martin isn't home," Mattie said. "He's in New Orleans on business and won't be home until sometime tomorrow."

"You could stay with Aaron."

Mattie frowned. She'd grown up knowing about Marcella Campion's powers. She'd been witness to them more than once, but she had no way of knowing if this woman was gifted in the same way. Then it hit her. This woman was the single reason Rachelle Mouton was still alive. Her eyes widened with fear.

"Are you sure?" she asked.

Laurel nodded.

Mattie's composure shattered, her voice dropping to just above a whisper.

"What do I do?"

"Stay here. Come home with me. Anything but what you were going to do," Laurel begged.

Before Mattie could answer, the door swung inward. Everyone looked up. It was Mattie's twin brother, Aaron. He was as stocky and blond as Mattie was slender and dark. They didn't even look like brother and sister, let alone twins.

"There you are," Aaron said. "I've been looking all over for you. I'm ready to go home. How about you?"

Mattie pointed to Laurel.

"Aaron, this is Miz Marcella's granddaughter. She says—"

Aaron Clement frowned. "I know who she is," he said shortly, nodding briefly at Laurel without actually speaking to her. "Come on. We need to be going. I have to get up early in the morning to take a load of watermelons to Houma."

Justin stood. He'd known Aaron all his life, and he also knew that Aaron was one of the few people in Bayou Jean who had made fun of Marcella Campion and scoffed at the powers she had claimed to possess. Convincing him of Laurel's vision would be far more difficult than it had been to convince his sister.

"Aaron, listen to me, okay? We've known each other all our lives, right?"

Aaron's frown deepened, but he nodded reluctantly.

"Yeah, so what does that have to do with anything?"

Laurel stood abruptly.

"Someone is going to kill your sister tonight. Is it you?"

Aaron staggered backward as if he'd been punched. His eyes bugged. His mouth went slack. Then he grabbed Mattie by the arm and yanked her toward the door. When she resisted and started to argue, he tightened his grip.

"We're getting out of here," he shouted.

"But, Aaron…she says she saw it. Please…I don't want to die."

Aaron rounded on Laurel like an old dog fighting to retain territory someone was trying to usurp. It was all he could do not to hit her as he pointed a finger in Laurel's face.

"You're crazy," he muttered. "That's all this is…just crazy talk! You don't say that crap about me or my sister. You hear me? You do, and I'll make you sorry."

Justin pushed Aaron's hand aside as he stepped between them.

"No. You're the one who's going to be sorry if you ever threaten her again." Then he grabbed Aaron by the shoulders and shook him, desperate to make him believe. "For God's sake, man. Even if you don't believe…what's it going to hurt to be safe rather than sorry? Take Mattie home with you. Her husband is gone. What can it hurt?"

"You heard me," Aaron said, casting a furious look toward Laurel, then propelled his sister out the door.

Justin started after them when Laurel stopped him with a touch.

"Let them go," she said. "I've been through this before. There's nothing else to be done."

Before Justin could answer, the baby on the love seat started to fuss. Laurel wiped away the tears on her face and straightened her shoulders, then picked up the child.

"Shh, little darling," she said softly, then put the baby on her shoulder, sat down in the rocker and started to rock.

But Justin wasn't ready to give up.

"Laurel, we can't just let her—"

Laurel looked at him then, and the pain in her eyes stopped him cold.

"Welcome to my world," she said, her words tinged with bitterness and defeat.

Justin didn't know what to say. The little he knew about Laurel told him that she was right, but that tiny part of him that still didn't understand how she did it wanted to believe she could be wrong—at least just this once.

"I'm sorry," he said softly.

The baby in Laurel's arms was starting to fuss.

"Go find this little girl's mama," Laurel said. "She needs to be home in her own bed."

Justin's shoulders slumped in defeat. At last he was beginning to understand the responsibilities that went with this kind of power. Seeing death before it came and not being able to stop it could make a sane person mad. How she still maintained even a semblance of normalcy was beyond him.

He bent down and kissed her cheek, then rubbed the soft hair on the top of the little baby's head.

"I'll be right back," he said gently.

"Don't worry," Laurel said. "This one is safe from my voodoo."

Justin flinched. "That's not fair," he said shortly. "I don't doubt you. Don't blame me for the ones who do."

He was gone before she could apologize, and it was just as well. If she'd had to talk again right then, she would have wound up bawling instead.

She cupped the back of the baby's head with one hand while cradling her little bottom with the other and started to sing, hoping it would soothe the fussy child until the mother could appear.

And that was how Justin found her when he returned with Lorraine—slowly rocking, with her mouth next to the baby's ear, humming a scattered little melody that had no words.

"I'm so sorry," Lorraine said as she hurried into the room. "I didn't realize Mattie had left. I don't know why she didn't bring the baby back to me."

"It was my pleasure," Laurel said, and reluctantly

handed the baby back to her mother. "By the way, what's her name?"

Lorraine smiled. "Genevieve, after my grandmother, but I think we're going to call her Ginny."

"It's a beautiful name for a beautiful little girl," Laurel said. "You're a blessed woman."

Lorraine nodded. "Yes, I am." Then it dawned on her what Laurel had just said and wondered if there had been a hidden meaning. "Am I...I mean, are my children going to..."

Laurel sighed. "I can't just see the future and tell you your life will be perfect, but I can say truthfully that I didn't see anything at all, which, in my case, usually means everything is okay."

"Oh, thank you!" Lorraine gushed, then looked at Justin and blushed. "I'm being all silly and all, aren't I, but we're just so glad that Miz Marcella's granddaughter is going to live at Mimosa Grove, just like Miz Marcella did."

"Yes, I'm glad she's there, too," Justin said, and then took Laurel by the hand, giving her fingers a slight squeeze as Lorraine breezed out of the house with her child. The moment she was gone, he turned to Laurel. She was pale and shaking.

"Take me home," she said softly.

He nodded. "Just let me tell Cheryl Ann and Tommy we're leaving."

"I couldn't see the face of the man who does it," Laurel said.

The hopelessness in her voice sent cold chills up Justin's spine.

"I'll call Harper Fonteneau, tell him what you saw. He can swing by the Lewis farm and check on her."

"Call whoever you want. Tell them whatever you

want to say. It won't change what's going to happen.''

Justin took her in his arms.

''I'm sorry, baby,'' he said softly, then rocked her where they stood. ''So, so sorry.''

''Don't be sorry for me,'' Laurel said, and then started to cry. ''Be sorry for Mattie. This was her last party.''

# 11

Justin's call to Harper Fonteneau went as far as the night dispatcher, who informed Justin that the police chief was working a wreck with injuries. Justin left his number with an urgent message to call as Laurel buckled herself into his truck.

The dispatcher tossed the message on Fonteneau's desk and went to pour himself another cup of coffee, while Mattie Lewis cried all the way home, despite her brother's assurances that she was going to be fine. In a culture where voodoo and people who claimed to see spirits were everyday business, some were still skeptics, and her brother was one.

Justin knew Aaron Clement well enough to know that he wasn't going to give any credence to Laurel's vision. And although Laurel was sitting quietly in the passenger seat of his truck, he knew she was anything but serene. Her fingers were curled into fists in her lap, and her eyes still glistened from some unshed tears. The few times he'd spoken to her, she had been unable to answer with anything other than a shake or a nod of her head. He didn't know how to deal with her like this, but he knew who would.

Marie LeFleur.

And in his urgency to get Laurel home to Mimosa Grove, he found himself driving on the high side of the speed limit, taking curves in the road close to the inside and wide at the corners. The desperation in Laurel's eyes was catching. He felt her anxiety and, at the same time, her defeat. It occurred to him then why, upon her arrival, Mimosa Grove must have seemed like the answer to a prayer. She'd thought she was coming to a place where nobody knew her or expected anything from her except being the new woman in town. How shocked, then disappointed, she must have been to find out that Marcella Campion had been Bayou Jean's Taj Mahal—their eighth wonder of the world, so to speak.

Lose a pig. Call Marcella.

Lose a child. Call Marcella.

Suspect a spouse was cheating. Call Marcella.

And Laurel had walked into all that completely unaware.

As sympathetic as he was to her predicament, he couldn't regret that she'd come, because if she hadn't, his niece would most likely be dead. And selfishly, he was most grateful that his dream woman had become a reality. But at what cost? Her happiness for his own?

Laurel was paying a high price for his peace of mind. But, though their relationship was new, never seeing her again would be a tragedy he didn't want to face.

He was still lost in thought when, from the corner of his eye, he caught a glimpse of something moving in the darkness to his left. His foot was already on the brake when a deer bounded out of the woods and then froze in the headlights of his truck.

"Hang on," he yelled at Laurel, then swerved to keep from hitting the doe.

The truck slid sideways on the road, breaking the headlights' mesmerizing glare. The deer disappeared as quickly as it had come, leaving Justin and Laurel shaking where they sat. He slammed the truck into Park and then reached for Laurel's arm.

"Are you all right?"

"I think so." She combed her fingers through her disheveled hair, moving it away from her face, then leaned against the back of the seat and closed her eyes. "That was close."

Justin scooted toward her, then pulled her into his arms.

"I'm so sorry," he said softly. "That was my fault. I was driving too fast."

Laurel shook her head. "It was no one's fault. It just happened." Then she looked into his eyes, unaware that the lights from the dashboard mirrored her sadness. "You would never have hit the deer."

"I almost did," Justin said. "I wasn't paying close enough attention."

"But you didn't. You didn't, because it wasn't meant to be. You can't change your own fate, you know."

Justin frowned. He knew she wasn't talking about the deer. She was thinking of Mattie Lewis.

"Do you really believe that?"

"Yes."

"Even though you saw what's going to happen to Mattie? Even though you warned her and she believed what you'd said?"

"Yes."

"Why?"

"Because she's also surrounded by people and things that play a part in her fate. She can believe anything she hears, but unless she acts on it, it's as if it was never said. Because of the way she was raised, she will not question a man's decision.''

''That would make me crazy,'' he muttered.

''Yes, sometimes that happens, too.''

His eyes widened as he remembered the gossip he'd heard about Marcella's daughter, Phoebe, and where she'd ended up before she'd died. He felt sick that he'd spoken so casually about something that had been a tragedy in her family.

''Oh, honey...I'm sorry. I forgot about your mother. I didn't mean—''

Laurel put a finger on Justin's lips, then shook her head.

''It's okay. Just take me home, will you?''

He took his foot off the brake, shifted into Drive and accelerated slowly.

Laurel scooted away from the door and closer to Justin. As the truck began to gain a little speed, she laid her head on his shoulder and started to cry.

''I'm sorry,'' she whispered. ''I can't help it.''

''It's all right, sweetheart, and I'm the one who's sorry. If I hadn't insisted on taking you to Tommy and Cheryl Ann's party, this wouldn't have happened.''

''Yes, it would,'' she said. ''I learned a long time ago that I have only two choices about how I live my life.''

''Like what?'' Justin asked.

''I can hide away from the world, never coming in contact with anyone or anything that could bring on my visions, or I can live like a normal person and deal with what that means. And for me, I'd rather deal than hide. It's that simple.''

Justin squeezed her fingers, then took his eyes from the road only long enough to give her a swift kiss on the forehead.

"And the world benefits from your bravery at your expense."

"Sometimes I can make a difference."

"Like with Rachelle."

"Yes…like Rachelle."

Justin frowned as he drove, staring through the windshield into the darkness and taking comfort from the limited illumination of the headlights, realizing that was the way everyone except Laurel lived their lives. They reacted and acted only upon what they saw, never having to deal with, or accept, the fact that there was more to the world than what they could see. But Laurel's world was, at times, a 360-degree sphere of pure light, where nothing was sacred or secret, and where only she had to cope with the consequences. His heart hurt for her, thinking of how isolated and lonely she had to feel, especially when others doubted her vision.

A short while later, he pulled off the road and started down the long driveway leading to the mansion. The front of the old house was brightly lit. He pointed and smiled.

"Looks like Marie left the lights on for you."

Laurel's anxiety began to ease.

"It's a comforting sight," she said, and then sighed.

Justin glanced at her, then back to the road, slowing down to allow a small opossum to pass before accelerating again.

"So you aren't going to pack up and leave?"

Laurel looked at him and then frowned.

"Of course not. Why would you think something like that?"

His chin jutted slightly, as if bracing himself for an answer he might not want to hear.

"I don't know…maybe because you've had nothing but trouble since you got here?"

Laurel laid a hand on his thigh. His muscles were as tense as the tone of his voice.

"That's not entirely true," she said softly. "*You're* here."

He braked near the front steps, then killed the engine before taking her in his arms.

"*Chère,* you take my breath away."

Suddenly the air inside the truck felt too thick to breathe. Laurel ached for him—wanted him, to be with him—needing the passionate cleansing of a physical release to assuage the sadness within her.

"I want to make love to you," she whispered.

"No more than I want you," he murmured, then cupped her face with his hands. "Let me come in?"

She hesitated, glancing toward the house and thinking of Marie and what she might say, then shrugged off the thought. She was a grown woman. It shouldn't matter what anyone thought.

"Yes."

Justin opened the door and got out, then took Laurel by the hand. She slid across the seat, then held his hand all the way up the steps.

The front door was unlocked. She opened it and walked in, half expecting Marie to be standing in the hallway with a judgmental expression on her face. To her relief, there was no one there. Justin locked the door behind them, then turned off the lights. For a moment they were left in utter darkness; then, slowly, their eyes adjusted, and they took to the stairs.

Halfway up, Laurel heard a door open downstairs; then Marie called out, "Laurel, honey, do you need anything?"

Laurel glanced at Justin, then smiled.

"No, Mamárie, we're fine. We're going to bed. See you in the morning."

There was a distinct moment of silence, then a soft chuckle.

"I'll make extra biscuits."

"Sounds good," Laurel said. "Sleep tight."

"Mmm-hmm. I probably be the only one sleep-in'," they heard Marie mutter.

She shut her door with just enough force to shatter the quiet within the old house, and then there was silence.

Justin heard Laurel sigh.

"It's all right, baby," he said softly.

Laurel turned to face him on the stairs, then put her arms around his neck.

"Oh, Justin…sometimes you almost make me believe that's true."

The despair in her voice was his undoing. Unwilling to wait any longer, he picked her up and carried her the rest of the way up the stairs.

"Which door?" he asked as they reached the first landing.

She pointed to the one that was slightly ajar.

He strode toward it, still carrying her in his arms as if she weighed nothing at all, then pushed the door inward.

He passed through the small sitting room into the bedroom. On the other side of the room, the parted curtains let in just enough moonlight to bathe the interior in a pale eerie glow. The covers on the old four-poster bed were turned back. Her robe and nightgown had been draped across the back of an old velvet settee beneath the window, while her slippers sat side by side near the foot, awaiting her pleasure. Marie had left a night-light burning in the adjoining bathroom, as well as a small lamp on a table beside the door. It was a scene straight out of the past, only Laurel and Justin were very definitely real.

Justin kissed the side of Laurel's cheek, laid her down on the bed, then crawled onto the mattress beside her. As he began to undress, he took his cell phone from his pocket. They both looked at the phone, then at each other.

"I'll leave it on in case Harper calls," he said.

Laurel shut her mind against what she already knew. No one was going to call, and Mattie Lewis was going to die. It was enough to drive her mad. Instead, she wrapped her arms around Justin's neck and pulled him down.

"Help me," she whispered. "I don't want to think about anything but the way you make me feel."

Justin thrust his fingers through her hair, raking them close to her scalp as he swallowed her sigh with a kiss.

"Ah, baby, this is heaven," he said softly, then began to take off her clothes.

When she was completely naked, he looked down upon her, marveling at the beauty before him.

"What is it?" Laurel asked.

He shook his head, almost smiling as he trailed a finger across the curve of her breast.

"We've been this way so many times before, but the real you is so much better than the dream."

Laurel shifted beneath his gaze, wanting to feel the weight of him, aching for the moment when he filled the emptiness inside her, then reached for him.

"Take off your clothes."

He heard the hunger in her voice and answered with a soft groan as he yanked his shirt over his head, then stepped out of his boots. By the time he came out of his jeans, Laurel was on her knees, helping him disrobe.

Her hands were shaking, her breath coming in short, urgent gasps. The need in her belly was coiling tighter and tighter. The ache between her legs was turning into real pain. She wanted him now, hard and fast.

Justin saw the urgency in her eyes, felt the thunder of her heart beneath his hands, and kicked out of the last of his clothes. Within seconds, he was on the bed, with her beneath him.

"Now, Justin...please," Laurel begged, and opened her legs for him to come in.

He took her without hesitation, piercing her warmth and then swallowing back a groan. So hot. So tight. So unbelievably good.

Laurel wrapped her legs around his waist and arched up to meet the first thrust. Soon she was coming undone.

"Oh...oh...oh, Justin...oh, God."

He hadn't known she was this far gone, but the tight, sweet pull of her body and the urgency in her voice were as potent an aphrodisiac as any drug could have been. He began to move, even as he felt the tremors of her first climax and laughed aloud from sheer joy.

"Ah, *chère,* he said softly. "The *petite morte* is so beautiful on you."

Laurel's mind was still floating, trying to catch up with what he'd done to her body, so it took her a few moments to catch on to what he'd said. When it connected, she had to ask, "*Petite morte?* What is the *petite morte?*"

Still inside her and throbbing with unspent passion, he raised himself up on his elbows, then thumbed the curve of her lower lip. It was damp and swollen. He traced the shape with the tip of his tongue, tasting her, knowing that, with her, his life could be complete.

"The little death? My darling Laurel, we have so much to share."

"So tell me," she pleaded.

He traced the shape of her nose from the bridge to the tip, then gently bit her bottom lip. When she groaned, he stopped.

"So…there are those who adhere to the theory that we are as close to death at the moment of climax as we will ever be without actually dying. For one fleeting moment, when we are undone by ecstasy, our heart pauses, as does our breath, thus the little death."

Laurel put her arms around Justin's neck.

"A little death seems a small price to pay for making love with you."

Justin nuzzled the curve beneath her chin. "Are you willing to die again…for me?"

"Oh, yes, love. Please."

Justin took her in his arms and began to kiss her

all over, as if memorizing her shape and face with nothing but his mouth and his tongue.

Laurel dug her fingers in his hair, riding the sensual high until she lost track of where she began and Justin ended. Outside, a storm began announcing its arrival with a grumble of distant thunder. Lightning spiked on the horizon, shattering the atmosphere with a surge of power that mirrored their passion. Somewhere between the thunder and the rain, Justin rose up on his elbows and resumed their dance of love.

And time passed.

Stroke after stroke, he drove himself near the edge of a climax, only to pull back at the last moment because he wanted it to be with her. Measuring his rhythm with the sound of her breathing and the urgency of her caress, he managed to control his need.

And it was working until she gasped. Only once, and so softly he almost didn't hear it. Seconds later, he felt her fingers digging into his arms, and then she moaned. The sounds were a trigger that loosened his control. She was coming undone beneath him as he came hard and fast in her.

Rain splattered against the windows, riding the gust front from the swiftly approaching storm. Wind tore through the mimosa grove with sudden fury, stripping fragile pink-and-white blooms from the huge trees and then scattering them about like confetti from heaven. Inside the old mansion, the lovers lay sleeping in each other's arms, weary, but replete from their lovemaking. On a night such as this, only the restless spirits moved about.

Laurel slept, held fast within the safety of Justin's arms. But though his presence was comforting, it was not enough to stop the dreams.

\* \* \*

Laurel was motionless, her head pillowed on Justin's shoulder as she slept. Somewhere in her subconscious, she knew they were being watched, and the knowledge gave her a faux feeling of power. No matter what visions might come, she would not face them alone.

Time passed with the storm, leaving the grounds of Mimosa Grove scattered with limbs, leaves and blossoms torn from the trees by the violence of the wind and rain.

*"Help me."*

Laurel moved restlessly as the whisper crept into her dream. The image of Mattie Lewis's face jumped before her mind's eye, the same as it had been during her vision at the party—wide-eyed and sightless, with blood streaming down the side of her face. Laurel watched in slumberous horror as the first shovelful of dirt fell down on her face and into her slightly parted mouth.

*"Help me."*

Tears pooled beneath Laurel's eyelids. It wasn't the first time she'd cried in her sleep. It would not be the last.

She wanted to help. God knows she'd tried to help, but no one had listened. Why did they always ask her for help when it was too late?

Still sleeping, she rolled over onto her side and curled up in a ball, pulling herself as far away from life as she could get, but it was still not far enough away to deafen her to the plea.

*"Please...somebody help me."*

A frown creased Laurel's forehead. Why did Mattie Lewis's spirit cry out for help now? There was nothing Laurel could do. Even now, the second and third shovelsful of dirt were being tossed down into the hole. Dirt was in Mattie's hair and completely covering one eye. As Laurel watched in dreamlike horror, the dirt continued to fall until she could no longer see Mattie's face. Still the voice persisted, begging for help. Laurel shuddered in her sleep, unaware that Justin had awakened and had become an unwitting witness to what was happening to her.

Laurel felt herself staring down into a disappearing hole. Shovel by shovel, dirt was returned to its proper place, covering the awful deed that had been done. Desperate to see who was burying Mattie Lewis, she tried to turn around, but her mind wouldn't let it happen. All she could see were the hands on the shovel, a Mickey Mouse watch on a man's left wrist and the toe of one large boot. She stared down into the hole again, watching as the killer tossed the last shovelful of dirt into the gap, then began patting down the mound he'd made, using the back of the shovel. As he was finishing, the first drops of rain began to fall. Laurel could hear them hitting the surface of a metal roof that was just behind her. She could smell wet feathers and newly turned earth, and then the thunderstorm hit. She saw the back of the man's head as he turned and ran for shelter, then nothing. She looked down, watching as the rain began to make tiny tunnels in the newly packed earth. Once more Mattie Lewis's face appeared, and then, to Laurel's horror, it began to morph into someone else. When the first shaft of lightning struck near the makeshift grave, the ghost of Chantelle LeDeux was reaching out to Laurel.

*"Help me,"* she begged.

Laurel woke with a start, then sat straight up in

bed. Shoving her shaky hands through her hair, she glanced toward the window. Raindrops were still visible on the glass, although the storm had finally passed.

"Dear God," she whispered prayerfully, and covered her face with her hands.

Now she didn't know what to think. It had made a sort of sense to her that Mattie Lewis's spirit might have been begging for help, but she didn't know what to make of Chantelle LeDeux's unexpected appearance. All she knew of Chantelle's history was that she'd run away from Mimosa Grove, leaving her husband and three children behind. Why was her spirit still earthbound—and here at Mimosa Grove, when it was the very place from which she'd fled?

She glanced over at Justin, then gasped. He was lying quietly beside her, watching her every move.

"I didn't know you were awake. How long have you been…?"

"Watching you?" he asked, finishing what she'd been about to say.

She nodded.

"Long enough to know that you were dreaming. You were, weren't you?"

She nodded.

"Want to talk about it?"

"Mattie."

He reached for her, pulling her close to him and then holding her tight.

"I'm so sorry, *chère*. I wish there was something I could do."

She looked away. "Yes, so do I."

He rubbed his chin near the crown of her hair, nuzzling the tangles and smelling the faint scent of her shampoo.

"Want me to call Harper Fonteneau again?"

"It doesn't matter," she said softly. "He'll know soon enough."

Justin tensed. "You mean she's, uh…"

"Already dead? Yes."

Justin's belly knotted. It seemed impossible to believe that the sweet, smiling woman of last night was no longer of this earth.

"You're sure?" he asked softly.

"I watched him bury her. I smelled wet feathers and the scent of rotting earth. He wears a Mickey Mouse watch and has a spot of white paint on the toe of his right boot."

"Jesus," Justin whispered, and then said a quick prayer, as if warding off the evil of what she'd just said.

He turned her in his arms, making her look him in the eyes.

"Talk to me, Laurel. I don't know what to do for you…how to care for you. Tell me how to help you deal with the hell that you see."

She wrapped her arms around him and then started to cry.

"Just the fact that you believe is all the help I need. I can't help Mattie. She's beyond that. All we can do for her is wait. Everything else will come in its own time."

Justin's eyes welled, then spilled over as he cried along with her, grieving for Laurel's burden and the loss of his friend.

"Just hold me," Laurel begged.

Justin wrapped his arms around her and then laid

them both down as they wept for the life that was wasted.

Just before she fell back to sleep, Laurel remembered Chantelle's plea. It was too late to help Mattie Lewis, but maybe if she could find out what it was that unsettled Chantelle's wandering soul, she could help her put her spirit to rest.

# 12

What might have been an awkward meal became, instead, a moment of bonding. Justin came down to the kitchen ahead of Laurel, following the scent of fresh brewing coffee and the sound of pans being banged about. Aware that he was going to be judged and probably found lacking, he decided to confront Marie with the news about Laurel's latest vision before she could begin. She was bent over the oven door, trying to take out a pan of biscuits by using the tail of her apron for a pot holder.

He reached above her, took a pair of pot holders from a nail beside the stove and slipped in front of her.

"Good morning, Marie. Something sure smells good," he said, and slipped the pan from the oven. "Where do you want this?"

She frowned and pointed to a cooling rack.

"That'll do just fine."

"Got it," he said, and slid the pan onto the rack, but not before he nabbed a piping-hot biscuit for himself. "Lord, this is good."

Marie tried not to preen, but she did take some pride in her cooking, and feeding a man who appreciated good food was always a pleasure.

"Well, you better have some sweet butter and preserves on that thing before it goes and gets cold."

Justin certainly wouldn't argue with such logic and moved toward the breakfast table.

"Sleep well?" Marie asked.

Justin slathered some butter on the biscuit, then took a big bite before answering.

"Um, sort of," he said, and then laid the rest of his biscuit on a plate on the table. "After what happened at the party last night, I don't think either one of us got much sleep. It was part of the reason I stayed with her." Then he grinned and shrugged. "Only part. The rest was selfish. I love your girl, Marie, and she loves me."

"Sure didn't take you two long to fall in love," Marie muttered.

"We've been seeing each other for months," he said.

Her eyes widened. Her lips went slack. Then she frowned.

"No, you haven't. She didn't know anyone down here before she came."

"She knew me...and I knew her."

"What you talkin' about?" Marie asked.

"The dreams... I've been dreaming of her...loving her...knowing her...for months. Every night. All night. And she was dreaming of me just the same. We didn't know it until after Rachelle was found, and trust me, no one was more stunned than I was to realize that my dream girl was a living, breathing woman."

"Sweet Lord," Marie said, and fingered the cross she wore on a chain around her neck. "You tellin' me true? You was knowin' each other...in your sleep?"

"Yes."

"Oh. Oh, my." Then she frowned. "What were you saying about trouble at the party?"

"Laurel had a vision."

"A bad one?"

"As bad as it gets."

"Tell me," Marie said.

"She saw Mattie Lewis die."

"Oh, Lord, oh, Lord," Marie moaned, then swayed where she stood. "Little Mattie... I remember when she and Aaron were born. Was Mattie there? Did she warn her?"

"Yes, but it did no good. Aaron got mad. Wouldn't believe Laurel. Even when Mattie was afraid to go home, Aaron took her just the same."

Marie grabbed his arm. "Maybe it's not too late. Maybe you could call Harper Fonteneau.... He could go—"

"Already did that. He wasn't in the office, and he never called back. Besides, Laurel said it was already too late."

Marie sat down in a kitchen chair, then pulled her apron over her face.

"This is bad," she wailed. "Poor Mattie...and poor Laurel. She gonna leave, I just know it. If this don't quit happenin', she gonna leave me."

"No, she won't," Justin said. "You underestimate Marcella's granddaughter. She's tougher than that."

"I pray that you're right," Marie said, and then suddenly froze and tilted her head, as if listening. "She's comin' down the stairs."

"So how about wiping your face and cooking me some eggs?"

"Yes, yes. It's time to start the eggs. How you like 'em?" she asked.

"How about over easy?"

Marie nodded as she stood. She started toward the stove, then paused. Justin looked up and caught her staring at him.

"What?"

She hesitated for a moment, then shook her head.

"Nothin'."

"Say what you think, Mamárie."

Her chin jutted slightly as she frowned.

"I was thinkin' that it's been a long time since a man's voice echoed within these walls."

"And?"

"And it's just a good sound, okay?"

It wasn't until she smiled and winked that he realized he'd been braced for a rejection. He relaxed and nodded.

"Yeah, it's okay."

"What's okay?" Laurel asked as she walked into the kitchen.

Justin pointed to the partially eaten biscuit on his plate, then picked it up and offered Laurel a bite.

"These biscuits," he said. "Only they're not just okay. They're fantastic."

"Baby girl, you wantin' one egg or two?" Marie asked as she stood at the stove.

Laurel walked to the stove and took the egg out of Marie's hand.

"Mamárie...I need a hug," she said softly.

Marie's eyes watered, but she blinked back tears.

"Well, sure you do," she said gently, and wrapped her tiny arms around Laurel's waist.

It didn't matter that Laurel was a head taller. Laurel was all she had left of Marcella, and that made her precious.

"Tula is gonna come over with her nieces again and help me tackle the top floor. Anything special you want done to the rooms?"

Laurel frowned, remembering that she had yet to do much exploring up there.

"I don't suppose so," she said. "Just clean them."

Marie nodded, then pointed toward the table.

"Go sit yourself down. Everything is done but your eggs, and they won't take long."

"I'll pour us some coffee," Laurel said, and got down three mugs.

Together, the two women—one very old and one young, but very sick at heart—finished the meal and put it on the table while Justin watched. It occurred to him, as he sat, that they drew strength from each other's presence. As long as Laurel remained at Mimosa Grove, Marie would be needed, and he knew from experience that feeling needed was what kept people young. And while, most of her life, all Laurel's physical needs had been met, she had been emotionally isolated until now. Her Mamárie and Mimosa Grove were her touchstones, and hopefully, Justin thought, there would be a permanent place for him in her life, as well.

"Okay...eat up," Marie said as she served up the last of the eggs.

Laurel carried the plates to the table, while Marie followed with the hot biscuits and a pot of fresh coffee.

Justin jumped up quickly and seated Laurel first, then Marie, who was right behind her.

Laurel smiled, accepting the gesture without thought, but Marie's life had been sadly missing in such considerations.

"Well now, I suppose a body could get used to such…if a body wanted to admit a man might have his place around a house."

Justin grinned, then, to add to Marie's confusion, he leaned down and kissed her quickly on the cheek.

"Here now! What you doin' all that for?" she asked.

With a straight face, Justin snagged another biscuit from the plate before taking his own seat.

"Damn good biscuits," he remarked.

The pleasure on Marie's face was obvious as Laurel picked up her fork. At that moment, she'd never loved Justin more, and the moment she thought it, she almost dropped the fork she'd picked up.

Love? Did she love Justin Bouvier? God knew she loved making love with him, and she did trust him in a way she'd never trusted another man before. Not even her father had gained such a place in her heart. She was thinking that she'd been so overwhelmed by everything that had been occurring that she'd taken his presence and their lovemaking for granted.

He laughed aloud at something Marie said, and Laurel watched the way his eyes crinkled at the corners, the way his head tilted just the least bit to the right as he sat listening. As her gaze slid to his hands, she remembered their gentleness and their strength as they'd made love. Now he held a biscuit in one hand and a butter knife in the other with the same sense of purpose. What he desired, he went after.

Laurel sighed, then let a small bit of the weight of her world slide sideways—toward Justin, whose shoulders were far broader and stronger than hers. He'd offered. She would be a fool to deny his strength—or his love, should he offer that, as well.

"Laurel, honey…can I pass you anything?"

She blinked. Justin was looking at her, smiling tenderly.

"Oh, uh, yes. The strawberry preserves, please."

"Your wish is my command," he said, and passed the small crystal compote of ruby-red preserves with an overdone flourish.

Marie snorted beneath her breath and then grinned.

"You better watch out there," she said. "You're talking so pretty that you're liable to sprout wings and take flight."

Both Laurel and Justin laughed aloud at the mental image, and the meal progressed.

They were finishing up with last cups of coffee when a knock sounded at the front door, echoing through the hallway and into the kitchen.

Laurel had started to get up, when Marie waved her back down.

"Probably Tula and the girls come to clean," she said. "You keep your seat. I'll get it."

Laurel nodded, then reached across the table to gather up the last of the dirty dishes as Marie exited the room. Laurel had barely gotten them into the sink before Marie was back, and with a look on her face that didn't bode well for the day.

"It wasn't Tula," Marie said. "It's Aaron Clement."

Justin saw the expression on Laurel's face and stood up. "I'll talk to him," he offered.

Marie shook her head. "No. He says he wants to talk to Laurel." Her voice was shaking as she added, "He says to tell you he says, 'please.'"

Laurel clutched her fists against her belly, then lifted her chin and nodded.

"Yes. All right."

Justin met her at the doorway and then took her by the hand.

"I'm still coming with you."

She nodded again.

Aaron Clement wasn't a man used to asking for favors, but he was scared. When he saw Marcella Campion's granddaughter appear in the foyer, all the breath slid out of his lungs in one swoop. He was still struggling to draw air when she reached him.

Laurel didn't know it, but she was holding herself stiffly, as if braced for another verbal attack similar to what she'd experienced the night before.

"Mr. Clement?"

Aaron stuttered, then briefly closed his eyes, gathering himself and his thoughts. When he looked again, she was still waiting.

"Miss Scanlon, I—"

Laurel stepped aside, then gestured toward the living room to their right.

"Laurel, please. And maybe we'd all be more comfortable in here."

She led the way without looking to see if anyone followed.

Justin might have glared a warning at Aaron until he saw his expression. Instead, he motioned for Aaron to proceed, then followed them both into the living room.

Laurel was already seated in a chair near the window. Unwittingly, she'd chosen the one place that put her in a small halo of light from the rays of the early morning sun. Given her reputation, appearing as an angel only added to Aaron's fears.

"Please sit down," she said, and smoothed her hands down the front of her shirt, thankful that she was wearing lightweight capri pants, rather than her normal attire, which would have been shorts. It was hard to maintain dignity with her long legs all bare.

Aaron sat with a thump, then stared down at the floor, unable to face the woman with his request.

Laurel sensed his distress, and while her first instinct was to protect herself, she caught herself leaning forward with the intent to help.

"Mr. Clement...Aaron...may I offer you some coffee?"

It was the ordinary gesture of refreshment that undid him. One minute he was shivering in his boots, the next he was struggling not to cry.

"No, ma'am, but thank you just the same," he said, then cleared his throat with a cough, unwilling to show how close he was to tears.

Justin took a stand beside Laurel's chair, making it plain to Aaron just where his loyalties lay.

Aaron didn't miss the significance, or the warning look on Justin's face, and because of the way he'd behaved last night, he knew the first thing out of his mouth had to be an apology.

"Miss Scanlon...Laurel...I need to apologize for my behavior last night."

Laurel's heart ached for the man and for the loss he was about to suffer. She swallowed to keep from weeping.

"You didn't need to come all this way to tell me you're sorry."

Aaron's fingers curled around his knees, and he absently watched them turning white at the knuckles as he stared down at the toes of his shoes and struggled to find a way to continue.

"I didn't come just to tell you that," he said, then forced himself to look up. "Mattie is missing."

Laurel's eyelids fluttered slightly. It was the only sign of her emotional state.

"And you know this because...?"

Aaron shifted uncomfortably, then abruptly stood.

"I let her off at her house last night, then went home. She was fine." Then he added, a little defensively, "And I went over this morning...but not because I believed what you'd said last night. It's just that she's my sister and I was checking up on her while her husband, Martin, is away. Only she wasn't in the house, and some furniture was overturned...and her bed wasn't slept in and—" He choked on the rest of what he'd been going to say and began to beg. "Will you help me find her? I thought maybe she'd gone out to check on the livestock and turned her ankle, or fallen into a ravine. It rained a lot last night, so I couldn't find her tracks, but—"

"I'm so sorry," Laurel said.

Aaron moaned. "What do you mean?"

Justin moved to his friend's side and put his hand on Aaron's shoulder.

"She told you last night. She warned you what was going to happen."

Tears were rolling down Aaron's face faster than he could wipe them away. Laurel could see where he'd run his fingers through his hair earlier in frantic confusion. His eyes were wide, and so filled with terror she could hardly breathe. If only...

She made herself stand, even though her legs threatened to give way.

"She's already passed."

Aaron fell to his knees. Laurel touched the top of his head, then staggered from the grief. Justin caught her before she fell.

"Laurel...let me—"

She shook her head. "Justin, would you please tell Marie to call Harper Fonteneau? Have him meet us at the Lewis place. We're going to be needing his services."

"I already called him," Aaron said. "He'll probably get there about the same time we do. That is, if you'll come with me?"

"I'll come."

Aaron swiped his big hands across his face, trying to regain his composure by removing the traces of his emotion.

"I thank you," he muttered, then pulled a small bit of fabric from his back pocket. "It's the handkerchief that Mattie had in her pocket last night. It was on the kitchen table. I thought you might—"

Laurel stepped back, unwilling to touch it just yet.

"Just hold it until we get to the property," she said.

"You don't need it to...uh, well, 'see' where she is?"

"I already saw it," Laurel said.

The veins in Aaron's neck were bulging. His face was flushing with anger and with rage.

"But maybe you can 'see' who did it. I swear to God, when he's found, I'm going to kill him with my bare hands," he said.

"Just wait," Laurel said, then looked to Justin. "Will you take me there?"

"Absolutely," he said softly, and put an arm around her shoulders. "There's no way you're getting out of here alone. Wait here. I'll tell Marie where we're going."

Laurel nodded. It was of some comfort to Laurel to know that Justin would be with her, but not enough to protect her from being swamped with regret.

Aaron Clement couldn't look her in the face.

"I'm so, so, sorry," she said.

"Not half as sorry as I am," he said shortly. "Tell Justin I'm heading over there now. He knows where she lives."

Laurel nodded.

Aaron was at the door when he suddenly stopped, then turned.

"You sure about this?"

"He buried her behind a place that smells like wet feathers."

Aaron staggered as if he'd been sucker-punched, then stumbled blindly out the door to his car as Justin came back.

"Where's he going?" he asked.

Laurel's voice was still shaking. "To his sister's house. After that...probably mad."

Spanish moss hung from the live oaks circling the single-story, tin-roofed house where Martin and Mattie Lewis lived. Two old tin buckets had been recycled into planters for the front porch and were overflowing with pink and purple petunias. An unused birdcage had been utilized for the same purpose and was hanging from the north end of the porch with a pot of bougainvillea inside. The trailing vines spilled randomly through the wires of the cage to sway lightly in the breeze. A hummingbird wind chime was on the south end of the porch. It marked the intermittent swells of incoming and outgoing air with clear, bell-like chimes. It was a gentle, welcoming sight for the arrival of guests.

As Justin and Laurel turned the corner in the driveway and got their first view of the place, Justin frowned, then groaned.

"Oh, no," he said. "Looks like Mattie's husband is just coming home. See, he hasn't even carried his suitcases into the house? How do you tell a man that his wife has been murdered?"

Laurel didn't answer. She was too busy watching the distant confrontation of brother and husband.

Moments later, they arrived. Justin parked next to Aaron's car and helped Laurel out of his truck. As they started toward the porch where Aaron and Martin were standing, Harper Fonteneau arrived and parked his patrol car behind Martin's white van.

Justin glanced at Laurel.

"Are you all right?"

Blinking slowly, she looked at him, then away without answering. The air felt too thick to breathe, and her limbs felt heavy—as if she were trying to walk under water.

Justin frowned.

"Laurel...honey?"

Laurel moved toward Aaron and Martin, unable to take her gaze away from both men.

Martin Lewis was a tall man—a head and a half taller than Aaron, and was dark where Aaron was fair. His skin was a warm, golden brown, toasted so by the sun. His hair was black and shiny, and at least two inches past a clean haircut, brushing the top of his collar as he stood. His shoulders were broad, his body long and lean. It was easy to see why Mattie Lewis had been attracted. Even his speech was mesmerizing—a thick Cajun cadence that drew the listener's attention to his wide, expressive mouth, as well as to what he was saying.

When he saw Justin, his eyes glittered with recognition, but he frowned when he realized Justin was not alone. And when Harper Fonteneau arrived, he became extremely agitated.

"What's happenin' here?" he asked, and then he looked toward his house, frowning. "Where my Mattie Faye? Why she not here?"

Aaron was struggling with words that wouldn't come. It was Harper who broke the news and the tension.

"I got a call that your wife was missing," he said. "What do you know about it?"

The shock on Martin Lewis's face was immediate. He looked at Aaron, then bolted toward the house, yelling Mattie's name.

Laurel flinched, but she didn't move.

Justin started toward the house with Aaron and Harper, but when Laurel didn't follow, he stopped.

"Laurel?"

"Wait," she said, and dug her fingers in his forearm as she struggled to stay focused.

He feared from the way she was behaving that the day that had gone so wrong was about to get worse.

"I'm here," he said quietly, then stood beside her without speaking.

They could hear shouts of dismay from inside the house, then Harper quickly ushering everyone out.

"This might turn out to be a crime scene," he argued, when Martin tried to push his way back in. "If it is, you can't go disturbing the evidence."

"She can't be gone," Martin said, looking wildly toward the pastures. "Maybe she fell out there. That's it! She's lying out there somewhere waiting for me to find her." He turned abruptly and started running toward the fence surrounding the yard, shouting Mattie's name.

"Go get him," Harper said.

Aaron and Justin took off after him and soon brought him back.

"This can't be happening," Martin said, then dropped weakly to the steps and covered his face with his hands.

Laurel's gaze was wide and fixed; then suddenly she focused on the men at the steps and moaned.

All four of them turned. Martin was the one who frowned.

"Who dat woman? Who she is?"

Harper Fonteneau was the one who dropped the bomb.

"That's Miz Marcella's granddaughter. Her name is Laurel Scanlon."

Martin's face turned from pale to a dark flush of crimson.

"De hell you say!" he said, and jumped to his feet. His expression changed from one of despair to that of the hunted. "Woman...stay away! Don't hold with no voodoo, me."

Laurel's legs were getting weaker as the evil that

had come to this place continued to grow, but she had to finish what had been started.

"The watch. He's wearing the watch," she said.

Harper frowned. "What you talkin' about, girl? We all got on watches."

Laurel didn't answer. Instead, she moved forward, intent on touching Martin Lewis. He saw her coming and jumped up, but Justin knew what she meant to do and grabbed him.

"No! No! Don't bring dat evil to me!"

"I'm thinking you're the evil," Justin said.

Harper frowned. "What's going on?" he said.

"Tell him, Laurel. Tell him what you saw."

"A man with a Mickey Mouse watch killed Mattie. There was a spot of white paint on the toe of his boot—like the one on *his* boot." Then she pointed toward a small building between the house and the barn. "I smelled wet feathers...then it started to rain."

Aaron's eyes widened in disbelief at the paint spot and the watch.

"Martin? Tell me this isn't true."

Martin Lewis twisted out of Justin's grasp.

"I did nothin' to my Mattie. Whatever happened to her, I was not here."

Laurel grabbed him by the arm, then fell backward as if she'd been struck. Justin spun, catching her before she hit the ground.

Laurel was turned toward Martin, but seemed to be looking through him, rather than at him.

"You were here last night. You saw her get out of a car. You waited in the dark until she came into the kitchen. You accused her of having an affair. You wanted to know where she'd been and who she'd been with. She tried to tell you, but you wouldn't listen. You hit her. She fell against the cookstove. She didn't get up.''

Martin started to shake like a man in a fit. His eyes rolled back in his head; then he started to scream.

"I live with no woman who sleeps with another man.''

Aaron roared in pain and then hit his brother-in-law with his fist. Martin's head snapped back. He fell backward into the dirt. Tears were pouring down Aaron's face as he stood over Martin's inert body.

"You fool!'' Aaron yelled. "You crazy, jealous fool. Tommy Moutan's baby girl got lost while you were gone. They had a party last night for everyone who helped in the search. Mattie wasn't going to go, but I told her it would be all right. She went with me. It was me who brought her home last night. She wasn't cheating on you. She was with me!''

Martin rolled over on his hands and knees, then hung his head.

"I didn't mean for her to die,'' he said, then started to cry.

Harper Fonteneau stared at Laurel, then at Martin, and shook his head in disbelief. He took the handcuffs from his belt.

"Stand up, damn it,'' he said, and began cuffing the man. "God Almighty, Martin. What have you done? What the hell have you done?''

"Not on purpose,'' Martin muttered. "Just an accident…wouldn't kill my Mattie Faye.''

Aaron grabbed him by the throat. "What did you do with my sister? Where did you put her body?''

Martin wouldn't answer, but he didn't have to. Laurel already knew. She pointed toward the barn.

"He buried her behind the chicken house. Dig below where he left the shovel."

"Don't touch anything!" Harper ordered when Aaron started toward the buildings. "This is out of your hands. I'm calling the coroner and the crime scene investigators. It's their business now."

Aaron's shoulders slumped in weary defeat. He turned toward Laurel, tried to talk, and wound up weeping openly instead.

Laurel shuddered.

"Justin?"

He was there beside her, right where he'd promised to be. She leaned against him, taking comfort in his presence and his strength.

"Yes, baby?"

"Take me home."

Before he could answer, her legs gave way. He lifted her off her feet and into his arms, then carried her to his truck.

Harper was on his radio calling for help as Justin drove away.

And while they were dealing with the aftermath of the tragedy, Trigger DeLane was on the move, following McNamara's orders before his world came tumbling down.

# 13

Although Cherrie Peloquin had turned her boss, Peter McNamara, in, she was living to regret it. Besides the fact that McNamara Galleries was closed and she was now unemployed, she was afraid for her life. The more she learned about her previous boss's real identity, the more convinced she became that he would not only find out that she'd been the one who'd told on him, but that he would have her killed for the betrayal.

Because she feared to leave her apartment, she was also not searching for a new job, which meant her savings were dwindling. Despite the promises from the offices of the attorney general that her identity was unknown and she was perfectly safe, she lived in constant fear. She couldn't remember when she'd had a good night's sleep and cried often.

Her parents lived in Oregon, and going back was sounding good to her, because the thing she wanted most now was safety. The ordinary life that had been so boring to her before now called to her on an hourly basis. Her high school sweetheart, Andy Preminger, still wanted to marry her. At least he had the last time she'd gone back for a visit. Being an apple farmer's wife was a lot more enticing to her now than it had been when she'd come home from college, dying to see the world. She'd seen it, all right—just enough that she might actually die because of it.

She paced the rooms of her apartment, contemplating every manner of getting out of her promises that she could imagine, but it all came down to running away, and she'd given her word that, when the time came, she would testify against her boss.

As she moved from room to room, peering through curtains and listening for unfamiliar sounds in the hall outside her door, she became more and more certain that her days were numbered. And with that came the realization that she wasn't patriotic enough to die for her country—not for any reason. She didn't quite know how she was going to do it, but she was going to get out of D.C.

Confident, now that she'd made up her mind, she ran to her bedroom, yanked a suitcase from the closet shelf and started to pack. At that point, everything began to fall into place. With her suitcase packed and a cab on the way to her apartment, she had only one more stop to make at an ATM before heading to the airport. The only thing that bothered her was the fact that if her apartment was being watched, as she suspected, then they would follow.

But she wasn't beaten. Not yet. She ran into the bathroom, got a pair of scissors from a drawer and began hacking at her hair, chopping it off in chunks and hanks until there was nothing left of her pretty blond tresses but straggly tufts. Still, she wasn't completely satisfied. Digging through some old cosmetics, she found a can of colored hair spray left over from Halloween last year and picked it up. It might scare the heck out of her parents when they saw her, but, if it kept her alive, it would be worth it. Aiming the can toward what was left of her hair, she began to spray and emptied the contents onto her head.

A few minutes later, she was out the door and on her way down to the waiting cab, satisfied that not even her own mother would recognize her.

The cabbie didn't even blink when a short, skinny woman with pink hair, green shorts and a ragged blue denim shirt came running out of the apartment with a suitcase banging against her shins. Compared to some of the people he'd picked up, she looked almost normal.

"Take me to an ATM first, then to the airport," she said.

He tossed her suitcase in the trunk of his cab and then slid behind the wheel. Within seconds, the only witness to the government's case against Peter McNamara had disappeared.

The attorney general was furious, as was Robert Scanlon's superior, but there was nothing to be done. Scanlon had refused to deal with Peter McNamara and removed himself from the case, which threw the whole process into a standstill. Even with another prosecutor being assigned, there were the obvious delays that would have to be dealt with. Then, the fact that McNamara had fired his lawyer and was, for the moment, without legal representation, brought everyone back to square one.

The new lawyer assigned to the case took Scanlon's files, his notes and the tape of Cherrie Peloquin's deposition, and went to work. Deciding it would be prudent to inform Miss Peloquin that a different prosecutor was now in charge, he made a phone call to her apartment.

The phone rang.

And rang.

And rang.

Without an answer or even an answering machine.

Still, he was not unduly concerned, but to be on the safe side, he sent an assistant to her address, only to be informed by a disgruntled manager, who had just received the information via a telegram, that Miss Peloquin had forfeited her deposit, donated her remaining belongings to whomever wanted them and was no longer in residence, with no forwarding address.

McNamara had spent his life taking pride in his superior intellect and skill at deception. He'd amassed a small fortune playing off those very talents and had no intention of spending the rest of his life behind bars. There were deals to be made and offers he had yet to make. There was little he didn't know about the old Soviet Republic, and while much of that information might no longer be pertinent, he knew plenty that was. The United States was still unsettled about servicemen missing in action from both the Second World War and Vietnam. He knew for a fact that the Mother Country had secreted both without ever coming clean. That alone would be enough to get him out from under the circumstantial evidence they had against him. And while selling out the Russians would mean he could never go back, there was always the Tropics. He'd always planned to buy a home in Bermuda. There was no time like the present. When his next meeting with Scanlon came up, he would offer something even Scanlon could not refuse.

* * *

Billy Mack Thompson had been a teenage farm boy with a passion for fishing and hunting when he'd been drafted and sent to the jungles of Vietnam. The man who'd come back had been nothing like the fresh-faced boy from Wichita, Kansas. To cope with the constant hell of jungles and war and dead babies, he'd gotten hooked on opium. From there, it was just a stone's throw to heroin, cocaine, and anything else that would stop the nightmares and numb the pain.

And during all the horror of war, something odd had happened. He'd become accustomed to bombs and blood and being afraid to sleep, which made going home a transition he couldn't handle. After all the years and the deaths and learning to become a killer, the war had ended. Just like that. As if he'd been to summer camp and it was now time to go home and resume life as he had once known it.

So they sent him back. But something had happened back in the States, too. The general public had become critics of the war that had stolen his soul, and they'd taken out their anger and sense of injustice on the returning vets.

The first time he was spat on, he spat back, then beat the hell out of the spitter and wound up in jail. There wasn't anything that going home could cure, although, to his credit, he tried. But his life went to hell along with his dreams, and when his parents finally died, he took his inheritance, invested in a trunkful of street-ready weed and didn't look back. Not until he was caught and sent to prison.

The fact that he was now incarcerated was no big deal to a man like Billy Mack. But being under the same roof with a traitor was. He had gone into a life of crime, but he'd been a soldier first, and being incarcerated beneath the same roof as McNamara was intolerable. There was a guard he knew with an old and, as yet, undiscovered weakness for blow, and now, having thought about it ever since he'd learned of McNamara's arrival, Billy Mack was about to make the deal of his life.

Peter grimaced as the toilet flushed. The lack of privacy in prison was disgusting. No wonder recidivism was such a huge problem within the American penal system. Only animals could exist under these conditions, and everyone knew animals were creatures of habit, thus the constant release and return of repeat offenders. The way he looked at it, the only ones who escaped the vicious cycle of crime were the ones who died in the process or were rich enough to buy their way out.

He washed his hands with care as his frown deepened. His nails were atrocious. He needed a manicure in the worst way. He needed a haircut, as well, but he wasn't letting some prison barber get hold of him. He would let it go until he could get back to his regular salon.

Without the use of a towel, he dried his hands on his pant legs and then strode to the bars that separated him from the general population. His belly told him it was almost time for the evening meal, although he did not look forward to the menu. To a man with a sophisticated palate such as the one Peter had developed, the food served in here was nothing short of appalling. At previous meals, he had dissected the food with the tines of his fork, half expecting to find bits and pieces of cockroaches or weevils. The inmate population had jeered at him and hassled him to the point of inciting a brawl. After continuous complaints from his now-fired lawyer, Peter had been taken out of the general population and put in isolation. He welcomed the quiet. It gave him the time he required to make plans.

So when he heard the solid clank of the metal door at the end of the passageway opening, then closing, he took notice. And when the sound of approaching footsteps started his way, he moved to the front of his cell, expecting the evening meal. But it wasn't the trustee who normally brought the food that he saw, although he recognized the man who was approaching.

The man was huge, even by prison standards, and had obviously spent many hours lifting free weights, one of the privileges offered by the prison. His face was lined and scarred, his long gray hair hung halfway down his back, and the once-black bandanna he wore around his head was gray from age and countless washings. His leg and arm muscles bulged against the constraints of prison garb, while his shoes made an odd squeaking sound as he walked. It took Peter a few moments to realize it was because of an uneven gait.

He leaned closer to the bars, expecting to see a guard, even two, close behind, but he saw no one. At that point his gaze moved back to the man's face. It was then that Peter McNamara née Dimitri Chorkin knew fear. It occurred to him that he might never get that needed manicure or live to spend another dime of the millions he had accumulated.

"What the hell are you doing here?" he demanded as Billy Mack stopped at his cell.

But Billy Mack had only one thing to say. He slid

his hand inside his shirt, pulled out a handmade knife, and thrust it at Peter's face.

"Die, you egg-sucking Communist," Thompson said.

Before Peter could scream for help, he did as Billy Mack had suggested. He fell backward with a bone-breaking thud, minus his right eye. A small puddle of blood began to pool beneath his head, staining his graying brown hair and giving it the appearance of turning black.

Thompson slid the shiv back into his shirt and then stood at the cell, watching until McNamara's body had quit twitching. At that point he walked out of the hallway the same way he'd come in. The foray into enemy territory was over, and this time, the enemy had been defeated. It was a satisfaction he had not known since leaving Vietnam. The door to Isolation banged against the wall, then swung shut.

Silence reigned.

It was unfortunate that Robert Scanlon was already en route to the airport when the prosecutor's department learned of Cherrie Peloquin's disappearance. It was even more unfortunate that he was in the air to parts unknown when McNamara's body was discovered by a guard doing rounds. But the greatest misfortune belonged to Trigger DeLane, who'd taken it upon himself to follow Scanlon in hopes of finding the man's daughter. Had he known that the witness had skipped and McNamara was dead, he would have been in the clear. His worries would have been over and he could have gone into detox as his father had been urging him to do, forgetting that Peter McNamara had ever existed. But he was so focused on following McNamara's orders to keep his name in the clear that he had lost his sense of reason and all touch with the events of the world.

Scanlon had his boarding pass, a sandwich, a cup of airport coffee and the *New York Times*. Now all he needed was a place to sit until his plane to Louisiana was ready to leave, but there were two other flights that had yet to board and seating was at a premium. He finally found a spot between a woman with two small children and an old woman who kept sliding her false teeth in and out of her mouth as she crocheted.

The thought of eating amid the chaos turned his stomach, and there was no room to open his paper, let alone master the concentration to read it, so, he opted just to finish his coffee and pray for an early departure. A short while later, he was downing the last swallow when the old woman beside him got up and left. Before he could enjoy the extra elbow room, another person slipped into the seat beside him.

"Well, for goodness' sake. Mr. Scanlon, isn't it?"

Surprised to hear someone speaking his name, he looked up, then frowned.

"Yes, but I'm afraid you have me at a disadvantage. I don't believe we've—"

Trigger turned on the charm as he offered his hand.

"Yes, actually we have, but it was a couple of years ago at Dad's New Year's Eve party. I'm Trigger DeLane. General Franklin DeLane is my father."

Robert felt stupid. It wasn't like him to forget people of note, even if they'd only met once.

"Yes, of course. Forgive me," Robert said, and

shook the man's hand. "How is your father? Haven't seen him in a while."

"He's fine, just fine," Trigger said. "I'll tell him you asked after him when I get home."

Robert nodded. "Where are you off to?"

"Houma, Louisiana," Trigger said.

The coincidence was lost on Robert as the two small children on his left took the opportunity to start a fight at his feet. By the time their mother had ended the argument and apologized to Robert, their flight had started to board.

"Where are you seated?" Trigger asked.

"Second row, aisle seat," Robert said as he gathered up his belongings and moved toward the gate.

*First class. Should have known,* Trigger thought, and kicked himself for not thinking that far ahead.

"Have a nice flight," Trigger said. "Maybe we can share a cab when we arrive."

"I'm not staying in Houma," Robert said. "I'm traveling on south."

"Business?"

Robert shook his head. "No, I'm going down to see my daughter."

Trigger's smile widened. "Laurel! I haven't seen her in ages. Has she moved?"

Robert's instinct for privacy began to kick in, although, if he was truthful with himself, it was really too late. He'd already told more of his business to a man he didn't respect than he'd meant to.

"For the time being," he said. "Her grandmother recently passed away. Laurel inherited the family property and is in the process of deciding what to do with it."

Trigger managed a proper frown, when in actuality he wanted to shout for joy.

"I'm sorry for your loss," he said. "Please give Laurel my sympathies when you see her."

"Yes, of course," Robert said. "If you'll excuse me, I'm boarding now."

"Certainly, and it's been nice talking to you," Trigger said, and stepped back into the crowd to wait for general boarding.

He waited impatiently, anxious to get off the ground and get to Laurel Scanlon. The sooner he put her on ice, the sooner McNamara would be free, which meant his ass was almost off the hook.

Robert forgot about the coincidental meeting once he was on the plane, when he realized he hadn't even let Laurel know he was coming. He waved down the flight attendant assigned to first class.

"Miss...do I have time to make a phone call?"

"Yes, sir, but you'll need to be quick," she said. "As soon as everyone is on board, we'll be asking for personal electronic devices to be turned off."

"Thank you," he said, then scanned the address book in his cell phone and quickly dialed the number of Mimosa Grove.

Laurel was sitting out on the veranda watching Elvis doing a fan dance for one of the female peacocks. Justin had been gone for a little over an hour, and she was waiting for Harper Fonteneau to come by and take her statement. She didn't know how much she could tell him that he didn't already know, but she was anxious to get the incident behind her. Marie had heard through the grapevine from Tula that the Clement family wanted to hang Martin Lewis. If Harper

Fonteneau hadn't already been on the scene, Martin wouldn't have lived to be arrested. Laurel leaned her head back against the rocking chair and closed her eyes, welcoming the distraction of the sun's warmth and Elvis's intermittent screeches.

As she was sitting, she heard the phone inside the house begin to ring. Remembering that Marie was in the garden out back, she reluctantly abandoned her seat to go answer.

"Hello."

"Laurel, honey, it's Dad."

Her lethargy shifted, allowing a small spurt of delight to seep in.

"Dad! It's great to hear your voice. How have you been?"

"Never better," he said, and realized that he meant it. "Say, do you have time for a visitor?"

Laurel's heart lightened even further. "If it's you, then definitely yes! When are you coming?"

"I'm already on my way," he said. "I'm landing in Houma around two. I'll rent a car and drive down. Should be there before dark."

"I can come get you."

"No, absolutely not. I've already got the car arranged. I'll come to you."

"I'll look forward to it," Laurel said. "Don't eat dinner. We'll make something special for you."

"We?"

"Mamárie and I. Oh, Dad…it's so good to hear your voice. I can't wait to see you. Drive safe."

"Yes, I will. I'll have my cell phone with me, so don't worry."

"See you soon." Then, although it was out of character for both of them, something prompted Laurel to add, "I love you, Dad."

He smiled self-consciously, then replied softly, "I love you, too."

Laurel was still smiling when she heard the back door open. She hung up the phone and then ran toward the kitchen.

"Guess what?" she cried, as she took the basket of ripe tomatoes from Marie's hands and carried it the rest of the way into the house.

Thankful to be relieved of her burden, Marie followed Laurel in, then began washing her hands.

"I don't know," she said. "You tell me."

"Dad is coming. He's already on the plane. He'll be here tonight."

Marie kept the smile on her face, but she was going to reserve judgment until she saw Robert Scanlon again. She'd only seen him once and still remembered the disdain with which she and Marcella had been treated.

"That's just fine," she said, and reached for the towel to dry her hands. "We'll be needin' to fix somethin' special for supper, then. Does your daddy have any favorites?"

Laurel thought of the beef Wellington that her father favored, then shook her head.

"Yes, but I want to share Louisiana with him. How about some étouffée?"

Marie smiled. "Yes…I got plenty of shrimps. I'll make some rice and beans and the étouffée. Maybe some blackberry cobbler for dessert?"

"Yes. Yes. Perfect," Laurel said. "I'll help."

Marie frowned. "No. I don't need help in my own kitchen. You go wait for Harper. When he's gone, you can fix up one of the clean bedrooms for your daddy. Maybe take some fresh flowers up there."

"Yes, all right," Laurel said, then turned at the sound of a knock on the front door. Her shoulders slumped, and she made a face at Marie. "Rats. That's bound to be Harper." Quick tears shimmered in her eyes, but she blinked them away. "I'd rather do anything than relive Mattie's death again."

Marie put her arms around Laurel and gave her a hug.

"Want me to come with you?"

Laurel shook her head as she returned the hug.

"No, I'll do it," she said. "But you don't know how much it means to me that you offered."

"Then go on with you," Marie said. "I'm gonna wash up these tomatoes and make some gazpacho for lunch. How does that sound?"

"Wonderful," Laurel said, and hurried to answer the door.

As she'd suspected, it was Harper.

"Chief, come in," Laurel said, and stepped aside for the man to enter.

Harper took off his hat and smiled.

"I just came by to tell you that there's no need for me to take your testimony after all. Martin's confession will be enough."

"Thank goodness," Laurel said. "I wasn't looking forward to reliving that."

Harper nodded, then eyed her curiously.

"Miss Scanlon, can I ask you something?"

"Yes, if you'll call me Laurel."

"Yes, ma'am… I mean, Laurel."

"Then ask away."

"How do you do it? I mean...see the future and all?"

"I don't know."

He nodded, accepting the answer as he glanced around the great hall.

"Does it scare you?"

Laurel sighed. "You mean the visions?"

"Yes, ma'am." Then he frowned. "What else is there?"

She almost smiled. "Well, there are the ghosts, and the—"

He stuffed his hat on his head and began backing up.

"I'm real sorry I didn't get Justin's message in time to help Mattie, but I want you to know that I appreciate you just the same."

Harper bolted for his patrol car.

Laurel waved, although it was futile. Harper was already gone.

She looked toward the mimosa trees beside the old fishpond and smiled. Elvis was strutting back and forth on top of the rock ledge while a small brown female pecked at the grasshoppers in the yard.

"Just like a male. I'm already old news."

As she started into the house, she felt a cool breeze against her cheek, but when she glanced back at the trees, there wasn't a breath of air stirring. She touched the side of her face, then looked around, although she knew there was nothing to see.

"I know, I know," she said softly. "You're reminding me you're still here. Well, so am I. But I still don't know what you want me to do."

Having said that, she hurried back inside. She still had enough time to get ready for her father's arrival, then read some more from Chantelle's diary.

# 14

One of Justin's clients, an elderly man named Maurice, was going into the hospital for cataract surgery and needed to sell some of his stocks to pay for the procedure. Justin had just finished brokering the sale and was in the act of transferring the money to Maurice's checking account when his phone rang. He typed in the last bit of information and clicked on Send, then picked up the receiver.

"Hello."

"Justin, it's me."

All the muscles in his body went slack as he kicked back in his chair and smiled.

"Hello, me," he said. "Was it rough talking to Harper?"

"I didn't have to, after all," Laurel said. "Martin's confession takes care of everything, so I guess my part in the discovery of her body was moot."

Justin's smile slipped. He could hear tension in her voice and knew that Mattie's death had affected her greatly.

"Honey, are you all right?"

Laurel sighed. "I will be, but that's not why I'm calling. My father is coming for a quick visit. I was wondering if you would come for breakfast in the morning. I'd like for you two to meet…if you don't mind," she added.

"Sweetheart, not only do I not mind, I look forward to it. Tell Marie to make plenty of biscuits."

"You sure? I don't want you to feel like I'm pressuring you to—"

"It's not pressure, Laurel. It will be a pleasure. Besides…he may as well get used to me now, because I'm not going away."

Laurel shivered suddenly with longing. His rough-tender voice made her ache.

"And for that I am forever grateful," she said softly.

Justin groaned. "Ah, *chère,* your gratitude is not what I'm longing for."

Laurel grinned. "Hold that thought until next time."

"Love you, baby."

Laurel's heart tugged. It was the first time either one of them had voiced what was in their hearts, and she could no more have denied a like answer than she could have quit breathing.

"Love you, too."

"See you in the morning…about nine?"

"Perfect," Laurel said. "See you then."

She hung up, reluctant to break their connection, and shuddered lightly from the quickening she felt just hearing his voice. She had it bad, but that was good. Next thing on her mental to-do list was to put some fresh flowers in her father's room and make sure there were clean linens, as well.

She hurried back into the kitchen, where Marie was already busy chopping ingredients for the evening meal.

"Mamárie…where would I find a flower vase?"

Marie pointed toward a small closet off the pantry.

"They're all in there. Your grandmama used to love fresh flowers, but the sicker she became, the less she wanted them around. Said they made her feel as if she was viewing her own funeral."

Laurel made a sad face. "If only our lives had been different. I think she would have been a marvelous woman to know, and I'm sorry I didn't make the effort to stay in touch."

Marie shrugged. "She understood. Your daddy didn't hold with the sight and tried to deny it existed by keeping you and Phoebe away as much as possible. After your mama died, Miz Marcella began to withdraw. She quit trying, so don't blame yourself."

"Still, it would have been good to have someone who understood what happens inside my head." Then she smiled. "But I have you."

Marie's eyes widened perceptibly; then she shook her head in denial.

"Don't lay none of that 'understandin'' stuff on me. I don't understand one single bit of what you can do. All's I know is that you can do it, and of that I have no doubt."

"That's enough for me," Laurel said, and headed for the closet. Moments later, she came out with a tall crystal vase, wiped it clean with a dish towel, then set it on the table.

"I'm going to cut some flowers. Be back in a jiffy."

"Take your time, child. It's too hot to rush."

"Yes, ma'am," Laurel said, snatched a pair of kitchen shears from a drawer and took a shallow basket from the back steps as she headed toward the newly manicured grounds and flower garden, compliments of Tula's grandson Claude. She still had the exterior of the house, as well as the roof, to contend with, but it would wait until another day.

Down on her knees among the sweet-blooming flowers and the freshly turned earth, Laurel felt such peace and, at the same time, a sense of timelessness. How many women of Mimosa Grove had been in this same place, she wondered, doing this same thing for the men in their lives?

As she sat, a butterfly rode a faint current of air in front of her outstretched hand before settling silently onto the soft white petals of a gardenia. Laurel rocked back on her heels, watching as it drank from the nectar, its wings fluttering slowly now and then for balance. Near the base of the bloom, a pair of small black ants ran a race toward the ground, using the stem for a track.

"Run fast," she said softly, and then sat very still until they were gone.

Movement near her left foot had her shifting her focus and brought a smile to her face. Her appearance in the flowers had obviously disturbed a large fat toad from his nap.

"Well, hello, Mr. Toad. Nice to meet you."

At the sound of her voice, the toad hopped back beneath the deep shade of the gardenia bushes and then disappeared.

"Honey...you gonna stay out there all day? It's past time you got yourself in outta that sun."

Laurel looked up and waved at Marie, who was calling to her from the doorway. She glanced at her watch, slightly surprised that she'd been outside almost an hour.

"Yes, ma'am," she answered, then picked up her basket of flowers and stood, wincing slightly from a small stiffness in her knees.

The unexpected pain was a reminder that she hadn't followed her normal exercise routine. Maybe tomorrow morning early, before it became so hot, she would take a run. Then she glanced toward the grove behind the house. Of course, there was always the shade inside the grove. If she had time closer to evening, she might take a short run.

Shifting her basket to the crook of her arm, she tossed the scissors on top of the blooms and headed for the house. She was on the first step when a shrill, high-pitched scream sounded from the trees behind her.

She turned abruptly, her heart pounding.

"Marie!" She dropped the flowers and raced to the door. "Marie!" she shouted, then turned back toward the grove, half expecting to see a woman run screaming from the trees.

Within moments, Marie was there.

"What? What's wrong? Are you hurt?"

"No, no," Laurel said, her voice shaking as she pointed toward the grove. "I heard a woman screaming...out there!"

Marie frowned. "Ain't supposed to be anybody—"

The scream sounded again. Marie's frown deepened, but her posture relaxed.

"Honey girl...that's not a woman. That's a painter. Only they don't usually come up in the daytime."

Laurel grabbed the basket of flowers as she backed toward the door.

"A painter? What's a painter?"

"Girl, don't you know nothin'?" Marie shook her head, grabbed Laurel by the arm and yanked her into the kitchen before closing the door. "It's a cat. A big cat."

"Oh, do you mean a panther?" Laurel asked.

Marie shrugged. "I suppose some call 'em that."

"What do we do?" she asked.

"We don't do anything," Marie said as she moved toward the phone. "But Tula got a cousin who can help."

Laurel resisted the urge to roll her eyes. Tula's connections seemed endless.

"What on earth would we do around here without Tula and her kin?" she muttered.

Marie dialed the phone, ignoring Laurel's comment.

A shiver raced through Laurel's body as she set the flowers on the table, then went to the sink to wash her hands. Even as she was looking out the window, she was struck by the beauty of the pastoral scene beyond. Still, her gaze slid from the garden and flower beds to the thick grove of mimosa trees at the back of the property.

It was like looking at a grove of giant toadstools. The limbs of the mimosas, with their fernlike fronds spread like so many open umbrellas and the pink-and-white flowers adorning them, were not unlike the feathered topknots of the peacocks of which Marcella had been so fond. But the presence of a predator at Mimosa Grove was a reminder of the dangers that often lay beneath the calm, peaceful existence of ordinary life.

"He's comin' right over," Marie said. "Name's Manville, and he's bringin' some of his boys with him. Now, honey, don't you worry none. They'll find that cat. Just don't be goin' for any of your walks off the grounds until they kill it dead.''

Laurel shivered again. ''Don't worry about that,'' she muttered. ''I may never go in there again.''

Marie frowned, then slid a hand across Laurel's shoulders and patted her gently.

''No, no, baby girl…don't be talkin' like that. That cat just got hisself lost, that's all. It don't want nothin' to do with you any more than you want with it. Understand?''

''I guess,'' Laurel said, then made herself smile. ''Looks like I'm still a city girl at heart, with a lot to learn.''

''You'll do fine,'' Marie said, then wiped her hands on her apron and straightened her shoulders. ''Now, fix your flowers and then go take a nap. I got me some étouffée and cobbler to make.''

''I really can help,'' Laurel said.

Marie shooed her away. ''You'll be more help if you stay outta my kitchen. Make yourself pretty for your daddy, okay?''

Laurel frowned.

''I'll stay out of your way, but I'm not some helpless female. Just because that stupid panther scared me doesn't mean I'm going to faint away. I'll do the flowers like we planned, then—''

Marie laughed, then patted Laurel on the cheek.

''Lord, honey…I didn't mean you can't take care of yourself. I just want you to enjoy your daddy's visit, okay?''

Laurel made a face and then laughed, too.

''Okay. Didn't mean to get all huffy. I'm not un-accustomed to two-legged intruders, but this is my first encounter with a hairy four-legged one. Next time I won't overreact."

"Let's just hope there's not a next time," Marie said, then tucked a straggling lock of hair into the knot at the back of her neck before moving to the sink.

Laurel made quick work of the flowers, then carried them up to the room where her father would stay. Once she'd finished that task and put out clean sheets and towels, she headed to her room to pick out something to wear. But Chantelle's diary beckoned instead, so she kicked off her shoes and crawled up into the middle of her bed. Moments later, she forgot about everything but the life and times of a woman long since past.

March 1, 1814
I am with child. My husband is elated. I would be, too, but I am so ill. Winter was short and mild compared to the winters in Paris. Already the heat is beginning, and the mosquitoes, the horrible flying bugs that bite the flesh, have arrived. Where do they go in the winter? I wonder why they don't die. I fear I will die from this sickness. Will I have a son or a daughter? I do not know, and for now, I do not care.

Laurel shifted restlessly on the bed, then scooted back against the headboard and pulled her knees up, using them, instead of her lap, as a place to rest the book. She turned the fragile pages with care as she read, already drawn into the drama of Chantelle LeDeux's life. It wasn't until she reached the month of October that she realized how fragile Chantelle's existence really was.

October 14, 1814
Last night I became a mother. My husband named our son Jean Luc. He seems to be a pleasant baby and is nursing well, but the birth was not easy. The midwife would not attend me. She feared I would put a curse on her, should the birth not go well. Were it not for Joshua, our houseman, and his wife, who stayed with me during the birth, I don't know what might have happened.

I love my child with all my heart and am happy I am now a mother, but I wish I had never left my dear parents. I do not know how to live amid such distrust and fear.

Oh, that I had never been born with this curse.

Laurel held the small book to her heart and closed her eyes, well aware of the anguish that Chantelle had been suffering. In an odd sort of way, it gave Laurel comfort to know that she wasn't the only one who'd had to endure ridicule and judgment because she saw things other people could not.

As she turned to the next page, it occurred to her that Chantelle had yet to make one believably positive mention of her husband or of her affection for him. It was then that she remembered that during this time in history, most marriages were arranged. Her heart hurt for the young French girl and her loneliness in the wilds of a new world. It began to make sense why a wife and a mother such as this might even consider running away.

She looked down at the next page, squinting to read the faded words, and turned on the table lamp beside her bed before continuing. Many pages later, another entry caught her attention.

December 25, 1815
Jean Luc is walking and into everything. I love his curiosity. I think he might be a scholar. My husband would not be happy about this. He wants a son to carry on the family business of cotton. When I mentioned the possibility that raising cotton might one day fall out of favor as a lucrative occupation, he shouted at me and told me that women did not have a mind for business, and that I should keep my opinions to myself.

So I shall.

We had a festive holiday. Neighbors came to share in our bounty. Cook roasted a great haunch of venison. I tried to show her how to make a flaming pudding like we have back home in Paris, but she did not welcome my presence in her kitchen, and the pudding was not a success. I do few things here in this new world with success, but I am a good mother, and obviously I breed well.

Again, I am with child.

Weary from trying to decipher the tiny, spiderlike writing, Laurel laid the diary aside, then rolled over on the bed and closed her eyes.

Just for a few minutes.

Just to rest her eyes.

Instead, she fell asleep.

And she dreamed.

\* \* \*

*Darkness was all around her, but fear kept her moving. Something sounded in the woods behind her, and she started to run, enduring the slap of limbs on her face as she moved blindly through the night. She knew she was in the grove, because the scent of mimosa blooms and rotting earth mingled with the coppery smell of fresh blood. Vines along the forest floor caught and tugged at her ankles before breaking as she struggled to get free. Her lungs were burning. It was getting harder and harder to breathe. She needed to stop. She needed to rest. But there was someone behind her—moving faster than she—coming closer and closer. Someone who'd already brought blood. Someone who wanted her dead.*

The light in Laurel's room was shifting from the floor to the wall. The sun was beginning to move closer to the western horizon, but she didn't know. In her sleep, it was already night, and she was about to die.

She moaned, then rolled over on her back. As she did, she flung her arms outward.

*Something hit her in the back of the head, then in the middle of her back, and then she was falling—off the riverbank and into the water below. She thought she screamed but couldn't be sure, although it was the last sound she heard as she was suddenly submerged.*

*Down, down, down, she fell…below the swift-moving surface. Water was rushing up her nose and into her eyes. Breath was gone.*

*She died—then found herself floating between heaven and earth, pulled toward a bright and pulsing light, but, for some reason, equally locked into the gravitational pull of an earthbound soul.*

*She struggled to go forward, aching to know the solace she could sense in the light, but something kept holding her back.*

*"Help me. Help me," she begged, reaching upward toward heaven, and still the weight around her ankles wouldn't let go.*

*Then, as suddenly as it had come, the light was gone. The weight, too, was gone from around her ankles, but it was too late. She was trapped in the dark between heaven and earth, with nowhere to go but mad.*

Laurel woke up, gasping for air, her arms and legs flailing. Still locked into the dream, she believed she was beneath the water and trying to swim up. She groaned in disbelief as reality dawned, then crawled out of bed and staggered to the bathroom. Splashing cool water on her face took away most of the horror, and by the time she got back to her bed, it was fading fast.

She dropped onto the side of the mattress and then picked up the diary. Her hands were shaking as she gently let it shut. Reading about Chantelle's life was sad, but not nearly as sad as the truth about her death. There might be a mystery as to what happened to her, but there was no mystery as to where she was now and why she kept begging for help. And this she knew, because Laurel had not been the woman in the dream. That fugitive had been Chantelle. Now she was caught between heaven and hell, and for whatever reason, she needed Laurel's help to move on.

"But how?" Laurel muttered, and held the diary close to her chest. "Help me, Chantelle...show me."

She sat, waiting for a miracle—waiting for what was left of a young woman's soul to conjure up enough energy to make the connection. But nothing happened, and finally she set the diary aside and began to undress. She needed to shower and change before her father's arrival, and despite Marie's insistence to the contrary, she was going to help with dinner, as well.

Robert Scanlon picked up his luggage and headed for the rent-a-car desk to pick up his vehicle. Minutes later, he was on his way out to the lot. The sun was bright. The air was hot. Soon he shed his suit coat and donned a pair of sunglasses. When he found his car, he tossed everything into the trunk and quickly started the engine, cranking the air conditioner up to high. Even with the vents all aimed in his direction, the air inside the car was still miserable.

A woman ran between his car and the next, then straight toward an approaching man. He watched the man's face light up, saw him drop his suitcase as he caught her on the run and swung her up in his arms. A sharp pain hit Robert square in the heart, and he had to look away. Angry that he'd been emotionally moved by two complete strangers, he jammed the car into Reverse and quickly drove away. It had been years since he'd let himself think of the loneliness of his existence, but with Laurel's absence and not having the job to compensate, it was no longer possible to ignore.

The rental clerk had given him instructions on how to get from the airport to the highway he needed, but the traffic was worse than he'd expected, and the route she'd mentioned had a detour due to some highway reconstruction. It took him a good forty-five minutes before he was clear of the city.

Although he had a general idea of how to get from Houma to Bayou Jean, he wasn't taking any chances on getting lost later and had requested a car with an in-vehicle navigation system to make his trip as quick as possible. There were things that needed to be said to his daughter, and the sooner it was done, the better he was going to feel.

He drove south out of Houma with Laurel on his mind. He hated the way they'd parted, and hated even more that he'd been the cause. It wasn't entirely her fault that she'd let herself buy into the idea that she was psychic. Her mother's influence had started it, and his busy lifestyle had let it fester. Now it was too late to change her, but not too late to change their relationship. He didn't believe for a moment there was such a thing as people who could see into the future as well as the past, but he wanted to believe in her. She was a good woman with a gentle heart, and she was his daughter. That was going to have to be enough.

As he drove, the air inside his car cooled off and his temper with it. He was so intent on following the proper route that he never noticed the gray SUV a short distance behind him.

Trigger had picked up a rental, as well, but had cursed his way through the city while trying to keep up with Scanlon. He wanted to talk to McNamara. He'd told Trigger he would call, but he hadn't, and Trigger could hardly call him. The last thing he wanted was to draw attention to the fact that he even knew the man beyond having attended some of the same parties over the years. All he had to go on was the last thing McNamara had told him to do, which was to snatch Scanlon's daughter, and come hell or high water, that was what he was going to do. He felt smug about his plan, letting Scanlon take the lead, show him where she was, and then, when Daddy dear was gone, Laurel Scanlon would be his.

But Robert Scanlon's rental car was not in on Trigger's plans. Thirty-five minutes later, every caution light on the dashboard came on at once, followed by a loud dinging sound not unlike that of a medium-size bell. At first Robert was too startled to be concerned, but concern quickly followed, as he barely managed to steer the car off onto the shoulder of the highway before it died.

Neither the fancy navigational system nor the fine Corinthian leather seats made a world's bit of difference to the fact that the engine beneath the hood was a dud. Frustrated beyond belief and cursing motors in general, he made a quick call to the rental agency, which promised a tow truck would soon be on the way.

"Fine," Robert said, "but I also need another car. I have a meeting tonight that I can't miss."

"I'm so sorry, sir," the agent said. "We don't have any more vehicles available until tomorrow morning."

"You've got to be kidding," Robert said. "No cars...of any kind?"

"No, sir. There's a quilting convention in town, and a lot of the women rented vehicles to go sightseeing."

"Oh, great. Just great. I don't suppose any of your competitors have anything, either?"

"I doubt it, but I'd be happy to give you their numbers."

"Yes, thank you. I'd appreciate it."

The clerk rattled off the other numbers, then disconnected, with a reminder that the tow truck would be arriving soon. Meanwhile, Robert was left sitting in the heat at the side of the road.

He got out and kicked at a rock on the side of the road, then looked up and down the highway, as if expecting a miracle to occur. And when he saw the turn signal of a late-model, silver-gray SUV suddenly blinking as the driver began steering the car off the highway and onto the shoulder of the road behind him, he realized he'd gotten his miracle.

But then he recognized the driver, and his suspicious nature kicked in. The coincidence of seeing Trigger DeLane in the airport, then being on the same flight, and now about to be rescued by the man, seemed too good to be true. But it was too hot and he was too pissed off to miss the opportunity.

He dropped his cell phone in his pocket and then stepped aside as Trigger DeLane pulled up and waved.

When Trigger, who had dropped back to follow several minutes behind, saw Scanlon's car pulled off the highway, he panicked. What the hell was he going to do now? He could hardly follow a man who was going nowhere. Then reality hit, and he laughed at himself. He was going to do the proper thing one acquaintance would do for another. He was going to stop and offer his assistance. How priceless was this going to be? He was looking for Laurel Scanlon, and without skulking about or subterfuge of any kind, she'd just been delivered.

He put the SUV in Park, put on what he hoped was a surprised expression and got out of the car.

"Mr. Scanlon?" Then he shook his head in pretend disbelief. "It *is* you! When I saw you get out of the car, I couldn't believe it. What are the odds of running into each other like this twice in one day?"

Robert had already asked himself the same thing, but it was too damned hot to delve too deeply into coincidence.

"Whatever they are, I'm grateful," Robert said. "Where are you headed?"

Trigger shook his head. "I was heading south to the Atchafalaya Bay to do some fishing."

"I would appreciate a lift to the next town. I need to try to rent another car."

"Certainly," Trigger said. "Let me help you get your things. Are they in the back?"

"Yes," Robert said, and popped the trunk.

Within minutes his luggage had been transferred, and he'd called the rental company to let them know what he'd done.

Robert slid into the passenger seat with a sigh of relief and aimed an air conditioner vent directly in his face.

"Hot one, isn't it?" Trigger said as he slid behind the wheel.

"This place is as close to hell as anything on earth," Robert muttered, then buckled his seat belt and managed a smile. "Of course, I'm slightly prejudiced in that regard."

Trigger arched an eyebrow as he pulled back onto the highway.

"You've been in Louisiana before?"

Robert hesitated, then sighed. "My wife was born and raised here."

"Really?" Trigger said, then eyed Robert anew. "I don't believe I've ever had the pleasure."

"She's dead," Robert said shortly, then turned to look out the side window.

Trigger was dense in some respects, but he knew when a faux pas had been made, and obviously, mentioning Scanlon's marital state had been one. "I'm sorry," he said quickly. "So, where were you headed?"

"A place called Mimosa Grove. It's outside a small town called Bayou Jean."

"Then that's where we're headed," Trigger said.

Robert looked surprised.

"Oh, no. I couldn't ask you to go that far out of your way."

Trigger smiled.

"On the contrary, Mr. Scanlon. It will be my pleasure."

"I don't suppose you have anything to drink?" Robert asked.

Trigger smiled. "Check in my duffel bag. I believe there's an unopened bottle of water."

"Great," Robert said, and turned around, unzipped the bag in the seat behind them and felt inside for the bottle. Instead, he felt the outline of a pistol wrapped up in some clothes, and froze.

"Find it?" Trigger asked.

"What? Oh…yes, here it is," Robert said, as he jerked away from the gun and quickly retrieved the water.

# 15

Robert stared out the window into the side-view mirror outside the car, watching the miles disappearing behind them and wondering why the hell Trigger DeLane was carrying a gun. Of course, lots of people did carry them, but after the restrictions on flying had tightened so drastically, there was no way he could have boarded that plane with a gun on his person or in his luggage. That meant he must have purchased it after getting to Houma. And since there was a waiting period for buying handguns, the only way Trigger had come by that gun was illegally. And what the hell did he need a gun for, anyway, just to go fishing?

He glanced briefly at the man again, considering asking him outright about the gun, then stopped, telling himself that he was probably being too suspicious. The man's father was a four-star general, for God's sake. There was no telling what Trigger did for a living. He could be some kind of undercover agent and the world would never know. If he was, he wouldn't have needed to buy a gun. He could have brought it with him and passed through security without question.

Convinced that he'd answered his own questions about DeLane, he relaxed and began to enjoy the scenery. But almost an hour had passed before Robert felt relaxed enough to start a conversation.

"You fish down here often?" he asked.

Trigger looked truly surprised. "I'm sorry?"

Robert frowned. "I thought you said you were going fishing. Did I misunderstand?"

Trigger gave himself a mental cursing, then laughed.

"Sorry. I was lost in thought when you spoke. No, I haven't been this way in several years, but I have a friend who lives on the coast. He invited. I accepted. That's me. Always acting on impulse."

"I see," Robert said, but he didn't really. He'd been a prosecutor long enough to recognize lies when he heard them.

"How about you? Do you enjoy deep-sea fishing?" Trigger asked.

"Can't say as how I've ever been," Robert said. "Not much on fishing."

"Oh, best thing in the world to relax and clear your head."

"I never felt like I had the time to relax," Robert said, and then grimaced. That sounded pompous, even to him. "Sorry," he said. "It's not that I couldn't take the time. I just didn't. I'm a bit of a workaholic."

Trigger nodded. "Just like my father."

"Yes. Your father is a good man," Robert said.

Trigger stifled a sigh. "That's what everyone says."

Robert absorbed the answer, mentally dissecting it and coming to the conclusion that, as a son, it must have been difficult to live up to the reputation of a man like Franklin DeLane.

"So Laurel is playing lady of the manor, is she?" Trigger asked.

Robert blinked. The transition from Trigger's father to his own daughter was more than abrupt, but he chalked it up to the fact that DeLane probably didn't like being compared to his old man.

"For the time being," Robert said. "I'm sure it's nothing permanent."

*Nothing was ever permanent,* Trigger thought, and pointed to a roadside sign.

"I'm going to pull off here and gas up. I'm told that towns are few and far between down here. I don't want to get in the middle of nowhere only to find myself out of fuel."

"Good idea," Robert said. "And you must let me pay. It's the least I can do for the ride."

Trigger gave him his best hundred-watt smile. "I won't hear of it. Just sit back and enjoy the ride." *It may very well be one of your last peaceful days for some time.*

"Thank you," Robert said. "While you're filling up, I think I'd better give Laurel a quick call to let her know I'll be a bit late."

Trigger frowned slightly as he angled off the highway, then headed for the small gas station and luncheonette. For some reason, the idea that Laurel Scanlon might know he was with her father made him nervous, but he didn't know why.

He pulled up to the self-service island, and Robert Scanlon picked up his phone and began punching in numbers. Trigger was out of the car and reaching for the hose as Robert put the phone to his ear. Trigger ran his credit card through the pump before he thought, then cursed himself for doing it, knowing he'd just left a trail, should the question ever arise as to where he was on this day. However, it was too late to fix it now. He shoved the nozzle into the tank and then stepped back, eyeing the hand-painted sign on the window of the quick stop.

Chicken and Catfish—Fried Fresh Daly.

He snorted beneath his breath as he read the sign. Ignorant bunch of hicks. Can't even spell *daily*. God only knew what the cooking would be like.

The heat of the day and the mingling scents of fried chicken and gas fumes were all but staggering as he waited for the tank to fill. He thought about getting a couple of cold drinks and started toward the store when he remembered the stories about Laurel. Now he knew why he'd been leery of Robert calling his daughter.

He pivoted sharply, staring through the windshield at Robert Scanlon's face as he talked on the phone.

Shit! It was too late!

Laurel was sitting by the windows in her bedroom, still reading from the diary, when the phone began to ring. She looked up, absently glancing out the window as she moved, and realized that Marie was outside in the herb garden. Reluctant to break her concentration, she made herself get up and answer the call.

"Hello?"

"Laurel, it's me."

"Dad? Is everything all right?"

"Sort of," he said. "I've had car trouble."

"Oh, no!" She dropped down onto the side of the bed and kicked off her shoes. "Do you need a ride? I can come get you. Do you know where you are?"

Robert chuckled. "No, I don't know where I am, but strangely enough, I don't need a ride. You will never guess who was driving along behind me and picked me up."

The moment the words came out of her father's mouth, Laurel was struck by an overwhelming sensation of fear.

"Oh, God…oh, Daddy…don't get in the car! Do you hear me? Don't get in the car?"

Robert frowned. "What the hell are you talking about? It's not like I got in a car with a stranger. I'm not that stupid, and please…don't start with this psychic stuff now. Everything is perfectly fine."

As soon as he said it, he thought of the gun in Trigger's bag and then chided himself for letting Laurel get to him—even for a moment.

"Dad…Daddy, please! You have to—"

The moan that came over the phone sent cold chills up Robert's back.

"Laurel? What's happening?"

She stuttered, then slid from the bed onto the floor. There was pain in the back of her head; then she felt cold. Her senses were assaulted by the smell of damp earth and rotting vegetation. She tried to see where she was, but everything was dark. She could hear her father's voice but couldn't respond. Every sense she had was locked into the vision.

Then suddenly she saw a face and words came out of her mouth that she didn't understand.

"McNamara. He's there because of McNamara. You have to get out!"

Robert's mind went blank. Laurel didn't know about McNamara's threats to him and his family, so why would she say something so off the wall? Then he flashed back on the coincidences of seeing Trigger at the airport—of being on the same flight, of breaking down, then being rescued from the side of the road, of the offer to drive him all the way to Mimosa Grove. At that point, another memory kicked in. Just before he'd left D.C., Estelle had mentioned Trigger DeLane calling for Laurel, only to be told that she was no longer in residence. His fingers tightened on the cell phone as he looked out the window—and straight into Trigger DeLane's frantic gaze.

The look on the man's face was a combination of panic and guilt, and for Robert, the last piece of the puzzle that was McNamara's case fell into place. He had never been able to put together a good enough explanation to convince himself, let alone a jury, as to how McNamara had access to so many military secrets. Yet what better partner than a four-star general's son?

"Son of a..."

"Daddy? Daddy?"

"Tell them it was DeLane," he muttered, then hung up and reached for the door.

It was momentary panic that made Trigger hesitate, but he knew why he'd been bothered about Scanlon calling his daughter. He remembered the little tidbits of party gossip that he used to hear about her on a regular basis. There were those who swore she was a bona fide psychic, and if that was the case, then there was the chance that he'd just screwed himself up the ass by letting Scanlon even talk to her. What if she could tell, just by talking to her old man, that he was coming to get her? What if—

Suddenly everything seemed to happen in slow motion.

Scanlon looked up.

Their gazes locked.

He saw the shock on Scanlon's face, then watched understanding dawn.

Even though he couldn't hear him, he saw Scanlon saying his name, then reaching for the door.

At that point, he bolted toward the car.

The fact that the gas cap was on the passenger side of the car gave Trigger the edge. He'd parked fairly close to the pumps, which inhibited Scanlon's escape attempt.

Trigger circled the car from the front and hit the door with his full weight just as Robert was trying to get out. The momentum slammed the back of Robert's head against the door frame, trapping him between the door and the car and, at the same time, rendering him unconscious.

Trigger took one look at the blood dripping from a cut on Scanlon's forehead and began to curse. Without looking up to see if anyone was watching, he shoved Scanlon's unconscious body into the car, slammed the door shut, hung the gas nozzle back on the pump and jumped into the driver's seat.

The receipt from the gas purchase was printing as he started the car. Then, as if his day wasn't already screwed, a man pulled a dilapidated truck up to the pumps and parked directly in front of him. Slamming the car in Reverse, Trigger saw the receipt dangling from the pump as he began to back away. The impulse to retrieve it was strong, but he could tell by the look on the other driver's face that he'd seen the blood all over Scanlon and was already pointing.

There was nothing to do but haul ass and hope that the driver was too busy looking at Scanlon to get a good look at him.

Justin was coming out of the grocery store in Bayou Jean when he was struck by a wave of fear so strong that he almost dropped the sacks he was carrying. He turned abruptly, looking behind him, then up and down the street, but he saw nothing except the usual assortment of cars and trucks and familiar faces. There was nothing here that should cause such concern. But the feeling was still there—deep in his gut, hammering at his head—telling him to run.

Startled by the intensity of the emotion, he tossed the sacks into his truck and then slid behind the wheel. No sooner had he put the key in the ignition then it hit him. It wasn't his fear he was feeling. It was Laurel's.

Marie was coming in from the herb garden when she heard a car pulling up in front of the house. She glanced at the clock, surprised that Robert Scanlon would be arriving this soon, then remembered the men who were going to hunt the painter and set her herb basket on the table.

Before she could get out of the kitchen, she heard loud knocking on the front door, then the sound of running footsteps inside the house.

Frowning, she stepped out of the kitchen just as Justin came running down the hallway.

"What on earth?" she murmured.

He grabbed her by the arms. "Laurel! Where's Laurel?"

"Uh…upstairs in her room, I think. What's wrong?"

"I don't know, but something is," he muttered, and bolted up the stairs.

Marie grabbed the stair rail and started up behind him.

Justin's heart was hammering against his chest as he reached the second-floor landing. The door to her bedroom was slightly ajar. He hit it with the flat of his hand as he ran inside, sending it banging against the wall.

She was on the floor, motionless. All he could think as he ran toward her was, *Please, let her still be breathing.*

He felt for a pulse, relaxing only after he felt it beating steadily against his fingers. Then he examined her head, searching for a wound, or a knot that would indicate she'd been injured. When he felt nothing, he began running his hands over her body, searching for something that would explain her state.

"Laurel…darling…it's Justin. Can you hear me?"

"She must have had a vision," Marie said.

At the sound of her voice, Justin jumped. He rocked back on his heels and turned around.

"Does that happen often?"

"Enough," Marie said. "Put her on the bed. I'll get a wet cloth."

Justin lifted her gently, then laid her carefully on the bed.

She moaned.

"Laurel…honey?"

She opened her eyes, then grabbed Justin's arm.

"Daddy."

"No, baby, I'm not your father. It's me, Justin."

She rolled over, then sat up on the side of the bed.

"No, no, that's not what I meant."

Marie appeared, then handed Laurel a cool, wet cloth.

"Here, baby girl. Maybe this will clear your head."

Laurel wiped the cloth across her face, then handed it back to Marie.

"I'm gonna go call Tula. She'll bring some of her tea. It'll help calm you down."

"No, I don't—"

But it was too late. Marie was already on her way out the door.

"I've got to call his office," Laurel muttered.

"Whose office?" Justin asked.

"My father's office. He's in trouble. It has to do with McNamara."

"You're not making sense," Justin said.

Laurel took a deep breath, then shoved her hands through her hair. Red curls tangled and caught in her fingertips as she looked at him in frustration.

"I know. I know. It's always like this. I see what I see." Then she slid her arms around Justin's neck. "Help me," she whispered. "Help me find my father. I don't know how to explain it, but I know something is very, very wrong."

Justin frowned and then pulled her close against him. She was trembling, and her tears were so close to spilling over. He wanted to make everything okay, but he didn't know how. All he could do was be there for her.

"Then let's go make that call," he said gently, brushing his mouth across her lips.

When he would have pulled away, she took his face

in her hands and held him close, kissing him back with a slow, hungry need.

Justin groaned.

"Oh, Laurel, Laurel...you are in my heart so deep I don't know where I stop and you begin."

"I know," Laurel whispered. "I feel the same." She started to move, then stopped. "Justin?"

"What, baby?"

"How did you come to be here?"

He slapped a hand up the side of his head.

"Damn... I've got melted ice cream on the seat of my truck."

"What?"

He grimaced. "I was coming out of the grocery store when I felt this...for lack of a better word... *overwhelming* sense of fear. It took me a few moments to realize it wasn't my fear I was experiencing. It was yours. I drove straight here and found you on the floor."

Laurel was listening, but it was difficult for her to wrap her mind around everything he was saying.

"You *felt* fear?"

"All the way to my toes. Scared the hell out of me. So I'm telling you now, for future reference, you can't ever accuse me of not knowing how you feel, because honey...I was inside your skin."

"Oh, Justin," she whispered, and hid her face against his chest.

"Look at me," he said, then put a finger beneath her chin and pushed just enough to tilt it upward.

Her eyes widened as their gazes locked.

"Sometimes what you do scares me, but not in the way you're thinking. I'm afraid for you...not of you. Do you understand?"

She nodded.

"So let's go make that call, and remember, no matter what they say, I'm behind you all the way."

"Ah, Justin…"

He saw it on her face, but he wanted to hear it from her lips.

"Say it, baby. Say what's on your heart."

"I didn't think I would ever find a man like you."

"What kind of a man is that?" he asked.

Saying the words was as frightening as anything she'd ever said before, but she could no more deny her heart than she could have quit breathing.

"A man I could love."

Justin sighed as he slid his arms around her waist.

"And am I that man?"

"You know you are."

"Then say it," he urged. "I need to hear it."

"I love you, Justin. So much."

Emotion swelled within him, making his answer much harder to say than he'd intended.

"You'd better," he said gruffly. "Because I'm so connected to you that I'm discovering I don't know how to function without you."

She smiled. "I don't have anything to do with that."

"It wasn't a complaint. It's just overwhelming, that's all."

"I know. For me, too," she said, and took him by the hand. "Now, let's go make that call."

Marie was off the phone when they got downstairs.

"Tula's comin' right over with a tisane. It'll make you feel better, baby girl."

"What's a tisane?" Laurel asked.

"Sort of a cobbled-up assortment of herbs that'll make you feel better."

"Well, okay," Laurel said. "But it better not taste bad."

Marie rolled her eyes.

"It's tea. You'll drink it and like it."

Laurel managed a grin.

"Yes, ma'am."

"Go make your call," Marie said. "I'll tell you when she gets here."

# 16

For the first few minutes out on the highway, Trigger drove like a man gone crazy, weaving in and around traffic, trying to put as much distance between himself and the gas station as possible. He kept glancing in the rearview mirror, afraid that he would see a highway patrol car on his tail, but when the miles passed and it didn't happen, he began to realize that if he got stopped by the highway patrol, it would be for speeding and not kidnapping, so he slowed down.

Scanlon had bled all over the front seat of his rental, but that didn't concern him as much as the fact that the man was still unconscious. This shouldn't have happened. If he'd left well enough alone and kept driving, then followed Scanlon like he'd planned to do, he wouldn't be in this fix. But he hadn't, and now he had a whole new set of problems. He needed to talk to McNamara, and he needed a fix. He cursed the man for miles because he had not called. The fact that he was in prison was not an excuse. All prisoners were allowed phone time.

A short while later, he realized he was approaching another small town, which meant he was going to have to slow down. The last thing he needed was to get caught in some local cop's speed trap.

He glanced at Scanlon, grimacing at the blood all

over the man's face and hair, as well as down the front of his clothes, and knew it would be a miracle if he got through the town without being seen and stopped.

That led to a panic he didn't know how to control. The easy way out would just be to get off the main road, finish Scanlon off and bury the body. But he didn't have a shovel and wasn't sure how Scanlon's death would play out for McNamara. If Scanlon was gone, they would have to assign another prosecutor to the case, and then McNamara would demand that Trigger get involved even deeper to make things go his way. He even thought about turning his gun on himself, but he was too big a coward to linger long on the thought. He wanted to live, but to do that unfettered, he still had a loose end to tie up. Scanlon had been talking to his daughter when he'd gotten suspicious, which meant he'd probably told her who'd given him the ride. And that meant that when Robert Scanlon went missing, the first person they were going to want to talk to was the last person to see him alive. Since that wasn't an option Trigger wanted to consider, now he really needed to find Scanlon's daughter, but not to put her on ice, as McNamara had suggested. He needed to shut her up permanently, so she couldn't report where her father had been—and with whom—and hope that the new SOB that took McNamara's case was more willing to deal than Scanlon had been.

As he continued to drive, he noticed a small cemetery up ahead on his side of the highway. Like all cemeteries in Louisiana, there were tombs and crypts of all sizes and shapes in which to leave the dead. With the land being prone to flooding and at sea level or below in most areas, coffins had a tendency to float up from the ground, never staying where they were planted. To alleviate that problem, centuries ago people had begun leaving their dead in what amounted to small houses above the ground.

It occurred to him then that it was the perfect place to hide Robert Scanlon. He wasn't dead yet, but this would be as good a place as any to let it happen. The authorities damn sure wouldn't think to look for his body in a place like this.

Confident, for once, that he was doing the right thing, he drove through the open gates of the cemetery and took one of the small, narrow roads toward the back fence. He drove slowly, as if looking for a loved one's final resting place, when in fact he was constantly looking into his rearview mirror for the moment when he could no longer be seen by traffic on the highway.

A large clump of willows grew on the northwest corner of an area near the fence, right beside two matching crypts with a large concrete angel standing between them its arms outspread. Trigger tapped the brakes, glanced in the mirror and smiled. He couldn't see the highway, which meant that no one could see him.

He stopped, then killed the engine and got out. A quick reconnoiter of the crypts revealed that both doors had been sealed, but a tire iron from the trunk of the car proved just the right tool for prying.

The ground was hard and dry, the grass thin and wispy, due to the shade of the trees and obvious lack of rain. It seemed impossible to believe that anything buried beneath ground this hard would come up like a bad meal, but he knew for a fact that it did. With one quick glance around to make sure he was still unobserved, he headed for the crypts.

A half hour later, with blisters on his palms and skinned knuckles on both hands, he'd managed to get the door open and was dragging Scanlon's limp body inside.

The air inside the old crypt had been stale and all but nonexistent until the door had opened. Now the heat of the day and the constant buzz of cicadas and other insects intruded upon the inner sanctum of George Henry Gooden's final resting place.

Trigger dumped Scanlon and his personal belongings against the concrete pedestal upon which George Henry's coffin had been laid to rest and moved toward the door without looking back. Even though he didn't believe in ghosts, the place gave him the creeps.

He stepped outside, then tried to pull the door shut. As he did, dust shifted on the floor, lightly coating Robert Scanlon's shoes and the legs of his pants. When the movement of the door suddenly stalled, it felt as if an unseen hand had caused it to stop. Trigger's heart skipped a beat. Then he saw the small rock that had gotten wedged beneath the door and laughed nervously at himself, kicked it aside and finished his task.

The door swung shut with a solid thump, and as it did, something clicked. Trigger tested the door by giving it a strong push, and when it didn't budge, he began to grin.

He'd done it. By God, he'd done it. He looked around again, just to make sure he was still undetected, then tossed his tools back into the SUV. When he slid into the driver's seat, he was reminded that his job wasn't quite finished. There was blood on the seat that had to be removed. Luckily, the upholstery was leather, so in lieu of water, he used a bottle of his after-shave and one of his undershirts to clean it off. After tossing the undershirt across the fence into the neighboring pasture, he got into the car. The scent of after-shave was everywhere, sickening in its intensity, and he was forced to drive for some distance with the windows down.

By the time he got to Bayou Jean, it was nearing twilight. He stopped for gas and something cold to drink, and began a conversation with one of the locals, intent on finding the location of Mimosa Grove. The sooner he finished what he'd come to do, the sooner his life was going to be back on track.

He smiled at a couple of kids who were riding by on their bicycles, then began washing his windshield with the squeegee furnished by the station. As he was moving to the passenger side, a young woman in a vintage Mustang pulled up to the pumps and got out.

"Nice car," Trigger said.

She tugged at the hem of her T-shirt and flashed him a grin.

"It belonged to my daddy when he was young. He gave it to me for my seventeenth birthday."

"What a great dad," Trigger said. "You're a very lucky lady."

"Yeah, I guess," she said, and began pumping gas in her own vehicle. "You done with that?" she asked, pointing to the dripping squeegee dangling from Trigger's fingers.

"Oh! Yeah. Forgot I had it," he said, then handed it to her and smiled, as if it was a joke on him. "I've been driving so long I'm punchy," he said. "Don't suppose there are any bed-and-breakfast places around here? I was checking online before I left California. I think I remember a place called Mimosa Grove in this area. Do you know it?''

She laughed out loud. ''Mister, everyone around here knows that place, and trust me, it's not any bed-and-breakfast.''

''Are you sure? I could have sworn—''

''Yeah, but you don't have to take my word for it. Go see for yourself. Take the highway south out of town five miles. You can't miss it. You'll know you're there when you start seeing all those creepy mimosa trees. The old house is just up the drive, but you're not gonna find a place to stay there.''

''Hmm, I was certain that was the name, but I could be wrong.''

''You're wrong, all right,'' she said. ''The only thing moving around there are ghosts and voodoo.''

He frowned. ''I don't believe in that stuff.''

She winked. ''If you go out there, you will,'' she promised, then returned the nozzle to the pump, tossed the squeegee into the bucket of dirty water and sauntered into the station to pay for her gas.

Trigger was still watching as she drove off without looking back, but for once, he didn't care that he hadn't scored. He'd gotten the information he needed. He paid for his gas, then headed out of town. His pulse accelerated as he thought of what was to come. Before the night was over, he would be in the clear.

Laurel sat curled up in an old overstuffed chair near the front window, staring blindly out onto the grounds. Her hair was in tangles where she'd run her hands through it over and over, and her white T-shirt and seersucker shorts were crumpled from having slept in them.

She'd called her father's office and spoken directly to Clausing, his boss. Clausing's reaction had been about what she'd expected. He'd chided her for claiming "psychic" abilities had led her to believe her father was in danger. Then she'd tossed out the name DeLane, and he'd stopped laughing. Accusing a four-star general of kidnapping and treason was crazy, but nothing to ignore. He'd said he would check it out. Now she had no recourse but to wait.

Light was fading, sending long blue shadows creeping toward the fishpond near the road. Parrots and cockatoos were coming home to roost. A pair of barn swallows kept flying through the air in long, graceful swoops, snagging mosquitoes in flight as they skimmed close to the ground.

Outwardly, it was an idyllic setting, but Laurel knew better. She'd learned the hard way that there was no such thing as peace on earth. Not when the evil men practiced spilled over onto the innocent. Her father was either dead or dying. She could feel it, but she didn't know where he was. It wasn't fair. All the times she'd been able to help others, and the one time she needed it to help herself, her powers wouldn't work. She needed a connection—something of her father's or some place he'd recently been. She kept going over and over her last conversation with him, hearing him say that he'd had car trouble, knowing when he'd told her that someone who was not a stranger had given him a ride, and certain that whoever it was, was going to do him harm. He'd told her DeLane's name, but he hadn't told her where he was, and she didn't know where to start looking.

Then Justin walked in, carrying a cup.

"Tula's come and gone, but she left your tea. Said for you to drink it slow."

He handed her the cup, and she took it without speaking, then had a first sip. It wasn't as bad as she'd expected, so she continued to drink until it was all gone.

As soon as she set the cup aside, she felt Justin's hand on the back of her head. She looked up, saw the concern on his face and dissolved into tears as he held her in his arms.

"He's dying," she said. "I can feel it, but I don't know where he is."

"What can I do? Tell me and I'll make it happen," he said.

Her arms were around his neck, her fingers clutching the fabric of his shirt as if he was all that was keeping her upright. Her voice was shaking, and she felt sick to her stomach.

"Oh, Justin…God…just tell me this is all a bad dream."

He hurt for her in so many ways and would have done anything to keep her from harm. But this was something completely out of his experience.

"Honey…I would tell you anything if it would make this better, but I don't know what to say."

"I know, I know," she muttered, then hid her face in the curve of his neck. "I'm losing control, and that can't happen."

She pulled herself out of his arms, then swiped angrily at the tears on her face.

"Damn this helplessness!" she shouted, and stormed out onto the veranda.

The suddenness of her arrival sent a pair of roosting

peacocks into a frenzy. Their squawks and shrieks were echoes of the way she felt inside, but if she started screaming, she might never stop. She strode down the steps and started walking with no destination in mind, unaware that Justin was only a step behind.

He caught her before she got far, then spun her around and into his arms. His breath was warm on her face, his grip firm as he held her close.

"Stop it," he said.

She struggled to get free.

"Damn it, Laurel. Stop it! Where the hell do you think you're going?"

"Crazy! I'm going crazy!" she yelled. "Just like my mother!" Then she went limp in his arms. The anger was gone as suddenly as it had come, leaving her weak. She looked up at Justin, ashamed that he'd seen her like this. "Just like my mother," she echoed softly, and let him hold her as night crept onto the land, swallowing the shadows and hiding everything, both good and bad, within the darkness.

Finally Justin picked her up in his arms. Her head lolled against his shoulder, but she didn't fight him. She couldn't feel her father within her anymore. At that point, hope died.

Justin carried her inside as lights from the hunters' lanterns danced intermittently through the trees. They were looking for the trespassing panther she'd heard earlier in the day. Somehow, it didn't seem right that man was willing to hunt a four-legged enemy quicker than a two-legged one.

Attorney General Andrew Clausing was sick to his stomach but with no time to throw up. Interrogating a four-star general in his own home had been daunting, but he was up to the job. He hadn't, however, expected to see someone of John Franklin DeLane's integrity crumple like yesterday's newspaper. But after a search of the house that had revealed bank accounts and trips out of the country coinciding with large deposits into a bank account in the Cayman Islands, it hadn't been the general who'd come up guilty. It had been the son.

DeLane's culpability had been by blood alone, and he had been willing to take the blame for his son's treason until his wife had slapped him square in the face and told him that it was high time their son took the blame for the messes he continued to make. Listening to her recount all the times that they'd paid off injured parties for their son's misdeeds had made Clausing thankful he'd never taken the time to become a parent.

He left without any answers as to where Trigger DeLane was, but certain that the son had just ruined his father's career, then he amended the thought. DeLane had ruined his own career by pandering to a weak and spoiled son. It was a shame, but truth often hurt.

He drove away, leaving the authorities in charge of gathering evidence to reopen the case. McNamara might be dead, but Gerald Dupont DeLane, nicknamed Trigger for the quick temper he'd had as a child, was about to get a lifelong wish fulfilled in a way he'd never imagined. He'd wanted to be famous, not infamous—but as he would learn, beggars can't be choosers. Before this mess was cleaned up, the name DeLane would be on everyone's lips. Now Clausing needed to call a woman about an apology and hope it wasn't too late to help her find her father, after all.

He called his office.

"Elaine, do we still have a number to reach Laurel Scanlon?"

"Yes, sir."

"Give it to me," he said, then jotted down the number as she read it off. "Okay, thanks. I'm on my way back to the office. Have Gabe Clancy meet me there. I think we've got a kidnapping on our hands, and I want the best agent the FBI has to offer."

"Yes, sir. Anything else?"

He sighed. "Have you ever eaten crow?"

"Sir?"

"Nothing," he muttered. "Just delaying the inevitable."

He hung up, started the car so that the air-conditioning would be running, then made the call.

Supper had been a quiet affair. Justin had coaxed Laurel to eat, succeeding only because he'd reminded her how hard Marie had worked all day to fix the meal. And strangely enough, it had tasted good. Laurel thought that maybe it had something to do with the company at the table. Marie had slipped into the role of caretaker for Laurel as easily as she'd done it all those years for her grandmother, and Justin was more than the man who warmed her bed. He loved her. She knew, because she felt it in his touch, even heard it in his voice. And because of them, she took an odd sort of comfort from knowing that, if they couldn't find her father, she was not going to be alone in the world.

Justin and Laurel were clearing the table while Marie made coffee to go with dessert when, once again, the telephone rang.

The trio froze, a study in solemn patience, waiting to see who was brave enough to face what could only be bad news.

Justin was the first to move, but it was Laurel who stayed him with a touch of her hand.

"I'll get it," she said. "You help Marie."

"Honey, let me—"

"I've let you do enough already," she said. "I've got to face my own troubles. You're here. It's enough."

He relented but kept a wary eye on her as she moved toward the phone.

It was on the third ring when Laurel picked up the receiver.

"Hello?"

Robert regained consciousness in darkness—or at least he thought he'd come to. There was always the possibility that he had died and gone to hell, but there was enough pain in trying to think and breathe at the same time to make him think he was still among the living. He tried to move, but when he did, pain shot through his head so fast that lights went off behind his eyelids. He groaned, and the sound had an odd sort of echo. He tried to roll over but found himself wedged up against what felt like a concrete wall. So he rolled the other way and took solace in the movement, small though it might be.

Slowly, slowly, he felt his head, groaning again when he felt the knot in his hair. His fingers came away wet and sticky, and when he held them to his nose, he smelled the coppery scent of fresh blood.

He tried to think what the hell had happened and remembered talking to Laurel, hearing her frantic warning not to get in the car and ignoring it as nothing than more psychic garbage until she'd said McNamara's name. Until he'd heard her shouting that the man who'd picked him up was connected to McNamara. He remembered looking out the windshield and locking gazes with DeLane, seeing the panic come over the man's face and knowing she was right, and that he'd left it too late to get away.

He knew that Trigger DeLane had been in D.C. looking for Laurel. And when he himself left for Louisiana, Trigger must have followed, using him to get to her. Robert groaned. If Laurel fell into their hands, then he was screwed. He would make a deal with the devil himself to keep his daughter safe, and McNamara knew it. He tried to sit up, but the world started to spin. He needed to get out, to warn Laurel that her life was in danger, but he was too hurt to move. He fell back onto the floor, trying to think, but the pain was too great, and he felt himself going under.

Time passed. He didn't know how long he'd been there, but when he came to again, it was still dark and he still hurt. Only something was different. It took him a few moments to figure out what it was, and when he did, his heartbeat skipped, then picked up a new rhythm. The air felt different—as if it had a bad taste. He was running out of oxygen.

A film of sweat broke out on his skin as he rolled over on his belly and began to crawl, hoping he could find a way out of whatever hellhole DeLane had put him in.

Within moments, he'd crawled into a wall. He felt one of his shoes fall off, but he didn't stop. Determined not to quit, he moved to his right and continued to crawl, using his hands and elbows for leverage as he tried to pull himself up to his knees. But as soon as his belly left the floor, he passed out.

Dirt was in his mouth when he came to again. Remembering what had happened the last time he'd tried to get up, he settled for the belly crawl on the off chance that if it happened again, he wouldn't have far to fall. He kept thinking about Laurel. McNamara had warned him, but Robert had been so determined to play out the hand his own way that he'd put Laurel in harm's way.

As he was cursing himself, he came up against another wall. Frowning, he realized that this was the second wall he'd come to within a very short distance. Using his fingers as eyes, he felt along the floor, found where the wall and floor met, then followed it further. Again he hit a corner and again he continued to crawl. But when his hand landed on what was obviously his shoe, he rocked backward, staggered by the knowledge that in this very short space of time, he'd made a complete circle.

Now he knew there was nothing around the perimeter of his prison, but he wondered what lay between the walls. Uncertain what he might find but afraid not to try, he backed himself into a corner, took a moment to orient himself to move what felt like forward, then started to crawl.

Within seconds, he'd come to an obstacle. Like the walls, it was concrete, but with some sort of decorations. He traced the base of it with his fingertips, felt different shapes in relief, but couldn't tell what they were. By the time he'd crawled around the entire base, his breathing was labored and the pain in his head was once more hammering against his scalp. Fearing that he would pass out again, he stopped, lowered his head and waited for the feeling to pass.

When it did, he reached up. Almost immediately, his fingers landed on what felt like cool metal. He gripped it fiercely, using it as leverage to pull himself upright.

Immediately the world started to spin, and he leaned forward, bracing himself against the object to which the metal was fastened. He stood like that for several minutes until his head began to clear and he could steady himself, taking great care to temper the length of his breaths.

He began to run his hands around and over the object against which he'd been leaning. Time passed; then, as he was tracing the shape for what seemed like the hundredth time, it dawned on him what this was.

It was a casket.

He was leaning on a casket.

Knowing that, and knowing he was most likely still in Louisiana, where they did not bury their dead below ground, he deduced that he had to be in a crypt.

He took a frightened step backward, as if being locked in with the dead could somehow hasten his own demise. It took a few moments for his heart to stop pounding and his hands to quit shaking.

Now he knew why the air was running out. Crypts were built to be airtight. The dead certainly didn't need to breathe. He moved once again toward the walls, ignoring the dizziness in his brain and trying frantically to find the door. There had to be a door. There was always a door. DeLane put him in here.

He could get out the same way. All he had to do was find it.

But the seal was tight, and even after he'd found what felt like hinges, there was no handle inside. Frantic, he cursed the men who would design a building, no matter what the intended use, and not leave an exit. It took him a few minutes of anger and grief to realize that in a crypt, there was also no one inside who needed to get out.

At that point his legs gave way and he slid to the floor with a thump. His head rocked back against the wall, reopening the wound and rendering him unconscious once more.

From time to time afterward, he came to just long enough to feel like he was slowly being strangled. The last time he woke up, he began taking off his jacket, then his shirt, in a crazy effort to relieve his body of any and all weight, hoping that it would extend his life for one second more.

As he tossed his jacket aside, he heard something bang against the floor. Frowning, he reached for the jacket but found only air. He rolled over on his side, extending his arms outward as he felt along the floor for the clothing that he'd tossed. Finally he found the jacket, and he ran his hands along the pockets, curious as to what he'd heard. It was then that he realized he was holding his phone.

God in heaven! Why hadn't he thought of it before? But when his head started to hammer again, he answered his own question. Logic had been impossible through such pain.

He felt along the face of the phone, trying to picture the layout of the buttons, then made himself relax. He laid the phone down by his fingers, slowed his breathing even more, then picked it back up. Without thinking, his finger automatically hit the redial button. He listened to the numbers clicking in, praying that the battery would hold out and he could get a signal.

He caught himself struggling for breath as the phone began to ring. It rang once, then twice, and when it began the third ring, he laid his head on his arm and slowly closed his eyes.

Then he heard his daughter's voice, and he wanted to cry. He tried to say hello—anything that would constitute an answer. He tried so hard but could manage nothing but a faint gasp. His fingers went limp. The phone was lying in his palm, and through what sounded like a tunnel, he could hear Laurel screaming his name.

He needed to tell her that he loved her, and that all these years he'd been so wrong about her mother and her, but it was going to be too late.

Laurel was still clutching the phone, listening to nothing but silence, and then what sounded like a sigh. Almost instantly, her stomach knotted.

"Daddy! Is that you?"

Justin spun and ran out of the room, heading for an extension in the library as Marie moved toward Laurel.

Laurel's knuckles were turning white from her grip on the phone. She was pressing the receiver so hard against her ear that it was actually painful, and still she could hear nothing but the faint sounds of labored breathing.

"Daddy! Daddy! Whatever you do, don't hang

up,'' she begged. "If you can't speak, it's okay. Just don't hang up.''

She closed her eyes, using the tenuous connection as the only link she was likely to get.

Almost instantly, she flashed on panic, then blood. Blood running down his face and onto the front of his shirt. She saw hands pushing her father into a car. She saw the back of the car as it was driving away.

"Louisiana rental LA 4122,'' she muttered.

Justin was on the other line, and the moment the words came out of her mouth, he picked up a pen and began to write down everything she said.

Trees and sky passed by in a blur of blue and green, and Laurel knew that her father was not where he'd been when he called.

"Daddy…can you hear me? Put the phone to your ear. Say something, Daddy. Anything…just keep breathing.''

Robert heard her, but the effort it took to move was almost more than he had in him. Still, unwilling to break the only connection he had left and knowing her voice would be the last thing he would hear on this earth, he wrapped his fingers around the phone and held on with what life he had in him.

Laurel swayed. Marie caught her where she stood, then dragged a kitchen chair beneath her legs and pushed. Laurel sat down with a thump. Almost instantly, she saw a cemetery and all sizes and shapes of crypts. Some concrete, even one or two that appeared to be of some sort of granite.

"Cemetery…trees…off the highway. Moving, still moving. I see an angel standing between two crypts. His arms are reaching toward me. Daddy…Daddy. Talk to me, damn it! You can't die! Don't you dare!''

Robert jerked. The shout pulled him up from the depths into which he'd been sinking. Before he knew it, he'd rolled over onto his side, and when he did, he felt a tiny bit of difference in the temperature on his face. It took a few moments for the reason to sink in, and when it did, he wasn't sure that he had enough energy left to make it worth his while. He could still hear his daughter's voice, and he followed it, using his fingers as a guide, until he realized he was touching one of the corners in the wall.

He dug into it with his fingernails, and as he did, he felt a faint stirring of heat against his skin. Heat meant air, and air meant life. He dug harder, and he felt a tiny bit of concrete crumble. He thrust his fingers into the crack. Concrete came away in small chunks. Whatever time and weather had done to the body inside his casket, it had done to the crypt as well.

In a short time there was a large-enough crack in that corner that Robert could put his thumb through. With his last ounces of strength, he pulled himself forward, laid his cheek against the floor as close to the crack as he could get and inhaled.

It was dusty and rank and smelled hotter than the insides of hell, but it was air, and better than what was left inside some stranger's final resting place. He took another breath, then another and another, until enough oxygen had filtered through his brain that he trusted himself to speak.

The phone was still in his other hand. He lifted it to his ear, making himself focus when it would have been far easier just to sleep, and heard his daughter screaming his name.

"Laurel."

Her name on his lips was like music from the angels. She pressed her fingers against her mouth to keep from crying and then made herself focus.

"Daddy. I see things...but nothing specific that will help us find you. Do you know where you are?"

"In a crypt."

"Oh, God...oh, God," she muttered, then made herself calm down. "Do you know where it is? Are you close to a town or a city? Did you see a name on any road signs?"

"I told you everything I know," he mumbled, then tried to laugh. It sounded more like a sob, but she wouldn't let herself think of what that would mean. "I don't know where I am." Then he added as an afterthought, "There's a casket in here."

Laurel closed her eyes. "Touch something, Daddy. Touch the walls. Touch the casket. I need something to lock onto."

He tried another laugh. "This is crazy."

"Humor me," she begged. "Where are you?"

"Lying on the floor. Running out of air."

Fear shattered her concentration. It was a sharp shake from Marie that made her focus again.

"Touch the walls, Daddy. Do it for me."

He sighed, then opened his hand. The wall was damp and slightly cool, reminding him of how desperately he wanted a drink of water, but he did as he'd been told.

Almost immediately, Laurel saw twin crypts and again the angel with hands reaching toward her. Then the vision suddenly narrowed, and she saw the door of a crypt, then a name carved in stone above it.

"George Henry Gooden—1904-1980."

* * *

Justin scribbled the name, yanked his cell phone out of his pocket and called Harper Fonteneau.

"Harper! Don't ask me why, but can you find the final resting place for a man named George Henry Gooden? Born 1904. Died 1980."

"Yes."

"Then do it! As fast as you can. It's worth a man's life. Call me back at this number." He rattled off his cell phone number, then disconnected.

Laurel was still talking to her father, but his side of the conversation was starting to break up as the battery in his phone started to go dead.

He could hear a faint beep against his ear and knew what it meant. His tenuous connection with her was almost over.

"It's not your fault," he said hoarsely.

"Daddy...don't die. Please don't die. I'm sorry for all the fights we've had. I'm sorry for everything that made you unhappy. Just please don't die."

His answer faded with the weakening battery, leaving her with only half the truth.

"...love...not your...sorry, too. You're...danger. Tell Clausing...Trigger..."

The line went dead. Her connection with her father was gone.

The phone slid out of her grasp, dangling from the cord against the wall as she buried her face in her hands.

Marie laid a hand on the back of Laurel's head.

"I'm sorry, baby girl."

Laurel turned around and buried her face against the old woman's breasts. Marie hung up the phone, then wrapped her arms around Laurel and held her close.

Justin came running into the kitchen.

"We're not out of this yet," he said, and laid his cell phone on the table, then put his arms around them both. "Don't give up, honey. Not yet."

As always after a vision, Laurel felt herself weakening. She needed to sleep but was afraid that if she did, she would wake up to find herself having to plan a funeral.

"Help me," she begged, and with their help, she managed to stand.

She staggered to the kitchen door, then opened it and walked out onto the back porch. Almost immediately, she saw the occasional flash of light moving through the grove.

"What's that?" she said, pointing toward the trees.

Marie put a hand on her back.

"That's the men huntin' for the painter."

"In the dark?" Laurel asked.

"That's when the big cats hunt. The men…they playin' on the painter's turf, so they have to do as he does."

Laurel shuddered. "I never knew life could be so…so…visceral. It wasn't like this in D.C."

Marie sighed, gave Justin a worried look and went back into the house.

Justin hated the sound in Laurel's voice and feared that she was pulling away from him and the land that he loved. He put his arms around her, then held her close, resting his chin at the crown of her head and feeling the weight of her breasts against his wrists.

"Are you sorry?" he whispered.

"For what?"

"For coming to Mimosa Grove?"

"No."

"You need to know that I would die to keep you happy."

Laurel turned in his arms and then realized true night had come when she couldn't see the features of his face. She reached up, taking comfort in the shape of him beneath her palms.

"And you need to know that your death would break my heart, so don't waste the gesture."

"Something your father said..."

"What?"

"Something about you being in danger."

Laurel frowned. In the heat of the moment, she'd let that go over her head, but now that he'd reminded her, she remembered.

"Yes, he did, didn't he?"

"From the man who kidnapped him?"

"I guess so."

"He said something about a trigger. Do you think he was talking about a gun?"

And in that moment, she knew.

Before, her father had said to tell them it was DeLane. And all the while she'd thought he was talking about the general who sat on the President's cabinet. But it wasn't him. It was his son, Trigger. She vaguely remembered seeing the blond playboy at various parties over the years but hadn't given him a thought. Now she realized she'd better think twice.

"It wasn't a gun. It was a man. His name is Trigger DeLane, and somehow he's connected to McNamara, the man my father's prosecuting for treason."

"Then you could be in danger," Justin said.

"Maybe," Laurel said. "I don't know why."

"I do," Justin said. "Think about it. If he knows you, then he knows what you can do. Your father was talking to you when your call was cut short, right?"

She nodded.

"Then it stands to reason that the man who took your father might believe you know his identity, if for no other reason than your second sight. Obviously, wherever he left your father, he intended for him to die. So it follows he'll want to get rid of anyone else who could still identify him."

Laurel turned, then stared out into the darkness.

"Come inside," Justin urged.

She followed without hesitation.

# 17

Within seconds after Justin reentered the house, a phone began to ring, but it wasn't the residence phone. He hurried toward the table where he'd left his cell.

"Harper?"

"Yeah, it's me," Harper said. "I got your information. The man is buried in a small cemetery near St. Lorraine."

Justin groaned. "That's nearly an hour's drive from here. We don't have that kind of time."

"Yeah, I gathered that from what you were saying," Harper said. "I've got the parish police from St. Lorraine on hold on the other line. What do you want me to tell them?"

"Just a second," Justin said, and ran from the kitchen to the library, where he'd written down the information. "Here it is," he said. "Tell them someone kidnapped Laurel's father, Robert Scanlon. It's too complicated to explain right now, but we think he's in their local cemetery and locked inside one of the smaller mausoleums. Laurel said to look for two identical crypts standing side by side with an angel between them. The angel's arms are reaching forward. Scanlon will be in the one that has George Henry Gooden's name above the door."

"Holy Moses," Harper muttered. "What's going on out there?"

"Just tell them to hurry and, Harper, call us the moment you hear anything more."

"You got it," Harper said.

Justin disconnected, then realized Laurel was standing beside him. She'd learned to mask her feelings so well over the years that he couldn't tell what she was thinking. Then she spoke, and he heard the tremble in her voice.

"Justin…please tell me something good."

"Gooden was buried in a small cemetery outside St. Lorraine, which is about an hour's drive from here. Harper had the local authorities on the other phone waiting for instructions. They can be there within a matter of minutes. I gave them the directions. If he's there, they'll find him."

"Oh, Lord," she muttered, and covered her face with her hands.

"It's going to be all right," Justin said, and took her in his arms. But as he held her, he wasn't so sure that he hadn't told her a lie. After everything that had happened, he didn't see how anything could ever be all right again.

And then, once again, the phone began to ring, but this time it was the phone at Mimosa Grove.

Laurel turned away from the sound and put her hands over her ears.

Justin reached for the receiver and picked it up.

"Mimosa Grove."

"This is Attorney General Andrew Clausing. I need to speak to Laurel Scanlon."

"One moment, please," he said, and handed Laurel the phone. "It's Clausing."

After the way he'd dismissed her before, she was in no mood to talk to him again. She was frowning as she took the phone.

"Yes?"

Clausing sighed. The distance in her voice was unmistakable.

"Miss Scanlon, I just called to apologize and to tell you that your father was right. We have issued a federal arrest warrant for Gerald Dupont DeLane, aka Trigger DeLane, for charges of treason against the United States of America, as well as conspiracy to commit treason."

"You can add kidnapping and attempted murder to that," she said shortly. "And if my father does not survive until the arrival of the St. Lorraine authorities at the burial vault where DeLane left him, then you can amend that to murder."

Clausing sat down.

"What?"

"You heard me," Laurel said. "I told you he'd been kidnapped. I told you he was in danger."

"Where—"

"If you have any further questions regarding what happened to my father, contact the parish police here in Bayou Jean. The man in charge is Harper Fonteneau. Or you can call the parish police in St. Lorraine, Louisiana. They're in the act of recovering my father...or what's left of him."

"But how—"

"We have nothing to say to each other," Laurel said, and handed Justin the phone.

"She might be through with you, but I'm not," Justin said. "One of the last things Robert Scanlon said was that Laurel was in danger. So I'm giving you fair warning. If anything happens to her because of your reluctance to react or any kind of negligence on behalf of the federal government, I will drag you and everyone connected with you through the dirt in front of every media outlet in the Northern Hemisphere. Do I make myself clear?''

Clausing's face paled as his fingers tightened around the phone. ''Yes.''

''Do you know where Mimosa Grove is located?''

''No, but I can—''

''Five miles south of Bayou Jean, Louisiana. Make yourself known upon your arrival or you're liable to be shot on sight for trespassing.''

The phone went dead in Clausing's ear. He stared at the receiver, then slowly laid it back on the cradle and took a deep breath. The clock on the wall opposite his desk began to strike the hour. He looked up in disbelief. It was almost nine. He looked out the window. It was dark.

''Eileen?''

His secretary appeared in the doorway.

''Why are you still here?'' he mumbled.

''Because you are, sir. Is there anything you need?''

''Yes. Get Gabe Clancy on the phone. I don't care where he is or what he's doing. We need to talk.''

Robert Scanlon came to just long enough to realize something was crawling on his face. He swiped it away and then shuddered, trying not to think what it might have been. His lungs felt heavy, as if someone was sitting on his chest.

He shifted slightly, then rolled over, feeling the roughness of the floor against his bare belly as he pressed his nose toward the crack in the wall, then took a small breath. Before, he'd taken the act of breathing for granted, but never again. He'd never realized that air could be tasted as well as smelled, but he knew it now. He lay without moving, savoring the faint scent of night that had come to the land, and thought about his life. He'd always heard that when a man was near death, his life would pass before his eyes, but since his death was taking longer than usual, he had more time than one might expect to contemplate his failures.

At the thought, he wondered what a psychiatrist would make of the fact that the first thing to come to his mind had been his failures, rather than his successes. He supposed it might be construed as not having enough successes to contemplate. Lord only knew how many mistakes he had made. His marriage had been a mistake. Then he edited the thought. It hadn't been the marriage so much as the way they'd behaved. That had been the mistake, and both he and Phoebe were to blame. Looking back over her behavior, he knew that if it had happened now instead of almost thirty years ago, her condition could have been treated. Even after she'd started blaming her psychic abilities on her inability to cope, he'd gone along with the notion because it seemed to give her some sense of relief. But it wasn't true, and to his shame, he'd never told any of the family, not even Laurel, the truth. Phoebe hadn't killed herself because she couldn't bear the trauma of what she claimed she "saw" during psychic episodes. She was manic-depressive and had killed herself during one of her downswings. If he didn't die in this mess, he was going to tell Laurel the truth. He owed that much to her, and more.

He lay for a few minutes with his nose to the crack, breathing and thinking how loud true quiet really was. He could hear his heartbeat, the sound of his breath. Even the sound of time ticking away seemed real, although he knew that was a crazy claim to make.

He wondered if the lack of oxygen was making his brain turn to mush, then supposed it was possible. If it was true, unless someone rescued him soon, it wouldn't matter. If heaven was all it was cracked up to be, then God wouldn't care what his earthly condition had been. It was Robert's immortal soul that would be His concern.

Something was digging into his right leg near the knee. He shifted his position enough to alleviate the pain, then realized it hadn't helped. At that point, he couldn't really determine where the pain began. All he knew was that he hurt all over. And that he was sorry he was going to die before he got a chance to tell Laurel he loved her.

Tears came suddenly, followed by harsh, choking sobs. He wanted to curl up and weep for all the wasted years, but if he moved, he would not be able to breathe. So he cried, anyway, with his face against the wall and his fingers curled into fists, and thought of his mother and father, who'd been gone for years, and a childhood friend who died from polio when he was seven.

Two cars from the St. Lorraine police department were running lights and sirens as they sped out of town. The fire-rescue unit was behind them, as was the police chief in his private car. It was the largest display of local authority that had been seen since an eighteen-wheeler hauling for the Townsend pig farm had picked up a load of weanlings, then gone off the Fourche Maline bridge, dumping upwards of seven hundred just-weaned pigs into the river. It was the first time some had ever seen pigs swim, while others claimed little pigs were climbing up on shore for days all along the river. And since there were a good number of wild pig herds in the area, most decided there was more truth to the story than fiction.

But this time the deputies in the lead were less certain of the emergency. They had orders to drive out to the cemetery and pop the door on Old Man Gooden's crypt. It seemed like the worst possible thing to do to a man's final resting place, but orders were orders, and neither wanted to admit to the other that it gave them the creeps.

Marty grabbed hold of his seat belt and braced himself against the dash as Harvey drove headlong toward what felt like imminent disaster.

"Dang it all, Harvey, what is it we're doing out here again?"

Harvey took the curve in the road too high and felt the tires on the passenger side of the patrol car sliding off the pavement. He corrected the skid and accelerated, relishing the feel of speed and the sound of the siren blasting in his ears.

On the other hand, Marty was not a man who enjoyed confrontation and, from time to time, thought about following in his daddy's footsteps and joining the family funeral business. The only thing that kept him from pursuing it was the fact that he hated embalming dead people worse than he hated confrontation with the living.

"Somebody's supposed to have stashed a kidnap victim in Old Man Gooden's crypt. We're goin' to see if he's really in there."

"And if he's not, who's gonna tell Old Man Gooden we made a mistake?"

Harvey snorted. "You're scared, aren't you. Scared you'll find a ghost in there."

"No, I'm not scared. I just don't like bothering a man's final resting place, that's all."

"Look at it like this," Harvey said. "If the victim is in there, he'll be real glad we bothered."

"I guess," Marty said, and then pointed. "Slow down, Harvey. Up yonder is the gate."

Harvey tapped the brakes, took the turn off the highway too fast, hit the old wire gate that was put up every night at sunset and drove clean over it.

"You drove over the gate!" Marty yelled.

"So? It's not like anyone in here is gonna suddenly jump up and run out," Harvey said, and headed toward the back of the cemetery.

He knew where George Gooden was buried because he'd been a pallbearer at the man's funeral, but everything looked different in the dark.

"Look for two crypts with a big angel in between them," he told Marty.

Marty leaned forward, squinting as they flew past one marker after the next without seeing anything familiar. "You need to slow down some," he said.

"There they are!" Harvey shouted, and turned abruptly, then came to a halt, parking so that the headlights shone directly onto the door of George Gooden's final home.

"Get the tools out of the trunk," Harvey ordered,

ignoring the still-blasting siren as he started toward the crypt.

Marty grabbed a sledgehammer in one hand and a tire iron in the other, opting to leave the pickax behind unless they ran into trouble.

Harvey was already at the crypt and pushing on the door when Marty thrust the tire iron in his hand.

"Here! See if you can wedge it into the crack, then I'll drive it home with the hammer."

Harvey hesitated, then shoved the tire iron in Marty's hand and took away the hammer.

"Hell no. I'm not holding anything for you to hammer until you get your glasses back from Doc Bartlett."

"I can see fine," Marty argued.

"Good. Then you can watch me while I do the hammering."

Marty thrust the tire iron into the crack beside the decorative knob, then turned his head as Harvey drew the hammer back. The blow from the sledgehammer was hard enough to make his arms tingle, but he managed to hold on. Two more blows and the door gave way, almost as if someone—or something—had decided to let them in.

"Christ," Marty muttered, and took a sudden step back.

But Harvey had seen something that Marty could not. The headlights from the cruiser were aimed a little too far to the right to give him a perfect view, but there was still enough light to see the casket on the pedestal—and the body lying next to the wall.

"Tell the chief that he's in here," Harvey said. "And get the ambulance up here fast."

He grabbed his flashlight from his belt and strode through the door as Marty turned on his heel and ran.

Harvey barely gave George Gooden a glance as he hurried past, then went down on his knees near the wall. When he put his hand on the man's neck to test for a pulse, the skin felt clammy against his palm. He rolled him over on his back, uncertain what to expect.

"Mister! Mister! Can you hear me?" Harvey said.

Robert thought he was dreaming until someone moved him. At that point, he realized that either DeLane had come back or he'd been rescued after all.

He tested the air by taking a deep breath and almost cried when oxygen filled his lungs, then went rocketing through his system. Then he choked and spent several precious gasps trying to catch his breath before a normal breathing rhythm kicked in.

"I'll be damned," Harvey muttered when the man showed signs of life.

"Hurry up!" he shouted. "He's in a bad way."

Robert wanted to tell them they were wrong, that he'd been in a bad way before they came, but not now. Only he couldn't seem to remember how to breathe and talk at the same time. He figured that would come back to him with time.

When the man started to get up, Robert panicked. He couldn't—no, wouldn't—be left alone in here again. Not even if the door was still open. Not even if the entire 45th Infantry Division was standing guard outside the door to keep him safe. He grabbed Harvey's wrist and wouldn't let go.

"Stay," he begged.

Harvey rocked back on his heels, trying to imagine

the hell of being shut in here to die, and then reached down and patted the man's shoulder.

"I'm not going anywhere," he said. "I promise."

It wasn't until they had loaded Robert into the ambulance and were driving away that Harvey realized they'd left the door to George's crypt standing ajar.

"Do we have to go back?" Marty said. "Couldn't we at least leave it until daylight?"

"Damn it, Marty. Sometimes you sound too much like my old lady for my peace of mind. Can you honestly tell me that you could go to sleep tonight, knowing you'd left old George to fend for himself?"

Marty frowned. "There's not a feminine bone in my body," he muttered. "And Old Man Gooden was mean enough in life. I reckon his ghost can take care of hisself, too."

"We're going back," Harvey said. "And you can stay in the car while I shut the door."

Marty frowned but remained silent. When they drove back into the cemetery and then parked in front of the old tomb, he pretended to be looking at something out in the Marshalls' pasture that adjoined the cemetery lot.

"You might want to tell Doc Bartlett that you don't need those glasses of yours after all," Harvey said as he opened the door.

"What are you talking about?" Marty muttered.

Harvey grinned, then pointed off in the dark.

"There's no moon, and I can't see six inches in front of my face without the headlights of the car, but you seem to be enjoying the view at the Marshalls' just fine without benefit of either light or glasses. So, I figured you'd suddenly been healed of your vision affliction and—"

"Shut up, Harvey. Just shut the hell up and go close that door," Marty said, and sat back in the seat with his arms crossed across his chest and his chin thrust forward in a defiant gesture.

Harvey chuckled all the way to the old crypt. When he got to the door, he peered inside.

"Sorry for the interruption, George. Have a nice night."

Then he pulled hard at the door. When it started swinging toward him, he jumped back. When the old door hit the facing, something clicked, and once again, George Henry Gooden was left to his own company.

Laurel was standing near the kitchen phone when it began to ring. She grabbed it the second it made a sound.

"Hello?"

"Miss Scanlon, this is Harper Fonteneau. I thought you would like to know that they found your father. He's alive. They've got him in an ambulance at police headquarters in St. Lorraine, waiting for a Medivac chopper to pick him up and take him to the trauma center in New Orleans."

Her legs went weak with relief as she turned her face to the wall.

"His condition…is it serious? Is he in danger of—"

"All I know to tell you is he has a head wound and he's a bit out of it, but still fairly coherent when answering questions. They said he keeps repeating your name and telling you to hide. He says that you're in danger and not to leave the property until DeLane is arrested."

"Yes. All right," Laurel said, and then, reluctant to break the connection, added before the police chief could hang up, "Chief, thank you. Thank you for believing me enough to check out what I saw. Thank you for my father's life."

Harper cleared his throat and then smiled.

"You're welcome. As for believing you...well, you need to remember that us folks here in Bayou Jean had a lifetime with Miz Marcella before she passed. She broke the ground you stand on. So to speak."

"Yes, I guess she did," Laurel said. "Do you have the number of the hospital where they're taking my father?"

"Yep. Got a pen?"

She picked up the pad and pen that Marie used to make her grocery lists.

"I do now."

He gave her the address and phone number, then told her they would be out that way to check on her soon.

Laurel wrote quickly.

"Was that good news?" Justin asked. It was the first she'd noticed that he'd come into the room while she was talking to the police chief.

"They found Daddy," Laurel said. "He's alive and talking."

"Praise God," Marie said, and sat down in a chair as Justin took Laurel in his arms.

"You did good, love," he said softly.

Laurel put her arms around his neck and leaned into his embrace.

"Yes. I did, didn't I?" Then she added, "But I couldn't have done it without his help. Whether he believed me or not, he went along with what I asked him to do.''

''And it turned out all right.''

''Harper said he kept begging them to tell me I was in danger. He said that DeLane is coming for me.''

It was reflex that made Justin look over her shoulder to the windows and then beyond.

''He'll have to come through me to get here,'' he muttered, then turned so that he was between her and the windows and pulled her close against his chest.

Trigger was crouched down in the trees surrounding the back yard of the old mansion when a woman suddenly walked past the kitchen windows. He got a brief glimpse of her before she moved out of sight, but the red hair was unmistakable. It was Laurel Scanlon.

His first instinct was to get closer. There was no moon, and the night was dark enough to hide his presence. But just as he started to move, a man appeared at the windows and pulled the curtains, and then he could no longer see.

He cursed and stepped back, then leaned against a nearby tree trunk. He was hot and hungry, and every place on his body that was uncovered, itched. All he needed was one good shot and this trip would be over. But he didn't have his rifle, and a handgun was no good from this distance.

When he'd known he was going to follow Scanlon to Louisiana, he'd made a quick call to one of his father's army buddies, using the excuse that he didn't want to travel alone in unfamiliar territory without some kind of protection but couldn't bring his own weapons on the plane.

The old army buddy, who had more than an affinity for carrying arms of his own, not only understood but had been waiting for him outside the airport with the handgun he was carrying now.

It occurred to him as he was waiting for the lights to go out that the army buddy might be another loose end that needed tying up, but he would worry about that after this was over.

Then a buzz near his ear warned him that another mosquito was approaching. He slapped at the sound. He had no idea whether he'd killed the mosquito or not, although the buzzing was gone. Somewhere in the distance, he kept hearing the familiar sound of baying hounds. He didn't like dogs and shuddered, then stood. As he did, something shifted in the bushes behind him. He spun abruptly, the handgun aimed into the dark. His heart was pounding as a fresh wave of sweat beaded on his brow.

*Son of a holy bitch. Who would willingly live in a place like this? Give me a city with its homeless and druggies, even its muggers, any day.*

Finally he decided it was his imagination that was making him jumpy and looked back toward the house, continuing to mark people's locations by taking note of the lights coming on and going off.

He thought about moving closer. There was always the possibility that he would get a good shot at her through a window. The getaway would be a cinch in the dark, he decided with confidence based on the cocaine he'd sniffed two hours ago. When another mosquito began buzzing about his ear, he decided the idea was good enough to act on.

He began walking toward the house and was only yards from the front door when a loud, raucous shriek sounded over his head. He fell to the ground and rolled onto his back, his gun aimed upward into the limbs of the trees under which he'd been standing.

Again the shriek sounded. It was somewhere between a Hollywood version of a banshee and a girlfriend he'd once had. He didn't know whether to stay put or take cover back where he'd been. But the longer he lay there, the more certain he became that the residents inside the old mansion were not coming out. Obviously, whatever ungodly creature was making the sounds was familiar to them.

With one last look upward, he rolled to his feet. Anxious to get away from whatever was up the tree, he abandoned the last of his caution and ran the rest of the way toward the house.

There were lights on in the foyer, as well as some to the right of the front door and also upstairs. He crept along the boards of the old porch, then paused when one squeaked.

Cursing the situation in general, he went flat against the wall, half expecting someone to come running outside to investigate. But again he was pleasantly surprised by a lack of interest and decided that the age of the place was working in his favor. There were bound to be any number of odd creaks and groans from a place like this.

He shifted the gun to his right hand, then stepped away from the wall and moved directly into view of the first of the front windows. Had anybody been looking out at that moment, they could have seen him, or at least the shape of his body, but there was no one there.

Silently, he moved on to the next, and the next, then realized that everyone must have congregated in the kitchen at the back. Anxious to finish what he'd started, he jumped off the veranda and began to circle the old house, dodging clumps of greenery and bushes as he ran.

He heard the dogs again but thought nothing of it. This was low country. Hunting country. There were bound to be dogs.

Now he was standing on the back steps, and through the window in the door, he could see the back of an old woman's head, the profile of a man, probably the one who'd closed the curtains, and then Laurel herself. At that point, he grinned and raised his gun. She was directly in his sights. All he had to do was squeeze the trigger and it would be over.

He shifted slightly to accommodate the difference in elevation, holding his breath as his finger tightened on the trigger.

At the same moment he squeezed off the shot, something came at him out of the darkness. The shriek that came with it was unnerving and loud. Whatever had been up that tree had followed him and was in the act of attacking. He was so startled that his aim went wild.

It came at him in a rush of sound and feathers, and he fell backward off the porch and into the dirt. The gun went flying from his hand, landing somewhere to his right. It was attacking him now in a thunder of vicious stabs and shrieks. Somehow he got to his feet and then ran toward the safety of the trees without stopping, without looking back.

Laurel was worried about Marie. The old woman had stayed faithfully by her side all during the day, but the toll was beginning to tell in her expression. Her café-au-lait skin had taken on a pale, ashy hue, and her steps were dragging as she moved from stove to sink. Now that they knew her father was safe, she was willing to end this day.

"Mamárie...please go to bed," Laurel begged. "I can't bear to see you like this."

Marie straightened her shoulders and frowned.

"Like how? You trying to tell me I'm too old to stand a little upset now and then?"

"I'm not telling you anything. I'm asking because I care," Laurel said.

"It's been a long day," Justin added. "I'm beat, too. If you two don't mind, I'd like to stay the night. Just to make sure everything stays okay."

Laurel wouldn't look at him. She didn't want to see the worry on his face, knowing that he was worried about her father's warning, though no more than she was.

"Yes, please," Laurel said. "I would appreciate the company."

"Well, that's different, then," Marie said. She'd hung up the dishcloth she'd been carrying and was on her way out of the kitchen when the shot came through the window in the door. She turned toward the sound as glass splintered.

"Get down!" Justin yelled, and saw Laurel drop flat. He grabbed the old woman, taking her down with him.

There was a moment of stunned silence, and then they could hear Elvis's repeated shrieks on the porch out back.

Justin rolled over onto his side, saw Laurel staring

at him in shock from beneath the kitchen table, then grabbed for Marie.

"Are you all right?" he asked.

"Except for those crazy hunters, I'm fine," she muttered, then winced. "I think I bumped my knee."

"I'm so sorry," Justin said.

"I've a good mind to go out there and give them a good tongue-lashing," Marie said.

"No!" Laurel said. "You could get shot."

"It must have been a stray shot," Justin said. "We can thank God that it missed."

Laurel rose up on her elbows, then to her knees.

Justin frowned. "Honey, I don't know if it's safe to—"

She pointed toward the wall.

"If it had been a little more to the left, it would have gone through my head."

Justin paled.

"I want both of you to stay down," he said. "I'm going to call the men in and send them home. We're safer with a panther in the grove than a bunch of men with loaded guns."

But Laurel wasn't convinced. "Something isn't right," she said. "That shot sounded like it was right outside. Would it have been that loud if they'd fired from inside the grove?"

Justin rocked back on his heels. He'd been so focused on getting both women out of the line of fire that he hadn't thought that far. But as soon as she asked, he knew she was right.

"No, it wouldn't."

"Elvis is still pitching a fit," Laurel said.

"He's a pretty good watchdog," Marie added.

"Never would let the neighborhood children onto the place for trick or treat at Halloween."

Laurel's voice quavered. "What if it wasn't the hunters?"

"Are you talking about the warning your father gave you?"

She nodded.

"Damn it. I don't like this," he said. "I think we need to call Harper."

"Wait," Laurel said, and pointed to the wall. "See if the bullet is in there."

"Why on earth would—"

"Let me hold it. If it was DeLane who shot at me, I'll know it."

"Oh…yeah…all right. But don't get up. Not yet, okay?"

"I'm gettin' up," Marie said. "And I'm goin' to my room and take a hot bath before I seize up so bad I can't walk tomorrow."

"I'll help you," Laurel said. "Crawl over to me."

"Not before I pull the drapes in the other rooms," Justin said. "Sit tight."

He took out his pocketknife, dug the slug from the old plaster wall, then dropped it into Laurel's outstretched hand.

Even before her fingers closed over the lead, Laurel knew.

"It was DeLane." She could see him running, feel the brush of limbs across his face, and knew he'd gone into the grove. "He's in the trees," she said, then let the bullet fall to the floor as if the mere touch had contaminated her skin.

"Damn it," Justin muttered, then reached for the phone and dialed the number for the police. While he was waiting for an answer, he flipped off the light switch. Immediately the room went dark, lit only by a faint bit of light from the other rooms beyond the hall.

"Police department. How can I help you?"

"Harper there?"

"Who's calling?"

"It's Justin Bouvier. Get him on the phone now."

A few moments later, he heard Harper pick up.

"Justin?"

"The man who kidnapped Laurel's father just took a shot at her through the kitchen door."

"Christ Almighty," Harper said, then turned around and yelled into the dispatcher in the other room. "Get everyone on duty out to Mimosa Grove." Then he put the phone back to his ear. "Everyone okay? Do I need to send an ambulance?"

"We're good. Marie hurt her knee when I took her down, but I don't think she needs an ambulance."

"Lord, no," Marie said. "Don't think I'm goin' off in one of those crazy contraptions. They drive too fast."

"She says no," Justin repeated. "Tell your men to hold their fire until we can get the hunters in from the grove."

Harper sighed. "Why do I get the feeling I should have heard about them before I jumped the gun and sent out my men?"

"Laurel said it wasn't them."

Harper resisted the urge to roll his eyes. "Well, she hasn't been wrong yet, so no reason to doubt her. Right?"

"That's the way I see it."

"We're on the way."

"Thank you. We'll be waiting." He hung up the phone, then pointed to the two women still crouching on the floor.

"Wait here. I need to make sure the doors are locked and the other lights are out before you get up."

"There's a flashlight in the drawer by the sink," Marie said.

Justin found it, then ran out of the room.

Laurel had heard the fear in Marie's voice and was instantly filled with guilt.

"Mamárie, I'm so sorry this is happening. I would do anything for you not to have to endure this."

"Just stop it," Marie said, and clasped Laurel's hand in her own. "It wasn't your fault, and no one is hurt. That's what we have to think on."

Laurel leaned back against the wall, then clutched Marie's hand. "Mamárie?"

"What, baby girl?"

"I'm scared for my father."

"I know."

"Even though we don't often get along, he's been the only parent I've had since I was ten. I want him to walk me down the aisle. I want him to play with my babies and spoil them the way he never did me."

Marie sighed. She wasn't going to mouth platitudes just to make someone momentarily happy. It wasn't the way she was made.

"I pray to God that he lives, but you have to accept the fact that we don't always get what we want. Sometimes life kicks you when you're down."

"So when that happens, what do you do?"

"Well…I suppose I'd cry for a while. Ain't nothin' wrong with a good cry. Then I suppose I'd pick myself up and get on with my life, 'cause if I didn't, then whoever or whatever got me down would have won."

Laurel sighed, then gave Marie's hand a soft squeeze.

"Do you think that if I live as long as you have, I'll ever be as smart as you are?"

"Maybe," Marie said, and then laughed.

Seconds later, Justin was back.

"Ladies," he said, and held out his hands. "I think you'll both be safer on the second floor, so follow me."

When Marie tried to get up, she winced and then groaned.

"Oh, honey," Laurel said. "You *are* hurt."

"No, I'm not. I'm just old," Marie said. "Wouldn't matter whether I'd been tackled down or got down here on my own. I'd still be havin' trouble gettin' up."

Justin chuckled. "Allow me," he said gently, then handed Laurel the flashlight and picked Marie up in his arms. "Honey, will you lead the way?"

"Gladly," Laurel said, and together, they went up the stairs.

# 18

Justin had carried Marie to Laurel's room and then gone out to call in the hunters. But doing it without getting shot at again was going to be a trick. He thought for a few seconds, then remembered how his daddy had called him in from the creek below the house when he was a kid. He hurried to his truck, unlocked the door and began to honk his horn. After using three long, then three short, then three long honks again, to signal an SOS, he soon heard the hunters calling in their dogs. He ran to the back porch to wait, and when he saw their lights coming toward the house, he knew he'd accomplished his purpose.

Tula's nephew, Manville, was a big, burly man nearing sixty, with a thick red beard and equally thick curly red hair. He had seven sons and two daughters, and a wife he loved so dearly that just the thought of her still made him weak in the knees.

He'd gotten the word from Marie LeFleur that there was a panther in the grove. And being the hunter that he was, he had gladly loaded up his dogs, four of his sons, enough lanterns to make sure they could see where they were going and headed into the trees.

They'd found sign almost immediately and turned the dogs loose, expecting to find the cat before midnight. Only it hadn't happened as easily as he'd hoped. The dogs had lost the scent more than an hour ago and had yet to strike it again. Then they'd heard what sounded like a gunshot, then a distress signal from the old mansion. After that, Manville had called in the dogs. By the time they reached the grounds of Mimosa Grove, they were running. Less than a hundred yards from the back of the house, Justin Bouvier suddenly appeared out of the night.

Manville stopped abruptly, startled by the man's appearance.

"Justin? That you?"

"Yeah, it's me. Didn't mean to startle you."

"What's happenin' man? We heard a shot, then I guess that was you honkin' your horn."

"Yeah, it was me. We have trouble."

Manville nodded. "Figured as much. What happened? Did our dogs scare the cat way up here?"

Justin shook his head, then put his hand on Manville's shoulder and gave him a slight push.

"Keep moving toward your trucks as we talk. It's not safe for you to be here right now."

Manville frowned, but did as Justin asked.

"Let's go, boys. Load up the dogs."

His sons started toward their trucks at a jog, while Manville followed behind with Justin.

"What's happening here? What was that shot?"

"It's complicated, but the short of it is, someone kidnapped Laurel's father, and now he's come after her. He took a shot at her through the back door, then ran into the grove. It missed her, but Marie got hurt some when I took her down with me. So we needed to get you and your boys out of there before he took a shot at one of you…or decided to take someone else hostage.''

Manville froze. Even in the shadows, Justin could see the expression of shock on his face.

''Tryin' to kill her for true?''

''Yes.''

''And you tellin' me that son of a bitch is still around?''

Justin shrugged. ''Can't be sure, but since he missed her, and if I had to guess, I'd say, yes.''

Manville shifted his rifle from his right arm to his left and looked up toward the house. The only light visible was a very small glow from a second-story window.

''Where's the law?'' he asked.

''On their way…I hope.''

Manville glanced back toward the grove, then at Justin.

''I reckon we'll be staying around a bit…at least until help gets here.''

Justin took a slow breath, understanding immediately what had just been offered. These men, who barely knew Laurel, had just put their lives on the line to make sure hers didn't end.

He put a hand on Manville's shoulder and gave it a brief squeeze.

''It won't go unappreciated.''

Manville shrugged. ''We take care of our own, is all.''

''Yeah, I know, and I'll make sure Laurel knows, too.''

Manville turned toward the trucks.

''Boys…you got the dogs loaded?''

''Yes, Daddy,'' one of them called.

"Then come on back here. We're gonna stay here for a bit and take us a rest."

All four of his sons, who were full-grown men, suddenly appeared out of the dark. They nodded their hellos at Justin, then fixed their gazes on Manville.

"What's goin' on, Daddy?" one of them asked.

"That shot we heard?"

They all nodded again.

"Well, someone's tryin' to kill Miz Marcella's granddaughter. He missed. I thought we might stay around here awhile until the law arrives and make sure he don't get a second chance."

"Yes, sir," they said in unison. "Where you think we oughta be?"

Manville looked to Justin for orders.

Justin hated to ask but was secretly thankful that keeping the two women safe wouldn't all be on his shoulders until the authorities arrived.

"Whatever you do, stay in the dark," Justin said. "We don't want you men becoming targets."

They nodded.

"I need to make sure that all exits to the house are covered, and that no one gets close enough to take a second shot."

"What kind of gun he usin'?" one of the men asked.

"Unless he's saving it for hard times, he doesn't have a rifle," Justin said. "The shot was fired from a handgun. Not sure what kind."

Manville grinned. "Then we got it made," he said. "'Cause my boys can shoot a fly off a deer's antlers at fifty feet."

"Lord, Daddy, the older you get, the wilder your stories get. You know good and well it's not more than thirty feet, and I'm a little rusty about doin' it in the dark,'' one son said.

Manville laughed at his son's brag, and then they left. Justin watched them disperse, leaving a man at each corner of the house while Manville went to the back porch and took a seat next to the wall beside the door. With the lights out and the lack of a moon, no one would ever know they were there until it was too late.

Justin breathed a quick sigh of relief, then hurried back into the house. He raced up the stairs, then into Laurel's room. When she saw him, she put a finger to her lips and pointed to Marie, who'd fallen asleep on the bed beside her.

Justin nodded, then lay down on Laurel's bed and pulled her close against him. Their whispers were soft, audible enough for their ears alone.

''Is she okay?''

Laurel nodded. ''Just tired. Did you find Manville and his sons?''

''Yes.''

''Good. I would hate to think they might come to some harm because of me.''

''They didn't leave.''

Laurel grabbed Justin's arm, urgently begging him to make them see sense.

''They have to,'' she whispered.

''They won't leave you unprotected. Said they'll wait until Harper and his deputies get here.''

For a few moments, Laurel was silent. Then she swallowed.

Justin saw her lower lip tremble.

''It's all right, baby,'' he said softly.

''Oh, Justin.''

"I know."

"No, you don't. I will never forget this night, but not because someone tried to kill me. Instead, it will be the night when I learned what it meant to be accepted…to belong."

Justin put his mouth against her ear. His words were soft—so soft, and warm, so warm—and what he said filled her heart with such joy that her eyes quickly teared.

"You belong to me, too, love. Since the first night when you slipped into my bed as quietly as you slipped into my mind. You are always in my thoughts and in my heart. I love you, Laurel. So much."

She shuddered on a sob, then took his hand and pulled it to her lips.

*Love you, too,* she mouthed, then closed her eyes and let the tears fall.

Trigger didn't know when it first occurred to him that he might not get out of this mess as easily as he'd planned, but it was certainly his first thought upon seeing the armed men and their dogs coming toward him in the distance.

Even though it was dark, the lights from the lanterns they were carrying illuminated each of their faces enough for Trigger to believe he'd been found. He thought about shooting at them before they got any closer, then realized that, even if he killed every one of them, there would be no ammunition left for the dogs.

And Trigger was deathly afraid of the dogs.

Uncertain what to do or where to go, he froze, and it was the single thing that kept his presence unknown.

Downwind from the dogs, and too far back in the trees to be detected by the minimal beams of lantern light, he watched five armed men and four leashed dogs pass within twenty yards of his location.

Certain that they would hear his heart pounding or, at the least, his shattered breaths, he couldn't believe it when they passed him by and then disappeared into the night. When he could no longer see them, he began to shake. His stomach knotted, and then suddenly he spun around and retched—over and over until there was nothing left in his belly to come up.

When he was through, he leaned against a tree trunk and wept. He cried for the life that he'd ruined, the innocence that he'd lost, and the man he'd left to die. There was a brief moment of lucidity when he knew what he had to do. To hell with McNamara. To hell with his father's good name. He had money in the Cayman Islands under an assumed name—enough that he could live comfortably for the rest of his life. All he had to do was disappear. There was a moment of grief as he thought of never seeing his mother again, but then reality raised its ugly head. If they caught him and convicted him of treason and murder, he would either be put to death or die in prison, anyway. He would rather be lonely, rich and alive, than miserable, incarcerated and dead.

Having come to that decision, Trigger felt one-hundred-percent better. He had fake ID stashed in a locker in the Miami airport for just such a moment as this. Now all he had to do was get the hell out of this place and keep driving. He would be out of the country before McNamara even knew he was gone. Then it wouldn't matter how much talking he did, they would never find him.

He glanced all around him, making certain that the
armed men were not coming back, then dared to use
his flashlight just long enough to check the compass
on his watch. He knew where he'd parked the car.
And he knew the direction he needed to go to get
back to it. Even more to the point, he was fairly confident that he'd hidden it sufficiently so that it would
be all but impossible for someone else to find it in
the dark. When daylight came, he would be long
gone.

So he'd shot at Laurel Scanlon. So what? He'd
missed her, hadn't he? She didn't have all that much
to complain about. As for her old man, he decided
that he would give the authorities a call and let them
know where Scanlon was, but only after he'd made
it out of the state.

Turning himself until the compass on his watch
indicated that he was facing true west, he started to
walk. In the distance, he could hear the occasional
bark from the hounds, and each time he did, he in-
creased his stride. The farther away he moved from
the old mansion, the faster he ran. But it wasn't easy-
going. The undergrowth was almost as thick as the
trees, and more than once Trigger stumbled and fell.
And each time he would stop and listen before he got
up, making sure he was not being followed. No bark-
ing meant no dogs, and no dogs meant no one on his
trail. Despite the rips in his pants and the scrapes and
scratches on his face and hands, he moved on with a
smile.

As he walked, he kept hearing the sound of running
water off to his right and vaguely remembered study-
ing a map of this part of the state and seeing a river
somewhere near. Confident that he knew where he

was, he let down his guard. He didn't hear the shifting of dead leaves in the underbrush, or the low, guttural rumble of a big cat on the hunt. He didn't even know it was there until it leapt into the path in front of him, and he saw the yellow glitter of its eyes.

Trigger gasped and then froze, unable to think. His heart began to pound, and he had a sudden and unavoidable need to pee.

"Shit…shit…oh, shit…" he groaned, and then remembered his gun.

Slowly, he slid his hand into his pocket. Even when he felt nothing but the inside of his pants, he didn't believe it. The gun must have fallen out during one of the times when he'd fallen. In desperation, he looked around for something else to use as a weapon, but in the dark, it was hopeless.

The black cat crouched, its ears flat against its head.

Trigger shined his flashlight directly into the panther's eyes, hoping to startle it enough that it would leave.

But the cat was already in a bad mood. Thanks to the hunters and their dogs, it had lost two different chances to feed. Now, with the dogs gone and no scent of the men with the guns, the cat lifted its head and let out a scream.

Trigger stared in disbelief. If he hadn't been looking at the cat, he would have thought it was the desperate, heart-stopping scream of a woman in distress.

Again the cat growled, then bared its teeth in a snarl.

Trigger started to move backward.

The cat crept forward.

"Oh, God, oh, God, oh, God," Trigger gasped, then picked up a rock and flung it toward the panther.

It missed by a good three feet and only served to antagonize the big cat further.

''Get!'' Trigger shouted, and waved his arms in the air.

The cat snarled and then started toward him.

Trigger pivoted sharply and began to run, shouting and begging for help as he went.

The cat's scream shattered what was left of his control. The warm surge of urine was already running down the inside of his leg when the cat leaped. The blow sent Trigger sprawling, and he was still screaming as he tried to get to his feet.

But the cat had downed its prey and had no intention of letting it get away.

The first bite went through the back of Trigger's neck, crushing two vertebrae and rendering him helpless. He couldn't feel his arms or his legs and it was becoming difficult to breathe, but he could still scream, and scream he did.

For help.

For mercy.

Then for God to let him die.

And, blessedly, He finally did.

Trigger's last thought ended the moment the panther's mouth closed over his head. He felt a fang in his ear and, from a distance, heard the crunch of tooth against bone, and then it was over.

Gerald Dupont DeLane, only son and heir of four-star general John Franklin DeLane, had lived a privileged life without appreciation of the sacrifices his parents had made on his behalf, taking it all as his just due. He would never have imagined that it would all end in a bayou in one of the country's southernmost states, and at the mercy of a four-legged carnivore with no consideration for the social status of man.

Justin had stayed with Laurel until she'd fallen asleep beside Marie. After that, he'd gone downstairs and slipped out the back door. He was sitting on the steps, talking quietly to Manville, when Harper Fonteneau drove up in a patrol car, followed by two other cruisers.

"'Bout time," Manville muttered, and followed Justin off the steps.

"We're not alone," Harper said, as he pointed over his shoulder to the headlights of two other cars that were driving up behind his deputies.

"What's going on?" Justin asked.

"Feds. They were just coming into the office as we were going out. They got all territorial on me, and we had a discussion about Robert Scanlon's kidnapping. Came to an agreement. They get the man who snatched Scanlon. I get the man who shot at Laurel."

"But it's the same man," Justin said.

Harper grinned. "You know that, and I know that, and I'm gonna bring in the guy in the woods. Did you know that possession is nine-tenths of the law?"

"I don't care who jails him first, I just want him behind bars and away from Laurel."

"Yeah, right. And as soon as the suits get their asses in gear, we're going in after him," Harper said, then eyed Manville and his four sons. "What are they doing here?"

"We were invited, and after the shooting, we thought it would be neighborly to stay with Justin here until you guys decided to show up," Manville drawled. "Now that you're here, we're goin' home."

Harper frowned.

Manville spat off to the side, then shouldered his gun.

"Come on, boys. It's past my bedtime. Your mama will be worried half out of her mind."

"You're gonna have to wait until these men visit with you a bit."

Manville spat again, then stood, watching as four men in suits walked up with the deputies who'd come with Harper. A tall, stocky man with a blond crew cut and a dimple in his chin stepped forward.

"Agent Gabe Clancy from the Federal Bureau of Investigation. These are my associates, Agents Smith, Harwell and Bronson."

Justin nodded, briefly identifying himself without explanation as to why he was there. "Justin Bouvier."

Clancy glanced at Harper, then frowned. "Okay, I'm the new guy in town, but we're all here for the same reason."

"And that would be?" Justin asked.

"To apprehend the man responsible for kidnapping federal prosecutor Robert Scanlon."

Justin stifled a snort. "You people didn't even believe Scanlon was in danger until it was moot," he said. "And because you didn't, you let the bastard get too close to Scanlon's daughter."

Clancy frowned. "We understand there was a shooting out here, but given the presence of these five armed men, it remains to be seen as to who might have been doing the shooting. If they were hunting on the premises, it could have been a wild shot from one of their guns."

Manville bristled, but it had to be said that, to his

credit, he didn't punch the man in the nose. Instead, he stepped forward and shoved the rifle under Gabe Clancy's nose.

"Take a whiff, Irishman. It ain't been fired, and neither have the guns my sons are carryin'. We was huntin' painter, not man, and if we'd been doin' the shootin', we wouldn't have missed."

"Painter? Why were you hunting a house painter?"

"It's a colloquialism for the word *panther*," Justin said.

Clancy's eyes widened briefly as he glanced into the darkness beyond, then shoved the gun back in Manville's face.

"Don't point that thing unless you mean to use it," he snapped.

"Am I gonna have to?" Manville countered.

"Look, mister," Justin said. "The shot came from a handgun, not a rifle. The slug is on the kitchen table inside the house. These men came at Miss Scanlon's request to get rid of a panther that has strayed out of its territory."

"Did you get it?" Clancy asked.

"Didn't I just tell you that we didn't fire a shot?" Manville muttered.

Clancy frowned. He didn't like to be caught in a slip-up.

"So there's a panther on the property?"

"Couldn't say," Manville said. "There was. We found sign, but we didn't find no cat. We're goin' home now. Justin knows how to find us if you got more you think needs to be said. Personally, I said my piece."

The five men turned around and headed toward

their trucks without waiting for permission. Clancy didn't like their attitudes, but they weren't who he'd come to get, so he let the matter slide.

"So what do you want to do first?" Harper asked.

"Go find my man," Clancy said.

Harper shrugged, then stepped aside, waving his arm in a generous gesture.

"Be my guest," he said.

Clancy frowned. "Aren't you coming with us?"

"Not in there—and not at night."

"Come on, officers. There are seven of us. We're all armed. You can't be that afraid of one wild animal who will probably run the other way."

"Maybe your cats are cowards where you come from," Harper drawled. "But down here, ours mean business. Besides, it's not the living I'm afraid of. This is Mimosa Grove. Here, it's what you can't see that will get you."

Clancy frowned. "What the hell are you talking about?"

Justin sighed. This was going nowhere fast. "Some people claim they've seen ghosts," he said.

Clancy snorted. "Ghosts. Holy Mary, Mother of God, what manner of place have we come to?"

He glared at Harper, who glared right back; then he turned to Justin.

"You look like a reasonable man. Have you seen these ghosts?"

"Yeah, actually, I have," Justin said.

Before anyone could answer, they heard the first scream. It was faint and obviously quite distant, but it raised the hair on the backs of their arms. It was followed by another, then another, and then what seemed like a constant and never-ending scream of unimaginable pain.

"Jesus!" Clancy muttered. "What was that?"

"The first scream was the panther," Justin said, then looked at Harper, who looked as sick as Justin felt.

"And the others?" Clancy asked.

"Not having seen it, I can't say for sure, but if I was guessing, I'd lay odds that neither one of you men is going to take a suspect into custody."

Harper motioned toward one of his deputies.

"Go call the coroner. Tell him to be out here by sunrise."

"Yes, sir," he said, and headed toward the cruiser.

Clancy was more than a bit taken aback by what had just happened.

"Are you saying that the other screams were human?"

Justin nodded.

Clancy muttered a quick prayer, then motioned to his men. "Get the rifles and spotlights out of the trunk."

"We're going in there?" one of them asked.

Clancy stiffened.

They didn't ask a second question.

Harper sighed. "Well, hell. If ya'll are going in, then I suppose we'll have to go, too. I can't let you city boys show us country boys up, now can I?"

"Much obliged," Clancy muttered as he headed back to his car.

As they were standing in the front yard in the dark, the front lights of the old mansion suddenly came on. Everyone turned toward the lights like moths to a flame, watching as the door slowly opened and a tall woman in a long white gown and robe walked out to the steps.

"Is she real?" Clancy mumbled.

"Yes," Justin said. "And she's mine."

He started toward her as she began to run.

Laurel heard the screams in her dream before she heard them for real. She came awake within seconds and was out of the bed and reaching for her robe even before her heartbeat had settled back into a normal rhythm. She glanced toward the bed. Marie was still sleeping.

She ran out of the room and then down the stairs. When she didn't find Justin anywhere, she looked out in the yard. It took her a few moments to determine that numerous vehicles were there that hadn't been before. She turned on the porch light and then headed for Justin.

"Justin! Did you hear that—"

"Yes, we heard it," he said, and then put his arm around her shoulders and pulled her to him as the other men approached.

Harper tipped his hat.

"Miss Laurel...I'm sorry it took us so long to get out here." He motioned to the federal agents who were bringing up the rear. "We had a bit of a delay."

It was all Gabe Clancy could do to remember why he'd come. The woman, who must be Laurel Scanlon, was obviously a stunner. He kept trying to remember all the particulars he'd read about her on the way out, but the only thing that stuck in his mind was that she was unwed.

"Miss Scanlon?"

She nodded.

"Clausing sent us. I'm Federal Agent Gabe Clancy. We've come to—"

"He's dead," Laurel said.

Clancy reeled as if she'd struck him.

"Who's dead?"

"The man you came to get. He's in the grove about a mile to the west, not far from the road. If you take a car and go down the highway, heading west for about a mile, then walk back east into the grove, it will be easier to remove his body."

Clancy's mouth was gaping. He knew it because he could feel the air on his tongue, but for the life of him, he couldn't find the gumption to shut it.

"She's never wrong," Harper said, and motioned toward his deputies. "You heard her. I'm thinking we oughta call Manville back with his dogs. I'm not partial to walkin' into those trees without a little protection."

The other deputy got on the phone, leaving Clancy to do as he pleased. "What are you talking about?" he finally asked. "How can you know where this man is…or that he's dead?"

"Didn't you hear those screams?" she asked.

Justin leaned down and whispered something in her ear. Clancy watched as she looked up and then smiled. His heart sank. Whatever dream he'd been having ended.

"Yes, ma'am, we all heard them."

"Well, I saw them," Laurel said. "It was awful." Then she shivered and turned to lay her cheek against Justin's chest.

"What am I missing here?" Clancy asked.

Justin held Laurel just a little bit tighter.

"She sees things," Justin said.

It was then that Clancy remembered. Laurel Scanlon claimed she was a psychic. He wanted to laugh, but considering all she'd been through, he resisted the urge.

"Miss, with all due respect, any one of us could have made that claim after hearing the screams."

"You won't find his right arm," Laurel said.

Chills ran up the back of Clancy's neck.

"The hell you say," he muttered.

Justin gave the man a warning look, then turned around.

"Come on, baby. Let's get you inside."

# 19

Marie was coming down the stairs, carrying her shoes, when Justin and Laurel entered the house. Her dress was rumpled from lying in bed, and her hair, normally done up in a tidy bun at the nape of her neck, was in soft, loose curls all around her face.

"Anyone gonna tell me what's goin' on out there, or do I have to wait and read it in the paper?"

"Give me a minute and I'll fill you in," Justin said, then gave Laurel a quick kiss and pushed her toward the stairs.

"Go to bed, *chère*. I'll be there soon."

But Laurel didn't move. She kept looking at Justin, locking on to his presence as her anchor to staying sane.

"Is it really over? Are they sure it's over?"

Justin frowned, then pulled her back into his arms.

"Yes, baby, it's over. Manville and his boys will have to come back another night to hunt the big cat, but the danger to you is over. You should know that better than us. You saw what happened to DeLane, didn't you?"

She nodded.

He touched a curl against her forehead, then lifted it back in place with his finger. "So, then, it is done."

"You're gonna be fine, honey," Marie said. "Soon

everything will be back to normal, which means the only male that will be giving you any more trouble will most likely be Elvis.''

Laurel laughed, but it didn't sound very happy. She kissed Marie good-night as she passed her on the stairs and kept walking without saying a word.

Marie frowned, then fixed Justin with a look that meant business.

''I slept through part of the action, so start talking.''

''Manville and his boys have gone home, although Harper is calling him to come back with his dogs and help them find what's left of Trigger DeLane.''

''What happened to him?'' Marie asked.

''The panther got him.''

Marie's eyes widened, but she refrained from comment.

''Harper and two of his deputies are going to the west end of the property to wait for Manville and his dogs. The four FBI agents that Scanlon's boss sent here are trying to figure out who to follow...Harper or Laurel.''

Marie frowned. ''All I want to know right now is...are we safe?''

''Yes, ma'am.''

''Then I'm going to sleep in my own bed,'' she said. ''Lock up before you leave.''

''I'm not leaving,'' he reminded her.

She stared at him for a moment, then smiled.

''I knew that. I was just testin' you.''

Justin's shoulders slumped. ''This whole night has been hell on earth for us. I can't imagine what it's been like for Laurel. Not only did she know some of this in advance, most of the time she was helpless to stop it.''

''God doesn't give out gifts like hers to people who aren't strong enough to handle them,'' Marie countered.

''Yes, I suppose you're right,'' Justin said.

''Course I'm right,'' Marie muttered.

He grinned, but the expression slipped when he saw her grimace with pain.

''Still hurting?''

''Some.''

''Would you allow me to carry you to your bed?''

She smiled primly.

''I suppose I might.''

He picked her up as gently as he would a baby, then started down the hall to her room.

''I'm still sorry I hurt you.''

Marie patted him on the cheek as he set her down on her bed.

''What you did probably saved my life, and I thank you.''

''You're very welcome,'' he said, then kissed her on the forehead. ''Sleep tight.''

''I plan to. You might try to do the same.''

Justin stifled another grin. He knew she was digging at him for staying with Laurel.

''I would never hurt her,'' he said softly.

''Oh, I know that, boy. Now go on with you. I need to get my sleep. And don't forget to lock all the doors.''

By the time he had checked all the exits, swept up the broken glass in the kitchen and taped a piece of cardboard over the place where the pane had been, almost an hour had passed. He thought of Laurel, guessing that she'd probably long since gone to sleep, and turned out the lights.

As he started up the stairs, he could hear Marie snoring. He smiled to himself and was thinking how good it felt to be in a house where love dwelt, when it dawned on him that he was no longer alone.

He paused on the stairs, looking down into the foyer, then up to the second-floor landing, thinking he would see Laurel, but she wasn't there. All was quiet, and nothing moved. Still, the sensation was slightly unnerving. Finally he tossed out his best answer without having heard a question.

"Bear with me," he said. "I'm doing the best I can."

There was a movement of air on the side of his cheek; then the sensation of being watched disappeared.

He didn't know how loving Laurel was going to play out in his life, but he knew that there were going to be some big changes involved. There were things afoot in this house that he'd only read about in books. But if it took learning how to live with ghosts to keep his woman, he was ready to give it a try.

Laurel had just hung up the phone when Justin walked in. He moved to her side, caressing her face with the palm of his hand, then leaned down and kissed her.

"*Chère*, I'm sorry I took so long. I put a temporary patch on the broken pane in the door, but it will have to be fixed in the morning. I didn't think you'd still be awake, but I'm glad that you are."

"I was talking to Dad's doctor. He has a concussion, a broken nose and some cracked ribs, and they're keeping a close watch to make sure he doesn't come down with pneumonia. Other than that, he said Dad's in surprisingly good shape for what he's been through.''

"Did you get to talk to him?"

"No. They said that wouldn't be possible before morning.''

He nodded. "We'll leave tomorrow as soon as we can get someone to come stay with Marie."

"Tula will do it," Laurel said, and then her chin quivered. "This is all my fault. None of this would have happened if I hadn't come to Mimosa Grove."

Justin sat down beside her, then took her in his arms.

"Honey…sweetheart…don't even think like that. Tonight, my heart stopped when that shot shattered the window in the door. You mean more to me than words can say. Besides the fact that I would be the loneliest man in Louisiana if you had not come to Bayou Jean, Marie would still be grieving for Marcella's passing and wondering what to do with the rest of her days. Most likely Rachelle would have drowned, and Martin Lewis would have gotten away with murder.''

Laurel leaned against him, letting his words wash over her in warm, gentle waves. He brushed the tangles of her hair away from the side of her face, then began taking off her robe.

"Evil doesn't follow certain people. Evil just is. It's only a very special few who know how to see beneath its pretty disguises.''

He took off her shoes, then straightened the covers and tucked her in bed.

Laurel lay back, watching how the light reflected

on his hair and thinking to herself that she'd never seen hair so black or eyes any softer a brown. She felt that she'd loved him forever.

"Aren't you coming to bed?"

"As soon as I take a shower."

"I'll wait up," she said, and then blushed when he bent down and stole her senses with a slow, hungry kiss.

"Whether you're awake or asleep, we'll still be making love, remember?"

She sighed, then nodded wearily.

He winked as he straightened, turned off all the lights except a small lamp near the bed, and began to undress.

Laurel watched as his shirt came off, then his shoes, then his jeans, and thought to herself that he was as nearly perfect a man as she'd ever seen.

"Justin?"

He turned, unashamed of his nudity. "What, baby?"

"Do you know how truly beautiful you are?"

He looked a bit taken aback, then smiled. Slowly. With promise in every nuance of his expression.

"Are you throwing out pretty compliments in the hope of getting laid?"

She grinned. "And if I was…?"

"Then you need to know it worked," he said, and started toward her.

"I thought you were going to shower," Laurel said as he pulled the covers from her body and started taking off her gown.

"I didn't say when," he growled, and tossed the nightgown off the side of the bed onto the floor.

"Justin…"

"Shh," he whispered, and then straddled her legs.

At first he was just touching her body, but the more intense their lovemaking became, the more clear it became to Laurel that it was her heart that this man touched most.

For Justin, it was love, enhanced by the fear of how close he'd come to losing her tonight, that made the act more special than it had ever been before.

Her smooth golden skin was satin to the touch. Beneath it, he felt the pulse of her heartbeat as it raced through her veins, and then he remembered the sound of shattering glass. He heard her moan, then sigh, and was reminded of the terror in her voice only hours ago. Her hair was like fire spreading on the pillow, and with every curl that tangled in his fingers, he felt consumed.

He moved slowly down her body, taking his own sweet time in tracing the shape of her breasts and peaking her nipples into hard little pouts. He dipped his tongue into the depression of her navel, pushing, swirling, drawing to a point the connection between him and the ache between her thighs.

And with every soft, desperate gasp that slipped from between her lips, with every urgent sweep of her hands across his body, she pulled him under, too.

"Justin…enough…enough. I want you with me… in me. Please, baby, come inside."

Her plea shattered what was left of his control. He rose up, then slid in, piercing her sweet warmth, and then lost his mind. For every hard, body-slamming thrust, she met him halfway, wrapping her legs around his waist and her arms around his shoulders, sending them both to heaven.

\* \* \*

Clausing was finishing off a bite of bagel, washing it down with the last swallow of coffee in his cup, when his phone began to ring. It was six-fifty in the morning. He wasn't due into the office before eight. Whoever was calling him at this time of day better have a good reason.

"Clausing," he said, making no effort to disguise the irritation in his voice.

"Sir. It's Clancy. Robert Scanlon was rescued from a crypt in St. Lorraine, Louisiana, where Trigger DeLane had left him to die. He's in a hospital in New Orleans. Some injuries, but none life-threatening, although if they'd been much later, he would have suffocated. Then, last night, DeLane tried to kill Scanlon's daughter, Laurel. He took a shot and missed, then ran into the nearby woods, presumably to try again later. There were hunters in the woods, and we think he was betting on Miss Scanlon and her family assuming it was an accident…a wild shot from the hunters. He did not, however, take Miss Scanlon's… uh…for lack of a better word, psychic abilities…into consideration. She claimed she knew who did it, and where he'd gone."

"Hold on! Hold on!" Clausing yelled. "This sounds like you're trying to pitch a plot to the Sci Fi Channel. For God's sake, you're a federal agent for the United States of America. We do not gather intel from psychics."

"If they're anything like Miss Scanlon, then maybe we should," Clancy snapped.

"I don't want to hear anything except the bottom line. Do we have DeLane's son in custody or not?"

"What we have, sir…is what's left of him."

Clancy heard a short intake of breath on the other end of the line, and then Clausing sighed.

"Are you telling me that Gerald DeLane is dead?"

"Yes, sir."

"At whose hands?"

"Not a who but a what, sir."

"Goddamn it, Clancy! Quit dragging out this farce of a report and tell me what happened."

"The hunters who were in the forest behind Laurel Scanlon's property were looking for a panther that had strayed from its regular habitat. When Trigger tried to kill Laurel Scanlon, the hunt was called off. They pulled their dogs and left. Trigger was hiding out in the same woods. The cat got him."

"Oh, Jesus," Clausing muttered. "The press is going to have a field day with this. They're already all over the fact that McNamara was taken out in prison by a Vietnam vet. They're making the inmate out to be some kind of folk hero for saving our taxpayers the cost of a trial and incarceration. Now you're telling me that McNamara's partner in crime has been eaten by a wild animal? I can't even begin to imagine how they're gonna put a spin on this."

"He wasn't eaten entirely. Only his right arm. Just like Miss Scanlon said we'd find him."

Clausing picked up the phone book and threw it across the room.

"I don't want to hear another damned word about Laurel Scanlon or her psychic abilities. Do I make myself clear?"

"Yes, sir."

Clausing was pacing now, his thoughts racing with the twists and turns the case had taken.

"Okay…here's what we're going to do. McNa-

mara is dead. DeLane is dead. General DeLane and
his wife have already been through enough hell.
There's no need ruining his fine military career by
dragging his son's dirty laundry through this mess.
I'm going to run this by the President, but the way I
look at it, justice has already been served. So do not,
under any circumstances, talk about DeLane's part in
the treason. Tell your men to forget everything they
knew before they went to Louisiana. All the media
needs to know is the general's son died in a tragic
hunting accident.''

Clancy frowned, but he knew better than to argue.

''It's your call, sir,'' he said.

Clausing gripped the phone as if he were gripping
Clancy by the throat to make his point.

''That's right. It *is* my call. I will expect a full
report on my desk upon your return.''

''Sir. Yes, sir. And I have a question.''

''What?''

''About the report…do you want the truth…or do
you want your version of the truth?''

''I want the truth, damn it. The file will be sealed.
End of story.''

''Yes, sir.''

Clausing disconnected, then threw the phone across
the room, in the same direction that he'd thrown the
phone book. He grabbed his briefcase and his car keys
from the hall table and took off out the door. It was
going to be a long day at the office, and the sooner
he started, the sooner it would be over.

The moment he got in his car, he reached for his
cell phone and punched in a number. Moments later,
his caller answered.

''Mr. President, this is Clausing. We need to talk.''

\* \* \*

Cherrie Peloquin had changed her mind twice, delaying her trip home by days. But she knew the moment the cab turned down her old street and pulled up to her parents' home that she'd made the right decision. The sick feeling in the pit of her stomach was gone, and if she didn't look too closely in the mirror at the shorn pink hair and weird clothes, she could still believe that she was the same fresh-faced college graduate she'd been when she first left home to make her mark in the world.

Her parents knew she was coming. She'd called them from the road, but she hadn't told them why, only that she wondered if they would mind her staying in her old room until she found a job and a new place to live.

Her mother had started crying and laughing all at the same time, then told her that her old boyfriend had asked about her just the day before.

It had been all Cherrie could do not to cry with her. And now that she was here, she couldn't hold back the tears. Green Trees, Oregon, population 723, had one more to add to the count. A prodigal daughter had come home.

She paid the cab driver as he unloaded her suitcase, then turned toward the house. The door was opening. Her mother was coming out on the run, with her father not far behind.

"Cherrie…Cherrie…you're home! You're home."

A short while later, she was at the kitchen table, listening with rapt attention to her parents rattle off the news of the day, while in the background, the national news was being broadcast on a small portable TV on a sideboard that had once belonged to her great-grandmother Mabel. It had shocked, then delighted her that neither of her parents had even mentioned her looks, although she was anxious to take a shower and wash the pink hair spray away.

In the middle of her mother's story about the waitress down at the diner who was getting married for the third time to the same man, a picture of Peter McNamara's face was flashed on the TV screen.

"Daddy! Daddy! Turn that up! Quick!"

"...was found murdered in his cell two days ago. He had been in solitary confinement ever since..."

Cherrie's heartbeat skipped a few beats as elation dawned. There was never going to be a trial. The fact that she'd run out on the federal prosecutor's office was never going to be an issue. They would not come looking for her after all.

"Oh. Oh, my," she whispered, then started to laugh.

Her mother stared at her as if she'd just lost her mind.

"Cherrie! I taught you better manners than that. You shouldn't be laughing about that poor man's demise, even if he was a criminal."

"You're right, Mother. I don't know what I was thinking. For a minute there, I thought I knew him. When I realized I'd made a mistake...that I didn't really know him after all, I laughed. But not because he'd been murdered. Only that I'd been so foolish."

Her mother's expression lightened. "Well, I wondered," she said, then chuckled. "I should have known it was something like that." Then she glanced at her husband and giggled. "Imagine...our Cherrie thinking she might know a criminal."

Cherrie leaned back in her chair and smiled.

"Yes, Mother. Imagine that."

* * *

A similar sense of relief was taking place at the Russian embassy in Washington, D.C. The Russian ambassador was about to set out for a meeting with a group of farmers from Iowa about exporting their wheat to his country when an aide hurried into the room and handed him a folded note. He took it without comment, opened it absently, then stopped in his place.

*Dimitri Chorkin is dead.*

He folded up the note again and slipped it into his pocket. He didn't care how it had happened, or who'd done the deed. All he knew was that the killer had done them a huge favor. With this man dead, the conversations regarding old spies and Cold War secrets would certainly die a death on its own, if for no other reason than that there was no one left to remind them of their international faux pas.

Robert Scanlon was propped up in bed and watching the national news when Peter McNamara's face flashed across the screen. He fumbled for the remote control and managed to up the volume just in time to hear of the man's demise.

Startled, his hands went limp, his lips slack, as he listened to the news anchor retell the story that was ricocheting all over the world. Then he thought of Trigger DeLane, wondering how he'd gotten caught up in McNamara's web, and wondering how things would have played out if the news of McNamara's death had aired two days earlier. No one had known of Trigger's involvement. The facts would have died with McNamara. Instead, according to the anchor, who thought he was reporting the unrelated death of another Washington, D.C., resident, the son of General John Franklin DeLane had died in a tragic hunting accident in Louisiana.

Robert immediately recognized the political spin that had been put on the story and couldn't have cared less. It was still unclear what Trigger had hoped to accomplish by doing Robert in. But it was certain that whatever his reason, it had died with him.

What Robert did know was that he had his daughter to thank for his life. He didn't understand it, but he was going to have to learn to accept it. Call it crazy, call it the most phenomenal guesswork of the century, but there was no way anyone would have found him unless—

''Daddy?''

He looked up. Laurel was standing in the doorway.

''Laurel...darling, you didn't have to come all this way. Didn't they tell you I was fine?''

Laurel stared at the bandages on his head, the machine that they'd hooked up to register his heartbeat and the IV connected to his arm, and then shivered, thinking how close they'd come to being too late.

''I'm more like you than you might like to believe, okay?''

He grinned, then winced at the pain that shot through his jaw and across the bridge of his very broken nose.

''And how's that?'' he asked.

''I like to see things for myself, too, you know?''

Suddenly he understood that she was giving him an out for never having believed her before. He thought of all the years he'd ridiculed, belittled and, in her youth, even punished her for being different.

''Come here,'' he said softly.

She crossed the room, then, very carefully, put her arms around his neck and started to cry.

Justin watched from the doorway for a moment, then closed the door and left them alone. He knew just enough about their situation to know that what was happening inside was what could only be construed as Robert Scanlon's first act of contrition, as he finally told her the truth about Phoebe's death.

*A week later: Mimosa Grove*

It had been raining for three days straight. Flood warnings had been issued, and people who lived in the lowlands were preparing for the worst.

Whatever else Jean Charles LeDeux had been, he had been a wise man in picking a building site for his home. It sat on a rise about a half mile from the river, and never once since the last nail and peg had been driven had it been underwater. The river had run over its banks plenty of times, but never coming close to the mansion. Even when it receded, it was doing the place a favor by leaving the silty loam from the bottom on the higher ground. And over the years, the few mimosa trees that had been growing wild on the land had grown into the green jungle that now surrounded the place.

Justin had absented himself from Mimosa Grove over the past two days, only because his sister and some of her neighbors were close to losing their homes. With his own house in no danger, he'd moved his sister and the baby there; then he'd moved in with her husband, Tommy, and, along with a good portion of the residents of Bayou Jean, continued to build a temporary levee.

He called Laurel every time he got a chance, and she could hear the loneliness and exhaustion in his voice. More than once, she'd sensed his fear that they were fighting a losing battle, but this was one time when she didn't have an answer. As hard as she tried, she couldn't see into the future of Bayou Jean, because she was too locked into the past of Mimosa Grove.

She had but a few pages left to read in Chantelle LeDeux's diary and had intended to finish it last night, but the power had gone off during the storm. By the time it had come back on, she and Marie were sound asleep in their beds. Then, this morning, there had been so much to do in cleaning up the grounds. Limbs from the trees had broken off during the high winds and were scattered all about. The fishpond had overflowed, giving up what appeared to be an ancient padlock, heavily encrusted with rust and with a single link of chain still attached.

Laurel had been elated by the small find until she'd read of it in the diary.

Our house servant, Joshua, was whipped today for breaking one of the serving bowls to our best set of china. I begged my husband not to do it. I even tried to take the blame myself, but I am not good at lying. He saw right through me and, as a result, has locked me in our bedroom until I know my place.

But I already know my place, and it isn't here.

Joshua is screaming for mercy at the whipping post in the backyard. I can hear him as I write these words. I hate this way of life. One should not own another. It is not civilized. But then, what do I know? I was not born for a life such as this. I do not cherish my husband as I should, although he has given me three beautiful children. I should not be so selfish. They are joy enough to make living with him worthwhile.

Except in times like this. Mon Dieu…how can he be so cruel? It was only a bowl.

If I do nothing else in my lifetime except this, I will have that whipping post taken down and throw the padlock and chain into the pond. If my husband wants it back, then he will have to read my mind to find out where it's gone.

Laurel's chest hurt too much to breathe. The horror of the simple words in the diary brought home but a small bit of the truth of what being a slave had entailed.

She laid the diary facedown on her bed and walked out of the room. When she came down the stairs, there were unshed tears in her eyes.

Marie was coming out of the library with a dust cloth in her hand when she saw the expression on Laurel's face.

"Laurel…honey…is something wrong? Are you ill?"

Laurel stopped and, for a moment, experienced such a feeling of déjà vu that she staggered.

Another face, darker and younger than Marie's, superimposed itself over her image. The plain green-and-white seersucker house dress that Marie was wearing seemed to morph into a long gray duster with a white, full-length apron tied around her waist and a white kerchief tied around her head to keep nappy black ringlets away from her face.

Laurel gasped, then shuddered. The woman started to cry, holding her hands out to Laurel in a begging, beseeching manner, and in that moment Laurel knew she was seeing Joshua's wife—the mother of the child whose life Chantelle had saved. And she knew, as sure as she was standing in this place, that these ghosts had been resurrected when the pond had regurgitated the lock from its depths and Laurel had brought it back into this house.

Marie frowned.

"Laurel…are you havin' yourself a vision? Is everything all right?"

Laurel shuddered, then made herself focus as she pulled away from the image.

"Yes, I was, and no it's not, but it will be soon enough," she muttered.

Marie's frown deepened.

"You're not makin' any sense. I'm gonna get you some iced tea and something to eat. You skipped lunch. That's what's wrong. You just need to eat."

"No, Mamárie…I'm not hungry. I'm just sick to my soul. What did we do with that padlock that washed out of the pond?"

"Why…it's in the kitchen on a saucer. It's so rusty and all I didn't want it stainin' my counter so—"

"I'll be right back," Laurel muttered, and strode out of the foyer. Moments later, she was back, the padlock and its single link of chain dangling from her fingers.

"What you gonna do with that old thing?" Marie asked.

"Put it back in its grave."

Marie's eyes widened, and she crossed herself out of habit, although, having lost faith with the priest who'd reviled Marcella for being a witch, it had been more than thirty-five years since she'd set foot in a church.

Laurel yanked open the front door and then ran down the steps. At that point Marie came to herself and followed her out onto the veranda.

"Baby girl, you get yourself back in this house before you get struck by lightning. Can't you see it's comin' down a strangler?"

Laurel recognized the reference to the heavy downpour as another one of Marie's colorful phrases, this one about it raining so hard it would strangle a toad, but she was not amused.

The rain was warm, almost hot, in spite of the wind whipping through the trees. The pink-and-white blossoms from the mimosas lay plastered to the grass and stuck to her feet as she ran. The rain flattened her hair to her head and her clothes to her skin within seconds. The soaked ground could absorb no more, and water was ankle deep and splashing into her tennis shoes as she dashed across the grass.

The padlock was heavy in her hand, the thick casing of rust rough against her skin. The closer she got to the pond, the more overwhelmed she became.

Then she was standing at the pond, looking down into the black, murky depths, and it hit her that once, almost two centuries ago, a young woman not unlike herself had come here from another place and had stood in this very spot, with this same padlock in her hand.

Laurel could only imagine the despair that Chantelle must have felt and the pain that had been inflicted upon so many people by the fact that they'd been fastened to a whipping post with this very lock and chain.

"God help us," she said, and when she looked down at the hunk of metal, saw not the iron-red rust of time but the coppery color of blood.

Without further hesitation, and oblivious to Marie's shouts to come back, she threw the lock into the deepest, darkest part of the old pond, then watched until the water that had parted to let it in was washed back into place with the constant downpour of rain.

Still struggling with the ugliness of what she'd unwittingly brought into her house, she turned. Marie was standing at the edge of the porch, still waving frantically for her to come in, and beside her was the swiftly fading image of the young black woman in the long gray dress.

Laurel stood until the only thing she saw was Marie and the door of Mimosa Grove, standing open behind her, waiting to take Laurel in. She started toward the house, and by the time she got to the steps, she was running.

"You lost your mind. That's what you did," Marie said, and grabbed Laurel by the arm and dragged her into the house. "You get yourself upstairs and into some dry clothes. And dry all that hair that's dripping on my clean floors while you're at it." Then she pointed in Laurel's face, trying to prove her power, when it was evident that it was nothing but worry that caused her tirade. "And don't you go tellin' me that you been seein' ghosts, 'cause I don't want to hear it. There's too much of the past still alive in this house, and I'll be glad for the day when these restless spirits go and put themselves to rest. You hear what I'm sayin'?"

Laurel nodded. "Yes, ma'am, and I'm sorry about the mess. If you'll give me a couple of minutes to get out of these wet clothes, I'll mop up."

Marie frowned and waved her dust cloth toward the stairs.

"You run your own business, missy. I tend to this house. Now, get out of those wet clothes, like I said."

Laurel didn't have the guts to argue further. She could still hear Marie muttering to herself as she reached the landing. She was coming out of her clothes all the way to her room, and as she shut the door behind her, she heard the soft sound of laughter. She turned quickly but saw nothing.

"Laugh if you want to," she muttered as she headed for the bathroom. "I'll bet you wouldn't have argued with her, either."

# 20

Justin called after supper. Laurel was just getting out of the shower when the phone rang. She dropped her towel and hurried to answer, and when she heard his voice, all the tension of the day disappeared.

"Justin, sweetheart, you sound exhausted. Is everything okay?"

"The levee is holding. It's about all we can say."

"I think it will quit raining tonight."

Justin had been pulling off his wet boots when he heard what she said. He stopped immediately, sat down with a thump and traded the phone to his other ear.

"Did you see this, baby?"

"Sort of," she said, and then laughed. "It's what the weatherman is forecasting."

Her self-deprecating humor surprised him. It was the first time he'd heard her make a joke about herself, and he liked that. He chuckled, then bent down and kicked off his other boot, wiggling his weary feet in relief.

"You're a comedy queen, aren't you, *chère?*"

Laurel laughed again. "I'm sorry. I just couldn't resist."

Justin closed his eyes and leaned back.

"What are you wearing?" he asked.

"Nothing."

He groaned. "God. I didn't need to know that," he said. "You could have lied."

"Then you shouldn't have asked."

"I miss you, baby."

Laurel hugged herself, then rolled over onto her bed and curled into a ball.

"I miss you, too," she said softly. "How's Tommy?"

"He took my truck and drove over to my house to check on Cheryl Ann and Rachelle. He'll be back after a while, I suppose."

"Have the others gone home, too?"

Justin shoved a hand through his wet hair and then massaged the muscles at the back of his neck.

"Yes. We ran out of sacks. After that, Tommy thanked everyone for coming and told them to go home and get some sleep."

"Oh, no!" Laurel said, and quickly sat back up. "Is there anything I can do? I can make some calls. See if there are any available in the next town and go—"

"No. We tried. And don't you set foot out of that house. The only thing that gives me peace of mind right now is knowing that Mimosa Grove does not flood."

"All right, but if—"

"No buts. Just promise."

She smiled to herself. "I promise."

"Have you heard from your daddy?"

"Yes. He's home. Estelle is nursing him and, I think, driving him crazy. He says when the doctor releases him, he's still going to Fiji or Belize, or wherever it was he was headed before all hell broke loose. And those are his words, not mine.''

Justin chuckled. ''I like him, you know.''

Laurel thought back to the short time they'd all spent together, and how easily Justin and Robert had bonded.

''He asked me my intentions,'' Justin said.

Laurel gasped. ''He didn't!''

''Yeah, actually, he did,'' Justin said. ''I told him they were fairly honorable, but that I'd never really had a chance of getting away.''

''You didn't!''

He laughed. ''No, I didn't. I kept our dream-time rendezvous to myself. Besides, who'd believe me?''

''I would,'' she said softly.

''Yeah, but you're special that way,'' Justin said.

Laurel smiled, then rolled over onto her belly.

''Please be careful,'' she said. ''I've waited so long for someone like you that I couldn't bear to lose you.''

She almost said the word ''again'' and wondered where that had come from.

''You're not going to lose me,'' Justin said.

Then he frowned. He'd almost added the word ''again'' and wondered why.

''Still reading that diary?'' he asked.

She frowned. ''Yes. There's something I want to tell you when I see you, but it's nothing that can't wait.''

''Okay. Sleep tight, my love. I wish I was there to hold you.''

''No more than I do,'' Laurel said. ''Stay safe. I love you.''

"Love you, too," he said. "I'll see you tomorrow."

"I'll be waiting."

The click in her ear was distinct, and, she thought, the loneliest sound.

A few minutes later, she had dried her hair, slipped on a fresh nightgown and was back at the diary. With only three pages left to go, she knew she couldn't sleep tonight without knowing how Chantelle had ended her solitary conversation.

I have done the unforgivable. My husband is furious. By taking down the whipping post in his absence, I have defied him and his ways in front of the slaves. He has been shouting at me for hours, proclaiming that what I've done will lessen his power over them and cause an uprising. But I don't care. His behavior has solidified a feeling I've had for some time now. I came to this country to be a bride. Instead, I became exactly the kind of chattel that my husband covets. I may be white and educated, but I am his slave as certainly as the blacks who work his land.

I can't bear to live this lie any longer. Tonight I am telling him that I am leaving. I'm taking the children and going home to Mama and Papa. I will not have them grow up thinking their mother is some mindless, spineless female whose only skill is being ridiculed for a gift that has been in her family as long as can be remembered.

I will tell him. God help me. I greatly fear his wrath.

Laurel laid down the diary with a frown. This confirmed the legend that had come with the place, that the first woman of Mimosa Grove had run away from her man. Yet it was a contradiction, too, because, according to that same legend, she had left with another man, leaving her children behind. They lived, grew up, married, bore children and, according to Marie, were buried in the cemetery outside Bayou Jean. Yet according to the diary, Chantelle had planned to take them with her.

Still frowning, she pulled back the covers and turned out the lights. Outside, the occasional shaft of lightning still lit up the sky, and the belch and grumble of thunder still rattled the windowpanes. She went to the window and pushed the curtains aside, watching the darkness and waiting for the next bolt of lightning to illuminate what she already saw in her mind's eye.

Even without opening the window, she could hear the rush and rumble in the distance that was the river in flood. She thought about the grove, and of the big cat that hadn't been seen since Trigger DeLane's death.

Manville and two of his boys had come back the next day after the police and the coroners had allowed them on the property and tracked the cat until they'd lost its trail. For two nights afterward, they'd combed the grove, but with no results.

On the third day, a panther had been sighted about five miles downriver. The farmer on whose land it was hunting had killed it outright with a blast from both barrels of his shotgun. People said it was the same one that had killed the man at Mimosa Grove. Laurel liked to think it was so. It was part of that night. Part of a time she didn't want to relive. And if the panther, too, was dead, then the ordeal would be over.

As she stood, lost in thought and wondering if Justin was as restless as she, a bolt of lightning suddenly snaked out of the sky, striking so close to the house that she was momentarily blinded. She staggered backward, then stumbled over a chair and slid down to the floor. In a panic that something on the property had been hit, she scrambled back to her feet and ran to the window, worried about what had been struck.

But the darkness was blinding and the rain still fell, and since nothing was on fire, whatever it was would have to wait until morning. She went to bed with a prayer of thanksgiving that it had missed the house.

Then she started to dream.

*"You bitch! You ungrateful, foreign bitch! I will not be humiliated like this. You will not leave me, nor will you take my children."*

*"They're my children, too!" Chantelle cried, and then fell backward against the fireplace when he struck her with his fist.*

*As blood poured into the inside of her mouth, Chantelle knew she'd made a horrible mistake by telling him of her plan. She should have waited for him to take one of his trips, then slipped away with the children on her own. Now it was too late. Before she could get up, he fell upon her and began beating her in earnest.*

*Chantelle began screaming, begging for help and, at the same time, praying her children would not witness her debasement.*

"Stop! Stop! For the love of God, you are killing me!" she cried.

"It is what you deserve!" he shouted. "If you will not be my wife, then no other man shall know you, either!"

He continued to pummel her with his fists until she could barely see from one eye. Her nose was surely broken, because she could no longer draw air through one nostril. And just when she thought it was over, he was gone—lifted from her body and flung through the air like a rag doll.

She moaned. Someone was pulling her up, begging her to run. Begging her not to look back. But she did.

It was Joshua.

He stood between her and her husband like a dark and avenging angel. His hands were still curled into the fists that had knocked her husband from her body. The breadth of his shoulders and the long, strong length of his legs had proved too much for her husband to fight.

"Please, Missus," he begged. "If you don't run, we both dead."

Then she did something outrageous. Something she would never have imagined herself capable of doing. She thought of the beating he had suffered, then grabbed him by the hand and begged him to go with her.

"Come with me," she said. "He'll kill you if you don't."

Joshua looked down at their hands, at the fingers that were entwined, and was so shocked that she'd touched him in this way that he couldn't speak. She kept talking and talking, but he was still staring at the contrast of light and dark. Then he shuddered and

*made himself look up—right into her pale blue eyes
and a face that was so battered, and knew he had to
tell her no.*

*"No, Missus…no. I can't leave my woman…and
what about my baby girl?"*

*"I'll find a way," she said. "All I need is to get
word to my father. He'll buy you away. He'll pay for
you all. Then you'll be free, just like me."*

*Joshua looked down once again at her hand, ab-
sently thinking how tiny it looked against the size of
his own. And he knew that in another time, and in
different lives, he would have loved this woman who'd
dared to live true to herself.*

*He shuddered once, then moved his hand away.*

*"You run now."*

*Then Chantelle's face crumpled.*

*"My babies. I can't leave my babies behind with
this man."*

*Joshua's wife stepped out from behind a curtain.
She'd been an unwilling witness to it all, even the
shocking interchange between her husband and the
master's wife. As she looked down upon her unconscious master, she started to cry.*

*"Oh, Joshua…Joshua…what you gone and done
to the massuh? He won't just whip you again. He'll
kill you fo' shore."*

*And in that moment, LeDeux moaned.*

*Joshua grabbed Chantelle and turned her toward
the door.*

*"You run, Missus. It's still dark. He can't see you.
Run toward the river. I got a boat hid out down there,
and I'll take you to someplace safe." Then he turned
to his wife, and as he did, she began to cry. "Listen
to me, woman, and you listen good. You been the best*

*woman a man could have. We got us a pretty baby girl that we love, just like Missus here loves her babies. But we got us some trouble, too. If I don't get her out, he gonna kill her for shore. Then he gonna kill us both for knowin' she dead. You understand?''*

*Her dark eyes widened with fear as she nodded her head.*

*''You get back to the cabin. You lay down with our baby and you sleep like you never slept before. And when he wakes you up and asks where I gone...you start wailin' and cryin' like your heart done broke. You carry on so loud and long that he'll know for shore you don't know nothin' about what's been done.''*

*''But my babies,'' Chantelle moaned. ''I'd rather die than leave my babies.''*

*Joshua's woman stared as if she'd seen a ghost. Suddenly it dawned on her that this woman was just like her, that she would do anything to protect her children.*

*''Missus...you get my Joshua to safety, and I swear on my life that me and mine will look after your children and their children and their children after, for as long as we all lives.''*

*Chantelle hesitated again, until she saw her husband beginning to stir. And at that moment, her decision was made.*

*She looked up at Joshua, unaware that all her hopes and her trust were there on her face for him to see.*

*''You'll be waiting for me?''*

*''Yes, Missus, iffen I have to, I wait forever until you come.''*

\* \* \*

Laurel woke up. Sunlight was shining through her bedroom windows. She rolled over on her back, then sat up. But she didn't move, and at that moment, wouldn't have been able to speak.

She already knew what had happened to Chantelle when she'd made a run for the river. Someone had caught her. Someone had hit her in the middle of her back with something that had dealt her a deadly blow, and if she had to offer a guess, she would say it had been the man to whom she'd been wed.

Then she thought of Joshua's wife, and suddenly she understood the depth of her promise. She didn't have to ask to know that Marie LeFleur was a descendant of that woman, just as Laurel was a descendant of Chantelle. History had kept repeating itself, looping from generation to generation upon the promises that three people had made to one another.

And then there was Justin. She wouldn't tell him, because it served no purpose he would ever understand, but she knew, as surely as she knew her own name, that in another lifetime his name had been Joshua, and he'd given a promise to a woman that he was still trying to keep.

But what of Joshua? Had he made it to the river? And if he did, how long did he wait? Did he witness Chantelle's untimely death, or did he, too, fall prey to the fury of a rejected husband who valued pride above those he'd promised to love?

As she sat staring out the window, Marie knocked on her door.

"Laurel...honey? You awake?"

The knob turned, then Marie pushed the door inward and came in carrying breakfast on a tray.

Laurel got out of bed, took the tray from her and set it aside, then put her arms around Marie and tried not to cry.

Marie frowned but held tight to Laurel, sensing she was in some distress.

"That was a bad storm last night," she said. "Did you have some bad dreams? Here now…you get yourself back in bed and have some of my hot biscuits and jam."

"Not unless you sit with me," Laurel said.

Marie looked a bit taken aback, but when Laurel dragged the tray into the middle of the bed, then sat down, the old woman followed. Laurel buttered a biscuit half, then topped it with jam and handed it to Marie.

"For all you have done, for all the years you've done it."

Marie smiled a bit self-consciously but took the bread and ate.

"Not bad, if I say so myself."

Laurel fixed the other half for herself and, sitting cross-legged in the bed, shared her meal and her dreams.

It was hours after that when Laurel remembered the lightning strike, and immediately, she had to go see. She changed her shoes and then went to find Marie to tell her where she was going.

Marie frowned at the news. "What if that old painter still prowlin' around in the trees?"

"They say it's already dead," Laurel said.

"There's more than one cat in this state," Marie argued.

Laurel frowned. "So…do we have a gun?"

"Your grandmama wouldn't have slept a wink if she knew there was a weapon on this place."

Something about the way she answered made Laurel suspicious.

"Okay...but do you have a gun she didn't know about?"

Marie blinked; then she started to grin.

"I knew you was somethin'. First time I laid eyes on you, I knew you gonna be hard to match."

"Well?"

"Can you shoot?" Marie asked.

"I'm not afraid of guns. I can certainly take aim, and I can pull a trigger. Have I ever shot one before? No."

Marie shrugged. "Me, neither. But two old women livin' alone out here in the bayou didn't make sense without something to protect us. Wait here."

Laurel grinned. The more she got to know this feisty little woman, the more she hoped to grow old just like her.

Marie came back with a shoe box and handed it to Laurel with a flourish.

"It's in there," she said. "Loaded an' all. I had the man at the pawn shop load it when I first bought it, and since I haven't had call to use it, it's still full up."

"How long ago was that?" Laurel asked as she untied the string around the box and lifted the lid.

"Um, nearly ten, no, eleven years, I guess."

"Lord," Laurel muttered, and then took out the gun.

It was a revolver, and she didn't want to know how old it was before Marie had bothered to purchase it. But it was loaded, that much she could see. She picked it up gingerly, then let it hang between two fingers while she debated the best place to carry it on her.

"Here," Marie said, and took a small canvas tote bag from the back of the kitchen door. "This is what I use when I pick apples to make pies. This bag holds just enough apples for two pies. I reckon it can hold one gun."

"Okay," Laurel said, and put the gun inside.

"Just sling it over your shoulder like a purse," Marie said. "I don't think the gun will go off...do you?"

Laurel grinned. "Don't ask me. You're the expert, remember?"

Laurel rolled her shoulder to test the weight of the bag, then traded it to the other side and rolled it again. Both times, the handles slid downward and she just caught the bag before it could fall.

Marie snorted beneath her breath and took the bag off Laurel's shoulder before she started out the door. "We don't neither one of us have sense enough to pound sand in a rat hole, and if you tripped and fell, likely you'd shoot yourself in the ass, so I'm thinking you just leave this here with me, go see about your lightning strike, and then get back here on the double."

"I think you're right," Laurel said, and started out the door as Marie called after her, "You have any troubles, you just holler. I've got the gun."

Laurel kept on walking without letting herself consider the consequences of that remark.

"In a shoe box. Eleven years. Lord have mercy," she muttered, then laughed.

It felt so good to be outside after three days of rain that she began to jog. The ground was soft beneath her shoes, still spongy from the storm. Drowned flowers and downed limbs were lying everywhere, and she made a mental note to give Tula a call and have her grandson, Claude, come help her clean up the mess.

The closer she got to the trees, the louder the roar of the river became. When she was at the edge of the grove, she turned and looked back at the house, aligning the windows of her room with where she was standing, then turned around and closed her eyes. In her mind, she saw darkness and rain pouring against the windows—then the flash. It had been left of center of the view from her windows, which meant she needed to go a little bit west. It shouldn't be hard to find, because, from the sound she'd heard, it had certainly struck something.

She opened her eyes and struck out in a westerly direction, but always looking inward toward the grove, looking for a blackened tree or one that had fallen, or maybe one that had split. She'd heard that lightning would travel through a tree and then come out through every root, ripping up the ground as if there had been an underground explosion. She was curious to know if that was an old wives' tale or true.

A pair of white cockatoos flew past her head in a parallel race near the ground, while a raucous blue jay hopped about beneath a tree, feasting on worms that had been flooded out of their holes. On the outside, it made Mimosa Grove look like her own portion of paradise, but there had been snakes in paradise and a cougar in hers. She approached with caution.

Even then she almost didn't see it. If a half-dozen birds and a small squirrel hadn't erupted from the same spot and taken to the trees, she might have missed it. Curious as to what had caused them all to gather in **one location, she** shoved through a tangle of bushes **and vines, then had to** catch herself from falling **into the hole.**

She'd found the tree. **It appear**ed to be one of the older ones. Lightning had split it right down the middle, and, weakened by the separation and age, it had toppled, taking centuries of dirt and the entire root system with it as it fell.

"Oh, my, what a shame," Laurel said, thinking of all the life and years this tree had survived and stood witness to, only to be felled by a simple act of nature.

She leaned over carefully and stared down into the hole where the roots had been, squinting slightly as her eyes adjusted from bright sunlight to the darker qualities of shade.

The hole was deep. Far deeper than a grave. And there were all sorts of underground denizens that had been uprooted with the tree. Earthworms roiled together in small, muddy clumps as if disoriented by the weightlessness and light. Rocks of various sizes and shapes had been partially revealed, like shy strippers showing only bits of their skin. Something in the roots caught her eye, and she moved a bit closer to see, only to be startled moments later when she saw it was a small black snake.

Still a city girl at heart and unable to tell good snakes from bad, she stepped back to give it a wide berth, and as she did, tripped on an exposed root from another tree and fell backward onto the ground.

It was the unexpected motion that startled her, more than the impact of the fall. And she was already laughing at herself when she started to rise. Then she froze.

Being prone rather than upright had drastically

changed her view of the fallen tree—and what lay tangled within it. They were unmistakably bones, caught within the spidery, weblike network of roots, then washed clean from the downpour after the tree had fallen. She was wondering if they were animal or human when she saw the small skull and somehow she knew. For the first time in centuries, Chantelle LeDeux, or what was left of her, lay exposed to the bright light of day.

She moaned softly, filled with regret, then rocked back on her heels, and as she did, she saw a second skull. It was larger than the first, and with a crack that ran from the eye socket to the top of the head. These people had not died a natural death.

"Oh, God...oh, God," she whispered, then pushed herself upward and took a couple of steps back. Taking a slow breath and making herself calm down, she retraced her steps to the edge of the hole and then knelt. If she stretched just the least bit forward, she would be able to reach the second skull. Without thinking of what might happen, she leaned forward, and time stood still.

*Joshua was scared. As scared as he'd ever been in his life. The night sounds on the river were frightening, but not as frightening as facing his angry master would be. He'd been whipped near to death just for breaking a dish. He didn't want to think what would happen for knocking the man out and helping his wife get away.*

*So he sat and he waited, praying for the sound of her voice, waiting for the touch of her hand to give him courage to do what must be done.*

*Morning dawned, and still he sat huddled down in*

the canoe, afraid to stay, needing to run, but he'd given her a promise he wasn't willing to break.

As he sat, he thought he heard dogs, and the sound made him sick. They weren't just the barks of dogs in the woods. If they were hounds, they belonged to the massuh and were most likely on his trail.

He stared up at the riverbank, willing Chantelle LeDeux to appear, but all he saw were the trees beginning to be defined by color, as well as shape, as the light continued to spread.

Mist was rising from the water now as the warmth of the sun kissed the surface. He stared downriver, wondering how far he would be able to get before they shot him on sight. He thought of his woman, and then his baby girl, and knew he would never see them again. Something had happened. Something bad, or Chantelle would have come. It took him a few moments to realize that when he'd thought of her then, he'd thought of her by name. It was the first time he'd let the familiarity into his head.

With one last look toward the banks above, he reached down into the canoe for the paddle, and as he did, color in the river caught his eye. He swallowed a moan.

A flash of yellow, then a shadow of pure white. Chantelle had been wearing a yellow dress when he'd last seen her. Dear God, he didn't want to be right.

He looked again, and as he did, huge tears filled his eyes.

"Poor baby...poor tiny little thing...I shoulda killed him where he lay."

He shifted his weight so that he was balanced on both feet, then bent over and lifted her half-submerged body from the stream.

*Her face was swollen, both from the beating and from being in the water all night, and something, probably a big catfish, had eaten the small finger from her right hand.*

*He pulled her across his lap, then tried to straighten her dress and fix her hair.*

*"So, little missy, you done tried to keep your word to me, didn't you? You came, jus' like you said you would."*

*Then he closed his eyes and lifted his face to the morning.*

*Upriver, the hunters froze, stunned by the high, keening sound of animal pain and the roar that followed.*

*"God have mercy," one of the man muttered. "What was that?"*

*But it was LeDeux, bandaged and bloody and at the head of the pack, who turned his head toward the sound like a wolf suddenly scenting prey.*

*"It's him," he said. "And when we get him, don't forget that he's mine."*

*The men nodded, none willing to look at their friend who'd been so shamed. They all believed his story and were incensed on his behalf. None of them wanted to think one of their women might turn to a Nigra's bed. It was different when a man took one of the women. It meant nothing and, to most, was simply a way of strengthening the seed of his chattel. But for a woman to take a black was a sin most foul. They empathized with LeDeux in many ways and yet secretly wondered what had been lacking in him that would have caused his own woman to do such a deed.*

*"Let's go," LeDeux said, and unleashed the dogs.*

* * *

*Joshua heard them coming before he saw them. He glanced down at Chantelle's body, where he'd laid it out upon the ground, then picked up the club he'd made of a piece of deadfall and waited for fate to catch up.*

*Yesterday, when he'd gotten out of his sweet woman's bed, he'd had no thought of dying on the morrow, but yet it had come, and he would not leave Chantelle behind just to try to outrun it.*

*Suddenly the dogs came out of the trees and were upon him, snarling and snipping at his arms and his legs as he swung the club, trying to keep them back. But when one of them got past him and bit at Chantelle's leg, he lost control.*

*It didn't matter that she was far past the pain, or that she was immune to the indignity of her condition. He turned his back on his two-legged enemies to fight the animals from her. Wielding the club now with more anger than fear, he brained all but one of the hounds, leaving their bodies on the ground and the last one crippled and waiting to die.*

*His breath was coming in short grunts and gasps, and he kept seeing blood spots before his eyes. It took a bit to realize that it was the blood from the dogs that had splattered his face. He swiped at his eyes as he turned and saw the butt of LeDeux's rifle coming toward him, then threw up his arm and tried to duck.*

*But it was too little and too late.*

*The blow shattered his skull. He went down like a felled giant, with the upper half of his body lying across Chantelle. It seemed that even in death, he was trying to shelter her.*

*The hunters said nothing, instead watching Le-*

Deux's face as he dismounted from his horse. He took a shovel from the saddle, then turned to the men with a look of such malevolence that they all shrank back in fear.

His voice was shaking with rage, and there was a drop of spittle at the corners of his lips. To a man, they believed him to have the look of a mad dog, and none wanted to be bitten.

"Get out!" he said, his voice trembling in fury. "Leave me and never voice a word of this to another. If you do, I swear to you, on my children's lives, that you will never know another day without fear. I will burn your homes to the ground while you sleep, and if you think to escape, I will be sitting outside with my rifle to pick you off as you run screaming from the flames."

They paled. One turned and threw up his breakfast. Another mounted his horse and rode away without speaking.

LeDeux waited until they were gone, then walked to the nearest mimosa tree and started to dig.

Within weeks, word had been spread—by LeDeux himself—that his wife had become homesick and gone to Paris for a visit. By the time six months had passed, he was claiming that she'd written him a letter, saying she was never coming back.

He'd played the part of the bereft husband to the hilt, raised his children, spoiled his grandchildren, and died with the stains of her blood and Joshua's on his soul.

Laurel moved her hand, then fell backward on the ground, for a moment too shocked to move. Ever so slowly, she began to understand what Chantelle had been trying to tell her. She just wanted to be found. Her spirit had needed the truth to be revealed before it could be set free.

Laurel crawled to her feet and, without a backward glance at the hole, started toward the house. Soon she was jogging, then in an all-out run.

She was running to get help, just as Chantelle had begged her to do.

Marie was filling a vase with fresh flowers when she heard Laurel shouting. She dropped a stem of pink crepe myrtle into the sink and reached for the gun. She was on the porch before it dawned on her that the gun was still in that bag. Laurel was coming out of the grove, waving her arms as she ran. Without thinking of her own safety, Marie ran off the porch and started toward her, intent on protecting her, if necessary with her life.

They met halfway between the grove and the house as Laurel fell into Marie's outstretched arms.

"What's wrong? What's wrong? Is it the cat? I brought the gun!"

Laurel was still in shock and shaking, but when she saw the fierceness of Marie's expression, she almost managed a smile.

"No, Mamárie.... I'm sorry. I didn't mean to scare you. It's not the cat."

"Then talk to me, girl. What in blazes you mean, comin' outta the grove, shouting and scarin' me half to death?"

"Oh, Mamárie...I found her." Then she started to cry.

Marie grabbed Laurel's hand. "Honey...you not makin' any sense. Who did you find?"

"Chantelle LeDeux."

Marie's eyes widened, and her mouth dropped open in shock. She looked past Laurel toward the grove, as if expecting to see a specter come floating out of the trees.

"God have mercy," Marie muttered. "You saw her ghost?"

Laurel knew she wasn't making sense, but the emotional impact of what she'd seen was heartbreaking.

"No...no, not her ghost," Laurel said. "I found her...or what's left of her. The storm...last night... the lightning...it hit a very old, very large tree. It split in two and fell, roots and all, ripped right out of the ground."

Then she took a deep, shuddering breath, trying to put the horror of Chantelle's and Joshua's deaths from her head. There was no one to bring to justice. There was no one left alive to blame. But now they could finally be put to rest. She took Marie's hand, then impulsively pulled it to her cheek and laid her face against the small, work-worn palm.

"There were two skeletons all tangled up in the roots. One was Chantelle's. The other belonged to a slave named Joshua. He was married to a woman who was your ancestor."

Marie staggered as if she'd been slapped.

"Oh, Lord, oh, Lord...what we gonna do?"

It was that simple question that began to calm Laurel's senses, because she knew exactly what needed to be done.

"We're going to call Harper and tell him to bring his coroner and his crime-scene people, and they're going to collect the remains of the two murder victims. Then, when the authorities are finally done with all the fuss and hoorah they feel they have to make over two-hundred-year-old bones, we're going to have us a couple of funerals and bury Chantelle...and Joshua...right up in the family plot in Bayou Jean, where they should have been buried all along.''

Now Marie was the one whose eyes filled with tears. She took Laurel's hand as if she were a little girl who was about to learn a hard lesson and started to explain.

''Laurel, honey...you might not want to go buryin' the bones of some slave in the family plot. Times have changed some across the country, but there's a whole lot of the old ways that still hold down in the South.''

Laurel's chin jutted, her eyes suddenly glittering with far more than tears.

''I not only intend to bury that man in the family plot, I'm going to bury him next to Chantelle herself.''

Marie gasped. ''Oh, no, that wouldn't be right. She should be laid out beside the man who was her husband.''

''Not that son of a bitch...not in my lifetime,'' she muttered.

''Why on earth not?'' Marie asked.

''Because he's the man who killed her. He killed them both. Now, quit worrying, pick up that gun and come with me. It's way past time to right a terrible wrong.''


It was a cool day in September when the medical examiner finally released the remains. Laurel had an undertaker waiting. The caskets she'd chosen were the finest Bayou Jean's funeral parlor had to offer. The burial sites she'd had opened were the ones next to her grandmother, Marcella, and her husband, Etienne. The way she figured it, Chantelle would be happier in paradise if her earthly remains were as far away from Jean Charles LeDeux as they could be.

The day was gray and overcast as Justin drove her and Marie to the cemetery in Marcella's old Chrysler. The ride was quiet—each of the three lost in their own private thoughts. Although Laurel had told them everything she'd seen and what she knew to be true, neither of them could truly appreciate what she had experienced. They had not been in her head, or known the depths of Chantelle's pain and despair, or felt the strength of a slave—a man with no last name who'd made the ultimate sacrifice for a woman he admired.

As they arrived at the cemetery, a fine mist began to fall. It seemed a fitting tribute for lost souls—a washing away of the wrongs as they reached a final resting place that would make everything right.

Later, as they stood hand in hand beneath the wide shelter of the black umbrella that Justin was holding over their heads, Laurel felt as if she were being released—as if she'd finally been pardoned from some internal prison.

At Laurel's request, the local Catholic priest had administered last rites before the caskets had been closed, and he was now reading what Laurel guessed were meant to be comforting verses from the Bible, only she'd let the sound of his voice fade into the background of her mind so that she could hear what really mattered on this day. It was hardly more than a whisper—others, if they'd heard it, would have thought it to be the sound of water dripping from the large waxy leaves of the nearby magnolias. But she knew better.

It wasn't rain. It wasn't even the sound of the wind that was beginning to rise, whipping the hems of their skirts against their legs and blowing mist against their faces. She leaned against Justin as she looked down at the ground, absently noting the grass and mud on the toes of her shoes, while taking comfort from his strength and the warmth of his embrace.

Then, in the middle of the priest's last words, there was a lull in the wind and then an absence of sound.

Laurel looked up just as the sun broke through the clouds. A long yellow-white beam of sunshine was shining through the break, like a beacon showing the way home.

A breath caught in the back of Laurel's throat, and she remembered again the moment of Chantelle's death, when she'd tried so hard to go toward the light and instead had become earthbound.

But that had been an eternity of yesterdays, and this was today, and the priest had said all the right words and blessed their earthly remains.

*Safe journey,* Laurel thought.

*Blessed be your life* were the words that came straight back into her head.

And then she heard the priest say ''amen'' and she echoed it with one of her own. It was over.